*from the ashes*

LYNN RHYS

EDITED BY
ASHLEY OLIVIER

Copyright © 2022 by Lynn Rhys

All rights reserved.

No part of this book may be reproduced in any form or by any electronic or mechanical means, including information storage and retrieval systems, without written permission from the author, except for the use of brief quotations in a book review.

From the Ashes is a work of fiction. Names, characters, places, and incidents are the product of the author's imagination or are used fictitiously. Any resemblance to actual events or locales or persons, living or dead, is entirely coincidental and beyond the intent of the author.

Edited by Ashely Olivier

Cover design by KB Barrett Designs

❀ Created with Vellum

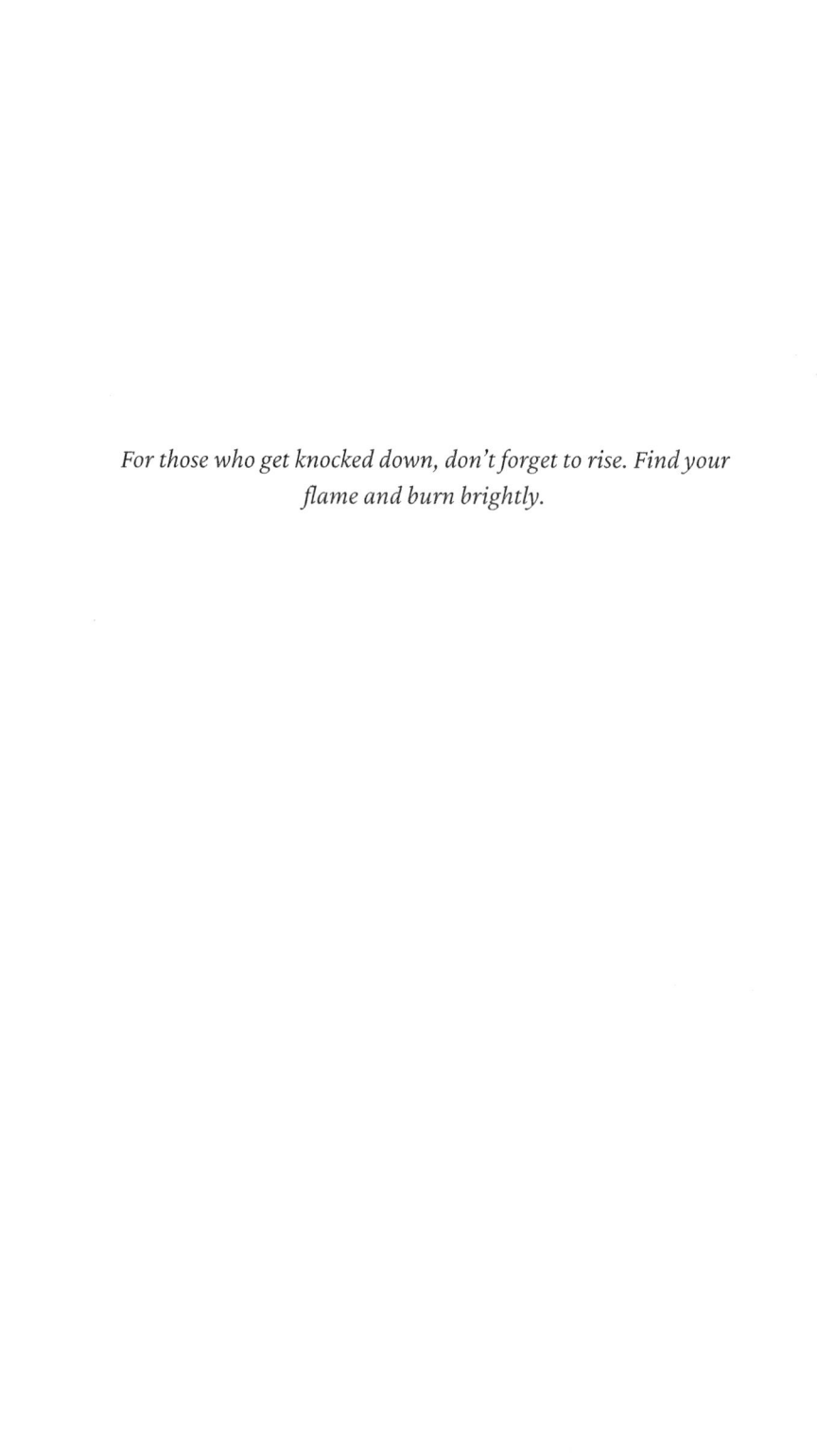

*For those who get knocked down, don't forget to rise. Find your flame and burn brightly.*

... Nor shall this peace sleep with her; but as when
    The bird of wonder dies, the maiden phoenix,
    Her ashes new create another heir
    As great in admiration as herself;
    So shall she leave her blessedness to one,
    When heaven shall call her from this cloud of darkness,
    Who from the sacred ashes of her honour
    Shall star-like rise as great in fame as she was,
    And so stand fix'd ...

WILLIAM SHAKESPEARE

*author's note*

THIS BOOK CONTAINS strong subject matter that may not be suitable for all readers, including scenes that may depict, mention, or discuss: anxiety, blood, bullying, death, depression, emotional abuse, self-harm, slut shaming, stalking, suicide and violence. There is profanity and sexual situations. Reader discretion is advised.

"MOM! MOM! ARE YA HOME?" I burst through the front door and throw my backpack onto the floor next to the front closet of our small ass apartment.

Letting out a sigh, I look around at what we currently call home. The place we live in is a dump. The floor's all cut up, the carpet's discolored, and the ceiling is covered in water stains. It's not the best place to live, but we make the most of our eight-hundred-square-foot one-bedroom apartment.

It's a shit town in Massachusetts, but Baybridge is now our home. It's a small town a couple hours away from the ocean. Not that I care about that; I've never been a fan of water, and I can't swim. There's plenty of drugs and crime that run through the streets of Baybridge. Graduation rates are low, and people work quite a few jobs to make ends meet. It's a lower income town, but it's where we can afford to live. And as long as Mom and I have each other, that's all that matters.

I stop for a moment to see if I can hear her maybe in her bedroom, but the house is silent. I shrug, throwing on my headphones and turning up some *Evanescence*. She probably got an extra shift at the diner, which means she'll bring home something for dinner.

I head over to the ratty brown couch we picked up from Goodwill and flop onto it. This couch also serves as my bed since we live in a one-bedroom. My mom deserves to get a good night's rest on a bed after all she's been through, after all she does to try to keep a roof over our heads. Our lives were destroyed by the loss of my father. My mother was destroyed by losing the love of her life.

This heap of fabric isn't my comfy bed in my own room, it's a lumpy reminder of where we have fallen.

Picking up my cheap as fuck phone, I scroll through Instagram and mindlessly like the posts. I'm seriously technology challenged, so music and social media are the extent of my world. Outside of that, God help me.

I could sit and do some homework, but I'm already weeks ahead in it all. It's April, and my junior year is almost over. It's been a bit stressful not knowing what I'm going to do after high school, though.

I miss my old life.

I miss my dad.

Mom and I have been left in ruins since he died, or as the police said, killed himself. Since it was ruled a suicide, we were denied payout on his life insurance. We fought them, but with barely any money, we couldn't prove otherwise.

We never believed what they ruled it as; we never could imagine my father, Trevor Hayes, taking his own life. He was happy, and he loved us. We had a perfect little family. Mom and I were his world, he would never leave us. Never take his own life.

But that's what they told us the accident was, a suicide. That he purposely used his vehicle as a vessel to end it all.

My heart squeezes at the thought that something was that bad that he felt he had to end his life. Still, I don't believe it. It's bullshit. What's worse is that lie has completely destroyed my mom.

The light in her eyes has dimmed, her skin has paled, and her mouth is always turned down in a permanent frown. She walks around here saying little and barely surviving on the minimum it will take to just make it through the rest of life. The rest of her life without the man she loves. With me as the constant reminder of what she created with my father.

She doesn't ever talk about him, though. We exist in our new lives without thinking or talking about our old one. It hurts, but I worry more about how she feels than how I do.

Because when I eventually leave for college, she'll be alone. Alone in her thoughts, alone in this shit hole, alone in existence.

I look at the time and see that it's close to six. I should probably get to work on the rest of the homework I need to finish for the semester. I have finals I need to study for and a couple of papers to write.

My stomach growls as I reach for my books. I need some study food. I pick up my phone and shoot a text to my mom.

**Me: Hey, can you bring me home a bacon cheeseburger please? Extra pickles. Lots of round hamburger pickles. Lots. Please. And thank you.**

I hit send and wait for her response. As I pick up my backpack to take out my math book, I hear a phone dinging in the back of the apartment.

*Huh, maybe she isn't at work.*

Standing up, I throw my backpack on the couch and take the short walk through the hall to the bedroom. I push open the door and see that the bed is still unmade, and clothes are scattered all over the floor. The nightstands are littered with water bottles and used tissues. There's a shoe box on the bed that I've never seen before, but I turn around and survey the rest of the room. It's in complete disarray. Drawers open, lights tipped over, and a garbage can on its side with the contents spilled everywhere.

My eyes catch an envelope on her dresser with my name on it. Mom's writing. I grab it and slowly peel it open, my stomach in complete knots and the lump in my throat growing by the second. I take a deep breath before reading the letter.

*My dearest little bird,*

*I'm sorry. I've let you down. Everything has changed, and I can't deal with this life anymore. So, I need you to fly on without me. Thrive. Become the woman I know you were meant to be. Take the box on my bed and keep it safe. It's yours. Please keep it from prying eyes. It's our life.*

*I love you more than you will ever understand. I'm so sorry for everything. I wish I could have been stronger for you.*

*Please call 9-1-1 and don't go into the bathroom. Just stay away. I don't want you to have that memory. Remember the family we were.*

*I love you, Phoenix. I'll be watching over you.*

*Love,*

*Mom*

My heart sinks, and tears spill onto the page. I lift my head and stare at the bathroom door, my lips beginning to tremble. The air is so thick I can't even take a breath. *No ...*

Slowly, I take a small step towards the door, then another. My hand reaches out of its own accord and grabs hold of the round door knob. Shaking, I slowly turn it and enter into the darkness.

"Mom?" I whisper. I turn to my left and with trepidation, flip on the light.

I shouldn't have come in here.

I should've listened to her.

At that moment, I feel myself leave my body. I watch myself from above as I scream at the top of my lungs. My body locks up, and I can't move and inch from the spot I'm standing.

Red water, a white pale body, dead dull eyes staring back at me. My mother lifeless in the tub. Gone.

My mother is gone.

She's dead.

And I couldn't save her.

I sink to my knees as I scream, tears falling from my eyes, the letter gripped tightly in my hand.

My entire world has just been obliterated.

## one

PHOENIX

SITTING ON MY BED, I stare at the box that I have not been able to open since I found it. I have no idea what's in it, and I don't care to. Not right now. The box and her locket are all I have left from my mother. Well, that and my hair and eyes. She had the same vibrant red hair as me, the same golden eyes. If it wasn't for our obvious age difference, we could have been mistaken as twins.

Nothing matters anymore. The two people I had in my life, gone. My mother and father, the people who were supposed to be here to celebrate life with me, gone. Two people who were supposed to stand by my side, gone. Leaving me here to fight for myself.

"Phoenix! Get your ass down here! You have your therapy appointment in thirty minutes!" my Aunt Julie calls from downstairs.

So, apparently, I have an Aunt Julie. Never met the woman in my life. From what my wonderful—and I use that term loosely—aunt tells me, my mom chose my dad over her. Or something like that. She doesn't get into specifics, and I don't fucking ask. Because I don't fucking care.

She has been cruel to me since the moment she found out she was now responsible for me. She yells, her words venomous, and apparently the way I eat and breathe are a problem. I guess her hatred of my mother automatically puts me on her shit list.

She lives in this giant house in Black Forest, which is about an hour east of Baybridge. Basically, it's the rich side of town. And her house doesn't disappoint. Her place is bigger than anything I've ever lived in. And it reeks of money. From the moment you step foot on the entryway under the portico, you're greeted with a set of wooden double doors that probably cost more than a Ford Focus to make and install.

Oh, but it doesn't stop there. The entryway is filled with luxury with its marble floors and expensive and gaudy chandeliers that sit high above you when you walk in. The wallpaper—yes, I said wallpaper—has gold flecks in it against a white background. The stairway in the grand foyer has a hand-carved wooden banister.

Or at least I'm told it's hand-carved. Bitch could be lying. I don't know.

The moment the car dropped me off after the move, looking up at the house that would now be my home, I hated it. I got lucky that my friends let me stay with them to finish school, but then having to move here after school ended makes me really hate it even more. There is a roundabout driveway with a giant fucking fountain in the middle of it. Sometimes I wish I could just take one of her cars and smash it into the fountain. Just because. No real reason.

"For fuck's sake, give me two minutes! It's down the street. It's not like it's an hour away!" I yell back at her.

Did I mention I hate living here? Well, I do. Every god forsaken second.

Apparently, somewhere in some will, my aunt was to be my guardian should something happen to my parents. Well, her and my uncle. Since he's no longer with us, it's just her. I wish I would have known, I could've made my thought known, because I definitely didn't sign off on this. She's an awful person who thankfully has no kids of her own because she doesn't have a maternal bone in her body. I'm a problem, a *disruption* to her. Thank God she didn't procreate. Those children would have been spawns from the devil.

And the last few months have been complete hell on earth.

Because everyone is gone. And I still can't unsee her. I close my eyes, and I'm transported back into that bathroom. It's a nightmare I live every day and night.

Hence the head doctor.

Kicking my legs over the side of the bed, I pick up my headphones and connect them to the phone. I move around my room and grab what I need to survive the next couple hours. Backpack, phone, kindle and I reach up and make sure that my locket is still hanging around my neck. It's the one thing that still connects me to her.

I shut my eyes and try to hold back the tears. I can't cry. I need to be strong. Just like I was at the funeral. The lonely and quiet funeral. There was no one there. My aunt, her *sister*, didn't even attend. So, it was just me and the guy reading off some crap that didn't even know her. Oh, and a couple coworkers from her diner came, but they only stayed for a few minutes.

Like everything else in life, I was left to bury my mother, alone.

But at least she wasn't alone; her grave sits next to my father's. So at least they have each other, while I battle life out here by myself.

Heading out into the hallway, which is also covered in some atrocious palm tree wallpaper, I shut my door and make my way downstairs. Don't want to keep Lucifer waiting.

"Do you even understand what this is doing to my schedule? You're messing up my day!" my aunt yells at me as I reach for the front door. Her face is all red, her lips turned down in a frown and her eyebrows pulled together. "This is taking up my precious time!"

Yeah, precious time. She sits at home doing nothing but living off the money of her dead husband. Apparently, he died of a heart attack or something. He never had any heath problems, but he also never went to a doctor. So, who knows? She doesn't talk to me much and again, I don't ask. I just know she lives the highlife and bitches that I'm taking up her precious time.

My uncle was some tech geek. Created software for companies. He was loaded and now she lives off his hard work.

Oh, and therapy was her idea because she didn't want "some depressed teen living in her house that could be trouble." I'm being forced to talk about my feelings because of her. She's fucking lovely, isn't she?

But then again, I do want to crash a car into her fountain, so maybe she's right for thinking that. Whatever.

Throwing myself in the backseat of the car, because I can't stand being close to her, I put my headphones in and blast the music for the short trip. Closing my eyes, I think of nothing. I envision blackness, a hole. Because that's what this life is.

Nothing.

* * *

"Phoenix, how have you been this last week?" Dr. Justin Parker sits across from me, his leg crossed over his knee and his hands in his lap. He's clean cut, young, probably in his late twenties. His brown hair is slicked back, his face is clean shaven, and his thick black eyeglass frames do nothing for him. He's a good-looking man, but very annoying with all his questions.

And yes, I know that's his job.

I give him a sarcastic smile. "You know, funny thing, Doc. I'm the same as I have been every single week I'm brought here to this fucking appointment." I sit with my legs tucked under me, my body turned away from him. "It's always the same."

"Hm. Well, here's the thing, this is part of my job as your therapist to see how you are doing. Each and every week." Dr. Parker's lips turn up, and he tilts his head.

"Oh! I didn't know!" I slap my thigh and roll my eyes. "Are you even old enough to do this? You look a little too young to be giving me advice."

He coughs through laughter. "I assure you, I'm old enough. Not to mention that I have the credentials and degrees needed."

"Yay me. So, I get you right out of junior college." I sigh. He ignores my attempt at insulting him and sits there staring at me. "I don't really care how many degrees you actually have. Are you really qualified to understand pain?"

Dr. Parker sighs, pushing up his glasses on his nose. "Phoenix, you experienced something very tragic. Not once but twice. Losing your dad to suicide—"

"He didn't kill himself!" My head snaps towards him.

The doctor is quiet for a moment. "Then what happened to him? What do you think happened?"

I let out a long sigh, "I don't know, Doc. But I know he would've never left us. He loved us." I shake my head, trying to keep the ball of emotions that's forming in my throat from coming up. *Don't cry, Phoenix. Don't cry.*

"Okay, let's talk about something different." He nods while shifting to placing his foot on the floor and leaning forward. "So, you start Darkwood Academy next week. A new school, your senior year. How do you feel about that?"

"So cliche there, Doc. 'How does that make you feel?'" I snort. "It's a new fucking school. It sucks ass. But on the bright side, I won't be living with my wonderful she-devil of an aunt. So, you know, totes excited." My last words are loaded with sarcasm as I look down and play with the hem of my tank top.

Dr. Parker shrugs. "Well, that's a good thing. You get to stay on campus, get out of the toxic environment you're in now. I heard it's run like a college campus, so you get to experience what it will be like when you go to college. Plus, you can make some new friends."

I huff, "Yeah, just what I need. Some preppy assholes who have more money than they know what to do with as friends. Wow, I can't wait. And there is no guarantee I can even go to college, so this may be the only 'college experience' in my book. Because let's face it, I don't have the money."

"Your aunt got you in, right?"

"Yup. Guess it pays to have been married to a rich guy. You know people."

"And she got you a scholarship there?"

"Yeah. I mean my 'poor me' story can basically buy me

an education. Woot! Don't have parents, but wow! I'll get the best education! If I milk it enough, maybe I can get someone to pay for college!"

"I'm sorry you have to go through this, Phoenix." He stays silent for a moment. "What you saw that day, it's traumatic. I know you have some walls up, and that's okay for now. But we do need to eventually talk about it. We need to work through it."

"I'm fine." I don't look at him. Instead, I stare out the window, watching the trees in the distance sway in the wind. The sun is filtered out by the leaves of the trees, cars zoom past each other on the street. People going about their daily lives, unaware that I sit here watching them.

"Are you?" he questions.

No, I'm not. My mother killed herself. I saw the grey look in her eyes, the blueish tint to her lips. I'm not okay at all. Both of my parents have abandoned me. I have no one. I'm alone.

But I refuse to tell him that.

"Yup. Totally fine," I respond with a smile.

I spend the rest of the appointment in silence. It's uncomfortable, but not as uncomfortable as sitting there and actually telling Dr. Parker what's actually on my mind. I don't want to rehash all that. I don't need to go down that road; I just need to pick up and move on.

Before I get up to leave, he finally speaks up. "So, after talking with your aunt and the school, they agreed to allow me the ability to visit the campus to have sessions with you there. Since you don't have transportation, and you will be busy with your studies. This way we can get in our time together and make sure you're adjusting to the school and your new surroundings."

My jaw drops before I clamp it shut, and I clench my

fists. "Are you fucking kidding me? I thought this was just for the summer."

"You went through something that doesn't get fixed overnight. The school and your aunt both think that this would be best." He stands and puts his hands in his pockets. "Can't hurt, can it?"

"Oh, my fucking God! So now, not only do I have to start a new school, but now they will look at me like the crazy one because I have a therapist coming to see me every week! Wow! Way to kill my chances of fitting in, Doc."

He gives me a firm look. "Everything will be done discreetly. No one will know that's why you're seeing me unless you tell them. They will have an office for us to have a session out of, and they said they can put it on the books as office time for you. Make it look like you are working there for a couple hours a week."

I rub my hands over my face and let out a groan. "This is bullshit." I pick up my things and immediately head towards the door, trying to get the hell out of there as fast as I can. I've had enough for today.

"Phoenix—" Dr. Parker calls out, but I run as fast as I can out the door and out of the office complex.

I turn out into the parking lot and head to the side of the building. I lean against the wall and slide down it, trying to catch my breath. Tears start to spill from my eyes, and I begin to hyperventilate. I can feel the ground spinning, and my vision starts to become tunnel-like. I close my eyes and drop my head to my knees.

These attacks have been happening since that day, usually at night.

But the fear of having to continue this at school, of having to deal with the loss, is too much for me. I wanted to leave it all behind.

Just like they left me.

Alone, scared. Having no one to talk to, no one to hug or even say 'I love you' to; they just left me.

Too selfish to think about me and my needs.

After a few minutes, I get myself under control and slowly stand up, keeping my back to the wall for balance. I'm supposed to text my dear Aunt Julie to come get me, but I don't really want to see the bitch.

Once I gather enough strength, I start making my way back towards the house. It's not far from here, but I could use that time to think. The sky is a vibrant blue, the wind cools me down with the sun beating down on me.

This town is beautiful, but it's full of rich snobs. Many who live off their investments or dead husbands. They run successful businesses and basically have more money than they know what to do with. They donate to the poor communities around Black Forest as a gesture to say "See? We care. We share our riches."

Yeah, money's great. You can buy anything you want. Go anywhere in the world at the drop of a hat. Have people groveling at your feet for a piece of you. You can get away with anything. Money is the greatest. It can do anything for you.

But you know what it can't do? It can't bring back the people you lost.

Being here, going to this rich-people school, does nothing for me. Except get me into a good college if I can somehow find a way to afford it. And then what do I do? What will that get me?

A good job, a good place to live.

Won't get me the one thing I need most in this world. Money can't buy love, and it can't buy me.

And it can't fill the absence inside my heart.

## two

PHOENIX

DARKWOOD ACADEMY, my home for the next several months as I start my senior year. Home of the Ravens, and home to some ridiculous school fucking uniforms.

Seriously, these black and hunter green plaid skirts for the girls are obscenely ugly. Pair it with a white button-down shirt, some white knee-high socks, and black Mary Jane's and you have yourself the most ridiculous outfit—which, of course, you have to wear five days a week.

What fucking century is this?

What's worse, my uniforms are used. Not new like all the other rich pricks, used. Donated by students at the end of the year who graduated. Thanks to all those who came before me to wear these atrocious uniforms. I forced my aunt to have these taken to a place and cleaned. I didn't really want to wear other people's cooties.

It's the Friday before school starts, and it's the day they allow seniors to move into their dorms for the year. Yes, dorms. As in, I'll have to stay on campus all day and night with people I really don't want to be around.

This past week, I went online and pulled up a map of this place. Darkwood is huge. This whole place is like a college campus. There are a ton of academic buildings and dorms, and it's evident this place loves its sports based on the athletic facilities scattered around the campus.

There are five sets of dorms on campus. The Blackwood Tower houses the junior and senior girls, and the Dark Pine Tower sits next door and houses the junior and senior boys on campus. Black Pine Tower is for the freshmen and sophomore girls, while the Forest Edge Tower houses the freshmen and sophomore boys. Then out in the corner of the campus is a set of apartments for the faculty if they choose to live here during the school year.

How weird is that?

As my taxi pulls up to the unloading zone near the gates, I take in the tall stone wall with iron gates and gargoyles perched on stone columns beside them. Creepy ass rich people shit. Turning to look out the other window, I see the parking lot packed with cars I don't even know how to pronounce. Wait, no, I see a Porsche. Okay, I know how to pronounce that one.

There are cars parked all along the sidewalk outside the school gates. Students with iPads and moving hand trucks circle the others like sharks. There are people talking on walkie talkies, directing others and pointing to areas for the drop off. It's a fucking circus. I let out a long sigh and open up my door, but the minute I step out onto the sidewalk, I'm attacked by a bouncy blonde girl holding an iPad.

"Hi! Welcome back to Darkwood Academy!" she says as she obnoxiously chews her gum. Her eyebrows shoot towards her hairline, and her eyes stare into me like they're trying to steal my soul. Maybe that's why she's so happy; she sucks the souls from her victims. "I love your hair! Is that a natural red? You have to tell me what salon you went to if it's not! Do I know you? You don't look familiar. And I know everyone here! Well, except the incoming freshmen. *Oh*, you must be a freshmen!"

I reply slowly, "Um, yeah, this is my first year, but I'm a senior. So, just point me in the right direction and I'll take it from there."

I take a step back towards the trunk of the taxi. The taxi driver opens the trunk and starts pulling out my bags. Before I can take them, speedy soul sucker is already there grabbing them and placing them on a flatbed cart.

She flips her blonde hair over her shoulder and chimes, "Oh no! That's what we're here for. By the way, I'm Lillian Harris. I'm going to help you to your dorm and then someone will be by to show you around campus. I just need your name so I can get you all checked in." She smiles at me, a wide, creepy, way-too-happy smile. What the fuck do they put in the water here?

"Phoenix Hayes," I tell her dryly.

"Oh em *gee*! I love your name. Oh! Here you are." She scrolls through whatever she's looking at on her iPad. Suddenly, her smile is a little more forced. "Well, your dorm is in Blackwood Tower. But um, you need to go to the office first, since you're, um, a scholarship student."

I don't understand what that has to do with anything, but sure. "Um, okay, but what about my stuff?" As I ask her this, I hear a door shut, and it pulls my attention momentarily. I turn to see the taxi driving off and turn my gaze back to Peppy Patti—I mean Lillian.

"Well, we'll have someone bring it to your room. The floor monitor has access to your room for today, so we'll just stick it in there. But in the office, they will more than likely have your welcome packet that will have your access codes for the room." She presses the iPad against her chest and tries to keep the smile on her face. "Okay then! The office is that big building there," she says as she points behind her. "Just follow this path and you'll find the Forthright Building. The office is on the main floor when you walk right in."

Before I can say thanks, she turns away and stalks off towards another unaware victim.

I grab my backpack and throw it on. This thing carries the most import of my items: my shitty laptop, a photo of my mom, and the box she told me to hold onto. I glance over at the cart and pray that it actually does get to the correct dorm room. I reach up and grab my locket, watching the chaos around me. The laughter between friends and the chatter of students trying to make sure they have everything. I roll my eyes and press forward.

I need to get to the office so I can find some sanity in the silence of my door room. The introvert in me is not enjoying the throngs of students milling about.

As I weave through all the commotion of students trying to gather their boxes of items, I realize how little I actually brought. One girl has a box stuffed to the brim with shoes. Another has bags of stuffed animals. They all look like they're trying to pack an entire house worth of worthless crap into whatever size cell we are going to be living in over the next several months.

But I also realize how alone I am. As I watch people hugging their loved ones, or friends becoming excited over seeing each other, I feel a dull pain in my chest.

There's no one for me. Everyone I once loved is gone from this earth. There's no one to see me off on a new adventure or my first day at a new school. No one to tell me that they love me, no one to send me a care package. I'm utterly alone in this world.

I bite my lip and force back the tears as I make my way around all the chaos.

I pass through the gates, and I get a sudden chill running down my spine. Something feels off about this place. There's a dizzying thought that this has been a mistake. That coming here was not a good idea. Then again, none of this was my idea. I just don't want to be here.

This campus is old, and it's been around for at least a century. The trees around me make a soft rustling as the wind blows through them. I cross my arms over my chest as I try to ignore the feeling that I need to run.

The path winds around, eventually leading me to my destination: the Forthright Building. It's a massive stone monstrosity. It looks gothic in architecture, and the grey stone has ivy growing on some parts. There are two massive towers that extend above the top of the building on each side. On top of each tower sit these beautiful, ornate iron details around the edges. This building looks almost medieval.

As I march up the steps, I suddenly feel like I have a set of eyes on me. I turn back around but find no one near me. The hairs on the back of my neck raise, and I bite my lip. I'm imagining things; I have to be. My imagination's a little overactive at the moment, with being here. Turning back around, I head into the building, trying to shake off the stalker feeling.

My mouth immediately drops open the moment I step inside. It's like I've been transported into a whole other universe.

The inside is nothing at all like the outside. It's the exact opposite. Where the outside is rugged and old, the inside is clean and new. Modern and filled with high-end technology. The floors are a pristine white marble with flecks of black and gold. The furniture that lines the halls are sleek and clean. There are black leather couches with stainless steel legs lining the hallways, coupled with metal end tables. It's cold, almost museum like. Glass cases sit between some of the benches, and pictures and awards sit preserved in them. It's all unapproachable, too clean. It's awful.

Looking around the museum of rich people stuff, I notice a glass partition wall with the word "Office" frosted over the massive pane. . Well, that would be where I'm supposed to go, instead of hiding out in my dorm like I want to.

I push through the glass door to find an older lady with her hair up in a bun sitting behind a desk. Her grey hair is neatly pulled back, and her face is devoid of any wrinkles. She looks good for an old bag.

"May I help you, young lady?" She looks at me, her eyes narrowing. I look to the side and see a name plate, *J. Hodgens*. Old dinosaur bones here has a name.

"Yes, Ms. Hodgens, the name's Phoenix Hayes. I was told to come here when I was trying to check in at the gates of hell out there. You know, for the Underworld, your intakers are quite cheery. They must love the hellfire. Or maybe it's the sweet accommodations in the torture pits?" I give her a smile as I grip the straps of my backpack, adjusting them under her stare.

She clears her throat and looks down at her desk, not amused in the least at my ramblings. "Ah, yes, Ms. Hayes. Headmaster Lockhart would like to talk to you."

"Okay, so we couldn't just do this little meet and greet after I moved into my room? Because I gotta say, I'm a little worried. Twiddle Dee and Twiddle Dumb out there just don't give me the confidence that they will get my stuff to my room." I shrug, but she ignores me, looking down at the papers in front of her.

"Go back to his office. It's the one that says Headmaster on it." She waves me back.

I stand there for a moment longer before heading towards the office. I reach the door that has a plaque on it that does indeed say "Headmaster". I tip my head back and let out a long sigh before knocking on the door.

"Enter," a gruff voice behind the door says. I open the heavy wooden door into yet another room that is drastically different from the office. What the fuck?

It's full of ornate wooden bookshelves that span across the walls on either side of me. A giant wooden desk sits in the middle of the room with windows out to the courtyard behind it. It stinks of money in this office and for some reason, I get a sinking feeling that this isn't a good room.

"Ms. Hayes, please have a seat." Headmaster Lockhart extends a hand out to two green leather high-back chairs in front of his desk. The furniture in here is the complete opposite of the hallway. It's not modern, it's not clean. It's ornate and detailed, hand carved crown molding that has probably been there since the opening of the school.

I shrug my backpack off and drop it next to the chair, plopping down. I lean against the back of the chair and place my hands in my lap, waiting for him to say something.

He's a bald man, probably in his late fifties. He has dark circles under his eyes and nose hairs coming out of his nose. Well, at least we know where the hair on his head went.

"Ms. Hayes, let me be the first to welcome you to Darkwood Academy." He folds his hands together on top of his desk as he gives me a weak smile.

I point behind me with my thumb. "Well, actually, your welcome crew did that. So, you wouldn't be the first."

He stares at me silently for a moment, then clears his throat. "Ms. Hayes, are you aware of the gift you received by being accepted here on a scholarship? Darkwood can unlock so many opportunities for you. Don't waste this chance." He pauses for a moment once more, and I contemplate just turning around and walking out. Fuck this guy. What opportunity? The chance of a lifetime to lose both your parents only to end up in this purgatory? No thanks.

"I know you have been through some tough things in life already, with the loss of your parents and all. We are here to support you. Your aunt and therapist both agreed that it would be best to maintain your usual appointments. We have set up an office next door to me. You will be using that for your therapy." He stares at me, his eyes narrowing. "Let me offer you a piece of advice. Do your work, get the grades, and then move on. Just keep your head down."

My body stills at this warning. I had already planned on being invisible, but his words cause me a bit of discomfort. What the hell goes on here that I need to heed his advice?

"Yeah, I'll keep that in mind as I run for class president."

He sighs and hands me the packet that was sitting on his desk. "Here. You are on the top floor. Room 821. Your passcode is in there, along with your schedule for the semester. Please, Ms. Hayes. Stay quiet, stay invisible," he pleads.

I jump up off the chair and take the packet, grabbing my bag and then hightailing it out of the creep's office.

Running out of the building, I head back along the paths that lead to the dormitories. The minute the air hits me, I breathe a little easier. I'm no longer feeling like I'm suffocating.

That's all I want to be, is free.

Free from my past, free from the death that hangs over me, free from the pain in my heart.

As I make my way across campus, I take in the beautiful landscaping, the lush trees and the chirping of the birds around me. It's calming. The only thing that's calming about this place.

I grab the map out of my back pocket that I had printed before I left. I had studied it on the way here, but I didn't expect to be making a pitstop. So now I need to figure out how to get back to the dorms. Once I locate myself, I head east along the pathways. As I get closer, I look up at yet another castle-like building. My money is on the inside being renovated. I doubt the rich pricks would want to live in anything less than expensive ass surroundings.

As I make my way in, I walk past the desk at the front check in desk. I turn to the left and see a bank of elevators. When I turn to the right, I see a lavish sitting area that screams money. They even have a coffee bar along the wall. *I'm sure the coffee is laced with gold.*

I shake my head and see if I can find a set of stairs to take. The elevators are packed with other students trying to get in, and I really don't want to socialize; I've done enough of that today already.

I round the corner and find the stairwell. Then I head up the flights of stairs until I get to the eighth floor. Thankfully my door's at the end of the hall right off the stairwell, no need to walk through the hallway of students trying to get all their shit into their rooms. I punch in my door code and hear it unlock. Taking a deep breath, I push it open.

Holy shit.

PHOENIX

THE MINUTE I push the door open, my jaw drops, and for a moment I think I may be dreaming. This is where I'm living? This place is a penthouse suite compared to my living situation in the past.

I slowly walk in, taking in the surroundings of my new home.

The floors are a dark hardwood, and there's a flatscreen television hanging on the wall to my left and a plush sofa and loveseat in front of it. When I turn to the right, I notice a kitchen area. Not just an area, but an actual kitchen with full-size appliances. Expensive-ass-looking countertops, stainless steel appliances, even the light fixtures look like they are out of a Home and Garden Magazine.

Do these rich assholes even know how to cook?

The entire summer at my aunt's house, Aunt Julie had people cooking and cleaning for her. I mean I guess if you have the money, that's one way to waste it.

As I survey the rest of the new surroundings, a door opens to my left and out comes a blonde with a huge smile on her face as she takes me in. I'm guessing she's now my roommate for the foreseeable future.

"Hi! I'm Elizabeth Denton, but you can me Liz or Lizzy. I really hate the name Elizabeth. Sounds so pretentious." She wrinkles her nose. "You must be Phoenix? I love that name! So different!" She bounces on her feet with excitement, again a smile stretching wide across her face. Is everyone at this school on happy drugs?

"Um, yeah. Well, I didn't pick it." I press my lips in a thin line as I take her in. Her eyes are as blue as the ocean, and she's about the same height as me, but her breasts are way more pronounced. There's no way those are real.

And here I am judging tits. Awesome.

"Okay, well, your room is going to be that one there, next to the kitchen. My room's here off the common area. The bathroom is through that door, and that's pretty much the tour of the dorm," she says with a laugh. "Go get moved in. I'll leave you be while you get settled!"

"Thanks," I mumble as I head back towards my room. I just need some space away from all these happy people.

I push open my bedroom door and gawk at the space before me. It's huge, with more space than I really even need. There's a queen-size bed that awaits me, with a desk and two bookshelves beside it. The windows look out towards the campus, and I can see students walking around. As I turn to my right, I see a door that leads into my walk-in closet. Yup, this dorm has a goddamn walk-in closet.

Not like I'll ever fill up the thing with clothes or anything. But whatever.

That's where I find my couple of bags that I brought with me. Just sitting there inside the massive closet, looking all sad. I'm sure Smiley Liz has a closet packed to the brim with clothes.

Which brings me to my next thought: Do they do their own laundry or send it out to be cleaned? Well, if they send it out to be cleaned, at least I won't have to fight over open washers and dryers.

You know what? This is all too tiring to even think about. I'll try to figure that out later.

I saunter over to my bed and grab my backpack from off the floor. I pull out the box that my mom left for me and place it on my lap. The worn box, wrapped heavily in tape to keep everyone out. One day, I will have enough strength to see what was so important to leave me. Why she left me only this box.

Today is not that day.

I pull out her photo from my bag and stare at it. Her hair was red like mine. A vibrant red, like a flame. Her eyes were an amber that matched my own, golden when the sun hits just right. Her face was covered in freckles, with the majority of them on her cheeks.

She was beautiful, lively. Full of love and always ready to experience new things. Until the death of my father.

Then she became a shell of the person she was. She hid away, always looking over her shoulder. She lived in isolation except to work. It's like she was always waiting on my dad to appear out of nowhere. She would always mumble his name.

I asked her about it once, but she told me it was nothing, and it was just because she wasn't used to not having my dad around. I never asked again.

Maybe I should've pressed the issue.

Maybe I could have helped her fight whatever was haunting her.

Or maybe she just really missed my dad.

That's the thing with suicide. It doesn't just make the problems go away. Just transforms them. Now I have to live with her death and my father's. It's on my mind, in my heart, taken over my soul. I have to go on without her. I have to live with the pain of losing them.

I lay down against the school-provided-pillows and curl up with the box and the picture. I should probably get my room set up, but I'm just too tired to do that.

I close my eyes and picture a happier time in my life. My mother and father cheering me on after a dance recital. Eventually, my eyes become heavy, and I let sleep win.

* * *

I wake up to a banging on my door. I look out the window to see the sun is setting.

Damn, I slept the whole day away.

"Hey! Sleeping Beauty! You awake?" my roomie calls through the door as I try to wipe the sleep from my eyes. I head over, unlocking it and swinging it open. She chimes, "Well, you're awake. Let's go. Get yourself dressed. Let's go get something to eat."

"Um, I'm okay," I say as I wrap my arms around myself and press my lips together in a thin line. Food is honestly the last thing on my mind; my bed is begging me to crawl back under the covers and forget about everything.

Liz pleads, "Look, I know you haven't eaten all day. Come on! I know you're starving." As she looks at me with sad eyes, my stomach chooses that time to betray me and rumble quite loudly. She tilts her head, knowing what she heard. "See? You need food. It'll be a good chance for us to get to know each other."

I close my eyes for a moment and let out a sigh. The introvert in me is not happy that my roomie is very much the opposite of me. I open them to see the hopeful look on her face. Shit. She's going to keep trying to be all friendly. Pick my battles. "All right. Let's go. I guess some sustenance wouldn't hurt."

Liz claps her hands. "Yay! Okay, I can also give you a bit of a tour of the campus on our way there," she says as she jumps up and down in obvious excitement. Oh my God, she is so excitable.

I walk over to my backpack and grab my meal card and ID before shoving them into the back of my jeans. I throw on my black hoodie and pick up my shitty phone. Not like I have anyone who wants to call me. My aunt was all too happy to shove me out the door this morning and get me out of her hair.

Liz is waiting at the door for me. I saunter over, and we head out of the room. I stay silent, hoping that she'll realize I'm not one for conversation. Except she doesn't realize that, and she doesn't seem to have an off button.

"So, they just remodeled these rooms a couple years ago. Which, I mean, they needed it. Did you see the shower? It's huge. The ones we had before had like that tub shower combo, ugh." She sticks her tongue out and fake gags.

"Sounds rough." That's all I can offer her.

When you have so much privilege that a tub shower combo makes you want to vomit, I lose the ability to even care about the rest of the conversation. Must be nice to be that excited to have an upgraded shower just so you won't feel so lowly.

God, I just need to survive this year without having to beat the shit out of rich bitches. Fly under the radar and keep my head down. *Survive.*

As we come out of the doors, we make our way down the paths towards the center of campus. The campus is not only huge, but it's also dark and eerie. The trees are tall and wide, shrouding the path and area around in shadows. Barely letting the light in from the light poles around the path. The buildings add to the weird atmosphere, being so old and creepy.

You know what else makes my skin crawl? The over excited, slap happy nature of everyone I've run across here so far.

Liz begins to ramble again, "So that's pretty awesome that they let you in your senior year. They don't usually accept seniors. Freshmen—even sophomores they will, but I can't remember ever truly hearing about a senior being admitted here." She clasps her hands together as we walk down the barely lit path.

"Yeah, not like I had any choice in the matter." I look away, trying to orient myself to where we've walked to.

"What do you mean?" Liz turns to me as we walk.

I shake my head, dismissing her. "It's nothing."

"Well, I'm excited. This is a great school, and you must be really special to get in for your senior year."

We come up to another building like the rest on campus, but smaller in size. It doesn't extend upwards like the dorms or the Forthright building. It's less intimidating.

"What is this place?" I ask.

"This is the dining hall. Dorian Hall."

"You all just have a whole building? Not just like a gym turned into a lunchroom?" I pull my brows in, confused with this whole set up.

She shakes her head. "Nope. It's a building. But other things do exist here. It's primarily for eating, but home economic classes take place here. The school decided they wanted to have a brand-new auditorium. Well, new, like they remodeled a whole building new, but they had to move some things around. And this is where they put them."

"Wow," I say with little enthusiasm.

Liz holds the door open for me, and the moment I step over that threshold, my jaw drops. This dining hall is high-end. It doesn't look like any cafeteria I've ever eaten in. There are round wooden dining tables that are scattered throughout the room. Massive, detailed bases, beautiful high-back dining chairs that have actual padding on them. The ceiling is vaulted with wooden beams spanning the space. Beautiful modern fans and chandelier lights stretch from one side to the other to cool and light the space. Then there's the food.

It's set up like a luxury buffet. As we walk closer, the combinations of all the different smells inside my nose. I look up and see chefs cooking behind the food stations, with the steaming food laid out in front of them. My mouth drops at the sight.

"What in the upper-class bullshit is this?" I can't turn my head away, but Liz knows I'm speaking to her.

She lets out a laugh. "What? Normal high school doesn't have a buffet filled with amazing foods such as sushi and lobster and made to order food from top chefs?"

I roll my eyes. "No, you asshole. Normal high school has normal fucking terrible food. Rubber, bland chicken nuggets and canned fruit. Oh, and square pizza every Friday." I can't even believe what I'm looking at. My eyes don't know where to look first. "This is seriously the school dining hall?"

"Yeah, it is. Welcome to Darkwood. Though, I'm sure more surprises await," she says mysteriously.

Before I can respond, she heads over to grab a tray and a dish. I follow and do the same. This isn't diner food. This is so much more. I'm standing in front of prime rib and whole chickens, watching the chefs carve it in front of us to place on the dish.

I turn to look at her. "Is there a station where I could get a burger?"

"You want a burger and not prime rib? Sushi?" Her eyes widen, and her brows raise up with her question.

"Yeah, I think I prefer the simpler foods." I nod and try to swallow the uncomfortable feeling I have standing in front of a luxury most normal students don't have. She points to a station towards the end of the line. As I head over there, I feel eyes on me. I get it, new girl. Apparently in the spotlight more, thanks to the unusual nature in which I got here, since they don't usually admit seniors in on scholarship.

It's not just their eyes, but the whispers. As if I have a neon sign on my back that says, "Hey! New girl here." Add in my social status, and yeah, circus freak.

I order a bacon cheeseburger and fries, standing there with unease as I wait for the on-demand burger to finish. This place is weirdly dark and animated at the same time. There's a weird fake vibe that people walk around with. But when you step outside, when you feel the wind blowing in your face through the trees, it's haunting.

It's the same sensation as when I felt those eyes on me earlier.

Placing the burger on my tray, I turn and find my smiling roommate behind me. I try to not react, but I flinch a little at the sight of her near me. *Warn a person that you're coming up behind them.*

"Ready? Let's go find a table," she says as she bounces

away, her blonde hair swinging as she approaches a table in the corner of the room by a window.

I plop my tray down and then fall into the disgustingly comfortable chair.

"So, tell me about yourself," my ever happy new 'friend' says as she takes a bite of her salad. I almost want to throw her comment back in her face. Sushi and prime rib, but she gets a salad?

"Nothing to tell." The last thing I want to do is share anything about me with anyone here. I want to get in, get out, and move the fuck on with my pathetic life. Just like the headmaster said.

"Well, there has to be something! You don't just get accepted in to Darkwood your senior year, unless you know people."

I take a bite of my burger, relishing in the juicy flavor bursting in my mouth from each bite. This bitch is better than any diner burger I've ever had. "I don't know. I just got accepted," I retort through a mouthful of food. Un-lady-like? Yep. Do I give a fuck? Nope.

Liz opens her mouth to ask me yet another assumably annoying question, but nothing comes out, and her eyes shift behind me. It's at that moment I notice the whole place has become quiet. Pin dropping quiet.

"Oh my God, they're here," she says as a pink hue forms on her cheeks.

"Who?" My brows pull inward, and I stare at her like she's grown a second head.

"Shhh! Them." She points to a set of three guys who have walked into the dining hall. I turn to take a look at the sex gods. Holy fuck me. "The boys that run this whole place. The Kings of Darkwood."

Turning back to her, I scoff, "The Kings of Darkwood?

What the fuck elitist bullshit is that?" She doesn't answer, and I turn back to the guys who have stopped time around us. Each one of them are cut from the molds of perfection.

She breaks contact with royalty and turns to me. "They run this place. They are who everyone wants to be around or be associated with. It means you've made it. You're on their level. Every girl wants to be claimed by one of them, marry into money."

I choke back a laugh. "You mean more money than they already have?"

"Yeah." She shrugs. "I mean, I would love to be hanging off the arms of one of them." She smiles and stares off like she's daydreaming.

"Sad." I turn back to my plate and start picking away at my fries.

"They're everything here. The guy with the jet-back hair? That's Daxon Emerson. Quarterback for our football team, wanted by almost every college out there. Will probably go pro at some point." She grins. "The blond guy next to Daxon is Mason Turner."

I take in his dirty blond hair, cut high and tight. He looks pristine. Turner ... I know that name.

"Is he—"

"The mayor's son. Yep. He drips sex, and from what I hear, is a god in bed."

There's a twinkle in her eye, and I can see that she definitely has the hots for Mason. Which, by her explanation of things, he's politician royalty. She could hang off his arm and be set for life.

Liz goes on, "The other one with the beautiful brown hair is Colton Langford. He's a little more quiet, more into nerdy things, but hotter than sin."

I stare at his very shaggy hair that falls slightly in front of his face.

"You do know guys are like shoes. The cuter they are, the more they hurt." My lips curl back in disgust.

Liz rolled her eyes. "Yeah, but I like the cute, pretty shoes."

As I watch the world stop moving for these three, I notice three very beautiful ladies coming up and greeting them. I cock my head back to Liz. "And they are?" I'm assuming they have some importance.

"The Queens of Darkwood," she says matter of factly.

"What the fuck did you just say? Am I being punked?" I draw my brows in and narrow my eyes at her.

She chuckles, "No. They really are. Self-proclaimed, but they are the Queens of Darkwood. To most everyone else, they are just the lucky ones that get to hang around the kings all the time. Bianca Bellecourt is the blonde and captain of the cheerleading squad." Of course the bitch is. I scoff at the information, and Liz continues. "Tiffany Ives is the small brunette to her right, and Jacklyn Greenwood is the taller brunette to her left."

"Wait, okay, I thought you said that girls want to be claimed by the almighty douchebags." I shake my head in confusion.

"The queens are associated with the kings; they belong to them in the hierarchy of things. Top of the food chain."

"So, what is everyone else?"

She shrugs. "Lowly commoners who are just fighting to get that crown."

"But I thought you all come from money?" This shit is too fucking much.

"Yes, but those six are richer than all of us. Their parents run this town, probably even beyond this town."

I gather up my tray and pick up my things. "This was a nice little dinner and all, but I'd like to get back to the room. This is all just too much for me to even deal with ... ever." I walk my tray over to the trash and dump the barely eaten burger. I place the tray on the belt next to the bin and turn around to head out of this strange wonderland I'm in.

As I make my way through the chattering crowd of annoyingly peachy students, I look up and meet the greenest pair of eyes I've ever seen. For a moment, my step falters, but I try to recover and hope to fuck no one noticed.

But he did. Daxon Emerson saw my misstep. His lips curl up into a sinister smile, and I shudder. I hold my head high and head out of the dining hall. The cool wind hits my face outside, and I take a deep breath.

I make my way back around the winding path towards the dorms, but a chill races down my spine as I get that feeling that I am being watched again. This time, I don't bother to look around; I head back to the confines of my dorm. This fucking place is a creepy mother fucking place.

*Head down, get through this year.*

Somehow, I don't think it will be that easy.

*four*
DAXON

BEEP! *Beep!* I reach over and pick up my phone to turn off my alarm. Seven fucking-o'clock. I could use another hour at least of sleep.

Rest is not something I have time for, though. I love playing football, but I really hate the constant conditioning and keeping up with the workouts. But if I want to make it into the NFL after college, I need to keep pushing myself and my body. Fuck, anything to get out from under my father's hold on me.

I'm an Emerson. My future has been written for me since the day I was born. I will run Emerson Industries. That is what my duty as an heir is. Except, it's not what I want. At least when my mother was still here, I had a better chance at pursuing my dream, not *his*. She always wanted me to be my own person, have my own dreams. But she abandoned me. She left me in his custody. Now I don't have that support anymore. I only have the Emerson way.

She left me. I wasn't worth protecting. The NFL is my only shot at a different life. A life not controlled by my father.

Therefore, I need to be at the top of my game. Get into college, land a spot as their top quarterback, and get drafted into the NFL. That's my plan out of it all. So, all these early mornings, these conditioning exercises I put myself through, they're my ticket out.

I throw my comforter off me and kick my legs over the side of my bed. The light from the sunrise is peaking through my blinds. I get up, make my bed, and saunter into my bathroom to shower and clean up. Yeah, I know, before I go get all sweaty, I take a shower. I just do. After rinsing off and brushing my teeth, I head to my walk-in closet to get changed.

The kings and I have the penthouse of dorm rooms here at Darkwood. At the top of the Dark Pine Towers, our massive dorm sits.

Our families founded this city and this school. They still contribute donations to Darkwood and even sit on the board. We are engrained in this school and the history. That's what makes us kings. By birth and by legacy. Our fathers were legacy, our grandfathers were too, and one day when we have our own kids, they will walk the halls of this school as well. It's expected. The expectation I'm hoping to change.

We live in luxury here. And with all the money funneled into this place, we damn well should. My room's huge; I have a private en suite, as all the rooms in the penthouse do. My walls are a dark grey, while my furniture is black and minimalistic. The tile floor is cold beneath my feet as I walk back to my bed. I don't spend much time in here, except to sleep and change. We hang out in the game room down the hall more than anywhere else.

I throw on some shorts and a shirt and grab my phone and headphones. I need to head over to the weight room to get in my lifts for the day. We have a free day today, but I can't let myself get complacent. I need to keep my regimen, keep my workouts going.

Once outside, I take a moment to let the cool air blow against me and take in the blue sky and bright sun rising in the east. The campus is so still at this time of day. Even with move-in for the seniors starting soon, it's quiet. It's nice to be up early before the chaos. I can think without all the noise. For a few minutes, I can get that quiet, that peace I need.

I look up and close my eyes, letting the coolness hit my face. I take a deep breath and let it out slowly.

It's only a moment of peace.

I throw my headphones on and crank up Breaking Benjamin. The weight room is across campus, so I take the opportunity to use that as an excuse to get my cardio in and run the whole way there. While I speed down pathways and sidewalks, my mind goes through my daily routine, my future, my mother.

I let out a sigh as I think about her. There are days I can't even stand to think about her. Today isn't one of them.

Was there something I could've done? Was it something my father did? What made her disappear? Run away from me? Why didn't she take me with her?

Listen to me; I've got mommy issues. I chuckle as I shake off the thoughts running around my head.

By the time I finish my session and grab a nice ice bath in the locker room to soothe my aching muscles, I realize it's now nine in the morning. My body is sore, and my stomach is growling. I was so in my own head that I forgot to bring a protein bar with me to at least hold back some of the hunger. As I run back towards the dorm, I notice the droves of students starting to gather everywhere, some with boxes and bags, some with suitcases.

It's official. Move-in day has commenced.

But then my eyes catch her. A redhead walking towards the Forthright Building. Quickly, I take cover behind a tree as I watch her. Goddamn, she is fucking beautiful. Sexy as fuck. Her long red hair hits the middle of her back, and her curves are fucking perfect. The way she sways her hips as she walks and the way her tits bounce, fuck. Her ass in her ripped jeans make me want to bite into it.

What I wouldn't give to slide my cock into her pussy. *Fuck.* I'm a creeper with a hard-on behind a goddamn tree.

I pull up my phone and locate the information I have on the new student, sent from my father. Phoenix Hayes. I pull up her picture and sure as shit, it's her. I push down my will to want to grab her and fuck her and just watch her. She walks with a confidence of not giving a fuck, but she falters for a moment. A false sense of confidence. She reaches the door and looks around.

That's right my little bird, I'm watching you.

She shakes her head and then heads inside. I take a deep breath and step away from the tree, running back towards the dorm. Once I get there, I push past the herd of new students to the only elevator made for us and head back up to my room.

Yes, the kings have their own elevator. We are a legacy. Privileged.

When I enter my en suite, I quickly turn the shower on and wait for the water to heat up. Once in I get under the water, I let it it cascade down my sore body.

I press my hands up against the tiles and close my eyes. The image of Phoenix pops into my head. Her curvy little body, her long hair I want to wrap around my fist as I fuck her beautiful ass from behind. Fuck. I reach down and slowly start stroking my cock, which is as hard as steel at the thought of her.

I start to move my fist up and down it as I imagine her riding me, her tits bouncing in my face. How warm her pussy feels, how tight. I squeeze my dick slightly, which makes me groan. Thinking about her on all fours as I slam into her, her perfect pert ass in the air as I leave my handprint on them.

I start to feel the tingle in the base of my spine, and then instantly I'm pushed over the cliff. I come hard, grunting as I spill all over the tile. I rest my head against the shower wall, breathing hard. I'm not nearly as satisfied as I need to be. But it took the edge off for now.

There's plenty of pussy currently moving in that have been salivating all summer for a chance to fuck me. Pick of the pussy litter. It's good being a king.

Once I'm fully dressed, I head out to the kitchen to get some water and finally find something to eat. As I stroll up, Colton's leaning against the counter on the island.

Colton Langford comes from old money. His family's a big player in the security technology industry, and he's expected to take over the company after he graduates from college. It's the last thing he actually wants to do.

Colt's also tech savvy. He loves his computers, and he loves hacking into things. Thing is, he hates people. Running a company would put him front and center as the face of Langford Tech. AKA, put him in front of people.

He doesn't even like being around people here at school. Well, except for us. We protect each other.

"Hey." I stroll up to the pantry and root around for one of my protein bars. Colt's quiet and has his head down looking at his iPad. "Did you get the stuff I sent you on the new girl?"

"Yeah, I'm just going through it now. So far, all I got is that she's an excellent student and could get into any college of her choice but has yet to apply to any of them or show interest in one."

I hum. "I ran into her on my way back."

"What?" He pulls his head away from his iPad and pulls his brows in. He adjusts his glasses and gives me his full attention.

"She was walking into Forthright. She didn't see me. But fuck, she's sexy as hell. Too bad my father says she's a problem. He's hell bent on us getting rid of her. I'd like to sink my dick into her." I bite my lip and internally groan.

"Awesome." He deadpans. "So, what's the plan then?"

"Not sure yet. Still working that out." I chug my water and then toss the bottle away. I rip open the protein bar and shovel it into my mouth, trying to tame my hunger.

"Hey, assholes." Mason saunters into the kitchen as I finish up my bar. "New year, Kings. New fucking year."

Mason Turner comes from a long line of politicians. Currently, his father's the Mayor of Black Forest with aspirations of running for the Senate. Mason has been primed to eventually get into politics. If he does, he's going to need a good team to bury the skeletons in his closet. He is a walking man-whore of a scandal.

"I just want to get out of here." I look over at him, shaking my head.

Mason's lips thin. "Well at least it's our last year here. We just have to make it through this bullshit."

"Yep. No new teachers this year, so they know the drill. Keep us happy." Colt nods. "Just hoping we don't have to deal with a lot of outside work beside our little problem student."

"Did your dad explain why we need to push her out?" Mase walks over to the barstool on the other end of the island and leans his elbows on the counter.

"Nope. I'm sure I'll know soon enough, though. That's why I want to know her background. Figure out what his angle is before he tells me. I want to be one step ahead of him on this. This is an odd request and truthfully, I don't know how comfortable I am with it. Something doesn't sit right." I shake my head and frown. "Watch the docks, handle transactions for the business, that I get. Kicking a girl out of school is just weird. But whatever Father wants, Father gets."

Mase shrugs, toying with a fruit from the bowl on the counter. "We could just make her life a living hell. That's easy enough to do."

"Did you get us into her classes, Colt?"

He confirms, "Yep. We are each in at least one of them, or all of us are. But someone is with her at all times."

"Good. Okay, I need to meet up with Coach Collins to go over some of the new recruits this year. You coming?" I turn to Mason. Him and I are starters on the Darkwood football team. He's my wide receiver, and we make an unstoppable team.

"Yeah. Let's roll."

* * *

When dinnertime rolls around, the guys and I make our way over to the dining hall. Most students have been moved into the dorms by now, so the campus is very active.

Students are probably walking around now, meeting up with friends and getting excited for the new year.

As we stroll through the campus, students part like the Red Sea for us. They know who we are, and they know their place. They bow before the kings.

A student walking out of Dorian Hall sees us as we come up to the door. He looks down at the sidewalk but holds the door open for us as we stride into the room. The entire dining area falls silent. All the eyes are on us as we head to our table in the center of the hall. Whispers greet us, and eyes hone in on us. And I know, most of the women here are coming up with some plan to try find an in with one of us.

Once we reach our table, a flash of red catches my attention. My eyes immediately find my distraction. Her.

This time, I get to see her up-close, and holy fuck. As she looks up, she sees me, and I watch her falter a bit in her steps. The side of my mouth goes up in a smile, glad to know I have some sort of effect on her. Even if she doesn't know who I am, she will soon.

Her eyes sparkle with a golden hue. Her long, fiery red hair comes down around her face. She's short, maybe five feet tall at the most. Her tits are huge, and so much more than a handful. Her hips sway as she walks, and I can't wait to see her walk past me so I can take in that ass. She has these pouty lips I want to see wrapped around my cock. Fuck.

She quickly moves past me, and that's probably for the best. I'm all but willing myself not to get hard, and I don't know if I can control myself and not want to grab her and take her off somewhere to have my way with her.

But for as much as I am trying to will myself to tame my dick, a certain shrill voice pipes up and does the job for me.

"Oh! I'm so glad you're back, Daxy." Yeah, my balls shrivel right back up.

"Bianca." It's all I'll acknowledge for her. Her and her mangy mutts are the most annoying creatures this world has ever created. I feel her fingers start to graze my arm and instantly, I want to recoil. Her touch burns like acid. The only reason we even put up with these bitches is because they're cheerleaders and high on the food chain.

She pushes her blonde hair back, and I catch a whiff of whatever shit-smelling perfume she has on. It's all I can do not to gag. "So, what are you three up too?" For appearances, I try to keep a united front. Just for appearances.

Bianca looks up at me with desperate eyes. "Oh, just missing our kings." Mase snorts and laughs. I narrow my eyes, shooting him a look to cut it out. "We went all summer without seeing you guys. It was lonely."

Yeah, something tells me she was anything but lonely. The three of them will spread their legs for any reason. Especially if that reason comes with a huge bank account.

"I'm so hungry. I think I'm going to go grab something," Tiffany whines.

"Well, make sure it's veggies, Tiff. You're getting a little heavy on the lift," Bianca spits at Tiffany. Tiff's mouth drops open, and her cheeks turn red from embarrassment. She turns and walks away from the table in a huff.

"Was that really necessary?" I turn to the queen bitch.

"Yes. We need to be in top shape to compete in regionals this year. I can't have a heifer on my team." She smiles at me, and I cringe. She is the worst kind of human. Well, really, we all are. We do tend to bulldoze anyone who gets in our way. It's who we are, who we have been groomed to be. Who gives a shit about their feelings?

Of course, there are times I hate being a legacy. But it

doesn't matter what I want or hate or like. I just have to do as I'm told.

I can feel a headache starting to form in my head. I pull away from her and get up to move away from the retched witch. I head over to the small cafe in the dining hall and order my usual coffee. Strong and black as night. I take a sip of the hot sludge and let it burn my throat as it goes down.

"Fuck, they are so goddamn annoying." Mason comes up behind me, no doubt needing to get away from the Witches of Darkwood.

"Last year we have to put up with them," I offer.

"Yeah, unless they conveniently get shipped to Harvard or Yale with us. And who knows what our families have cooked up for us? After all, kings need their queens." Mase sticks out his tongue and makes a fake gagging sound. He repeats the same statement our fathers have been telling us since we were little. That to rule the world, we need some queens by our side. Queens that can help us rule. Blah, blah, fucking blah.

"Won't happen." I shake my head.

He crosses his arms over his chest. "So, was that the new girl you locked eyes with back there?"

I shrug, sipping my coffee again. "Yeah."

"She was hot."

I roll my eyes. "Yes, she is. But remember she's off limits," I remind him. "We need to just get her out of Darkwood."

"Yeah, yeah. I get it. Any reason why our superiors want her gone?" Mase looks out at the dining area. He has a real problem with his father and ours. He refuses to acknowledge them as such.

"Nope. No idea." I take another big gulp of my coffee and let the bitterness rest on my tongue before swallowing.

"Well let's hope this chick is easy to get rid of. I really don't want to spend a lot of time on it. We have enough shit on our hands to deal with," he says as he walks away.

Something tells me she will put up a fight. Just by looking at her, she seems like she doesn't go down without swinging.

Personally, I'm looking forward to getting dirty.

## *five*
PHOENIX

TODAY IS BULLSHIT. Mondays are always bullshit. But today is more bullshit than just a regular Monday.

I stand in front of the mirror inside my walk-in closet, staring at the ridiculous uniform they expect us to wear. The damn skirt is so short, and I don't care if it's just above the knees. One slight breeze and the campus will get a front row viewing of my ass. The fucking socks and shoes take the cake, too. These things are ugly as sin, and now I'm supposed to be okay just strutting across campus in them. I stare at my Doc Martins, longing to rip these monstrosities off and put them on.

I'm starting to think that my aunt sent me here to torture me. Well played, Aunt Julie. Mission accomplished. I'm officially tortured.

The best part? This damn uniform has a plaid cross tie and blazer. I'm literally in hell. This is bullshit.

I finish buttoning up my blazer, making sure I look full-on geek presentable. At least everyone on this campus will look this awful. As I finish buttoning this horrid hunter green blazer, there's a knock on my door.

Swinging it open, I find my roommate standing there with a wide smile splashed across her face.

"Good morning! Are you ready for your first day at Darkwood?" She's practically bouncing.

"No. I would rather stick hot needles under my nails." I shake my head and purse my lips.

"Oh, come on! It won't be that bad. What class do you have first?" Liz pushes past me and helps herself to a seat on my bed.

"Sure, come on in, roomie." I pull my lips in a tight smile as I walk over to my desk. Then I grab my schedule and see what's in store for me. "U.S. Government."

She scrunches up her face. "Ew. Well, what's after that?"

"Pre-calc, English IV, then lunch and my Vocal Music class." I shove the paper into my backpack and then gather up my books, tablet, and stuff I need for the day.

Apparently at this fancy school, some of your homework is done a fucking tablet, so they hand them out like candy.

She frowns. "We don't have any classes together. Well, at least we will have lunch together."

I don't respond, but Liz doesn't even care. She bounces her happy ass right out of my room. Thank God she's gone.

Don't get me wrong, she's nice, but she way too fucking happy for me. She's basically the opposite of me. The sunshine to my dark, thunderous rain clouds.

And I prefer the rain.

As I make my way out of my room, I head into the living area and grab a granola bar to take with me to eat. I fill up my water bottle, throwing it my bag when it's full, and start to head towards the door.

"Wait! I'll walk with you!" Liz calls out as she's

finishing up a text on her phone. "This way you won't have to walk alone."

Alone. That word eats at me. And I know that she's trying to just be nice, but I'm better off doing things alone. But she doesn't know that and maybe she could be a good friend. At least then maybe I'd have someone.

"Yeah sure." I shrug and wait for Liz to get her shit together. When she finally finishes, she throws her bag over her shoulder, and we make our way out of the room and down the hall. As is everyone else.

Liz and I decide to head down out of the building via the stairs. I refused to wait for the elevators. Also, I make a note to leave a lot earlier to avoid the crowd.

When we finally make it outside, the wind whips through my hair as I try to keep it out of my face. Students are gathered in groups, walking to their respective classes, and I'm pulling out my map to figure out where the building is that I need to go to.

"You're looking for the Emerson Building." Liz throws a soft elbow into my arm. "See that castle-looking building next to Forthright?" I nod, and she explains, "That's Emerson. History, science, and business are all located in that building. I'm headed over to Forthright for English, so I'll see you at lunch!" Liz turns and walks away.

I'm left there, standing alone while other students huddle around each other.

Alone.

Shaking myself out of my pity moment, I steel my spine and hold my head up while I push myself through the crowds. Walking the path towards the Emerson building, I'm very aware of the stares and whispers. Obviously, being the new girl, I'm front-page fucking news. Can't wait until it becomes old news.

As I walk up to the building, I stand off to the side and pause for a moment. *Keep your head down and get the hell out of here.*

Taking slow breaths, I try to slow my wildly beating heart. In all honesty, I'm extremely nervous. I can feel my anxiety threatening to break free. This is all just too much for me. Too much change in such a short period of time. Dealing with the loss of my father, then my mother, and now being shipped off to some old, creepy-as-fuck school is just way too much to deal with.

Once my nerves are calm, I pull open the door and make my way to my history class. As I walk into the lecture-like classroom, I immediately run to the back corner by the window.

As I get my book and tablet to prepare it to take notes, I feel a figure standing next to me. I look up and am greeted with one of the kings Liz pointed out to me Friday.

"You're in my seat." The king with the dirty blond hair stares at me with his piercing blue eyes.

I may be sitting down, but even standing, he would tower over me. Oh, and his uniform? I think it may be painted on him, because I can see how giant his arms are through his blazer. His chin is sharp and chiseled, and I put ten bucks on him having that "v" that leads to the promise land.

I think Liz said his name is Mason. "Move. Fucking. Now."

Nope, his name is asshole.

I roll my eyes. "Yeah, not gonna happen. Feel free to find another seat." I look back down at my tablet and ignore the beautiful asshole of a man.

"You must not know how this works. I sit here in this desk, and you sit somewhere else." He leans in. One hand goes on the flat part of the desk while the other moves to the back of my seat. He's so close, his citrus and sandalwood scent is invading my nose.

I wouldn't mind him invading other places. *Shit, no, Phoenix*. Think with your head and not with the girly parts.

Meeting his gaze, I lift the corner of my mouth. "Is there assigned seating?"

"Yeah, I'm assigned to this seat," he hits back. God, why the fuck is he so good looking? It's a shame that hotness is wasted on a dick.

"Really? That's so fucking weird then. Because right there on the white board it says pick your seat for the year. So, I'm picking this one." I give him my sweetest fuck-you smile I can muster. "You can pick another one. Toodles!" I wave and bat my eyelashes at him, then look back down at my tablet.

I hear a low growl and he pushes up. "That's fine, Red." Taking the desk in front of me by the chair, he shifts it over, creating an annoying scraping sound, and he plants himself in the seat next to me against the wall. "I'll sit right here so we can be partners."

I let out a laugh but turn back to my tablet, trying to figure the damn thing out. "Yeah, no thank you. I'll find someone else less ... you."

He lets out a deep throaty chuckle but doesn't say anything. I can feel the heat of his stare on me. He's even sitting sideways in his desk so that he can lean over the aisle and be closer to me. There's a flush that starts to burn my cheeks and a flutter in my stomach, knowing his gaze is fixed on me.

Before I combust under his watch, a voice booms from the front of the room, causing me to look up.

"Welcome to U.S. Government, ladies and gents. As you

can clearly read from the board, the seat you are in is the seat you will have all year long. So, get comfortable."

I turn my head and shoot the asshole next to me a big smile.

"Now, my name is Mr. Patterson. Introduce yourself to the person on your right, because that person is now your partner from here on out." He turns to his desk, picking up a stack of paper to pass around, but I freeze at his words.

The king beside me snorts. "Hey, Red. Did you hear that? I told you we would be partners."

"My name is not Red." My eyes narrow at him. "It's Phoenix."

"Pretty name for a beautiful girl." He shifts in his seat so he's sitting more on the edge of the chair now.

"Worst fucking pickup line ever. And you haven't introduced yourself, by the way."

"Really? I get a lot of girls that way." he sighs. "Well, my name is Mason. Mason Turner." He holds his hand out to me as if he wants to shake my hand. I ignore his hand, and he pulls it back, acting wounded by placing his hand on his heart. "Do you have a last name, Red?"

I groan at his use of the dumbest nickname ever. I've heard it all my life, so old. "Again, it's Phoenix, and yes, I do."

He tilts his head, waiting for me to tell him what it is, but I don't. Fuck him and his very good-looking ass.

"Okay, the syllabus for the semester is coming around. Study it, know it. That will tell you what we are working on, your assignments, and even your group project. Please take note of the due dates." Mr. Patterson drones on about God knows what. I have completely tuned him out because of the idiot next to me. Mason hasn't taken his eyes off me once.

As soon as the bell rings, I'm up and out of my chair. I'm not even bothering to put my stuff away first. I just grab it and run out the door, heading to my next class, which is conveniently down the hall.

When I get to my pre-calculus class, I find a seat again in the back row, but this time away from the windows. This way, if any of the king douches are in this class, they can have their precious window seats. No sooner than I sit down do Mason and another king asshole walk in and lock eyes on me.

Well, fuck.

The new king seems to not be as rambunctious as Mason. He doesn't smile or show any emotion, and he doesn't really stare too long at me once he enters the room. He turns towards Mason and says something too low for me to hear.

I put my head down and hope that they head to the other side of the classroom. Of course, I'm not that lucky. They walk right up to me.

"Hey, Red. How cool is this that we have another class together?" Mason takes the seat next to me.

"Don't you have an assigned seat to get to?" I snap at him. I can feel myself clenching my jaw; I'm so tense around him right now.

"Yeah, I do. Next to you, of course." Mason shrugs. "Red, meet Colton. Colt, this goddess here is Red." Colton just stares at me, and I snap back to Mason.

"Hey! Douche canoe, my name is not Red," I growl at him. My fists clench at my sides.

I turn to get a look at my other tormentor and wow. He is the opposite of Mason. His hair dark brown, his eyes that he hides behind a pair of black rimmed glasses are hazel. His face is softer, rounder, but his cheek bones are high. He isn't as muscular as Mason, but I'm pretty sure there's a six pack under that uniform.

I mean birds of a feather all have abs to die for, right? Or however that saying goes.

"I know that, sweetie. It's a nickname I gave you," Mason says softly and condescending. He rolls his eyes and looks at Colt before returning his eyes to me. "Her name's Phoenix. There, you happy now?"

"I'd be happier if you were on the other side of the room."

He smirks. "No can do, Red." Mason shakes his head, and Colton takes the seat in front of me. Wonderful. I'm now surrounded by them.

I release a loud sigh and go back to my tablet, still trying to figure out how to access the programs I need to. Without warning, a shrill voice cuts through the air. I swear I lose some hearing after that.

"What the fuck, Mase? Why are you sitting there?" She rests her hands on her hips, and her mouth drops open.

Mase waves her off. "Because I want to, Bianca."

Her icy gaze cuts to me. "So, you're slumming it with the trailer trash whore?"

Ahh. There it is. I was waiting for that to come out. Apparently, since I don't come from money, I'm immediately classified as both trailer trash and a whore. Both typical and pathetic.

"You should close your mouth before a dick falls in it," I say to the very pissed off Bianca. Her mouth immediately closes, and her cheeks flush.

"You bitch! Do you know who you're talking to?" She comes closer to me, her eyes narrowed and her body shaking in anger.

"Well, he just called you Bianca, so I'm assuming that's

your name. Outside of that, I couldn't give a rat's ass about you." Shrugging, I turn my head away from her for a second before she comes at me. But before she can touch me, Colt steps in between us, halting her in her place.

She seethes, "I'm a queen, you cunt. A Queen of Darkwood. You're nothing but a charity case whore."

"Wow, that language is so becoming of a queen." I frown.

"Go sit down Bianca. Go!" Mase yells at her. Bianca huffs and stomps her foot, turning to a seat three desks down from me in my row. Great. She's still in my proximity.

Throughout the class, I can feel Mason's eyes on me. It's making me extremely uncomfortable. His other friend, Colton, ignores me the entire class, but I'm completely fine with that. I wish Mason would take notes and learn from his buddy. How to ignore the new chick 101.

"So, how about I take you out to dinner?" Mason leans over the desk and whispers to me.

"Well, first off, no. Second off, hell no." I don't even look at him. But as I say that, I hear a snicker in front of me and then a clearing of a throat. Mason narrows his eyes at his friend, who just laughed at him being turned down.

Honestly, it probably doesn't happen a lot for the guy since he is a coveted King of Darkwood.

"Aw, come on, Red. Let me take you out to a nice dinner. It will be like a 'Welcome to Darkwood' dinner." He make a sad face.

I shake my head. "Fuck off, Mason. It's never going to happen. I'm sure there's plenty of bitches that would kill each other over a date with you, but I'm not one of them."

Class comes to a close, and I can't move fast enough to get the hell out of here. Packing up my shit as I go, I walk down the aisle. Without warning, I trip and fall on the floor, my wrists stopping me from smashing my face into the ground.

Pain shoots through my wrist as soon as I move it. I immediately stand up to see Bianca in her seat with a smile on her face.

"You should be more careful, *whore*," she spits at me.

I grab my wrist and square off with her. "Really? Like you didn't purposely trip me? What the fuck?"

"Ladies! Is there a problem?" the teacher yells over from his desk.

I turn to him. "No, there isn't." I shift back to Bianca and stare at her.

"Okay, Red. Come on, I'll help you get to your next class." Mason comes up and places a hand on my shoulder. I shrug out of it, picking up my shit and walking away.

Fuck these people. Fuck these fake ass people.

As students pour out into the hallway, I walk as fast as I can, trying to get away from Mason and Colton. Last thing I need is to be anywhere near them.

Holding on to my injured wrist, I plow my way through the throngs of students, dodging bodies in my way. I turn my head back to see what distance I have put between me and the pricks of Darkwood, and I don't see them. Smiling, I turn my head back forward just in time to see myself hit a solid body, knocking me on my ass. My hands go down on instinct to try and break the fall, only to cause a shooting pain in my injured left wrist.

"Ow! Motherfucker!" I immediately roll to my right and sit up, clutching my wrist. The throbbing pain shoots through me, and I think I made it worse. At this rate, I'll end up in the emergency room by lunch.

I look up at the brick wall I just hit and see yet another king standing before me. Students have halted their trek to class, standing there and watching. Waiting to see what happens between me and their precious king. Daxon. I stand up and grab my bag up off the ground with my good hand.

He narrows his emerald-green eyes at me, his lips forming a thin line. His hand runs through his dark black hair. I don't cower under his stare; fuck the kings. "Do you normally just imitate a fucking wall in the middle of the hallway?"

"You should watch where you're going," Daxon says calmly.

"Or, and I know this will be an odd concept for you, maybe you could just move out of someone's way. I know you're used to having the commoners just part for you upon your arrival," I retort snidely. I hear gasps in the hall around me, students not believing what they're hearing.

"Well, aren't you just a little spitfire?" He tilts his head to the side and keeps his eyes on mine, not wavering one bit.

"No, just highly annoyed that one of your retched queens tripped me and your guard dogs have been a pain in my ass already on my first day, and it's not even ten-o-clock yet. Oh, and yes, I'm fully aware of the royalty that are the kings and the bitchy court jesters, but I couldn't give less of a fuck. Tell your friends to find someone else to annoy."

The corners of his mouth tilts up in an evil smile. He says nothing; he just bores holes through me. After what seems like an eternity, he walks around me, never looking back.

So much for keeping my head down. I have a feeling I just put a target on my back.

## *six*

DAXON

I SWEAR I got a little hard listening to that little spitfire just go off on me in the hallway this morning.

Phoenix Hayes.

If I didn't need to destroy her and run her out of this school, I would've pulled her into a vacant classroom, bent her over a desk, and fucked her into next week. Fuck.

Such a shame she won't be here much longer. It would have made my senior year a lot better to fuck with her the entire year. And actually fuck her. I bet she has a tight pussy. Damnit, I really want to fuck her now.

But she needs to go.

Though, I'll be honest, I have no idea why my father is hell bent on getting her kicked out of here. He's on the board for Darkwood; he could have denied the scholarship. Of course, I can't ask either. And I couldn't care. Whatever. I'll get her out of here and then move on with my life.

As I walk back to the dorms, my phone rings. Pulling it out of my pocket, my dad's name flashes across the screen.

"To what do I owe the pleasure of this phone call?" I roll my eyes as I greet my father.

Gregory Emerson is a man who takes no pleasure in being a father. From early on in my life, I can remember him always focused on the company more so than my mom and me. In fact, I can remember many times where he referred to his company as the only family he needed. Emerson Industries is his blood, sweat, and tears. His life source.

Emerson Industries creates and manufactures weapons. He handles defense and government contracts that bring in more money than my family knows what to do with. That's important to him. Money is his everything. I'm just a means to continue on with it all.

The man spends all hours on the docks, in the office, and traveling. He meets with politicians and celebrities, wheels and deals when it comes to defense and weapons. He is always researching new weaponry and putting it in front of our military and government.

Our family is very close with Mason's, and I'm sure it's to help make sure we can operate more 'efficiently', or do things under the radar. Having someone on the inside can only help my father. With Colton's family in the security technology sector, our families are powerful.

To him, I'm nothing more than an heir. A position he has been grooming me for since as far back as I can remember. He would take me to meetings and make me meet powerful people. And I hated every minute of it.

"Did you find our situation?" my father growls into the phone.

"Yep." I let out a sigh. This just feels like such a waste of time. "Can I please ask why it is that we get her removed from here?"

"Not important."

"Well, you say it's not, but if I'm going to be getting rid

of an innocent, I need to know why." I stop in my tracks and stare up at the dorms in front of me.

"She's far from innocent. She's out to destroy this family!" he yells into the phone. He pauses for a moment, and I hear him clear his throat. "And that is all you need to know. She will cause trouble, cause this family trouble. Do what I asked you to do, and don't give me a hard time about it."

"Yes, sir." I click end on my phone and throw it back into my pocket, running my hand over my face and letting out a long breath.

What is she connected to? She seems so aloof. She's different from the students here, not trying to fit in and not even trying to buddy up to us. How can that little spitfire destroy our family? And to that question, what family? After my mother left us, we became two strangers. Emily Emerson was the glue that held us together.

But trying to create a family with someone who wanted nothing to do with us became too much. My father is cold. Honestly, I'm surprised I'm even on this earth. Though he has always told me that his marriage to my mother was a contract. That's all marriage is, really. Her duty was to bear a child after they married, an heir. Basically, her marriage was a loveless contract that she was stuck in. Her only way out was to leave, so she abandoned me.

By the time I reach the top floor of the dorm, I can feel the tightening of my muscles. I rub the back of my neck and let out a sigh. Walking through the living area, I head straight to my room to drop off my stuff. I need to find Colt and see what he has found.

Before I step out of my room, my phone dings with a message, and I pick it up to see it's a text and video from Mason.

**Mason: Our little birdie can sing.**

I click on the video, and it's Phoenix in the theater with her headphones on, singing on stage. It's a song I recognize, *The End of the Dream* by Evanescence. And holy shit, she can sing. Her voice gives me goosebumps; its beautiful. I'm captivated by every single word she belts out. The notes she can hit, the confidence she holds up there on the stage. Fuck, it's spellbinding.

I replay it, completely enthralled by her. Fuck me.

**Me: When did you get this?**

**Mason: After study hall, she ran off to the theater. Followed her. Dude, she's mesmerizing up there. My dick got hard just listening to her.**

Not gonna lie. Mine did, too. But he doesn't need to know that. We all need to keep our focus.

**Me: Keep it in your pants. That's not what we need to be thinking with.**

**Mason: Buzz kill.**

I lock my phone and go off to search out Colt, finding him in his room.

Colton may be organized when it comes to his computers and whatever he needs for finding out information, but his fucking room looks like a bomb went off in it. There are clothes thrown everywhere, books laying haphazardly on every surface of the room, and his bedding has been tossed about. It's just a good thing he doesn't eat in here; I'm almost positive there would be science experiments growing by now.

Colton is a bit more introverted than Mason or me. He just doesn't really like being the center of attention. Which is rough, considering he's a king. But Mason and I tend to steal the spotlight away from him, and he's okay with that. He never really got into sports, but Colt's always down to work out with us. He's a brother, a nerdy-face-in-the-computer-all-the-time brother, but still a brother.

A very messy brother.

Maybe I need to call a weekly maid for him.

I knock on his open door. "Hey."

"Hey, what's up?" Colt says as he turns to face me, away from the four computer screens he has running.

"Find anything on our girl?" I sit on the corner of his bed.

"Actually yeah. A lot." He turns back to his computer screen and pulls some files up. "Phoenix Hayes, born September 13th—"

"She's got the same birthday as me? No way! What are the chances?" I grin. My little spitfire and I share a birthday.

"Well, technically there's a .27 percent chance ..."

I slap his shoulder. "It was rhetorical, Colt."

"Anyways," he continues, "currently she lives with her aunt, Julie Trivits. Well, before she moved here. So that's at least her home away from Darkwood."

"Trivits ... Why does that name sound familiar?"

"Well known software developer, Ronald Trivits. Made his money on startup companies. He actually developed the accounting software your father uses. He was also on the board of Darkwood right up until we got here."

"Yes! That's how I know that name. Shit, so she lives with them now? Maybe that's how she got in here."

"Well, he suddenly died well over a year ago. They say natural causes. Left everything to his wife, Julie. She still had contact with some of the people on the board, used it to get Phoenix in the academy." He clicks a few more things on his screen.

His setup is quite impressive. The clear panels allow you to see into the computer tower, which glows. Lights and lit-up fans blast color from inside the machine. This is nerd central. It's a command center.

"Okay, but then where are her parents?" I cock my head to the side, trying to make sense of everything.

"Dead."

My eyebrows shoot up. "What? How?"

"Well, that's where this gets messy. And I'm going to need you to keep a cool head with everything I'm about to tell you." He turns to me, but then his eyes flit over my shoulder for a moment.

"Hey, assholes, what are we talking about?" Mason interrupts, appearing beside me.

"Colt figured out some stuff about our little princess. Both parents are dead, and her aunt was married to Ronald Trivits," I catch Mase up on the information I have.

"That's the software guy. He had a lot of small businesses around here." He pauses for a moment. "And you said her parents are dead?" He looks between Colt and me, trying to gather everything we have so far.

Colt nods. "I was just about to tell Dax here why. But here's the thing,"—he looks towards me—"I don't know how this wasn't all over the news, or how this was hidden from reports that were put out, but it's fucked six ways to Sunday."

"Spill it, Colt." I glare at him. I'm on pins and needles waiting for him to spit out whatever it seems to be that has him looking pale.

"They both died from suicide." He pauses and looks at Mase and then me. "Her mom killed herself at the beginning of this year. Which police assume was because her husband killed himself a little over a couple years ago."

I shrug. "Okay, so both her parents were selfish and left

her to fend for herself. I'm still not following what would have me so upset."

Colt flits his eyes between Mason and me, his leg bouncing rapidly. He finally breaks the silence. "Trevor Hayes was killed in a vehicle accident when he ran himself off a cliff. No tire marks, nothing to suggest that someone hit him. Witness state that he just turned his car and careened over the cliff. That was on January 25th."

That date sends shivers down my spine.

"Okay. So, he killed himself the same day my mom ran out on us. So what?" I'm connecting the dots in my head, but I'm not liking the results that it's coming up with. My heart is ready to beat out my chest, and I start to feel extremely hot.

Colt looks to Mason and then back at me, taking a deep breath. "He wasn't alone in the car."

"Wait, I thought you said it was a suicide? Why would there be someone else in the car? Then that would be murder-suicide." Mason steps forward and sits on the bench at the end of Colts bed.

"Well, that's where I can't connect the pieces. There were definitely two bodies in that car, but the second body found was covered up to make it look like it was only Trevor in the car." Colt takes off his glasses and runs a hand down his face. "I'm sorry, man."

"Sorry for what?" I furrow my brows together and beg the heavens above that he isn't going to say what I think he is. But I can already see it in his eyes, and I know the answer.

"Trevor Hayes and Beverley Emerson were found in Trevor's car on January 25th. That's why she never came home. I'm sorry, Dax," he says quietly.

"Wait ... what? No. She left. Why would she be in his

car?" My breaths come out heavy, and there's a weight on my chest pushing down on me, making it hard to breathe. "There's no fucking way she was in that car with that piece of shit! My dad would've told me. He would've said something!"

"Are you sure, Colt?" Mason asks.

Every muscle in me tightens, and I clench my teeth so hard, there are lightning bolts of pain inside my mouth. This can't fucking be true.

"Yeah. Positive. I'm not sure how she got in that car, but it was her. And the reports on the car show there was no tampering of the car either. So, whatever happened, Trevor did commit suicide in that car—"

"Killing my mother in the process," I growl.

"Here's what I don't get. Why cover it up?" Mason turns towards me.

"My dad told me that Phoenix was a problem. A problem that could destroy our family. That's why she needed to be taken out of this school and ruined. Maybe my mother was cheating on my father with Trevor." I run my hand through my hair, unsure of what to make of everything I just heard.

"Okay, but then why kill her? Why kill himself in the process?" Mason questions.

"No idea. Maybe she was backing out of the affair? He didn't like that, so he killed them both," Colt suggests. "I mean, anything we come up with is just speculation. Your dad would obviously be the key to this."

My entire body is tight, my fists are clenched, and my teeth are grinding together as my mind is assaulted with the truth of what Colt found. My mom was taken from me. The only light in my life was snuffed out by the actions of

Trevor Hayes. I jump up off the bed and let out a loud scream.

"This fucking bitch has the nerve to come here? Act all high and mighty like we are scum when her fucking father killed my mother?" I vibrate with a rage I didn't know I was capable of. "She's done. She will wish she never stepped foot on this fucking campus."

"What do you want us to do?" Mason places a hand on my shoulder. "We will do whatever we need to."

"Kings, Queens—fuck, *everyone* at this school is going to make her stay here a living hell," I seethe.

"And then?" Colt asks.

"Eye for an eye." I swallow the pain I feel inside. Everything is gone because of the actions of her father. My life, my mother, my future, gone because of the actions of one man.

Well, she's about to pay for his sins.

## seven
PHOENIX

"HOW DID YOU HURT YOUR WRIST?" Dr. Parker tilts his head to the side as he looks over at the bandage I have around it.

We have been sitting in this office for about ten minutes, not speaking a word to each other. He let me just mull over my thoughts, staring at the empty and depressing walls of the office we're in. I sit on the white plush couch that was brought in for us to use.

"I fell." I pick at the hem of my shirt, trying to avoid eye contact with him. Because, well, he's going to try to get things out of me, since it's his job and all.

"You fell. How?"

"Two left feet, Doc. I mean have you seen these shoes? I don't know what sexist asshole came up with this outfit for the girls, but I'm sure he was getting his rocks off as he did it. I mean, the knee-highs, the shoes, the fucking skirt! A gust of wind will let everyone on this campus know what color my thong is today."

I meet his eyes for the first time. He shifts uncomfortably in his seat, and there's a redness in his cheeks as I bring up my thong. Doc must not get laid much. Ha!

He clears his throat and fiddles with his watch. "So, you tripped?"

"That's what I said." I lower my head and pick at the hem of my skirt again.

"You know, Phoenix, if something else is going on, you can tell me. I'm here to help you." His voice is steady, and I see out of my peripheral vision he has shifted so his arms rest on his legs as he leans forward.

My head snaps up. "You're here for me? For me? The way a mother or father should be for their daughter? Can I call you to tell you about my day? Any boy problems I have? Will you take me shopping and we can spend quality time together?"

"No—"

"Will you be there for dances to help me pick a dress? Help me look for colleges? Will we get to have family dinners and spend the holidays together? Will you tell me how proud you are of me, that I'm the best daughter in the world? No? No, you can't be there for me! The only two people in this world who would ever be there for me are dead. Dead! You are here because you are getting paid. Let's not mix that the fuck up, Doc." My heart is beating rapidly, my face heating up in anger and my eyes narrowing at Dr. Parker. I grab my backpack and storm out of the office.

Fuck this.

Walking across campus, I grab hold of my locket and try to center myself. I feel so lost. My body shakes and I want to just scream. Every part of me is consumed with grief and disappointment, and I'm hanging on to my sanity by a thread. I take a deep breath; I need to keep calm. I need to stay the course. Graduate and get the fuck out of dodge.

Looking around, I find the courtyard where some other people are sitting around studying and locate a tree to lean up against.

Taking out my shitty phone, I open it up and see that no one has given two shits to text me or call to see how I'm doing. And by no one, I mean my aunt. The only living relative that I even know about.

I never knew my grandparents on either side. They all died before I was born. My father was a single child, and my mother only had my aunt, her sister. As far as I'm aware, I'm it. Well besides the Wicked Witch of the fucking West, my aunt. But she doesn't count since she can't even be bothered to call me or, fuck, send a text.

The woman literally filled my checking account up and said, "This is all you get for the year. Spend wisely. I don't want a phone call saying you need more." Gee, thanks.

I haven't touched a single penny. I eat the school lunches and shop at the student center. That's it. I don't need her.

As I sit there and contemplate my wonderful fucking life, I'm suddenly hit by something against my face. I pick up a wadded piece of paper and see a couple condoms wrapped up with the note: *So you can afford your tuition.*

Rolling my eyes, I crumple it up and throw it behind me, tossing the condoms right behind me as well. How original. I hear snickers around me, obviously from those who thought this was pure gold comedy. I look down at my phone and see that I need to get to my next class. I pick up my bag and head towards Emerson.

Yay, biology.

Walking though the hallways, people are turning their attention towards me, staring at me, laughing and pointing at me.

Do I have a "kick me" sign on me back?

There are cat calls, hollering at me as I push through the students. I look back at someone whistling at me, "Take a picture! It will last longer!"

And then, once again, I'm on my ass.

"Do you fuckers just stand in the middle of the hallway?" I look up to see that I've run into Colt. His hazel eyes narrow at me through his black eyeglass frames.

Colt is actually the smaller of the three, but he's still giant. His brown hair is gelled to short spikes, and his arms that aren't as big as Douche Dax's. His face is a little more square than Mason's. And I'd put money on the rest of him being just as fucking chiseled as the other two.

He hovers over me as the people around us stop and watch the scene play out. Again, what the fuck? Is there nothing else going on that this is what stops the student body dead in their tracks?

Colt stands there, not saying a word to me. I stand up, thanking my lucky stars that I fell on my ass and didn't proceed to use my hands to break my fall. I'd like my wrist to eventually heal.

"Are you not going to apologize for just standing in the hallway like a damn statue?" I get closer to him, having to strain my neck to look up. At five-three, it's rare that I'm not having to look up at someone. "No words? Can we not talk? Do you not know how to say 'I'm sorry'?"

He brings his head down, close to mine. "I don't talk to insignificant trash."

Remember when I said I liked him more than the others? Yeah. That's not the case anymore.

I hate them all equally.

Colt saunters off in the direction I came from, and I bite

the inside of my cheek to keep from saying anything further. So far, my ability to stay low isn't working so well.

I'm like the goddamn bat signal.

When I stroll into class, I immediately try to find a table in the back corner. I'm praying none of the kings are in this class.

Of course, I can't be that lucky, because as I pull out my notebook and biology book, I feel a tingle in my spine. I look up to see Mason staring at me. He runs over to the desk and slides in the seat next to me.

"You've got to be kidding me. What did I do to deserve this hell?" I roll my eyes and look back at the biology book.

"Aw, Red, is that any way to treat your number one fan?" He places a hand over his heart and frowns like I hurt him.

"A stalker is more like it," I groan.

"How about that date? Come on. I'll take you somewhere nice. You can get all dressed up. Wine and dine ya. Even bring you roses. What's your favorite color rose? I'm going to go with black. You probably like black roses. Then you can come back to my place—"

"Finish that sentence and I'll stab you in the eye," I interrupt.

"I was going to say watch a movie, but okay. I guess you hate movies."

"It's not the movies I hate."

He gasps. "Ouch. Red. Why so mean? What else does a girl from the wrong side of town have to offer except her pussy?"

My head snaps towards him. Mason isn't usually that cruel.

"Wow. We are a bit bitter. Must suck that I won't bow

down to you and beg you to let me suck your itty-bitty cock. I'm sure you have plenty of willing holes that will fill that need. Now, please fuck off and don't talk to me."

There's a flash of regret in his face. But he turns back without saying anything, so for the moment, I'm at least fine with the silence.

\* \* \*

After lunch with my roommate, I head towards the fitness center for my gym class. I was informed that our first session in class is swimming.

I could feel my anxiety rise when Liz told me that. I don't swim. I hate pools. Not to mention that the only two people I've ever really loved died in water. The last thing I need is for it to claim me too.

Plus, I don't have a suit. So, it's possible I could get out of it for at least today.

Fucking of course this place has a pool. I internally groan at the thought.

When I reach the fitness center, I stop for a moment and take in this very out of place building. It's modern. It's new. There are glass windows and slopes in the front façade. Sharp angles in the architecture give it a much different vibe than the rest of campus. It looks like it was teleported from the future and dropped here.

This thing is a monstrosity.

I walk through the front doors and am instantly hit by the chlorine smell. My stomach turns, and I clench my fists. I'm trying my best to hold it together.

I follow the signs to the locker rooms and locate the teacher's office inside the woman's side.

I knock softly on the door.

"Come in," I hear a voice boom behind the door. Slowly, I open it and find a small woman sitting by a desk. Her long chestnut colored hair is pulled back in a ponytail, and her face is sans makeup.

"Um, hi. I'm Phoenix Hayes. I, um, was told we would be doing swimming to start the semester. But I don't have a suit, so can I just spend the time in study hall?" I push out a breath.

"Hi, Miss Hayes. I'm Ms. Thornton. Lucky for you, I actually have your gym uniform and school supplied bathing suit for you. Normally, we pass these out freshman year, then junior year we give those who need new sizes or new ones. So, here you go." She passes me the black bathing suit and the black gym uniform.

"Thanks. I think." I pause for a moment. I want to tell her that I'm really scared of the water, but I instead turn and head out to find a locker.

The inside of the locker room is huge. There are rows of lockers, benches, and even a wall of full-length mirrors. I guess when you're all stuck-up Barbies, you need enough mirrors to appease everyone so the claws don't come out.

Walking through the multitude of lockers, I stumble upon a section that has me groaning. The Bitch Triplets are in my gym class. Wonderful. Fucking wonder-fucking-ful.

"Oh, look what the wind blew in!" Bianca spits as she pulls her hair up into a bun.

"Well, maybe if you guys ate more than a carrot stick at lunch, you all would have some weight on ya to keep the wind from whisking you away," I throw back.

"We were talking about you, whore," Jacklyn snaps.

"So original with your insults. But I guess that's what

happens when you have exactly one brain cell. Does it hurt when you have to think?" I tilt my head to the side and feign concern.

"Girls! Suit up!" Ms. Thornton yells from the doorframe of her office. "Then get yourselves to the pool!"

I walk away from the gremlins and head over to a section of lockers that no one is around. I put my bookbag in and start to strip down, putting on the bathing suit.

Shit, I need to get a lock. A feeling of unease goes over me as I think about someone messing with my stuff, or worse, hiding my uniform. Granted, I only have one class after this, but I really don't think I want to sit in class in a bathing suit under a gym uniform.

Though my unease could be coming from the fact that I'm about to go stand in front of a body of water. A thing that takes lives, steals breaths. Suffocating you with its weightlessness.

I throw my hair up and pick up a towel that is on a bench for us to take. Following the others out there, I take a deep breath the moment I step over the threshold of the pool.

Chlorine attacks my nostrils, and echoes of conversations flood my ears as they bounce off the cement brick walls. Everything is so loud. Even my heartbeat sounds like a drum beating in my chest. The fear is starting to eat at me.

"Look a little pale there, Trailer Trash. Did Mommy or Daddy not have enough money to give you swim lessons?" Bianca taunts.

I ignore her and try to find the teacher. As I walk towards her, I notice how close she is to the edge of the pool. She's got her back to the pool, reading something with another teacher. Fuck. I can't do this. My breaths are coming out fast, my heart is racing inside my chest, and my hands are shaking. My steps falter, and the only sound I hear is the blood rushing in my ears.

Before I can turn around, I'm picked up and run over to the pool. I'm suddenly in the air and crashing into the water before I even have time to take a breath.

Oh my God, I'm underwater.

I struggle in the water, swallowing it as I try to come up for air. I start to panic, trying to expel the water from my lungs, coughing and wheezing. I flail in the water; I don't even know what to do, but I start to get lightheaded, and I'm not sure if it's from being in the water or lack of oxygen.

Suddenly, I'm pulled from the pool. I spit up water and cough out whatever left in my lungs. Taking deep breaths, I can feel the burn in my lungs as oxygen starts to fill them again.

"Ms. Hayes, Phoenix. Just breathe. You're okay," she says as I sit up and scoot away from the pool. "Come on, come over here." Ms. Thornton helps me up and walks me over to a set of bleachers off to the side. She wraps a towel around my shoulders to try to keep me from getting cold.

My body's shaking, but it's definitely not from being cold. I thought I was going to die. I thought the water was going to swallow me. Just like my parents, in water. Fuck.

My mind ceased all logical functions at that point. Images of my mother and father flashed in front of my eyes. I couldn't even process that I should be trying to breathe in the water. I just wanted to get out. The panic took over me.

"Are you okay? Can someone get the nurse?" Mrs. Thornton calls out.

"No!" I yell. "No. I'm fine. I ... I'm not a fan of pools or l-large areas of water."

"What happened? Did you slip in?" She rubs my shoulders. I look up, and my eyes meet Bitch Barbie number one, Bianca. The corner of her mouth is turned slightly up as if this was better than anything she had planned. She had discovered a weakness of mine.

"Yeah, I slipped in," I lie. I could've told on Bianca, but that would never have fixed anything. In fact, it would have made everything worse. "Sorry."

"No, honey, it's okay. Stay here on the bleachers for the rest of class, and just relax. I'll find something for you to do other than swimming for the next couple weeks, okay?"

I nod and she walks away to line the other girls up. I hang my head down for a moment and try to calm my still wildly beating heart.

Fuck.

By the time class is headed back to the locker room and Mrs. Thornton is still begging me to let her call the nurse, which I refuse, I sigh with a little relief. I can get changed, get through study hall, and get back to the safe confinement of my dorm room.

Then a bit of panic runs through me. I don't have a fucking lock for my locker. Shit. I'm praying that none of my stuff was stolen.

As I run back to the locker, slowly I open it and find that my stuff is right where I left it. I let out a small breath of relief as I begin to dress again. I don't have a brush, so I comb through my hair the best I can with my finger and throw it back up.

I open up my backpack and reach in to grab my locket, only it's not there. Are you fucking kidding me?

No, no, no. Please don't tell me they took that. I can feel the heat rising in my neck as I grind my teeth together. I pull out my bag and dump everything on the bench behind me.

It's gone. Fucking gone. Those fucking bitches. Fuck! I need to come up with a way to prove they took it and get it back. I really did not need this shit.

Grabbing my bag, I walk out of the locker room and ignore the stares and whispers around me. Yes, I know they are talking about the pool incident and no, I don't give a shit.

I make it into Forthright in time for my last class of the day. A study hall. And of course, royalty themselves are in this class. Daxon, Colton, and Mason all sit there surrounding the one unoccupied desk.

Seriously?

As I walk up to the desk, I reach around to the back of my neck. Nervously, I scratch it. Plopping down into the seat with utter annoyance over having to sit between these three. Colton sits in front of me, Mason next to the desk, and the self-proclaimed god himself, Daxon behind me.

"Hey, Red. How's your day been?" Mason leans over towards me. I start to feel the heat on my skin as he gets closer to me. I shift in my seat, trying to move away from him.

"Just fine," I say, not even looking at him.

"How was your swim?" Daxon asks from behind me.

My mouth thins, and I grind my molars together. So, they set that up. Awesome.

As I sit there, under the watchful eye of the kings, my skin starts to burn. My arms, my chest, even between my legs.

*What the fuck?*

Am I having an allergic reaction? I don't have any allergies that I know of but, I have never felt this itchy before.

My skin is literally burning. It feels like small pieces of glass are cutting into my skin.

I start to slowly scratch, trying to relieve the pain, but it becomes worse with each pass. My heart starts to race, and I'm trying to control my breathing, but Mason of course catches on that there is something wrong.

"Hey, you okay Red?" His corners of his mouth turn up slightly, and then it hits me.

They did something.

I squirm in my seat and try not to rub my legs together. But I fail miserably, only causing there to be more burning, more itching, between my legs.

I start panting, my eyes darting around the room.

"What's wrong, Spitfire? You seem to be a little squirmy," Daxon says smoothly. I turn around, and his lips turn up.

"What did you do?" I turn around and glare at Daxon.

He throws his hands up and feigns innocence. "Me? I didn't do anything."

"What's going on over there? This is a time to study, not a time to socialize!" the teacher at the front yells at us.

Daxon sighs. "We were, I apologize. It's just, see our friend here, Phoenix, seems to be having an issue. I think her STD is flaring up from a recent encounter."

My mouth drops open, and my cheeks heat up. I am doing everything I can not to haul off and deck him. For one thing, I don't feel like getting in trouble. Second, he is basically made of stone, so I'd hurt myself more than him.

There are whispers around the room, and people start to chuckle at my recent development.

Those fuckers did something to my uniform.

I grab my bag and race out of the room. My entire body is on fire. I need to get back to my room and immediately in the shower to rinse off what I am now realizing is itching powder.

If they thought this would break me, their *juvenile* attempt to break me, they were fucking mistaken.

Try harder, assholes.

## *eight*
MASON

I'M NOT GOING to lie, school became way more interesting the moment Phoenix stepped on campus. And goddamn, she's a sexy little siren. What I wouldn't give to see her lips wrapped around my cock, those beautiful eyes staring up at me.

Fuck. And now my dick's hard.

I need to pull a random into an open classroom and nut. Because if I don't, I'll be jerking it all night thinking of Red.

There's something about her. Not sure if it's her 'not giving a fuck' attitude, the fact that she doesn't take shit from anyone, or maybe it's the mystery that surrounds her, but I have this need to want to be near her. Even if it pisses her off. And I do enjoy pissing her off. The fire in her eyes, fuck, gets me hard as fucking steel.

She has been dealt a lot of shit the last couple days, and she acts like she doesn't care. The itching powder? Fucking that was going to happen no matter what, but her freakout in the pool? That just adds a whole other level of fuckerism that we can torment her with.

She's now known as a walking STD. Students taunting

her in the halls, throwing condoms on her. I heard through the grapevine that someone put hazard tape up on her door and covered it with condoms. A big note that said something about her pussy being infected.

That's the one thing about being in our position: What we say goes. We told the students to give her hell, and they have fully delivered. They are like our little minions. And some are cute enough to fuck.

"Where is our little spark?" I greet Colt at our table in the library. It's Thursday, thank fucking God, finally the end of the week. We're in the library for our morning study hall that we have every Tuesday and Thursday. Red is supposed to be here with us, but Tuesday she was MIA. She didn't pop in until biology.

"I don't think she'll be coming to these study halls," Colt says as he looks up from his iPad.

"What? Why? We made sure to mirror our classes." I swipe the chair across from him at the round table that has always been saved for the kings. This library is massive and two stories high. This table's the farthest from the librarians but allows us to see out into the study spaces and other tables scattered throughout.

The librarians sit up at the front near the entrance, and if you turn right when coming in, it takes you to the first area of books. Taking a left at the desk brings anyone here to the study area. There are study rooms upstairs and more books. But the nice thing about this library is that the second floor wraps around as a balcony, allowing the first floor study area to gather light from the atrium above us.

"I got word from Ms. Hodgens that she has a visitor on Tuesdays every week. On Thursdays, she just goes into the same office and spends her study time there." Colt clears his throat and opens his mouth to continue, but Dax saunters over with Bianca hanging all over him. Behind them are Tiff and Jacklyn.

"Hey, Mase," Tiff purrs as she comes over to me.

"Tiff." I roll my eyes and focus back on Colt. "Do you want to tell him what you were telling me?"

"Bianca, you and the whores need to leave." Dax pries her off the side of his body. She narrows her eyes and then scoffs at him.

"Whatever, Dax. Let's go, girls. Chad and the boys are over there," she says a little louder to try and get us worked up. Only we couldn't give less fucks than we currently do. Chad and his friends are douchebags. They are all second string players on the team. They dream about being us, being kings. Except they never will be.

"So." Dax turns the chair around so he can straddle it and leans forward on the back part of the chair. "What's going on with her?"

"How do you know it's about her?" I smile at him.

He shoots me a look and then turns back to Colt. "Spill."

"Well, it seems on Tuesdays, our new friend has a visitor that comes in once a week to talk to her." Colt stops there for a moment to let that sink in.

"A visitor once a week? What, like a doctor or something?" I cock my head to the side.

"A shrink." Dax looks at Colt, but I can see the wheels turning in his head.

"Exactly. For whatever reason, it's hush-hush. I mean obviously their conversations are, but the fact that the shrink is even in here is all on the down-low. The fact that our little office receptionist even knows is because she has to sign him in and out. Otherwise, everyone else just ignores the fact that he's here." Colt taps the table with his fingers.

"We need those conversations." Dax turns to me. "We need to know what that bitch is saying in there. She may know something, and patient confidentiality and all, she could be holding whatever my dad is after her for."

"And how do you expect that to happen? Just walk in and tell them that we're there to water the plants? Bro, I doubt we can get access to that room." I shake my head at him. He is crazy if he thinks they will just let us in there.

"Get Hodgens to let you in. She owes us for helping get her husband out of that debt pickle he was in."

I run a hand down my face. "Fine. I'll see what I can do."

"Meanwhile, Colt, you need to hook that room up so we can see and access what is being talked about in there. I need to know everything about her, anything I can get my hands on to destroy every single fiber of her being," he says through gritted teeth.

His dad is really pressuring him to figure out a way to get Phoenix out of the school. We just don't know why. But we do as our fathers tell us, because that's what's expected. Good little soldiers.

It's expected that I go to law school, become a lawyer and eventually a politician. Run the town like my father has with the Emerson and Langford seniors. Honestly, I really have no desire to go into politics. Being a lawyer? Yeah, definitely can do that.

But right now, our main concern is getting Red off of this campus. And apparently listening in on her private conversations with her doctor. Now, I know I'm no lawyer, but that definitely breaks a few laws. But let's be honest, now's not the time for a conscience.

I push back from the table and head to my biology class, where I get to be lab partners with the one and only Phoenix.

Man, the daggers she threw at me on Tuesday when she realized she was stuck with me for the semester was worth it. She was pissed. Her cute little face got all red, her eyes narrowed on me, and I could hear a cute little growl come from her. I was fucking turned on, and it was difficult to keep my dick from becoming rock hard.

I head out of the library and over to the Emerson building. Fucking Dax and his fucking family name. I shake my head because I know it drives Dax crazy that his dad had a building named after them.

As I walk through the building, I spot her a few feet ahead of me, and my eyes cannot move from her plump ass swaying back and forth as she walks. It's a crying shame she's the enemy in all this. Actually, it's torture. Fucking pure torture.

I speed up and get up next to her, draping an arm around her shoulder. "Hey there, Red."

She tries to shrug out of my hold, but I pull her closer and keep her right next to me. Other students are staring, their eyes wide and wondering what she's doing walking alongside me.

"Get off me, Mason." Her hand touches mine, and it burns with such an intensity that I want to push her up against a wall and take her right here in front of everyone. Fuck.

"Aw, come on, sweetheart. Is that anyway to treat your lab partner?"

"Feel free to switch partners. In fact, I'll ask for you. I'm sure any other girl in that class would jump at the chance just to breathe the same air as you." She sticks out her tongue and fake gags.

I smirk back. "Hm. That's true. They would. I'm a lucky guy. But sorry, no take backs. You, Red, are stuck with me."

She rolls her eyes but doesn't say anything. She adjusts her backpack, letting out a little grunt as she does, and its then I realize she's carrying her entire day's worth of books or whatever she needs for classes.

"Hey, why don't you put some of that shit in your locker?"

"What? What locker?"

"Um, the locker the school assigns to you. Didn't anyone tell you that?" I stop in the hall right before the classroom, and the look on her face tells me no one did. "I'll take you there before lunch. Come on, Red."

I follow her inside, and we walk back towards the tables along the back wall. We come upon our table, and she slides onto her metal stool, dropping her bag on to the tabletop.

She's quiet, but every now and then I see her eyes move to the corner, trying to catch a glimpse of me. "You can stare at me. I know I'm pleasing to the eye."

She scoffs. "Can you tell your hoes that I need my locket back?"

"Locket?" I pretend to not know what she's talking about, but I know full well what she's missing. She seems to think it was the girls who fucked with her while she was having a meltdown in the pool. It wasn't. I took the locket out of her backpack, and it's in a special little place. I opened it up, there was nothing special in it. Just the words, fly and little birdie. It means something to her, but fuckall to us.

"Yes. A locket. It was in my backpack and now it's fucking gone. Surely you know what a locket is? Tell your chihuahuas to give it back." Her fists curl up, and I can start to see the panic in her eyes. Sorry, Red, I'm doing this to break you.

"I'll ask, but I doubt they would mess with that. They have Tiffany and all that other high-end stuff. They don't need cheap jewelry from a scholarship student." Fuck. I'm an asshole.

Phoenix drops her head down to her book, and I can see her fighting with herself. Probably not sure if she wants to deck me or start throwing things at me.

I've noticed over the last couple classes I have had with her this week, she takes notes in her notebook instead of the iPad.

"You know, taking notes on here,"—I tap the iPad—"is a lot easier."

"Maybe I'm old school," she says as she scribbles away.

"*Or* maybe you don't know how to. I can show you." I pick up her iPad, grab an extra Apple Pencil I keep in my bag, and open up our notes app on it for her. I create a tab for biology class and get it set up and ready for notes today. "All you have to do is write like you would in that, but on this. You can keep it organized by date and class. And up here you can search for dates, classes, or specific terms. Save a tree."

For a moment, she stares at me, crinkling her face. I think it actually might hurt her to say something nice to me. She takes the pencil and her iPad and places it in front of her. "Thanks," she murmurs.

Yeah, being nice is killing her. I can visibly see her relax a little next to me.

So now I know how to break her down. Kindness. Thank you for showing me your weakness, Red.

"I can copy my notes from Tuesday into here for you. This way you won't have to rewrite them. Also, you can download the syllabus and add it to each section so it's easy to reference. You know, in case you lose the paper one they hand out."

"Why are you telling me all this?" She turns her head towards me, her eyes narrowing in disbelief.

I shrug. "Just trying to be friendly."

"Why?" she presses.

"Why not?"

"Because you're a king. You apparently rule this place and can get anything you want. Why be nice to me? All of the sudden, I might add. What do you have to gain? What's your end game, Mason?" She eyes me, waiting for me to give her the motive behind it all.

"Not all of us are assholes, Red. Besides, I'm still waiting for you to agree to let me take you on that date." I wink at her.

"Not happening, Turner. Not ever. Also, you are an asshole. Personified." She presses her lips into a thin line.

"Fine, I can settle for being friends."

Her beautiful little mouth drops open, but before she can come back with a retort, the teacher walks in, and class begins. I face forwards and smile, softly laughing to myself. I know it's killing her that I got the last word in.

Halfway through class, we partner up to do some stupid exercise together. I turn in my seat to face her as she scrolls through the iPad, reading the exercise for us to work on together.

"So, how come you weren't in study hall?" I place an elbow on the table and study her. She straightens up and tenses. She looks at me, and for a moment I see a slight panic in her eyes, but it leaves in a flash.

"None of your fucking business," she bites.

"Just trying to make conversation, Red."

"How do you know I had study hall? Are you in that

class too? Why the fuck do I have one of you assholes in each of my classes? You all are the most annoying gnats in the fucking world. Just won't go away. It's none of your fucking business what I do and when I do it. So please, and I say this as nicely as I can, get fucked." Her face turns red with obvious anger, and I'm honestly turned on by her attitude problem she has.

Before I can respond to her, she has packed up her stuff and is leaving the class. Except class isn't over.

"Miss Hayes, please take your seat. The bell hasn't rung," Ms. Barrens calls after her.

"Yeah, fully aware." Phoenix doesn't even turn around; she just pushes through the door and out into the hallway.

My dick is now rock-hard. Fuck.

## nine

PHOENIX

JESUS FUCKING CHRIST! Can I not just have a single moment without one of those assholes up my ass? They are constantly around me. It's been what, not even a full week of school, and everywhere I turn, there they are.

Colton's a brooding silent asshole. Well, except for the few words he did actually speak. Daxon's a stuck-up douche who sits on his throne while the girls throw themselves on his dick.

And Mason never shuts the fuck up! I don't understand how he gets laid. Does he talk during sex? Maybe that's the only time he shuts up.

I let out an exhausted sigh and head into the nearest restroom. I needed to march over to the office and find out about this locker nonsense. It would be nice to drop stuff off; my back has been killing me lugging all this around.

As I round the corner, I find the women's restroom and pull open the door. Even the restrooms are high-end. There's a little waiting area with a couch, the floor is all a beautiful dark tile, and the stalls have that glass that blurs when you lock it.

It's a fucking school. This shit is in a school.

Rich people.

At Baybridge High, we had to just hope we had a bathroom that actually worked. This here is ridiculous.

Walking over to the stalls, I stopped dead in my tracks as I see one of the queens fixing her caked-on face.

Shit. I do not need any more bullshit today.

"Since when do they let the trash in these bathrooms?" Tiffany Ives crinkles her face in disgust.

"Well, I guess that would be the day you stepped foot on campus," I retort.

"You better watch yourself, whore." Her fists are at her sides now, her eyes in thin slits.

I cross my arms over my chest. "Wow, how original. Call me a whore. Please, hit me with more of your amazing insults."

"You better watch yourself. You're not welcome here." She pushes past me, shoulder checking me as she walks towards the door. "And stay away from the kings. They're ours. They don't want any of your STDs."

"You can have them!" I sing-song. She's gone before I can get out any more.

God, these people are so frustrating. I just want to be left alone. That's it. Yet for some reason, they have it in their money-filled brains that I want to be part of them or need them bothering me. I don't want any of this.

The one thing I do want, I can never get back. My family. My hand immediately goes to where my locket was, and my heart breaks when I remember I don't have it. I checked with my gym teacher and the campus lost and found. No one has turned it in. And I'm positive I took it off and placed it in my bag as I was changing for the pool on Tuesday. I tore apart my room and eventually gave into the fact that one of those bitches took it. I should've asked Barbie number two about it, but she had me distracted.

My heart starts to beat a little faster, and I can feel a knot form in my throat as I try to keep the tears from breaking through. It was the one thing tying my mom to me.

*Why? Why did you leave me, Mom? Why wasn't I enough to keep you here?*

Images of her body in the tub flash through my head, and I have to shut them down immediately. The bloody water, the blank stare in her eyes.

A small sob escapes my lips, and I lean against the counter and try to breathe through the heartache. Once I have myself calm, I head into the stall and handle business.

Looking at my phone, I see that I have a text message. I pull up my beat-up phone with the cracked screen and unlock it.

**Unknown: You ok, Red?**

Are you fucking serious? How the hell does he have my number?

**Me: Lose my number, asshole.**

**Mason: Come on, I'm just checking on you.**

**Me: How in the world did you get this?**

**Mason: School Directory**

What the fuck is that?

**Me: I'm fine. Go away.**

**Mason: Aw, you wound me. Here I am just trying to care for you.**

**Me: I don't need it.**

I toss my phone in my pocket. I feel it go off, but I ignore it. I need to get to my next class. Business class. Yeah, nothing fun. In rich people land, they make you take a business class so you can take over Mommy and Daddy's company.

It's then that I remember who is in that class. Daxon Emerson. And I'm not going to lie, he's not hard on the eyes. He's way more muscular than the other two. He's so incredibly hot, not that I would ever tell him that. I mean, if I'm being honest, all the kings are.

And if I'm really being honest, I don't hate it that I'm partners with Mason. I mean, he smells amazing, the way his shirt clings to him, and having his ocean blue eyes stare at me is not something I would say sucks. He is just a man whore. And he's a king, which by default I want nothing to do with.

Colton is the leaner of the three. I actually liked him, until I ran into him in the hallway. I thought he was the nice one, and then he opened his mouth. But his hazel eyes watch every move I make. It's like he's engraining my movements to memory.

The three of them have somehow popped into every aspect of my life in under a week of me being here. I'm hoping the fascination with me will go away once something else shiny pops up.

I head out of the bathroom and find that the halls are littered with students milling about. I push through them and head to the section of the building where my business class is.

As I am walking along the hallway, I'm suddenly pushed from behind, and the force causes me to fall forward. Yet again, I use my bad wrist to try and stop the fall. I grunt at the pain and then my ears pick up the laughter around me. I push up onto my knees and turn around behind me to see the three queens standing with smiles on their faces.

"You should really learn how to walk, slut." Bianca glares at me, her mouth curling up on one side.

"Yeah, well, take your own advice. You should really learn new insults. Also, if you ever push or touch me again, I'll make it so you can't show your face for two weeks. And that could really impact your cheer abilities. And your dick sucking abilities. Though, if I knocked your teeth out, you actually might be better at it. Less teeth scrapings, if you know what I mean." I stand up and gather my things. My wrist is throbbing now.

Bianca opens her mouth to come back with something but is stopped when a voice booms over everyone. "Get to class. Nothing to see." I see Dax strolling up from my peripheral. He stares at me with disgust in his eyes. He looks around and sees people are still standing there watching. "Get the fuck to class." People start walking away, taking off to where they were originally headed to.

"Hey, Daxy, baby," Bianca purrs as he walks over to stand next to her.

I stare at him, not even sure what is going on or why he is looking at me like he wants to chew me up and spit me out.

"What's going on, sweetheart?" Dax says in a sickly-sweet voice. He leans in and gives Bianca a peck on the cheek.

"Well, the trash tripped and fell, causing us to now be late to where we need to be. I'm hoping I don't catch any STDs from her. She touched me," she says with a pout.

"Is that so?" His eyes meet mine, and I can feel the hatred rolling off him.

"Wow, so we like to tell little white lies?" I stare at Bianca.

She turns to her friends. "I'm not lying. Am I, girls?"

"No," the other two say in unison. Fuck them.

"Whatever." I stand up and smooth out my skirt, wincing once the pain hits again from my wrist.

"Watch yourself, Spitfire," Dax seethes.

"Fuck off, King," I spit back. Before I have a chance to turn around, I'm shoved up against the wall behind me, his hand wrapped around my throat. It's not cutting off my ability to breathe, but I take it for what it is, a threat.

"You don't belong here. So why don't you do us all a favor and pack your garbage bags and head back to your drug infested city and be the whore you were aiming to be? Spread those legs for the next disgusting lay, until the day you end it all," he growls in my ear.

My body freezes at his words. For the first time, I'm actually tensing being around him. My eyes widen for a moment, and I try like hell to not let him see how badly he touched a sensitive subject, but no matter how fast I put my walls back up, he grins at me. He knows he got to me. Fuck.

He releases his hand around my throat and runs his thumb along my bottom lip. As badly as I want to push off him and beat the ever living shit out of him, my body didn't get the memo. I can feel the heat building between my legs. A part of me doesn't want him to stop touching me. A sick part of me, but a part of me nonetheless.

But he pulls away, leaving me feeling so cold, almost missing his burn when he touches me. I watch him and the others walk away. For a moment, I close my eyes and wish to be anywhere else but at this god forsaken place. When I finally open them, I look around to see the halls empty and everyone in their classes. I take a deep breath and slowly let it out. I can't go to that class.

He's there. Dax will be in that room.

I just can't go.

I'm done for the day. They can mark me absent, they can give me detention. I have zero fucks to give.

I leave the Emerson building and head back towards my dorm. I need some silence, some solitary confinement of my own. I just need to regroup and get my head back on straight. Those three have some weird effect on me, not to mention they are everywhere I turn. I can't escape them.

They are in my classes, my breaks, everywhere. And their fucking minions remind me that they are too. They set the school to fuck with me, make fun of me, try to scare me off.

I'm supposed to be alone, flying under the radar. Yet somehow, just my presence has completely disrupted their way of life enough that they need to make me miserable because of that. I didn't even want to be here, yet here I am, taking the bullshit.

When I reach my room, I head back towards my bedroom. I let out a sigh as I push open the door, ready to feel the immediate release of all the stress that has been building up. But it never comes.

I'm frozen when I walk past the door and see what's laying on my bed. My made bed, a bed I know I just rolled out of this morning. And unless the dorms suddenly have a cleaning service I don't know about, someone was in my room.

I slowly creep up towards the freshly made bed and find my black lace bra and thong laid out on it. I know when I left this morning, it wasn't there. My bed was absolutely not made. That set was in my drawer tucked in the back.

Looking over at the dresser, nothing on it looks out of

place. Except the lace set laid out in front of me. My space, my room, my surroundings start to feel tainted, poisoned.

Someone was in this room.

I clench my fists at my sides, my surprise turning to anger. I walk over to my closet and head towards the back where I have a pile of clothes and my suitcase sitting in the corner. I shift the clothes and pull back the carpet that was laid there. Underneath is a little cut out that I found when I moved in. I lift the top of the hideaway and look inside to still see the taped-up box that my mom gave me.

I let out a sigh of relief. I hastily put everything back and roam around the room to make sure everything else is where I left it.

Crazy thing is, I'm doubting everything I see. My mind is playing tricks on me. Did my notebook move? Was that pencil there? Why just leave my stuff on the bed? Why just that?

I take a deep breath and walk over to the bed and scoop up the offending garments. I place them back into the corner of the dresser, definitely never to be worn again. God only knows who touched them.

I sit on my bed and stare at the framed picture of my mom on the night stand next to me.

"Why? Why did you have to leave me? I wasn't enough. Not for you, not for dad." I wipe the tears from my eyes. "Why were you so selfish to think I was better without you? I'm not, Mom. I needed you."

Since I've been here, I haven't heard a peep from my aunt. She has shipped me off and doesn't care at all about what's going on. And honestly, I'm not sad she's not keeping contact with me. The woman is horrible. I wish I still didn't even know I had an aunt. One less person to be disappointed in. One less person to realize that all they care about is themselves.

I get up and lock my door, making sure no one can disturb me. I head back into my closet and grab the box I hid. Then I bring it back out and sit on my bed, staring at it, waiting for it to do something. Combust, open itself, tell me what to do with it, just anything at this point.

This whole week has been shit. My life has been turned upside down, and now I'm stuck here playing with the one percent of Massachusetts in this closed-off rich kingdom of theirs. Why? Why did the dominos fall this way?

I peel back the tape slowly on the shoe box. My hands shake, and my heart feels like its ready to rip out of my chest. I carefully lift the top and place it to the side of the box. The inside of the box is confusing. There are newspaper clippings, receipts, printed letters, and a manilla folder.

"What the hell did you leave me, Mom?" I pick up the white envelope that has my name on it. Ever so carefully, I peel it back and take out the folded piece of paper.

My eyes widen when I see it's a note from my mom.

*My dearest little bird,*

*If you have this box, it means I had to move on from this life. And I'm so sorry. I didn't have a choice. I tried to fight it. I tried to come up with anything other than what I found. But I failed.*

*Especially if you are in fact reading this.*

*Please know I will miss you, and your father, and I love you. I hope you didn't see me at my weakest, and I hope you have grown strong since I've been gone.*

*Your aunt isn't the greatest person, but she will make sure you are in a good school so that you can thrive once you graduate. I don't want you suffering the same fate as me.*

*Protect what's in here. You and I both had our doubts about your father. Pieces are missing, things don't make sense, the story has holes. You can't trust those you should be able to trust.*

*I love you, my little bird.*

*Fly.*


*Love always,*
   *Mom*


I place the letter back in the envelope and before I have a chance to sort through the box, I hear the main door to our dorm open and shut. Shit. Liz.

"Phoenix? Are you here?" she calls out.

I jump off my bed and run to hide the box back into my closet. As I come out, I see the handle jiggle and hear a knock on the door.

"Phoenix, are you in there? Hey, I heard some shit went down. Just want to make sure you're okay." She tries the handle again, but the lock keeps her out. "Okay, well, if you need to talk, I'm here. Whatever happened, it'll blow over. I'll be in my room if you need me." With that, I hear her footsteps walk away from the door.

I internally groan and hate myself for not just letting her in. Yeah, she is beyond annoying, but in this moment, she was trying to be nice.

Except right now, I just want peace and quiet.

I crawl into bed and throw the covers over my head to keep out the light that is still filtering into the room. For tonight, I'll let myself cry and mourn what I have lost and what I was thrown into. But just for tonight.

Tomorrow, my walls get reconstructed.

Tomorrow, I won't let anyone make a fool of me.

Tomorrow, I will burn with fury.

## ten
PHOENIX

IT'S the last day of the first week of what has been an interesting start to my senior year. I have been pushed, tripped, called names, and injured all in the first week. Oh, and let's not forget about the itching powder debacle. My necklace is still missing, and I'm being stalked by the Three Stooges. If this is how week one is going to go, I have high hopes that every other week from here on out will absolutely get that much worse.

Bring it.

Friday has given me a renewed sprit. There's a buzz going through me, a need to fight harder against these trust fund babies. So, I throw on a piece of me, my Docs.

Let them suspend me, let them give me detention. I don't give a shit. I need my armor. And if I have to prance around this fucking campus, I'll do it in my own way. I'm not one of them, and I refuse to pretend that I am.

I grab my bag and my phone and slam my door behind me. Hearing the door slam, Liz peeks her head out of her room.

"Hey! You okay?" She pulls her brows together. "If you give me a few, I'll be ready, and we can grab—"

"Not today." I interrupt. "I got shit to handle. See ya at lunch." I storm out our front door and take the stairs. Once I make it out front, I push past some of the students already hanging out and gossiping about who is doing who and something about the kings.

Fuck the kings.

As I walk towards Forthright, my fists are clenched at my side. I notice Dax and Colt walking out of the building out of the corner of my eye. Immediately, Dax meets my eyes and squints. He leans over and says something to Colt, and he looks up from his phone. I swear for a second, I see his lip turn up, but he quickly lowers his head back to his phone.

As I walk up to the doors, Dax steps in front of them and stops me. "Those boots are definitely not school issued, Spitfire."

"Sucks to be anyone that has an issue with it." I try to step around him, but he blocks me. I look up at him and narrow my eyes.

"How's your wrist?" He tilts his head and looks down at my left wrist that's still wrapped.

"Move out of my way, Daxon." I can feel the heat in my cheeks as I stare at him, and I'm not sure if it's because I'm pissed he won't let me through or because of how I felt when he pushed me up against the wall yesterday. I'll pretend it wasn't the pushing me against the wall part.

The heat from his body when it touched mine, I could've melted on the spot just from that touch. Except I'll never admit that out loud. Ever. And I'll be going out of my way to avoid him touching me at all costs.

"Can't I ask how you're doing? I'm just trying to be nice." His eyes look me up and down.

That earns a loud laugh from me. "There's not a nice bone in your body, Daxon. Go kick rocks."

"So feisty all the time. Hey, while I have you, I've got a question to ask you." He crosses his arms over his chest, and all that does is accentuate his already pronounced muscular arms. I bite my lip and try to control the urge to moan over the sight.

"Actually, I have a question for you." I hike my bookbag on my shoulder, readjusting it and its weight. "Where's my necklace? Because if I have to, I'll tear this place apart looking for it, so just hand it over."

"What necklace?" Confusion comes over him as he pulls his brows together. Even Colton stops what he's doing and looks up at me with the same facial expression.

"My necklace that your minions stole out of my gym locker when they decided to put the itching powder on my clothes." I cross my arms over my chest.

"Spitfire, I don't mean this meanly. Well, actually I may." He stops and laughs. "No one wants your shitty necklace."

My stomach does somersaults as the possibility that I lost it becomes more my reality. But I know I had it when I walked into the locker room. I shake my head and lock my eyes in on Daxon. "Fine. Whatever. So, what was your question, Emerson?" I sigh.

His eyes sparkle in excitement, and he hums for a moment. "Does the carpet match the drapes?"

I scoff and push past him as he and Colt laugh at their little joke. Without turning around I flip him off and walk inside, heading towards the office.

I reach back to pull my phone out of my bag as I head

down the hall, and my shoulder bumps into something solid, and I start to fall. Giant hands grab ahold of me and help me to steady myself. I look up and see the giant hands are attached to a very good looking guy.

His blond hair is short on top and shaved on the sides. His shoulders are broad, and he barely fits into his blazer. His jaw is sharp, and his smile is blinding. His blue eyes pierce through me and keep me stunned. I'm sure if he turned around right now, his ass would be just as amazing as the rest of him.

"Are you okay? I'm sorry, I didn't see you." His voice is relaxing, smooth. There's a weird calmness I get from it. Entranced by his entire body package, I suddenly realize that he is still holding on to me.

"Sorry, I should have paid better attention to where I was walking," I say as he slowly lets go of me.

"It's all right. You looked like you were on a mission." He smiles at me, adjusting his bag that's hanging over his shoulder. I'm not sure if I should run the other way or engage him. He's nice. It's a strange thing here.

"Um, yeah, I was. I mean, I am. Apparently, there are lockers in this place, and the office failed to mention to me that I had one." I wave my hand in the air towards where the office is.

"Oh! You're the new girl. The one that was brought here on scholarship. I'm Chad Oliver." He holds out his hand for me to shake. I meet his hand and greet him. All right, so he definitely isn't like the others. Interesting.

"Yep. That would be me. Phoenix Hayes. Guess I'm just the talk of the town." I start to turn my head towards the other students walking around us, trying to avoid contact with another person who only sees me as that "new student".

"Well, no. It's just if you were a freshman, they do all that during orientation. Since you didn't get one, they probably forgot to include it because you keep the same locker all four years. Also, my mother is on the board. I had overheard her talk about the rare acceptance into Darkwood." He lifts his shoulders and tilts his head slightly to the side.

"Oh. Sorry. This, uh, this place is just a lot. I didn't mean to assume."

"Don't worry about. I get it. New school, new people, the whole hierarchy situation, it really is a lot. But look, I need to get to class, and you need to chew out Ms. Hodgens. If you ever need help with anything, just look me up. I'd be glad to help you around the campus or with whatever you need." He gives me a soft smile.

"Yeah, thanks. Nice to meet you, Chad."

He continues on the path he was one before I collided with him, and I burst through the door of the office.

"How can we help you, Ms. Hayes?" Ms. Hodgens looks up from her computer screen with her lips pressed together.

"So apparently, somewhere out there in Darkwood Land, there's a locker with my name on it. Problem is, no one told me I had one. So, can you be a dear and tell me where my locker is? These fucking books are really starting to become a pain in the ass to carry."

"Language. It was in your packet," she bites back, turning her attention back to the screen.

"Do you honestly think I would be here if it was? Do you not think I checked there first? So just tell me where it is."

She taps her finger on the desk and then sighs. She moves her hands across the keyboard and grabs a sticky note.

"Locker 407. Out this door and go to your left. Down the hall and then make another left. Go all the way to the end till you see the lockers." She slaps the note on top of the counter in front of me. I grab it and turn without even muttering a thank you. Screw the bitch. Her job is to help us when we need it, not act like I'm a problem child and interrupting some big things she's working on.

Following her instructions, I push past some of the students that are standing around in the middle of the hallway, as I work my way down towards my locker. I look up at the numbers until I come across mine. Locker 407. I enter the code on the lock, opening the door and being hit with an intense rotting smell inside.

I turn my head and start to gag from the smell that's invading my nose. Backing away, I take a moment to try and keep myself from dry heaving. When I look up at my locker, I notice rotten food and garbage sitting inside of it.

Are you fucking kidding me?

"What is that smell?" I instantly freeze at the sound of her voice.

Bianca. I turn and look at her, my right hand clenched at my side and teeth grinding together.

"Oh, it's just the trash they let walk in here. Stay there, slut. I don't want to get any of your STDs from you being too close to me."

Sounds of laughter start to echo through the hall, and red is starting to cloud my vision. Turning, I take a deep breath and try to calm myself. I reach down and pick up the bag that I dropped when I opened the locker. Screw this, I will just carry my shit.

"Wow, what the hell is that smell?" Mason's voice bellows through the hall as he makes his way over to where

Bianca is standing with the other Barbies. Yeah, that's exactly what they are. Fake ass plastic bitches.

"Someone wanted to give the new girl a welcome present. Seems they thought that trash would be fitting since she's used to living in it." Bianca places a hand on Mason's arm and rubs it.

Mason laughs and suddenly I am no longer mad, but more embarrassed. He's looking at me the same way that Bianca is. Disgusted.

"Man, and now I have to sit next to her in class." He shakes his head and holds his nose. Everyone around us is now laughing, and I'm frozen in the spot where I stand. I have no idea what just happened. Mason went from wanting to get in my pants to humiliating me along with everyone else in this school.

I turn and sprint away from the crowd around my now dumpster locker. How the hell did they even know it was mine? I didn't even know it was mine. Who knows how long that garbage had been rotting inside that locker? It could have been there since Monday.

I head out to the courtyard and people are staring at me, pointing at me. I hear some snickering and talk about my locker, and I steel my face and emotions. This is what they want. They want to break me, make me look weak. I close my eyes for a moment and think of my mom and dad.

A happier time when we were together, when we were a family. When everyone was alive and full of love.

I let out a long sigh. Opening my eyes, I start my trek to the Emerson building. A shiver goes up my spine just thinking about that name. I fucking hate Daxon Emerson.

Reaching my classroom, I take a deep breath and pray that Mason isn't a complete dick to me like he was in the hallway. My hope quickly evaporates when I see that the desks around my desk have been shifted so that there is a huge gap around me. I walk in and make my way to my desk with murmurs and whispers floating in the air.

I drop my bag on the floor and fall into my chair. I stare at the top of my desk, not wanting to look around. I can feel their eyes on me.

The air shifts, and I know Mason has walked into the classroom. The chatter dies down as everyone is waiting to see what he does. The minute I look up, I regret that decision.

He walks over to his desk that is pushed farther away from mine than it should be, as he holds his nose and scrunches his face.

I scoff and shake my head at him. "Real mature."

"Seriously, maybe use the shower in your dorm room, Trailer Trash." He fake gags as he slides into his seat.

My chest tightens over the fact that he didn't call me his usual nickname, Red. While it wasn't my favorite nickname, I would take it over the new one. While I can't stand any of them, his flirty ways were better that what he's doing now. He's being cruel. I expect that from Daxon, not him. "Seriously, Mason?" I narrow my eyes at him.

"Yeah, you seriously need to take a shower."

I can feel my cheeks heat and I'm about to say something when the teacher walks in.

"Miss Hayes, the Headmaster would like to see you now, please," Mr. Patterson says as he walks into the classroom.

Rolling my eyes, I gather my things and walk out the classroom door, actually happy for the slight distraction. I take a win where I can get one. Right now, not being in that classroom being made fun of, total win.

As I stroll back into the office, Ms. Hodgens narrows her

eyes at me and taps her pen on her desk. "Headmaster Lockhart wanted to see me?"

She nods. "Go ahead back there."

I slowly walk back to his office, knocking on the door. "Come in," comes from behind it, so I turn the handle and push the door open to find him behind his desk typing furiously on his keyboard. He looks up from his screen and points to the seat in front of him. I saunter over and take a seat.

"Miss Hayes, how are you this morning?" he says as he pushes his keyboard away and folds his hands on top of his desk in front of him.

"I'm fine."

He raises and eyebrow and stares at me. "Are you sure? Because we had a student come report that a locker was stuffed with rotting food and garbage. Turns out that locker was yours. So, I'll ask again. How are you this morning?"

"And I said I'm fine. I don't know what you want me to say." I cross my leg over the other and place my hands over my lap.

"You know those boots are not part of the uniform." He tilts his head. "Has something happened this week?"

"Nothing happened. And I can't walk across campus in those damn shoes. I'm sorry I'm not bred from better genetics that allow me to walk all over campus in the most uncomfortable shoes ever," I snarl as I cross my arms over my chest.

His expression darkens. "First, watch your tone. Second, watch your mouth. You are a student at a prestigious academy, so act like it."

I snort at his comment. If only everyone at this school would act like they were from some prestigious academy. Instead, they are vile humans who only care about

Daddy's money and who they can marry to get ahead in life.

I see the way people act, the way people talk. It's nothing but bullshit. In their world, everything has a price and can be bought.

Must be nice.

He straightens in his chair and narrows his eyes at me. "So, what happened with the locker? Why would you stuff the locker with garbage?"

My mouth drops open and I gawk at him in complete surprise. Does he really think I did this? That I would do that? What the actual fuck?

"I'm sorry, did I hear you correctly? You think *I* did that?"

He nods. "It was your locker."

"Why? Why would I honestly do that? Why would I humiliate myself in front of everyone? Why would I take gross, discarded trash and put it in my own locker?" My hands grip the arms of the chair, the sharp edges digging into my skin.

He takes a moment and stares at me, then finally letting out a breath, he says, "For attention. You're new here, and maybe you are trying to find what will help you fit in? Maybe you are trying to pin it on someone?"

"Did I take crazy pills today? I had to have taken crazy pills. No. No. Maybe this is all a dream. Yeah, I'm still fucking asleep. Because in no sane universe would someone suggest that I put garbage in my own damn locker when I didn't even fucking know I had one!" My voice raises with each word. My jaw clenches shut, and I see nothing but red.

"Detention after school today, Miss Hayes. And you will also clean out that locker." His face is crimson, and he curls his fists in front of him.

I'm too stunned to even say anything. How did this even happen? My mouth hangs open, and he writes something down and hands it to me. I see that it's a detention slip.

"Get back to class, Miss Haycs." He dismisses me and turns back to his computer. In my current state of fucked up confusion, I say nothing and head out of his office.

Before I realize it, I am sitting on the steps in the front of the building with my head in my hands. It's like I stepped into an alternate universe. It's not bad enough that I've lost everyone in my life that was important to me. It's not bad enough that I saw my mother dead in a tub. No, we pile on top of that. We strive to make me more miserable by making my stay here nothing but torture.

Pure fucking torture.

A tear falls down my cheek. I have no one to call. No one to talk to about this. No one to take my side. No one to defend me.

I'm utterly alone.

## *eleven*

PHOENIX

STANDING in front of the rotting mounds of God knows what in my locker, I hold the garbage bin next to me as rage runs through me. The rotting smell is burning the inside of my nose, my stomach turning with each shallow breath.

The last bell has already rung, and most students have already left back to do whatever it is they do. Some students linger in the hall, and a few have their phones out, I'm sure recording my humiliation to post on whatever social media site they think will make them go viral.

So of course, I flip them off. Because fuck them.

As I let out a sigh, I hear a deep voice coming down the hall that I recognize.

"Hey, Phoenix." I turn to see Chad standing next to me, looking between me and the locker. "You okay?" His lips turn down, and his eyes soften.

"Yeah, I'll be fine. I mean, it was always my life goal to get blamed for something I didn't do and then clean out disgusting slop from a locker, so my life's complete." The sarcasm drips from my lips, and Chad smiles.

"Why did they give you the job to clean it?" He adjusts his backpack on his shoulder and looks around the hall.

I shrug and shake my head. "To make my life hell."

"I can help." He takes hold of the garbage can and moves it closer to the locker. Then suddenly, he drops his bag and throws an arm over his mouth and nose.

"No, really, I can do this. This is my punishment." I step forward hold my hand in front of me, trying to get him to stop.

He frowns at the mess. "You didn't do this, Phoenix. You shouldn't have to clean it."

"Well, you're not the headmaster, so I'm stuck with the job and also detention." I step toward the locker, taking the bin from him and shoving it under the locker. I reach into the little canvas bag tied to the lip of the bin and grab a pair of rubber gloves. My whole body wants to recoil from the smell, but I need to just get this over and done with.

You know, so I can go sit in detention.

"Let me help. It's wrong that they're doing this to you. I don't know why the headmaster would make you clean this. There are plenty of people who can do this."

"Careful, Chad. Your privilege is showing." I side-eye him, and my lips turn up into a smile.

He shakes his head. "It has nothing to do with privilege. It has to do with what's right. You obviously wouldn't put rotting food in your own locker. That's stupid as fuck. And you don't strike me as stupid."

I stand there, stunned for a moment. He's the only person that has actually taken the time to talk to me besides Liz.

Chad reaches into the same canvas bag and pulls out another pair of rubber gloves. We both begin grabbing the slimy goopy substance from inside and throwing it into the garbage bin. The loud plop that comes from throwing it in the bag makes my stomach turn, but the retched smell that burns my nostrils has me turn away and dry heave.

While it takes only a couple minutes to get the shit out of the locker, I still have to wipe it down and try to bleach the smell away. Chad hands me some paper towels from the bag and takes the bottle of bleach cleaner off the side. He steps in to spray inside the locker.

Honestly, I'm a little relieved that Chad is here and didn't abandon me. He didn't have to do this. He could've walked away or stood there taking pictures of me. But he got right in the mess of this and helped me.

After a shitload of paper towels and enough bleach on the surfaces that it burns my lungs, we finally finish cleaning up the mess.

"Um, Chad, thank you," I say softly. I look up at him and see him smiling down at me.

"Not a problem." He picks up his bag and opens and closes his mouth a couple times, like he's trying to find something to say.

"You okay?"

He runs his hand through his hair and sighs. "Yeah, me just being a chicken I guess."

"A chicken? You're a barn animal?" I chuckle.

He gives me this big smile, his teeth so white, so perfect, I almost blush at the sight. "Well, I was going to ask you if you wanted to come to the party tonight." He looks at me and doesn't say much else.

"I-I didn't know there was a party," I stammer as I take off my gloves and throw them in the trash.

"Well, usually after a game, we head over to whoever's house and celebrate the win."

"Kinda cocky to assume you are going to win before

actually doing so, don't you think?" I tilt my head to the side and cross my arms over my chest.

"We're the Darkwood Ravens. We always win." He smiles. "Come on, go to the party tonight. It's at my dad's house, so you can ride with me, and I'll bring you back to the dorms after."

"Will there be booze?"

He nods eagerly. "Shit ton."

"Well, you did help me clean this shit, so okay. Yeah. Sounds good."

"Will you come to the game?" He takes a step closer to me.

"Now you're pushing it. Party, sure. I'm not going anywhere near a football field." I step back and grab my bag. "See you later, Chad. I need to drag this outside and get my ass to detention."

He grins wider and waves at me as I walk up to the bin and pull it out the first set of doors I see. I'm not sure who comes and gets this, and honestly, I could care less. I did my very unwarranted punishment, and now I need to serve my time.

I make my way over to the Emerson building and find the classroom. I walk in and hand the warden my slip.

"Pick a seat. Stay quiet. No homework. You are here to sit and waste my time." The old codger says, not even looking at me. He's bald with a few wisps of hair barely hanging on. His face is all wrinkly, and there are dark moles on the surface of his skin. This guy may have been alive at the signing of the Declaration of Independence.

I turn towards the desks and find one towards the back by the window. As I walk down the aisle, I notice I'm the only one in the room. Great, so first week here and the only one in detention on a Friday.

*Living the high life, Nix.*

I fall into my seat and fold my arms across my chest. I have to sit here for an hour. Awesomesauce. I let out a long breath and stare out the window. Sixty minutes of pure boredom. At least it's a beautiful day. There are no clouds in the sky, and the trees sway slightly from the little wind that is blowing. It would be nicer to be outside than being stuck here in this hell.

About ten minutes into my sentence, the door to the classroom opens, and I think that someone else is finally coming to join me in my solitude. The old lump in the front doesn't even flinch.

But the three guys that walk through the door are the last three people I expected to see.

"Fuck," I mutter under my breath.

"Hey, Spitfire." Dax turns the desk around in front of me and sits facing me. Mason and Colton pull up desks next to me.

I look at the teacher who hasn't looked up since the three came in. Obviously, they can do whatever the fuck they want, so I'm learning.

"What do you want?" I stare at Daxon, not blinking.

"Did you get your locker all cleaned up? Such a shame someone did that to you." An evil smirk forms on his face. He cocks his head and doesn't break eye contact with me.

"You know who did it? What the fuck? I'm sitting here because of it! You need to tell the Headmaster, you bastard." My hands grip the side of the desk, my knuckles turning white. Of course they know, and it's a long shot that they will actually help me, but one I'm willing to take.

"Can't do that, Red," Mason speaks up.

My head whips towards him. "Why the fuck not?" I know that fucking George Washington up there can hear this. He can hear I'm in detention for something I didn't do. Yet he sits there, growing older by the second.

"Because your undoing will be the best thing all year." Dax says. My eyes find his and I swear if they could shoot daggers, he would have twenty firing off at him right now.

"My undoing? What the fuck is wrong with you three? I don't care who you are or how much money you have. I want to graduate and get the fuck out of here. So just leave me the fuck alone."

"Can't do that, Red," Mason says again.

"Is that the only thing you can say?" I glare at him. "Look, this new person hazing is bullshit, so grow up. We ignore each other for a year, and you go marry the pussy your parents have lined up for you. I'll do my thing and forget every single one of you."

"What did Chad say to you?" Colton pulls my attention away from Mason. His voice is quieter than the other two. He adjusts his black rimmed glasses and clears his throat. "I'll ask again, what did Chad say?"

I look back and forth between all three and then laugh. "You're kidding right? Why the fuck do you even care? It's none of your business."

"It absolutely is my business, our business. So, what did he say?" Mason shakes his head.

"Really? Because he was there helping me clean a mess I didn't even do. Whereas you three know what actually happened and refuse to get me out of this." I swing my arms around the room. "So please, kindly go fuck yourselves."

"A dirty locker is the least of your worries. So is your little STD problem." Dax leans closer to me, his eyes dropping down to my lips, and I can feel my heartrate pick up. "Stay away from him. You're ours."

"I'm sorry, I think I'm hallucinating. Did I fall asleep? Is this a dream? I swear your pompous, rich ass just said I was yours. Please go take a long walk off a short dock." I shake my head and inwardly groan.

Dax reaches over and grabs my chin, and his touch burns me. His single touch ignites every inch of my skin on fire. Holy shit.

His eyes move from mine to my lips, and his vibrant eyes darken. I hold back a moan as his grip tightens on my chin. As I sit here, feeling his touch in every part of my body, I try to keep from rubbing my thighs together.

"We. Own. You." As he stands, his hand goes into my hair. He grips it and tilts my head back. He leans over the desk, brings his face to mine. I can feel his breath on my lips. "You're ours to play with, you're ours to destroy. It'd be best if you remember that."

"We don't take kindly to other people playing with our toys, Red," Mason says in my ear.

"Best to listen to us, Phoenix. It will make all of this easier," Colt says. I can't move my head because of the hold that Dax has on me, but out of the corner of my eye, I see him stand from the desk.

Mason's hand comes up to my cheek and strokes it softly, he pushes up from the desk and stands. Dax's finger brushes my lower lip, and I can feel my heart racing, and my breathing picks up. My brain and my body are not on the same page when it comes to these three.

"See you around, Spitfire." Dax drops his hold on me, and the fire I felt instantly turns to ice. I watch the three of them walk out of the classroom, not once looking back. The teacher still has his head in the newspaper he's reading, not once acknowledging what just happened.

I close my eyes and try to still my body, which is still

humming from being around those three. I don't open them until I hear a throat clearing.

"You may go now, Miss Hayes." The old man doesn't even look up from his paper as he says that. I look up at the clock and see that it has indeed been an hour.

I grab my bag and run myself out of the building. Once outside I take a deep breath and march towards the dorms.

They may rule the school, but they do not rule me. No matter what they say or think, they do not own me. They can't tell me what to do or who to talk to. It's funny that they think they can.

I'm no one's toy.

## twelve

COLTON

THE LAST PLACE I want to be is here. But the football team won tonight, so the kings need to make their presence known here at this stupid fucking party.

This place is a testament to Chad Oliver's douche baggery. It's set back in the middle of the forest, hidden away from prying eyes. When you walk into Palace de Oliver, it's nothing but a display of their wealth and influence that they have in this town. And while they have a lot, it's not nearly as much as our families.

The Olivers have been trying for years to get into our little circle. They come from new money, real estate investments. But our families don't want them. It doesn't stop them from flaunting their wealth across this city.

The walls are stark white, windows from floor to ceiling. When you walk into the house, you walk into the great room that shows off the windows that overlook their back property. I think at last count, they owned at least sixteen acres.

People are in every corner of the great room and walking in and out of the kitchen that is off to the left of the space. There's a balcony above the great room with a glass wall divider. Some students have taken to hanging out up there. Well, more like dry humping each other up top.

Expensive abstract paintings painted by no one I know hang on the walls. A family portrait hangs in the great room over their floating gas-fired hearth. They are situated and painted in a way to look like they are royalty. Like I said, douchebags.

People give us a wide berth as we walk around. They try to high five us, shake our hands, anything to get on our good side. But we didn't really show up to mingle and socialize like we normally do. There's a whole different reason we showed our faces today.

Phoenix.

She's a defiant one. I saw the look in her eyes when we told her that she's ours; she was determined to prove us wrong. She won't bow to anyone, not even us. She just doesn't realize we love the fight. We thrive off the challenge. She will burn out before we even lift a finger.

Fight us, little ember.

I can feel myself harden just thinking about her putting up such resistance to me, to us. Fuck, I love it that she's so feisty.

Where Mase and Dax have chicks constantly hanging off them, I really prefer to not walk around school like a man whore. I'm quiet and reserved. I've always been taught to listen and observe, and if I'm running my mouth or distracted, I'll miss the obvious.

With my family in the security business, it's been engrained in me how to read people, how to break them down. It's also great because being as smart as I am, I helped set up the technology for security systems in this town and state.

When you have a company run by a king, people flock to throw their money at you. The amount of trust they put into you is ridiculous. I could break into any house I choose to with a push of a couple buttons. The number of secrets, valuables, lives, that are protected by my father's company is overwhelming.

To have that level of trust.

I don't trust anyone but my brothers.

And I don't trust any chick on this campus enough to let them get close to me.

Now, I'm not saying I haven't fucked a chick; I've had plenty. I'm just picky about where I stick my dick and when. And right now, my focus is on one particular off-limits pussy.

"Hey, have you seen her yet?" Mason turns to me. We're all standing along the back wall near the fireplace of whatever room this is in Chad's mansion of horrors. We weren't kidding when we said he was not someone she should even talk to. Mommy and Daddy have gotten him out of a lot of shit that would have landed him some time in the slammer.

Fucking Chad.

Turning to Mason, I do another quick sweep with my eyes. "No. And I haven't seen Oliver either. So, my money is on him picking her up."

"That's what I'm afraid of. Shit. Maybe we should have approached that differently. She's fiery. Phoenix isn't going to take to being told what to do." Mason shakes his head.

"We aren't here to be her friend," Dax jumps in. "So, I don't care about her feelings or how she responds. She'll learn soon enough what happens when she crosses us. She will get what's coming to her."

Dax has a huge stake in all of this, and I understand why he's so hell-bent on making her his target. First, he's under orders from his father. And to be honest, his father is not one to be screwed with. Gregory Emerson's a very powerful man. Second, finding out that Phoenix's family had something to do with the disappearance of his mom and now shows up here at Darkwood is very fucking suspicious.

I just have this feeling that we are going about this all wrong. She seems too aloof. She doesn't want attention. She's not seeking Dax or any of us out. Something doesn't add up right.

But of course, I won't say anything. Our fearless leader calls the shots, and Mason and I respect him enough to follow. He has always made sure that we end up on the winning end, and I won't question him outright about it now.

"Hey, are you still planning on throwing your birthday bash at your place in a couple weeks?" Mason leans over to Dax, who throws back the rest of the whiskey in his glass and places it on a table in front of us.

He nods. "Yeah. Dad's going away on business, so we'll have the place to ourselves to throw it."

Mason and Dax go on about the party when I sense a sudden shift in the room. *She's here.*

I turn towards where the entry is, and her vibrant red hair stands out among the crowd of bleach-blondes and box-brunets. She has on a black skull t-shirt with a red plaid skirt. Her legs are covered in fishnet stockings, and she has on the damn black Doc Martins that caused a serious stir today. If it wasn't for her hair that makes her stand out, her outfit definitely would. Her makeup consists of just her eyeliner, heavy and black. Damn, she's a fucking knockout.

Phoenix is the complete opposite of every single girl on

this campus. That's why I think Dax has this all wrong with her. She isn't here to be married off to some rich asshole. She isn't here to find a trust fund. She isn't dressed in flashy and barely-there clothes.

Something has been bugging me with the information I found. I can't figure out what I'm missing, but there had to be a reason Beverly Emerson's death was covered up. She's an enigma.

"Hey. She's here, with Oliver." I hit Mason on the arm and point in her direction. Chad Oliver stands next to her, his hand on her back. She fiddles with the hem of her shirt for a moment; she's probably a bit nervous. This really doesn't seem like her thing.

"Red didn't listen." Mason shakes his head. "She's in so much trouble." He rubs his hands together in excitement, practically jumping up and down.

"Keep an eye on her. Don't let her out of your sight." Dax walks away, and I head over to a corner where I can keep lookout on her.

Phoenix looks around the room, trying to look at each face as if she's looking for someone. Or multiple someones. And I know who she's on the lookout for.

The kings.

But she won't see us. We all have taken up spots around the house to stay out of sight but still keep an eye on her to make sure that Chad doesn't try something. He won't take what's ours. And she may fight it, but she *is* ours.

It's our job to get her out of here, to ruin her.

She plasters on a fake smile, but when Chad looks away it disappears. I can tell she really doesn't want to be here. Phoenix wrings her hands together, only breaking them when she accepts a drink from Chad.

Shit.

I pick up my phone and text the group chat.

**Me: He gave her a drink.**

**Mase: Fuuuck.**

**Dax: Don't let him take her out of this room.**

**Mase: Should we cut in?**

**Dax: Not yet. Maybe he's not stupid enough to try something like that with her.**

**Me: It's Oliver. He is that stupid.**

**Dax: Just don't let him or her out of your sight.**

Chad moves in closer to her, placing his arm around her shoulder. She throws her head back in a laugh at something he said. He starts to rub her shoulder, and I can feel the anger inside of me start to come to the surface. He's too comfortable with what is mine. *Ours.*

I feel a tap on my shoulder, and I turn to find Jacklyn standing to my right. Her brown hair done up, her tits on display for the world to see. If her dress got any smaller, it would be a napkin.

"Hey, Colt." She runs her hand down my arm. "How are you doing tonight?" She beams at me, her eyes glassy from whatever she's been drinking or whatever drug she's on.

"What do you want, Jackie?" I turn my head to her and narrow my eyes. I try not to visibly recoil.

"It's Jacklyn," she spits.

"Doesn't matter. What do you want?" I roll my shoulder, trying to shrug her off, but her grip is tight on me.

"Well, you know, you and I really haven't had a chance to have any alone time since school started. I miss our special time."

"Special time? What the hell is that, Jackie?" I make a point to use that name again because I know it's like nails on a chalkboard to her.

She tuts, but then schools her features and her eyes are

hooded. "You know, when you would take me back to your room and make—"

"Fuck you? When I would use your pussy for nothing more than a place to stick my dick? That's all it was, Jackie. Nothing special about it or your worn-out pussy."

Her face scrunches together, and her eyes become slits. I swear if she had lasers in her eyes, I'd be a dead man. A dead man in about a thousand different pieces.

Except I don't care. Fuck her.

"Whatever, Colton. When you need a place to put your small ass dick, don't come and find me." She throws caramel-colored her hair back over her shoulder and struts away. I do all I can to keep from busting out laughing at her attempt at an insult.

I watch her walk away, her ass swaying to the beat of the horrid club music they have on rotation. My eyes wander back to where Phoenix is, and my heart stops.

She's gone.

My head spins around, looking for any signs of a fiery redhead, but I don't see her anywhere. I start pushing my way through the throngs of drunk classmates grinding on each other. Keeping my head on a swivel, I try to look for any sign that she is out here and not locked up in a room with Chad.

Taking my phone out of my pocket, I text the group.

**Me: Is she near you?**
**Dax: What do you mean? Did you lose her?**
**Mason: I don't see her either.**

Before I can even respond, Dax and Mase are standing next to me.

"What happened?" Dax says through his clenched jaw.

"Dude, I was standing here watching her and Jackie came over and tried to dry hump me. I turned my head for two minutes and she fucking vanished!" I yell over the music.

"Fucking Tiffany came over to me. She kept grabbing my dick, begging me to let her suck it." Mase sticks his tongue out and fake gags. "Never."

"But she actually has sucked it before," I point out to Mason.

"Okay, well, never again!" He puts his hands in his pockets as he turns to scan the area around us.

"Both of you, enough," Dax cuts in. "We need to find her. Let's split up. Locate Chad, too. Make sure she isn't locked in some room with him. We need to find her fast. If he gave her anything, it would be kicking in by now."

If Oliver gave her anything, I will murder the bastard. I don't give a shit who his father is. He has gotten away with too much for too long, and this time he messed with the wrong girl.

Phoenix is ours.

## thirteen

PHOENIX

AS WE ROLL up to a gigantic house, my stomach starts to twist a little. I'm not sure why, but being here after the run-in with the kings is making me a little nervous. I tried making small talk with Chad on the ride over, but honestly, I'm just not feeling it.

Also, Chad's been a little touchy feely on the way over, and it's starting to make me a little uncomfortable. He finds a way to touch me as we drive. Something turns in my stomach with each touch. But the point of this was to show the kings they don't own me, so I push forward and try to keep the bile in my throat down. Hence the small talk.

The one thing I was curious about was why people lived on campus when they lived so close to the academy. I found out that this area wasn't always populated like it is. Most shipped their kids in from all over the states to go to Darkwood. But the Emerson family changed all that.

They single handedly brought life to Black Forest. I guess that's why they get a building named after them. So even though they all live in the vicinity of the academy now, it has always been tradition to stay on campus and be part of the campus culture. There's also a lot of students who come in from elsewhere that need a place to stay. I guess it just helps to have everyone all in one area.

When we pull up to the house, my mouth drops. Holy shit, the size of this place is insane. I'm pretty sure like a hundred of my tiny ass apartment that my mom and I lived in could fit in this place.

The vertical wood paneling is dark, but the large windows break up the outside. It makes it feel not so monstrous, but hell, this place is fucking insanely huge, even with the huge ass windows.

I look around at the cars strewn about the lawn and driveway. "Aren't your parents going to be mad at the mess the cars are making to the lawn?"

Chad shakes his head. "Nope. The landscaper will fix it. Also, this is tradition. This house has been in my family for some time, so my dad had parties here, and my grandfather as well. It's expected."

"Must be nice," I mumble under my breath.

"Come on. Let's go celebrate our win." Chad gets out of his expensive ass SUV. I have no idea what kind of vehicle it is, but everything in it screams money.

I open the door and jump down. "How did all these people get in, if you were picking me up?"

"The staff let them in."

Oh. Silly me. Why didn't I think of that? *God, Nix, you're showing your poorness.*

We walk up a set of grey stone stairs to a huge set of brown wooden double doors. Massive windows flank the sides, and detail on the set of doors is ornate and looks hand carved.

But if the outside is the dark, the inside is the light. From the moment I cross the threshold, I'm greeted by white walls that contrast the outside. Colorful paintings take up some of the real estate along the walls. I can feel his hand on my back as he ushers me past the foyer into the great room. I want to recoil from his touch.

It's odd. Somewhere inside me, something is telling me this was a bad idea, that he's a bad idea.

Could just be my nerves and the bullshit the kings said today. So, I shake off the red flags and continue into the house, or should I say mansion.

And then my eyes fall upon one of the most pompous things I have ever seen. A fucking painting of what I'm assuming is him and his family over what looks to be a fireplace of some sort. I bite my lip to keep from making a remark, and man, I really want to say something about that atrocity.

Walking into the main area where others are hanging out, the hairs on the back of my neck stand up. *They're here.* I can feel their eyes on me, but I don't want to make it look like I'm searching them out, so I try to ignore their stares and follow Chad farther into the great room. We find a group of people that he starts talking with, and I'm assuming they're other football players since they're all talking about their coach.

Not meaning to, I start to turn my head around trying to locate the reason for the goosebumps along my skin. I don't see them, but I know they see me.

I grab the hem of my shirt, a habit I have when I am trying to distract myself or I get uncomfortable. Right now, I'm extremely out of my element. I'm going to need to find a place to escape to. I reach up to grab my locket, but then I realize it's still missing.

Chad throws me looks as he continues to joke, smiling down at me. I do what I can to fake myself through this conversation that I have not heard a single word of. I feel so fake, so not part of this crowd. Hell, let's be honest, I don't fucking belong at this school. Except for some luck of the draw, I was given a shot to finish my high school education here.

One week down, a gazillion to go.

"Hey, you want something to drink?" Chad leans over, his hand caressing my back. I fight a grimace trying to break through.

"That sounds great. Just beer if you've got it." I wring my hands together, trying to keep my nerves under control.

"Got it." Chad disappears for a moment before coming back and handing me a red cup with beer in it. I accept it and pretend to place it to my lips.

One thing I have always known, never take a drink from someone else. Always get your own drink. While I have no reason not to trust Chad, I just don't. Not yet. At the same time, I don't want to be rude. It's a balance, obviously. As soon as I can, I'll swap it out with one I've gotten for myself.

Chad turns to me with his lips turned up and wraps his arm around my shoulder. "I can't believe I got my hands dirty today helping you clean your locker."

I throw my head back and force a laugh. "Glad I could help you add something to help your college applications stand out amongst all the other Richie Riches."

Chad shakes his head and laughs. "You're seriously not like others, Phoenix. It's refreshing. Thank you for that."

The air gets a little thicker, and suddenly I'm needing to find myself a way out of this conversation. I need some fresh air. "Hey, can you point me to the bathroom?"

He holds his hand out behind us. "Go down that hall, past the doors that lead out to the deck. It's the third door on your right. No one should be down that way, so you should be good to use it."

"Thank you. Will you watch my drink for me?" I hand him the cup and head towards the hall he pointed out.

Before heading to the bathroom, I push open the doors to the deck. There is a bartender out there serving drinks, so I take the opportunity to get my own drink.

"Hey, can I just get a beer please?" I turn to the guy who nods to me. After about a minute, he hands me the red cup and I thank him, finding a clear spot on the railing. I take sip of the bitter tasting liquid. God, I hate fucking beer. But when in Rome. Also, I really don't want to start knocking back shots of tequila and lose any chance at being in control.

Looking out, I take in the beautiful land that sits behind the house. I wonder how long it goes on for. There's a ruckus below the deck and with the cup off to the side of me on a table, so I can lean over and take a look below me. Beer pong. I shake my head and stand up, realizing that I really do need to pee. I lean back over and grab my cup.

Turning, I bump into someone with my hand that's holding my drink.

"Oh! I'm sor—" I stop my apology when I see who is standing before me. Queen Bitch herself, Bianca. "Wow, good thing I stopped myself. I was about to apologize to you. And that will never happen."

Bianca shakes out her arm that now is wet with beer. "You stupid whore! Look what you did!"

"What I did? It's beer. It's easy to get out. Much easier than the cum stains you're used to." I knock back the rest of my beer in a big gulp. Gross. "Why are you standing so close to me anyways? Don't I have some poor person cooties that can jump to you because you're within a certain number of feet to me?"

"I came over to tell you to stay away from the kings," she growls.

"Oh, sweetheart, I don't want anything to do with the three Douche Kings. You can have their privileged asses and become their cum dumpster for all I care."

Her shrill voice cuts through me, "You don't belong here! You shouldn't be allowed here!"

"Well lucky for you, I'll only be here this year." I start to walk away from Bianca.

"Not if I have my way. You won't make it to graduation day, whore."

I take her ominous words and store them for later to try and figure out. I keep walking through the doors and find the third door on the right. I open it to find a massive bathroom.

Closing the door behind me, I turn around and my jaw drops. The bathroom is so sleek and modern. The floating counter and cabinets are a white marble. There's a black sink that sits on top of the countertop. A giant shower is behind me. I turn to see a walk-in shower that has several shower heads. There's a touch screen right outside the door, which I assume controls them.

Okay, I may be a little jealous of the fucking shower. Who wouldn't want a shower like this?

The windows are giant, and I'm not even sure how they give any privacy. Though maybe there's a button that brings down shades or something.

Fucking rich people.

I handle my pee business and then wash my hands in their waterfall faucet. Wow.

I look up in the mirror, and that's when I start to feel

off. I start to get a little dizzy. I shouldn't have slammed that fucking beer. I take a deep breath and try to steel myself, but my mind feels hazy. Shit. I need to find Chad and have him take me home. I don't feel good at all. See? This was a bad idea.

My movements feel out of my control, but I make it to the door. Holy shit, this isn't normal. I reach for the doorknob, and my arm feels so heavy. When I open the door, I am met with a pair of emerald eyes.

"Spitfire, are you okay?" His voice sounds tunneled, and I can feel myself start to walk back into the bathroom. Pushing myself, I find a wall and slide down it. I can't talk. I see Dax hovering over me, but I can't make out his movements or what he's doing. Next thing I know is the other two kings are flanking his side.

"Red? Talk to us. What's going on?" It sounds like Mason, but I can't be sure.

"She was drugged," another voice comes out of the air.

I try to open my mouth to say anything, to call for help, but my body starts to feel like a dead weight. I can feel my eyes getting heavy. The room is spinning. I feel hands on me, and I want to do nothing but fight off whoever is touching me, but my body doesn't move.

"Relax, Phoenix. We've got you. We're gonna get you out of here." It's Dax. I know that smooth voice. That's definitely Dax.

I'm trying to will any part of me to work, but nothing is.

"Listen Red, we won't let anything happen to you. We're going to get you somewhere safe. Just relax." I feel a hand on my head, pushing my hair back. Mason's voice.

I feel us moving and arms under my knees and around my back. The music playing is loud. How did I get here? Where am I?

My mind tries to stay focused, but I'm suddenly sitting next to someone warm. Their arm is thrown around me, keeping me upright.

"Just a little longer, Red. Almost there."

Someone adds, "Chad's a dead man."

"We can't prove it was him."

"But we *know* it was him. Who else would do this?"

Time seems to move at different speeds. I know I'm in a car, but next thing I'm aware of is being laid in a bed. My heartrate picks up, and my breathing quickens.

"Relax, CT. No one will hurt you. You're in our dorm. In Dax's bed." The voice sounds so far away.

My eyes close, and my body gives out. The voices become sounds I can no longer understand.

Then darkness takes me under.

\* \* \*

My head feels like there's a construction crew knocking against my skull. There's a pain behind my eyes, and I don't have the energy to even open them. It feels like I went twelve rounds in the ring with a professional boxer. My entire body aches.

Where the hell am I?

There's warmth coming from next to me, and I am struggling to move. My stomach starts to turn, and I suddenly feel sick.

"Oh, God," I moan.

"What's wrong, Spitfire?" Oh no, it's Dax. I tense the moment I hear his voice. "Phoenix? Are you okay? Are you feeling sick?"

I nod in response, not even sure if I can form the words. I feel strong arms lift me up and carry me to another room. I slowly peel my eyes open. The light hurts them, but I can make out that I'm now in the bathroom. He places me on my knees and before I have time to think about it, I'm puking into a toilet.

Dax pulls my hair back and rubs my back. "Just get it out, Phoenix. Get it out of your system."

I don't know what makes me want to throw up more, whatever made me sick or the sweetness rolling off Daxon. Either way, I'm not sure I like it.

Every muscle in my body tightens as I lose the contents of my stomach. I grip the sides of the toilet until there is nothing left but me dry heaving. I feel my hair fall and water running behind me. Dax crouches next to me and begins to wash my face with a warm washcloth.

"What happened last night, Spitfire?" he says softly.

I'm still woozy, but I'm able to speak. "I have no idea. I was at the party ..." I trail off as I try to remember the night before. Everything is a blur.

"Yeah, we found you in the bathroom, and it's a good thing we did. Come on." Daxon helps me up and wraps an arm around me. As we walk out of the bathroom and into his room, I see Mason on the couch and Colt on a chair in the room. Both still asleep.

"We took turns making sure you were still breathing. Don't think too far into it," he says sharply.

I internally groan as he places me back on the bed. Taking slow breaths, I try to steady myself. "I need to get back to my room."

"Well, until we know what happened last night, you're not going anywhere." Colt's eyes open, falling on me. His brows furrow.

"Why the fuck do you care? It doesn't matter," I seethe.

"Well, we took care of your pathetic ass, so yeah, it does matter," Dax bites back.

"Here's the thing, you can't make me talk. So, sucks to be you."

"Come on, Red. Don't be like that. Just tell us what happened so we know what went down," Mason says as he sits up on the couch.

"And then I can go?"

All three of them nod.

I bring my hand to my forehead and rub it. My skull still feels like it's being split open from the inside out. And my eyes still hurt in the light. Daxon comes over and sits next to me, handing me some ibuprofen and a glass of water.

"Small sips, slowly," he orders. I nod and knock back the pills, internally praying for quick relief. "Start from the beginning."

Taking a deep breath, I close my eyes and try to remember what happened. "Chad and I walked in, and we started talking to some people. I have no idea who they where. He went to get me a drink. I didn't know it was going to be in a cup. I thought, these are rich assholes, you all can afford to buy bottles for everyone. I remember him handing me the cup and I put it to my lips to pretend I was drinking it, but I didn't. I mean, I know he brought me there, and I didn't think he would do anything to hurt me, but you never know."

"Smart," Mason pipes up.

"I really did need something to drink, so I told him I needed to go to the bathroom. Plus, I just needed some fresh air for a little while. So, Chad pointed me in the direction to the bathroom. I went that way but snuck out to the deck and got myself a new drink, where I proceeded to drink it."

I stop for a moment, trying to remember everything.

"Oh!" I turn to Dax. "Your cunt of a girlfriend, Bianca, snuck up on me."

Dax growls in response.

"Bianca was there?" Mason questions.

"That's what I said. Yeah. She surprised me and I ended up spilling some of my drink on her." I bend forward and groan as my head pounds away. "I don't remember much after that. I walked away from her, but that's when things get a little fuzzy."

"We found you in the bathroom. Drugged out of your mind. But if you didn't drink Chad's drink, how did it get into your system?" Dax runs his hand through his hair and lets out a sigh.

"I was drugged? Like roofied?" I look up at Colt who nods.

"You were," he confirms. "We just don't know how or who did it. For all we know, you did it yourself."

My mouth drops open in complete shock. "Are you fucking serious right now? Why the hell would I do something like that to myself?"

"Attention. I mean, you're the new girl after all. Same reason you put trash in your own locker." Dax tilts his head towards me.

What the fuck is even going on at this point? I feel like I'm in crazy land. Maybe I'm still passed out and this is all a dream? Running my hands through my hair, I look at all three assholes. "I didn't drug myself. I didn't even know I was fucking drugged. But way to blame the victim in all this. Now if you will excuse me, I will be getting the fuck out of dodge and away from you royal assholes."

Slowly pushing up from the bed, I walk towards the door, noticing my phone sitting on the dresser along the wall. Without warning, I'm turned around and slammed up against a wall.

"Easy, Dax," Mason calls out.

Dax presses his body against mine, and I can feel him vibrating against me. His hand comes up to my throat, squeezing just enough to hold me in place but not cut off my breathing. My body hasn't gotten the memo that he is not someone it should be sexually attracted to. Instead, I can feel my nipples harden against my bra. I can feel myself become very aroused from his touch.

"What are you doing here, Phoenix? Why are you at Darkwood?" he demands through gritted teeth.

"What the fuck are you going on about? I'm here to go to school, fucker." My hands try to push him off me, but he is too strong for me.

"See, I don't see it like that. I think you are up to something. You have secrets, Spitfire, and I'm gonna figure them out and tear you down."

"Are you on medication? Your flip flopping is seriously giving me whiplash. I don't know what the fuck you think I'm hiding, but fuck all of you. I didn't ask for any of this!" I grab his wrist pinning me against the wall trying to wrench it away from me. I fail miserably at it.

"I'll give you this one warning, Phoenix, leave this campus and get the fuck out of town. You stay, you deserve everything coming your way. I will make you pay for what you did. Vengeance is a beautiful thing." His other hand comes up and caresses my cheek as his eyes darken. He pushes off me, releasing my throat.

My fists clench at my sides. "I don't know what you are talking about, but you can shove your threats up your ass. I'm not going anywhere."

"I'll love watching you break. Better run. Get out of here before we keep you locked up."

I walk back towards the door and open it, but not before getting in the last word.

"Bring it."

## fourteen
PHOENIX

I SPENT most of the weekend completely recovering from my incident at the party. My entire body just felt like it was hit by a train. Not to mention the confusion of waking up next to Daxon, the guys sleeping in the same room. It was just ... a lot.

Liz said she worried when I didn't come home, but also, she never called me or tried to contact Chad to see what happened to me, so I'm not quite sure what to make of that. She was nice enough to bring me food from the dining hall all weekend so I wouldn't have to leave the room, so points for that.

It took a while for my body to feel better after that. I decided against a police report because frankly I had no idea how I got roofied and nothing happened outside of being taken back to the kings' dorm. I just won't be drinking at any parties any time soon.

Monday was very uneventful; the kings even ignored me. In fact, the entire student body ignored my presence. None of that even bothered me. It was great. I could float through my classes without worry. So, if this was the kings' way of trying to force me out, it wasn't working.

It's Tuesday, and I have my weekly check in with the head doctor. I still don't understand the need for this. Yes, my parents are gone. Yeah, I discovered my mother's body. Sure, I'm sent to a fucking nightmare of a school. And no amount of talking with anyone will ever bring them back or change the events of the past. I stroll up to the office and head back to the boring ass room that has been designated for us to use for our sessions.

I walk up to the door and knock on the outside of the wall. Dr. Parker looks up from his laptop and gives me a smile.

"Phoenix, please come in. Sit." He points to the white plush couch that I really hate sitting on. He moves his chair that he was sitting in behind the desk to the side of it so that he can focus.

I turn and shut the door and then plop down on the couch, moving my bag to the floor before leaning back.

"How's your wrist?" he asks.

I hold it up, still bandaged. "It's better, but I keep it bandaged just in case of anymore accidental falls."

He hums but moves on. "So, how was your first full week here?" Dr. Parker crosses his leg over his knee and leans forward.

I let out a chuckle. "This place is ridiculous."

"What is ridiculous about Darkwood?"

"Look, Doc, you know where I come from. This place isn't for people like me. These people ironically think I'm some diseased infested whore, while in reality, they are so blinded by money and power that they just want to spread their legs and get knocked up by whatever golden sperm sticks. I just want to graduate and give myself a chance to survive."

"Hm. Are students here giving you any trouble?" He leans back in his chair and uncrosses his legs.

"Nothing I can't handle. I really don't want to talk about them. Giving them more than a second of thought is more than they should get."

Dr. Parker nods and frowns. "You turn eighteen soon. In a couple weeks."

"Yup. September thirteenth. Big one-eight." I fold my arms across my chest.

"Any plans to celebrate? Maybe with your aunt?"

I let out a loud, obnoxious laugh and clap my hands together. "My aunt doesn't even know if I'm still alive at this point. And I'm sure she's hoping I fall off the face of the earth. She couldn't give two fucks about my birthday. She shipped my ass here and washed her hands of me."

"She hasn't called?" His brows pull together.

"She put me in that taxi and never looked back." I run my hands through my hair, turning my attention away from him and looking at the room around us. The walls are bare, completely void of any sign that someone had used this room at some point. All that sits in this room is the cheap wooden desk and this couch.

"Okay, let's change topics. How have you been dealing with the loss of your mom?"

I sigh. "Same way I always do. I ignore it."

"You know that's not a healthy way to deal with the loss. You need to talk about it, share how you feel—"

"How I feel?" I interrupt. "That I feel fucking alone? That I have been abandoned by everyone in my fucking life? That either people at this school ignore me like I don't exist or want to get me kicked out of this place? That in a month when parents come in for a parent visit, I'll have no one? It's me against the world. I have been dropped into surviving on my own and fighting to not end it all like my parents did."

The doctor gapes at me. "Phoenix, are you—"

"No, I'm not suicidal. I'm not a quitter, Doc. My dad always told me that in life I would be tested and when I thought things couldn't get any better, I just needed to push through because better days were waiting. I just don't know why they didn't listen to their own advice."

He sits there silently for a moment, taking in what I threw at him. He shifts in his seat and leans forward, putting his elbows on his knees. "No, you're not a quitter. And it may feel like you're alone, but you're not. There are people who want to see you succeed. Your aunt was concerned enough to make sure I was here to support you. I want to see you graduate and do great things in life. And there will be people in the future you will meet that will have your back."

"I just don't get why they left me. I don't know why the kings have it out for me. Why people at this school are bullies? I don't know why I'm not worth protecting." Tears threaten to break through, and I steel my features and push the emotion back down.

"The kings?"

"Some stupid richey rich group that think they are royalty. They seem to have it out for me because I'm the new girl who is from the wrong side of the tracks. I couldn't give less of a shit about them, but they are hell-bent on pushing me out of here."

"Have you told the administration about this?"

"No, and it doesn't matter. I just need to get through this year. And I have tougher skin than they think. If they think they can hurt me any more than I've already been hurt in life ..." I trail off.

We are both silent for a moment before he breaks it. "You mentioned that both your parents ended their lives, yet you have always been adamant that your dad did not commit suicide. What has changed?"

I shake my head and bite my lip. "I don't know. What's the point of fighting that? I may not think it was suicide, but who's going to care? Who's going to listen? It's easier to take it at face value. Police reports say suicide, so that's what it is. But no matter what it is, they still aren't here, so does it matter? I'm tired of fighting that fight. It won't get me anywhere."

"I want to suggest something that might help."

I snort. "Oh, I can't wait to hear this. Please, give me your wisdom, doc."

"Start a journal."

I tip my head back and laugh. "What am I? In fifth grade? Do I have to write who I have a crush on? Can I put our initials in little hearts all over the cover?"

"Not a diary, Phoenix. A journal. Write whatever you want in it, but focus on your feelings, maybe situations you've been put in or people you've encountered. Focus on how you feel. Bad, good, however, just write your words. You may not think that would help, but writing might help you make sense of things. Organizing your thoughts or helping you through a situation."

I raise a brow. "Is this your official remedy, doc?"

"Let's try it for a couple weeks and see what happens. Can you do that?" he asks.

Slowly, I let out a sigh. "Sure. Why not?"

\* \* \*

Remember that thing about Monday being quiet? It

didn't last long. Tuesday has been anything but quiet. From the moment I step out of the office, I'm bombarded with wonderful messages by my fellow classmates. "Slut" and "whore" are two particular ones that stand out.

All this money for an education, and this is what they use it for. Awesomesauce.

To make matters worse, I'm headed into my accounting and finance class that I have with Daxon. I was berated in front of the class for missing Tuesday, but eventually Mrs. Leaver, our teacher, let me sit. And that was a problem all in itself. Because the last open desk was right next to the one person I don't want to be anywhere near, Daxon Emerson.

I walk in, and all eyes immediately go to me. I hear murmurs and laughs about my official slut status. Someone even throws an open condom at me. Gross. So, I roll my eyes and make my way back to my seat, next to fucking *him*.

"Suck anyone off on your way to class?" Dax turns towards me, leaning in slightly to encroach on my personal space.

"Why? Jealous you don't know what a good one actually feels like?" I retort.

"Sweetheart, I get the best blow jobs. And from any girl on campus I want."

"Huh. That's interesting."

"What's interesting?" He tilts his head to the side and smiles.

"That in reality, you're actually the slut." I grin as he drops his.

"Careful, I wouldn't want to make you cry in front of everyone," he says into my ear, sending shivers down my spine.

"Nothing you could ever do would make me cry in front of you or anyone in this school," I say as I look forward at the front of the class. "You all are nothing to me. I may be no one to you, but you will never be anything to me."

"Challenge accepted, Spitfire." When I look back at him, Dax turns back towards the front and takes out his phone.

Great. I just poked the goddamn bear. *Good move, Nix.*

We are almost done with class when my phone goes off. I pick it up out of my back and unlock it.

**Liz: Hey, I don't want to alarm you, but there's a picture of you floating around on Instagram.**

**Me: What the hell are you talking about? What picture?**

**Liz: One from the party Friday night.**

**Me: Okay? I'm not sure I understand. Who took a picture?**

**Liz: I don't know. It's under a fake account. @The_-woods_have_eyes**

**Liz: Meet me at the tree and we can have lunch together. We can figure this out.**

I close out my messaging app and open up my Instagram to search out that account. There it is, the only picture there on the app. I pull up the picture and see that it's of me standing on the deck knocking back the drink. The picture is grainy and blurry, but with my hair you can definitely tell that it's me. I look down at the caption:

*Little Birdie getting so drunk that three kings get to have their way with her.*

Then I realize that it's a series of pictures in that post. I scroll and see that there's a picture of them carrying me through the house and then putting me in the car. I'm completely passed out. The last pic is me in the back of an SUV with my head on Mason's shoulder with his arm wrapped around me.

My fist clenches around my phone, and I clench my

teeth. I'm not even that mad about the pictures. I could give a shit, but that name in the caption. My parents called me their little bird. I feel my heart squeeze at the thought. That was their nickname for me.

I push the emotion back, closing my eyes and refocusing myself. I take a deep breath and push through to the end of class.

When class finally does let out, I rush out trying to get out of that room as fast as I can. I burst out the doors and take in a deep breath as I walk towards the meeting spot where Liz and I meet for lunch. It's an old tree that stands outside the dining hall. I rest against it, crossing my arms over my chest.

Fuck, today has been a shit day since I woke up. I close my eyes momentarily when I hear footsteps come up to me. Opening, I see they are not the person I wanted to see.

"Hey, Phoenix." Chad stands there, towering over me. "How are you doing?"

"Fine."

"Um, listen, sorry about the party. I was actually looking for you. And by the time I got back, I had heard the three assholes took you."

"Yeah, did you drug me?" I spit out.

"What?" His face pales, and his mouth drops open.

"Yeah, they carried me out of there because someone drugged me." I cross my arms over my chest.

"No. Phoenix, I didn't. Fuck! I'm so sorry. I should have kept you closer, not let you go to the bathroom alone," he starts to mumble.

"Whatever. Look, I know it wasn't you. I never actually drank the beer you got me. So, don't worry. I just thought I would ask." I shrug.

In a weird move, Chad looks at me and then walks away. Says nothing. Just turns and walks away.

Okay.

I may have dodged a bullet with that one.

I look around me and can feel the stares. Eyes still pierce through me, and I know from the looks that they are indeed talking about me, but I just smile and wave with my middle finger. Fuck this school.

"Hey, you all right?" Liz comes up behind me.

I shake my head, "No, but does it even matter?"

Liz chews on her lip and then looks out at the student body that is filtering into the dining hall. "It will all blow over. You're just new. Once the newness wears off, they will move on to the next big thing."

I tip my head upward to the sky and let out a sigh. I look back down at her and smile. "Come on, I'm hungry. Let's eat."

We both walk into the den of whispers, also known as the Darkwood Dining Hall. Pointing, laughing, slut and whore being tossed around like they are the words of the day, and all I fucking want is something to eat.

Liz heads over to get her usual rabbit food. Salad with no dressing, the most boring and sad thing to eat ever. I head over to a section that has the Italian cuisine. Carbs. The best thing ever made. I point to the meaty looking lasagna and ask for a slice of it. I then grab the tongs on the end and add a couple pieces of garlic bread to my plate. The garlic invades my nose, and my stomach growls as it patiently waits for me to devour it.

I turn and see the kings and queens sitting in their usual spot. It's as if Daxon feels my eyes on him, he looks up from his phone and narrows his eyes at me. Mason and Colton both just stare blankly at me. Colton I expect that from, Mason is more the outgoing one. Shifting my head, I look over to where Liz is sitting, by our usual table next to the window.

I make my way over to her, but suddenly find myself slamming into the ground. My chest slamming into the tray of lasagna and my hands crashing into the hard floor. I can feel the squishy sensation of the cheese and sauce under me. My white shirt is definitely ruined.

There's a deafening silence that stretches over the dining hall until someone yells "dirty slut" and then everyone starts to laugh at my situation. I let out a growl as I push myself up off the floor. Noodles and sauce drip from my shirt, and my knees are red from banging them from the fall. My wrist that was finally on the mends now hurts again, and my entire body is vibrating with such a rage.

I turn to the kings and they sit there silently with faces of stone. The Barbie Bitches are cackling and jumping around for excitement over the fall.

I don't wait around to even begin to clean that mess up. I grab a glob of lasagna still on my shirt and throw it to the ground. Walking right past Liz and her protests, I head out of the dining hall and walk to the far side of the campus away from the students and their bullshit.

I head over to the auditorium and check to see if anyone is in it. It's very empty, and I thank my lucky stars it is. I need to go change since I smell like tomatoes and garlic, but right now I need to expel some of this rage that is boiling inside of me.

I get up on stage and throw my headphones on. Picking my phone out of my pocket, I scroll to Halestorm and start belting out my anger. I shouldn't be here. I shouldn't be left in this world alone like I am. My parents and I should be picking out colleges and talking about my fucking future.

But they left me. My mother had a choice. She had a choice to stay with me, but no. She was too fucking selfish. She took her own life to leave me.

I wasn't enough.

I have never been enough.

I'm not enough for them to love me. I'm not enough for this school to accept me as is. I needed a scholarship. The students on this campus don't feel I'm enough to even associate with them. I'm nothing.

From the moment my father left this earth, I have been fighting to be enough. All that does is enrage me more. Tears fall from my face as I emotionally belt out the music. It's not tears for what happened at the dining hall, it's tears that I'm alone.

It's tears of me fighting to keep my sanity.

Because after all that I have been through and seen, I'm holding on by a thread and trying to not combust from the rage inside me.

If losing my parents didn't break me, then I can survive this.

They will not break me.

## fifteen
PHOENIX

**THIS WEEK HAS BEEN FUCKING** hell. All of it. And it's still not fucking over. What started off nice and quiet is not ending that way. Oh, and it's only Thursday.

This morning, I woke up to trash at my dorm door. Actual fucking trash at my door. All over the floor and smeared into my door. They took the fucking time to smear ketchup and other condiments into the door. God only knows at what time in the middle of the night they did that, but nonetheless, it was a mess.

What's worse, it's not Liz's fault I am who I am, but yet she stood beside me to help me clean up the disaster that was left at our door. That was a complete nightmare.

I was late for my morning study hall, which got me dirty looks from the librarians and the teacher there. Fellow classmates were snickering as I entered and found a table to sit at. Of course, there were three sets of eyes staring me down from their own royal table. I obviously ignored them.

Then soon followed my science class where I was left with no chair at my table. The teacher ignored my pleas to find one. She told me I had the choice of standing at my desk or sitting at hers. Well, that was a no brainer, I stood at mine.

Mason proceeded to ask me if I wanted to sit on his lap the entire class. I told him in many different ways to go fuck himself. Though, if he wasn't a king and a giant asshole, I'd actually give him the time of day. But that's not happening.

In my business class, wads of paper were thrown at me every time the teacher turned around. Mrs. Leaver then yelled at me for making a complete mess around my desk. I tried to explain that it wasn't me, but she didn't care. I had to stay after class and pick them all up.

Did I also mention that we were supposed to work with our partner for the project, but Daxon completely ignored me and did his own thing? That left me completely clueless to what it was that I needed to do. I'm not some math wiz. I have no desire to go into business. Without his help, I failed the assignment for the day.

But now it's finally lunch. I finally get a reprieve from the bullshit classes and sitting close to the assholes that torment me. The three assholes that I'm sure sent the school after me this week. The three assholes who have fucked with me every chance they get.

Except now it's time where I can sit and eat in peace outside the dining hall. Liz went in and grabbed me a couple slices of pizza and a veggie tray for herself. I really need to work on getting her to eat more than rabbit food.

"How were classes today?" She turns to me as she nibbles on a carrot. We are sitting under a tree on the side of the dining hall. Away from prying eyes. Away from all of Darkwood's students.

I shrug. "Hell. They just won't stop." I pick at the pepperoni on my pizza.

"They will, I know they will. It will get old." Her eyes soften in pity for the shit they're putting me through.

"Has it ever been this bad?"

She doesn't say anything for a minute and then frowns. "No. Never like this."

"Then it's not gonna get better anytime soon. They have it out for me," I sigh.

"Any idea why?"

Shaking my head, I reply, "No. None. I have no idea why they have targeted me. But they for some fucking reason want me out of this school. I mean, maybe I threaten their GPAs. I don't know."

"It wouldn't matter how smart you are; money always buys their grades. Now, don't get me wrong, all of them are smart, but no one else has ever had the highest GPA other than those three. Teachers just hand them As like it's candy." Liz takes a bite of her broccoli with a frown. I don't know why she bothers eating that stuff; she doesn't look like she likes it.

"That's bullshit." I bring the pizza up to my lips and bite into the soft doughy crust. The gooey cheese and robust sauce hits my mouth, and I almost let out a moan. My eyes flit towards Liz, and she stares at me with her mouth open. Almost looking a bit jealous I'm enjoying this pizza and she's eating cardboard.

We sit there silently, enjoying our lunches. The weather has started to cool off, but it's still beautiful outside. Soon, I won't be able to escape out here to eat. I'm only hoping that this will all blow over by the time it becomes too cold to sit outside, so I won't have to sit through the bullying.

I start to open my mouth to ask Liz a question, when an ice-cold bath of something is poured over me. I shriek and am stunned but before I can turn to look more liquid is being poured over my head. I brush my wet hair out of my face and look up to see students standing around us.

"Here you go, trailer trash," a guy says before dumping his half-eaten tray of food on me. I now have spaghetti all over me, and now I'm starting to vibrate with rage. Before I can retort or beat their face in, a sticky liquid is being added to the top of my head. Fucking syrup.

Laughs are happening all around me. Liz has backed up and is standing there completely stunned. She's too scared to say anything, and I don't blame her. I look up and see the kings standing there, stoic and unmoving.

"Is this the best you've fucking got? Have your clowns do your dirty work and this is all they can come up with? This is so fucking amateur for the likes of fucking royalty!" I yell at them from across the courtyard area. The others that are here to torture me stand there stunned that I'm even squaring off with them.

Daxon nods to one of the students, and they all begin to leave. I stand up and try to shake off the excess shit that was dumped on me. The three of them just stand there and stare at me.

"Oh my God! Phoenix! I-I'm so sorry," Liz stammers beside me.

"Just stop. There's nothing you could've done." I'm sticky and wet. The stench of the mixed smells hits my nose, and I gag. "I need to get to a shower. Thankfully I have P.E next."

"I'll go with you," Liz offers.

I shake my head. "No. Just go to your class. Don't worry about me. I really don't need anyone." Before I grab my bag and turn, I use both middle fingers and flip them off. I grab my bag but carry it in my hand, not waiting to get it sticky or covered in the mess I am.

As I walk across campus, heads are turning and people are laughing. It takes everything in me to keep from completely breaking down in front of everyone. I keep my head forward and try to steady my anger.

None of this is flying under the radar.

I'm so over the radar at this point; I have flashing lights and a goddamn bullhorn.

I run quickly into the women's locker room of the fitness center and unlock my locker. I throw my bag in and look around for something to put the school uniform in. I have no idea how in the hell I'm going to get this all out. I scrape off what I can into a nearby garbage can. I definitely do not have the money for this to be sent somewhere, and God only knows if they would even be able to get this out. I don't want to use my aunt's money.

I find a sink and put the shirt under it and try to get off what I can. I lay it out on the bench, not sure what good that's going to do, but maybe it will be a little drier after class.

Awesome.

I take out my gym uniform and head into the showers, grabbing a towel off the shelf first. I have no shampoo or soap, so I'm hoping I can get the water hot enough to take everything off until I can get back to the dorm and get cleaned up.

I stand under the hot stream of water, letting the heat burn my skin just enough to turn it slightly pink. Closing my eyes, I fight the urge to scream. Scream for all the pain my mother and father left me by leaving me behind. Scream for the fear that I will always be alone. Scream for feeling like I am being punished for just being who I am.

And I don't even know who that is anymore.

My days are spent just floating through the taunts and

bullying. No one to talk to about it, no one to help me do anything about it. I just take it.

My heart cracks a little, the pain slicing through me that this feeling of loneliness grows deeper every fucking day. It makes it worse that I don't fit in here. At least when my mother was alive, we had each other. No matter how shitty the day, we had each other.

Without even meaning too, the tears start to fall as I stand under the water. A sob erupts from my throat, and my frustrations and sadness burst out. I place my hands against the wall and just let it all come out.

"Holy shit, she cries." My head snaps up to the voice that has entered the showers, and my eyes go wide with fear. Standing at the entrance is Daxon. "And wow, what an ass you've got." His eyes travel down my backside.

My entire body shakes with fear, and I can feel my anxiety start to grip onto me. I can't turn around, and I can't shield him from looking at my ass. "W-What are you doing here? Get out, Daxon."

He shakes his head. "Are you going to leave Darkwood?"

"Of course I'm not!" I growl.

Daxon chuckles. "Well, then, I'm not leaving here." He starts slowly walking towards me, and there is nowhere for me to go. "Tell me, why do you stay where you're not wanted? What's keeping you here?"

He's getting uncomfortably close. I watch him slowly stalking towards me as I try to curl into myself against the shower wall. "It's none of your business."

His hand reaches up to the shower dial, and he turns the water off, leaving me there, shaking and cold. I press myself closer to the shower wall as he presses himself up against my back. His hands box me in, and I can feel his breath on my neck.

"You're wrong, Spitfire. It abso-fucking-lutely is my business. What you do here, why you're here, everything about who you are is my business. I warned you, Phoenix. I warned you that it wouldn't be a good idea for you to stay."

"Fuck you and your warning," I spit back.

"And that's exactly why you're here, crying in a shower after getting trash dumped on you. It didn't have to happen. If you had left, none of this would have happened." He brushes my wet hair away from my neck, and the minute his skin touches mine, a fire is ignited throughout my entire body. He can't see my face; he can't see that I have my eyes closed or that I'm biting my lip trying to hold back a moan. I can feel his cock pressed up against my ass, and I swear I hear him growl as he slowly rubs against me. I'm dripping wet, and it's not from the shower.

What the fuck is wrong with me? These three have tormented me, bullied me. And I'm over here like the goddamn Niagara Falls. Fuck.

I feel his lips brush against my neck and then his body that was keeping my naked body warm is gone. Leaving me standing there, cold, naked, and alone. Now that the water is shut off, I hear the door to the locker room slam shut, and I know he's gone.

My chest heaves with the sheer panic that is now setting in. I need to get out of here before others come in here for class. Turning, I grab the towel and wrap it around me as I walk out of the stalls. When I get to my locker, I see the lock hanging there and the door slightly open. Panic sets in as I realize that Daxon wasn't the only one in the locker room. He was the distraction.

Opening the locker, paranoia seeps in my bones. What the hell did they mess with? I notice my gym uniform is missing but my clothes are still there on the bench. Slowly, I pick up my skirt and nothing looks tampered with. I pick up my shirt to see 'STD Slut' in black ink written across the back of it.

I drop down to the bench and let out a sigh. This is getting out of hand, and the last thing I want to do is run to the headmaster and tattle on them. I'm not that person. But fuck, I can't afford another uniform. As a scholarship student, I only get what I get. And now I'm down one.

I need to go back to my room. I need the comfort and silence that my four walls give me. Reaching into my locker, I root around for my bra and underwear. Only, they aren't there.

Seriously?

Those assholes stole my fucking bra and underwear?

Which means if a gust of wind hits just right, I'm flashing everyone my girlie bits. I let out a frustrated growl and throw on my now damaged uniform. Maybe I can call my wonderful and supportive aunt to help me get a new uniform.

I mean it's a long shot, but I don't know what else to do.

Yet that doesn't help me right now in trying to figure out how to exit the locker room and getting back to my dorm without a public indecency charge.

Throwing the ruined shirt on, I wrap the towel around my waist and then pull my skirt up around it. Have I mentioned how much I hate these uniforms? I look like a complete fool, but this is what I'm working with. I throw my blazer on, hoping that it will hide the marker, only to find a giant hole cut out in the back that provides the window to the message. And now I'm down a fucking blazer.

My fists clench at my sides, and I feel even more shitty knowing that while I was dick distracted in the shower stall, one of the other kings were in here messing with my stuff. All while taking my fucking underwear.

Checking to make sure that my phone is in my bag, I head out of the locker room and head down a back hallway towards the first exit I see. There is no way I can walk right through the campus like this.

I head out towards the edge of the campus and begin my trek around all the buildings back towards the dorm. I pray no one can see me like this. I can't take any more humiliation today.

Today, I think they may have won a battle. They got me to cry. They got me to break down and show a weak point. They are hell-bent on continuing this onslaught of breaking me to pieces. And yeah, I'm mad at myself for crumbling. But it won't happen again.

They have won this battle, but they haven't won the war.

## sixteen

DAXON

FUCK, these last couple weeks have been so much fun. We have been watching on the sidelines, watching the fun everyone has had with Phoenix. The students here, tormenting her relentlessly. They push her, yell things at her, someone even left her condoms with holes in them taped to her locker. I think the note with them said something along the lines of: *This will help you secure your financial future.*

They have been ruthless. And she stands there with her head held high and keeps moving. She fights back.

I thought after the visit in the locker room that she was at her breaking point. I mean, we destroyed her uniform and stole her bra and panties. She literally walked the perimeter of campus to get back to the dorm. With a towel under her skirt. Knowing she was sans her panties and bra, fuck I was hard as a rock while watching her.

Even hiding from all of campus, she dealt with what we threw at her. Fuck was I wrong. She's going to be tougher to crack than I thought.

She refuses to tell me why she's here. Why she's the

"special case" for the scholarship. No one has ever been admitted their senior year, yet here she is.

My father still has me in the dark, too. He's been tightlipped except for checking in to see how we are doing in taking care of the problem. Even when he has us run on little missions, he doesn't give us any more information than what we need. Honestly, part of me is too scared to ask. He's an asshole, a scary asshole. I don't want to be in his crosshairs. Son or not, if I'm a problem, he will take me out.

In all of this, we have one inside piece we're hoping brings us some answers. Honestly, I feel like a complete ass for it, but I have to do it. She will never tell us why she's here, but maybe her doctor knows.

We have been listening in on her therapy sessions. She's got a lot of issues. But I guess that's expected when you find your own mother didn't love you enough to stick around. Not to mention, your father was a cheating piece of shit who took him and the woman he was having an affair with and plunging them off a cliff. Yeah, that's bound to give you issues.

There seems to be two ways that she unwinds. Her therapist told her to start a journal. Since then, I've noticed her writing more around campus. She finds little spots to hide in and she starts writing. Against a tree, in the bleachers, or close to the edge of campus. Away from people and the taunting.

Then there's her other way. A way that I truly enjoy. She sings. Phoenix marches her beautiful ass over to the auditorium and jumps up on stage and belts out songs that could stop anyone listening in their tracks. She has the voice of an angel.

An angel who is seriously pissed off and dark as fuck,

but still, she gets me hard just listening to her sing.

Which is where we are right now. Hiding in the shadows of the auditorium, watching her on the stage with her headphone on as she sings. She's beautiful up there. So lively. So different from her normal everyday self. She's not stiff, no frowning, and her eyes don't look sad and lonely.

"Are you getting this?" I turn to Colt who has his phone out and is recording her up there.

"Every second," he says as he watches, as mesmerized as me. He's usually the quietest out of all of us, but I can tell that he wants nothing more than to slide his dick into her.

Mason groans. "Honestly, I kinda want to sit here and listen to her all day. While I rub one out." I shoot Mason a look and he just smiles. "What? It's hot as fuck."

He's not wrong. Her red hair falling around her face, her beautiful lips, her sexy body swaying to the song she sings. Everything about her is hot as fuck.

"No one knows she comes in here?" Mason turns and looks around.

"No. She has been coming here for weeks. It's been just her the entire time." I stare at her. Her beautiful long red hair flowing behind her as she sways to the music. Her eyes are closed, lost in her own world. "I also may have convinced the music teacher to move her after school activities."

Colt looks at me. "Damn, Dax. Power play."

"Not a power play. Just don't want to interrupt her flow. I need to know what makes her tick. What better way to get to know someone when they don't know you're watching?"

"Well, she sure as shit isn't putting up with the shit we keep throwing at her. I feel like we're spinning our wheels." Colt watches her closely. Studying every one of her movements, like he is engraining them to his memory.

Phoenix stops singing and takes a deep breath. She looks up at the ceiling and rafters. She closes her eyes, and her mouth pouts. I think I hear a small sob, but it's covered up by a clearing of her throat. Quickly, she steels her features and grabs her bag, heading outside.

"Let's go." I tilt my head. We quietly slip out of the building and stay back just far enough to be hidden. She heads to the northwest corner of the campus, past the pool and gym, to a small section of trees that heads out towards a lake off the campus.

She finds a tree right at the edge so that she can look out at the lake. She is a good distance away from the lake, and after the pool incident, I'm guessing she isn't a fan of large bodies of water. Most students get as close as they can to the lake, while she keeps it at a distance.

She pulls out her notebook and just stares at the lake. The guys and I hang back, all taking place behind a tree.

Brushing her hair out of her face, she begins to shake her head. "I don't fit here, Mom." She pauses and tilts her head back against the tree, and I can see she has her eyes closed. "I don't understand it. I didn't choose this. This school, this torment, none of this would have happened if you would have just talked to me. Told me what was going on in that head of yours. And why?"

She bows her head in her hands.

"I know. I know we both thought that he didn't kill himself." She raises her head, and I can hear her sniffles. "But Mom, I don't know anymore. You killed yourself. Why couldn't dad have done the same? Why did you leave me? I could've helped you. I could've saved you if I just knew..."

She lets out a long sigh.

"People are so mean here. I don't know what I did to deserve this. This school, this life. I don't want any of it.

Why do they want me broken? They are horrible people, Mom. Do you know how much I miss you? Did you even think about that? You left me here with them." She starts to cry harder. "You were supposed to protect me, and look where your selfishness put me. At the devil's fucking doorstep."

Her head drops again into her hands, and she cries into them. Her entire body is shaking from the pain and emotion she's shedding. For a moment, I actually feel a sense of pity for her. But I quickly push that down and shake my head. I can't let her affect me like that.

Her arms move to her face, like she's wiping the tears from her eyes. I turn to my brothers, and I see the look in their eyes. There is confusion, anger, sadness and an uncertainty in them. I see Mason with a hand rubbing his chest and Colton rubbing the back of his neck. They look at me, and I stare back with my lips thin and my face void of any emotions.

Slowly, I peel myself away from the tree and saunter over to her, Mason and Colton on my heels.

"Spitfire, so nice to see you here."

Her eyes go wide, and I can see the redness in them. I smile at her and crouch down next to her. I tuck a piece of hair behind her ear, and then take my thumb and catch a falling tear.

"You're crying. Again." I lick her tear off my thumb. "Mm. Tastes so sweet."

"What the fuck are you doing here?" she growls as she turns her head to each of us.

"We come out here sometimes, and it just so happens that we saw you sitting here. Sad and alone." I frown at her. "Is this where you come out and cry when all the kids are mean to you?" I say mockingly.

Her eyes start to water, but she pushes back the emotion and stands up. "Go fuck yourself. Am I just supposed to think that you were out here taking a stroll?"

"Yep. Because we were," Mason chimes in. He moves closer, on her right side, me on her left, and Colt moves to her front. We have her trapped, and I can see that she knows it when her eyes widen.

"Well, that's nice. Finish your little stroll. I need to leave." She starts to pull away, but my hand wraps around her throat and pushes her back against the tree. She lets out a sound that goes straight to my dick. She drops her notebook, and her hands immediately come up to mine to try to move it off her, but she has no chance.

"I didn't say you could, sweetheart," I breathe into her ear.

"Excuse me?" Her eyes narrow at me.

Mason steps up and wraps his hand in her hair to control her head. He leans down, tilting her head to the side so that he can run a tongue up her cheek. "Definitely tastes sweet," he groans.

I can hear her breathing come faster. "You like that, sweetheart? You like Mason getting to taste you?"

"You can fu—" Before she can finish her sentence, Colt comes up and places his hand over her mouth.

"Quiet, CT." He runs his other hand down her cheek. His leg goes between her legs, right against her sweet cunt.

"I bet you, if I stuck my hand up your skirt right now, run my fingers along your pussy, I would find out just how much you actually enjoy this." She shakes her head as much as she can under our grips. "Are you wet, Phoenix? Tell me how wet you are right now, Spitfire." I lean in and nibble her ear, getting her to release a soft moan.

Yeah, I knew this was getting her off. Mason continues

to kiss along her neck. Colton has removed his hand and is now taking his thumb to her lip. She is panting like a bitch in heat, trying to grind against Colt's leg. The sight of her, her cheeks flushed, her mouth opened with little moans coming out, her head tipped back as much as she can with Mason and my grip on her. It's a fucking beautiful sight.

"Please …" she groans.

"Please what? Please make you come? Please get you off?" I whisper against her cheek.

She squirms under my hold on her throat. "Yes, please."

Her entire body is vibrating, needing to find that release that we have now teased into her. I immediately drop my hand from her throat and the other two step back.

"We don't fuck desperate whores, like you." I clench my jaw and start to walk away from her. The guys following behind me.

"Are you fucking serious? You're the fucking man whore of this whole campus, Daxon. You fuck anything with legs that throws themselves at you."

Quickly I turn back to her and march up to her, grabbing her by her hair and pulling it back so she can look up at me as I tower over her. "Except you. I don't fuck desperate whores like you. Remember you are nothing more than a trashy cunt that got lucky she was allowed to breathe the same air we do." I drag her down and drop her to her knees. "That's where you belong. Know your place."

Walking back to the guys, we walk back towards campus. She lets out a frustrated scream about thirty seconds after we disappear into the trees.

That's it, Spitfire, get mad. Make this game fun for me.

Burn, baby, burn.

## seventeen
### PHOENIX

SEPTEMBER SEEMS to be moving at breakneck speed. And to that I say, thank fucking God. Today is not a day I wanted to even wake up to. I thought about missing classes today, staying in and locking myself away, but my roomie wouldn't let me.

Apparently, I'm not allowed to not celebrate my birthday. Especially this one, where I turn eighteen. It's a right of passage or something. Whatever.

September thirteenth was always one of my favorite days, not just because it was my birthday. My parents always made the day special, made me feel loved in so many ways.

My mom would cook me an amazing breakfast when I woke up, and my dad would give me a card. There was nothing inside the card but a poem that he would write for me. I always loved getting those, reading his words. It was always something I cherished. By dinner, we would all help cook up whatever the feast was for that night, all working as a unit, a family. But for my cake, my mom would always get me my favorite cake from a bakery in the city, Have Your Cake. A strawberry shortcake ice cream cake.

It. Was. Heaven.

The cake was layered with a vanilla frozen custard and swirled in was a strawberry puree. The icing was whipped cream dyed pink coated in crunchy croquant. This cake wasn't one they made often, but for me, this was one they made every year for my birthday.

And it was always the perfect birthday. Just me and them.

But then my dad died. And my birthdays were never celebrated again. Honestly, we stopped celebrating everything, holidays, birthdays. Mom and I even stopped spending time together. She worked so much to keep us afloat, and I really didn't complain about that. I understood the situation we were in was a shitty one.

Then she left me.

So today, I didn't want to celebrate my birth, because all I could think about were their deaths. I was brought into this world by parents who no longer were walking around.

When I woke up today, every part of me wanted to just stay there. My heart ached, my head was pounding, and my body felt heavy. So much of me is missing, and a birthday isn't going to make anything better or happier.

But Liz had other plans. And for the sake of not causing more issues I have to eventually deal with, I reluctantly am going along with her crazy.

I really wish I could have slept this day away.

I've been writing more in my journal. Dr. Parker insisted that it would help, and honestly, it has been a little cathartic. I can put words to my feelings, my emotions that I sometimes don't feel comfortable saying out loud.

I look over the entry that I just finished writing when I got back from class.

*That box haunts me. There are times that I want to burn it, rip everything in it to shreds, and set it on fire. Because that box isn't you. So, no matter what's in that box, it doesn't bring you back to me.*

*You told me that his death had holes, and honestly, I'm scared to go down that rabbit hole. Will I not like what I find? Will it make all this worse? Should I not just move on with my life as it is and try to survive on my own?*

*Every time I get up enough courage to read what's in there, I see you in that tub. Lifeless. Cold. Gone. That box brings me back to that day.*

*Why?*

*It's a question that I just have never been able to answer. I don't even know if I ever will. I'll wander in my life always wondering why you're gone. We didn't have Dad, but we had us. It was us against the world.*

*Now it's just me against whatever comes at me.*

*I miss you, Mom. I miss us. I miss our family.*

I close my book and place it under my bed. I lean my head back against the headboard and pick up my phone. I have a notification for a text message, so I pull up my app.

**Mason: Happy Birthday, Red.**

**Me: Yeah, thanks.**

**Mason: Can I take you out for your birthday?**

**Me: No. Stay away from me.**

**Mason: Aw, come on, Red. Let me treat a princess on her birthday.**

**Me: No.**

**Mason: You wound me.**

**Me: Good. Go away.**

**Mason: Never. I've had a taste. I need more. Like a drug.**

I don't even bother responding. He won't fucking quit. I throw my phone on the nightstand next to me. Those three have me so bundled in so many knots and in complete confusion. My mind wants to me run the fuck away, but my body responds to them, all of them.

I'm a fucking metal rod in a lightning storm when I'm near the three of them. They strike and every cell in my body is electrified.

When they had me against that tree, fuck. My body burned and craved every touch they were giving me. It was the most confusing thing I've ever experienced. But then they turned on their asshole mode and my brain caught up. But that still doesn't take away this deep-seated need of wanting them.

I'm so fucked in the head at this point.

Lost deep in thought and trying to find rationalization to whatever fucked attraction it is that I have to those three, a knock at my door startles me back to the here and now.

"Yeah?" I say at the door.

"It's me!" Liz squeals from the other side.

"Well? Come in." I roll my eyes at her upbeat tone.

She strolls in holding a chocolate cupcake with a candle in it. "Happy birthday to you! Happy birthday to you! Happy birthday, dear Phoenix, happy birthday to you!"

I can feel the heat in my cheeks as she places the cake in front of me. I blow out the candle, and she smiles excitedly at me.

"See? Birthdays are awesome!" Liz places the cupcake on the nightstand next to my phone. "Now, get dressed and get ready. We're going out tonight. Party off campus."

"I really don't feel like partying. Can't we just stay in?"

She shakes her head. "Not a chance. Get dressed. We're going to dinner and then we will head over to the party."

"Liz, there's no way I can show up to a party with any of these people. It's like I'd be flipping the switch to my own execution. You know what they do to me on a daily basis. Why would I want to go hang and party with them?" I cross my arms over my chest and let out a sigh.

"First, you are not partying with them. You're partying with me. Second, fuck them. Third, everyone's so self-absorbed and drunk no one will even care." She waves my concerns off.

"That's the other thing, I really don't want to drink. Not after what happened last time." I look up at her, and she's biting her lip, her hands on her hips.

"Yeah, well, I'll be there. And you don't have to drink. But you're coming out tonight. You need to live a little."

No, I don't. I think I've lived plenty for only being eighteen. Definitely had enough bullshit already.

What doesn't kill you makes you stronger, right? I should be fucking Wonder Woman then.

But it's not only not wanting to be around my fellow Ravens. I don't want to risk running into the kings. After what they did to me earlier in the week, I'm all sorts of confused.

I hate them with every bone in my body, but that same body was lit on fire the minute they *all* touched me. Mason's tongue along my cheek, Colt pushing his leg between mine, Daxon with his hand wrapped around my throat. My body was electrified by all three of them. And I didn't want them to stop. But then they did.

Daxon and them pulled away and forced me to my knees. He had the balls to call me a whore, when we all know his cock is always stuck in some pussy of the day. And then all three of them turned away and walked away from me. I was so shocked at the events that led up to that moment that I let out a frustrated scream. I shook in rage, my hair balled in my fists, and then I pulled myself up and went back to my room.

Fuck. Them.

And I know I shouldn't want to hide out, and that I need to not give a fuck, but being around them makes my head short circuit. So yeah, I have been trying to avoid the trio of assholes. They have not been in class for most of the week, and that has been very confusing and also awesome all at the same time.

First, must be nice to know that you can just skip a few days of class whenever you want, and teachers won't even care. They don't even bat an eye. And they're all gone. All three of them.

Second, I actually feel off about them not being around me. They're in all of my classes, at least one of them in a class. They constantly have eyes on me, they're always teasing or taunting me. But this week it was quiet. And I'm completely conflicted.

So, there's a small hope that they won't be at this party, but let's be honest. My body is hoping they will be.

"Fine. I'll go to this stupid party. But if anyone starts pissing me off, I can't be held responsible for kicking their ass."

"Yay!" She jumps up and down. "Okay, since I take longer to get ready, I'll go get ready now. You can shower after."

I give her a thumbs up as she leaves my room. I head into my closet, and I look over at the corner where the box is hidden. I bite my lip and think maybe it's time I at least take another peek inside. Just to be closer to my mom. Just to have something of her today.

I run to my door and lock it. I don't need Liz knowing I have it here. This is a secret between me and my mom.

Pulling it out of the space, I sit in my closet and pull out a folder that has emails written in it. I take out a piece of paper and read over it.

*To: BTrighton@gmail.com*
*From: TH913@gmail.com*
*Are we still on for tonight? I told her I had things to do, so I'm in the clear.*
*-T*

What the fuck? This is obviously from my dad, but this wasn't his email address. TH is Trevor Hays and 913 is my birthday. This has to be him just with a different email. Well, I mean he can have more than one, but still. And who is BTrighton? And who is the "her" they are referring to? Mom? My mind turns over on why these would be in there if they weren't my dad's.

My stomach sinks, but I pick up the next one.

*To: TH913@gmail.com*
*From: BTrighton@gmail.com*
*Yes. A room at the usual spot. Can't wait to see you.*
*-B*

My mouth drops open, and I can't begin to believe what I was reading. Was he having an affair? What I'm reading sure as hell seems like he was meeting up with someone. But I could be overreacting. I have no idea who this "B" person is. Could be a man that he was friends with. Maybe that's why mom had her doubts?

I hear the shower turn off. If I had more time, I could read some more. I place the emails back into the envelope and stick them on the top inside the box. This weekend, I need to dive into this more. Why my mom was so cryptic is beyond me, and I hate having to try and decode it. I make a mental note to set some alone time when I know the roomie will be out so I can go through the box.

A knock on my door startles me, and I quickly throw the box back in and run out of my closet.

Liz eyes me suspiciously. "Took you long enough to answer."

"I was in my closet picking out an outfit." I try to not give away that I'm full of shit. She sometimes gets a little clingy and strange when I lock her out of my room. It kinda weirds me out. Warning bells go off when she acts like this.

"Okay, well, the bathroom is free! Hurry!" She runs away excitedly, slamming the door to her room.

Rolling my eyes, I head into the bathroom and begin the process of preparing myself for a shitty night.

My only birthday wish is that I wake up tomorrow and everyone forgets I even exist. Or better yet, that all this has been a dream.

A fucking nightmare.

## eighteen
PHOENIX

WE PULL up to a stately looking house that sits extremely far back on the property. You can clearly see it from the street through the gate, but it's so massive that it's still giant hundreds of feet back. We pull around the driveway to an area, stopping and getting out. The valet takes Liz's keys and drives away with her car.

A goddamn valet.

We saunter up to the red brick mansion, and I look up at the three-story behemoth and suddenly feel incredibly small. I take a deep breath and try to calm my nerves. I don't want to be here.

"Come on! We have some drinking to do!" Liz pulls me through the front door, and my mouth drops.

This place is fucking insane. We walk through the front door into a foyer where the stair wraps up around above us. As I amble through, I look up and behind me to see other partygoers hanging out on the balcony above the front door. I then face forward and look above to find another balcony higher up looking down on the foyer.

We walk through a set of openings into an open area

that most people are standing around socializing with each other. There's a fireplace off to the right and no furniture to be seen. Three sets of French doors lead out to some sort of backyard area overlooking the ocean. The walls are painted a soft cool grey with very detailed crown molding at the top.

Whoever's house this is, they are loaded. Like Scrooge McDuck loaded. Maybe they have a money pit they swim in?

Liz drags me to the corner of the room where a bar's set up, and we each grab a cranberry and vodka. I wasn't going to drink tonight, especially with what happened last time I did.

But when in Rome ...

Plus, I think I'll need a little liquid courage to get through the night. We both look around at the insanity before us, and I realize how out of place I am.

Liz is dressed in a shimmery silver bodycon dress. I'm honestly not sure how in the hell she got into it. It currently looks like it was painted on. She's wearing silver stilettos that make my feet hurt watching her try to walk in them. But as I look around, every girl in this place is dressed almost the same.

Then there's me.

I picked a much more conservative dress, it seems. The top is solid black. There are three-quarter sleeves on it, with a v-neck. The middle of the dress is tied together like a corset that connects the top and bottom of the dress, which is asymmetrical with a deep red and black plaid. So I wouldn't feel the need to cut my feet off at the end of the night, I put on a pair of black fishnets and my Docs.

So basically, I don't belong here.

"Loosen up, Phoenix. Try to have fun tonight." Liz tips

back her drink. Did she just pound it down? Well, I guess I'll be the one driving home. As if she's reading my mind, "Don't worry. I'll call us an Uber."

"Or I can just not drink and drive us home," I suggest.

"No, drink." She places her palm on the bottom of my cup, bringing it up to my mouth. I take a small sip and smile.

As I stand there, I'm expecting the insults to fly. For someone to call me a bitch, or trailer park trash. Throw condoms at me, tell me I'm an STD, but no one seems to even care that I'm there. While my walls are still firmly in place, I do start to relax a little. And by a little, I mean I unclench my jaw.

We move into the kitchen to find a game of beer pong being played. We stand around and watch the teams play each other. The little bit of my drink has started to loosen me up. I start to actually have a good time. Relaxing enough to drink a little more knowing no one is being malicious towards me.

"So, whose party is this?" I lean over and ask Liz as I knock back the rest of the drink.

"Oh, well that's the weird thing. So, this is the Emerson mansion. It's actually Daxon's birthday too. Birthday twins!" she shouts, jumping up and down, and I pray that dress holds her in. I mean, she is already close to a nip slip, and any sudden movement could cause a wardrobe malfunction.

But when realization sets in that it's Dax's birthday, I nearly drop my cup, thanking my lucky stars it was empty. I shake my head as Liz turns back to the game. I immediately start to take off back the way we came, but I get shoulder checked and pushed back as I try to escape to the foyer.

When I tilt my head up, my stomach sinks. Shit, it's a wall of kings.

"Well, well, well. Look at who joined your birthday party, Dax. The birthday girl herself." Mason smiles like a cat that ate the canary.

"I just needed some fresh air and then was going to probably leave. If you'll excuse me." I try to penetrate the wall of muscle, but they just won't budge. I try again by going around them, but Mason grabs me and wraps his arm around my shoulder. My body heats up from his touch, and I swear my vagina's on its own fucking get-laid mission. She's all too happy Mason has his arm around me.

Backstabbing vag bitch.

"Actually, come celebrate with us," he says into my ear. His voice sends shivers down my spine, right to my goddamn core. Wow, she's feeling special right about now.

*Fuck. Fuck. Fuck.* This isn't good. Mason leads us down a hallway into a dark room. Holding on to me tightly so I don't bolt, he turns and flips on the lights.

We are inside a massive game room and theater. There are about twelve reclining chairs in front of a giant screen, with massive black leather recliners. Scattered throughout is a pool table and some arcade games. There's a small bar area in the corner and more French doors that lead out to what must be a giant ass patio looking out over the ocean.

"Look, sorry, didn't know this was your place." I look at Dixon. "Happy birthday. Okay, now that that's settled, I'm out." I go to head back towards the door but am immediately stopped.

"No, Red. Stay a little while. Let us help you celebrate your birthday, too," Mason says as he wraps his arms around my waist and nibbles on my ear. I'm doing some Jedi fucking bullshit to will my body not to react and my face not to give away that my body is absolutely turned on by Mason.

There's a sofa off against the wall to the side of the theater screen, and Mason leads me there. "No, I'm good. Look, it's very obvious that we don't like each other, so let's not keep tormenting ourselves with each other's presence."

"Who said we don't like you, CT?" Colt speaks up as he plops down on the couch.

"Really? First, what is with the stupid nick names? They're driving me crazy. What the hell does 'CT' mean? My name is Phoenix, use it. Second, you three have been complete assholes to me since I started, and don't even make me bring up the tree incident from earlier. You three have this weird power at school and that's fine, I'm just trying to graduate and move on in life."

"Are you?" Daxon narrows his eyes, towering over me. "You came to my house, Spitfire. You wanted to be here. So now, here you are." He takes me from Mason's grip as he falls back onto the couch. He drags me on top of his lap, wrapping his hand in my hair.

Jedi control, Jedi motherfucking control.

I stare into his beautiful green eyes and steel myself. "Yes, I am. And I just told you I had no clue this was your place. I'm offering to go." My entire body has every nerve ending on fire. I feel like I could combust at any moment. I am trying to hold myself just over his lap so that I am not touching him in an area I can bet is rock hard right now.

"And we want you to stay," Mason says has he comes up behind me.

"You're different." Daxon thumbs my bottom lip.

"No shit?" I retort. "We have well established that I don't belong at this fucking school."

Daxon chuckles as he moves his hands to my hips and

pulls me down on top of him. The only thing separating us are his pants and my scrap of material they call a thong. Note to self: avoid fucking dresses.

"We like you." Mason tips my head back so I can look at him.

My brows pull inward, and I frown. "I highly doubt that. You have been tormenting me since the day I got here. Then you left me high and dry against the tree. So, you've had your fun with me, so let me go. You're not doing that to me again," I snap at him, unable to move my head because of his hands wrapped in my hair.

"I doubt you were anything but dry," Colt pipes up from right next to us, watching what his friends are doing to me. "When we left you on your knees."

"In fact." Mason starts to kiss along my neck. "I know you are probably dripping wet right now. Are you making a wet spot on Dax's jeans right now?"

My breathing picks up and my entire body reacts to every single thing they are doing to me. My mind has lost all sensibility, and all I can think about is how it would feel to be fucked by one of them. Hell, all three of them.

Oh my God, what am I even thinking about? All three of them? My brain's completely misfiring.

"What do you want, Spitfire?" Daxon's hands travel up my thighs pushing under my dress. He pulls me closer, and I can feel how hard he is under his jeans.

What do I want? Right at this very moment, I want each of them to fuck me into oblivion. I want to come so hard I sleep for a fucking week. I want to be fucked into forgetting my name.

Mindlessly, I start to slowly grind against his cock. I'm so lost and turned on that I don't even care who it is at this point. I just need a release. Please just let them give me that release.

Mason tilts my head back and slams his mouth into mine, his tongue pushing against mine. He pulls back and uses his teeth to pull my lower lip, only to once again mold his lips to mine. I feel hands, that I can only assume are Colton's, caressing my breasts, finding my nipples under my shirt and pulling on them, as I start to feel the building of my impending orgasm.

"Do you wanna come, sweetheart?" Daxon says as he starts to move me back and forth along his hardened cock faster.

I pull away from Mason just long enough to let out, "Yes, please." My voice is hoarse with lust. His hands grip my hips harder, helping me hit the sweet spot I need.

Daxon shifts slightly and I can feel myself about to fall over that wall. My body tingles, and I can feel myself starting to peak. "Come for us, baby. Let us watch you come undone."

With his words, I come crashing down, my entire body shaking through a complete euphoric rush. My moans and screams swallowed by Mason's mouth as he continues to kiss me through it.

Mason pulls away, and I close my eyes trying to calm myself down. Except when I open them, I see a sinister smile on Daxon's face and feel his erection pressing against my throbbing and very sensitive clit.

"Mm, that was beautiful, Red." Mason strokes the side of my face, and that's when it hits me. What I let them do to me.

Shit.

Immediately I push off of Daxon and scramble out of

their reach. I shake my head and hold up my hands to keep them from advancing towards me. "No," I whisper.

Turning for the door, I run out of the room and try to weave my way through the crowd of bodies gyrating on each other.

I send a text message to Liz that I'm headed back to the dorm, that I don't feel good and then I call an Uber. Running out the same way I came in, I march past the valet people and head to the end of the drive. When I get far enough away, I turn back to look at the mansion and see three figures standing there at the front door.

The hair on the back of my neck raises, and I turn and run towards my destination. I'm only waiting about five minutes when my Uber pulls up and I get into the safety of the stranger's car.

Ironic that I am finding comfort in a stranger's car. But given my options, I'd rather take my chances with someone I didn't know than with the three I do.

And after what happened tonight? I'm royally fucked.

## nineteen

PHOENIX

I'VE SAID IT BEFORE, and I'll say it again. Fuck Mondays. Seriously. I get up a little earlier than I normally would because I want to avoid my roommate, who's extremely mad at me. I mean, I ditched her, but I didn't dare tell her why I ran out of the party on Friday. I don't need to relive that mistake, and she'll ask too many questions and probably plan my wedding to one of them. That, or she'll just think I'm a whore like the rest of the school.

Quietly, I leave the room. Well, as quietly as I can with a huge door that makes an extremely loud sound when it latches and shuts. Which is also why I'm taking the stairs. I won't have to wait for the elevator in case she decides to come stalking out of the room to ask why I'm leaving so soon.

I need some peace and quiet. I got a lot of that this weekend because she went home for the rest of the weekend, leaving me to have the dorm room to myself. It was pure fucking bliss.

But now it's Monday, damnit.

As I head into the very empty dining hall, the smell of

pancakes hits my nose, and my stomach immediately grumbles. I smell bacon and sausage and practically run to the serving area where all the pancakes are being made.

I make a huge stack on my plate and grab a couple sausage links and slices of bacon. Then I pick up an orange juice on my way to the table and am thankful that it's quiet and most students are not up yet.

While on Friday night everyone seemed to ignore my presence, I don't trust that it will be the same for today. Well, almost everyone ignored me.

A certain trio definitely did not ignore me.

They touched me, kissed me, made me see stars. Every touch lit my body up like it was ready to explode, and of course it did. My body wanted—no craved—more of their touch. My mind was the only thing trying to talk some sense into the rest of me, though obviously failing.

I push those thoughts back in my head and I dig into my fluffy pancakes. Minus the syrup. I hate syrup. I smile thinking about how my mom would always laugh and shake her head at me when I would eat pancakes or waffles without any butter or syrup. She said it was an insult to the food. I just didn't like the sticky feel of the syrup. The thought has me giggling, remembering a time I proved to my mom just how messy it was.

*"I can't believe you are my daughter. You will douse a hotdog or burger in ketchup, but eat pancakes plain." Mom laughs.*

*"It's sticky, Mom! No one wants to be sticky while they eat!" I stick my tongue out at her.*

*"What are we, cavemen? You can use a fork, knife, even a napkin while you eat. Oh, and then you can wash up after!" She throws a towel at me from the other side of the kitchen island.*

*"No, you don't understand. It never fails that even with all*

*the modern technology that utensils afford us, it still gets in hair, or on a shirt. Syrup seeks you out to make you sticky!" I throw the towel back at her. She turns her back to me for a moment and then spins around and my jaw immediately drops.*

*"Don't you dare, Mom!" I laugh as I get up from the kitchen stool. The corners of my mom's mouth tilts up, and she pops the top of the syrup bottle she is holding. "Mom! I'm warning you! Stay where you are!"*

*"I can't help it, little bird. It's taken control of me, and it's seeking you out!" My mom starts to walk around the counter. "It wants to find a shirt to stick to!"*

*"Mom! No!" I laugh as we both now run round the kitchen island, trying to dodge each other. She catches up to me and squeezes the bottle, but I dive away from the island at the last second and hear Mom gasp.*

*"Oh, honey. I'm so sorry. I—"*

*I look up to find Mom has covered Dad in a glob of the sticky sweet stuff. We are all silent for a moment until Dad grabs Mom and hugs her.*

*"And now you, woman, are covered in it too!" Dad laughs.*

*I double over in pain from laughing so hard and when I finally catch my breath, I look up at the two of them kissing each other and in complete bliss. "See?" They both turn to me, and I point to the mess they made. "It gets everywhere!"*

"Hey, Phoenix." A voice pulls me from my thoughts, and I see Chad hovering over me.

"Oh, hi." It has been a couple weeks since I've seen Chad. I thought maybe he had to follow the "Phoenix is diseased" rules of campus.

"Um, how have you been?" Chad pulls a chair out and sits down.

"Fine ..."

"Yeah, I had a visit from the kings since they thought I drugged you." His lips thin, and he starts to look around.

"What? Why?"

"I don't know, Phoenix. You tell me. Did you tell them I drugged you?" He lowers his voice, his eyes narrowing.

"No! I never said that to them. I have no idea who did it." The thought of someone having that control over me, being able to take advantage of me, makes me sick.

Chad looks at me like he's waiting for me give away any sign that I did indeed tell the kings it was him.

"Well you sure seem chummy with them. They ran out of my house carrying you. I heard they even whisked you away at the party this weekend. Say, did they have their way with you when they took you from my party? Did they fill each of your holes? They seem pretty protective of a slut like yourself. I kinda feel cheated that I didn't get any of that golden pussy—"

My hand slaps him across the face, and the echo grabs the attention of the few students that are in the dining hall.

"I was fucking drugged! The fact that you can sit here and make it my fault shows me who you really are. Calling me a slut, when I was given something that took away any control that I had over myself, is disgusting. I thought you were different. Not like the others. I was wrong. Stay away from me, Chad." I stand up and grab my bag. And of course, I can't help but get one last thing in. "Oh, and even if you had a giant golden cock, I wouldn't sleep with you. Creep isn't my type."

I hear a low growl behind me, but I dump my plate and exit through the door to my first class. U.S. Government. With Mason. I'm so not in the mood for bullshit. His bullshit, in particular.

When I get to class, I keep my head down and head over

to my desk. Again, no whispers or words are being thrown at me since the party Friday. I'm a little skeptical, but I'll take the reprieve.

As I sit down, I can feel him come into the room. The hair on the back of my neck stands up as if they know Mason walked into the room. I sit forward and try to not make any eye contact.

Mason slides into his seat, and I sigh. I lean over the left side of my desk and pick up my bag, placing it on the desk. I root around inside for my iPad but my hand touches something else. It's sharp point poking my finger.

Folded paper?

I pull out the foreign object. It's a red origami-shaped phoenix. Where the hell did this come from? I slowly look over it and see that there is some sort writing on the back. With caution, I start to undo the folds so I can read what has been written on it. Letting out a gasp, my hands shaking I drop the note onto my bag like its burning hot.

*You've been a naughty girl, Phoenix.*

"Hey, Red, you all right?" Mason leans over and grabs my chin, forcing me to look at him. "What's wrong? You tensed up all of a sudden."

I reach over and hand him the paper. He reads it, his brows pulling inward.

"It was in my bag. I didn't notice it until just now." I say as I wrap my arms around me. A sick twisting in my stomach forms as I try to remember if I had left my bag anywhere this morning. I know I didn't.

"This was in your bag?" I nod as he looks over the handwriting again. "And I take it you have no idea who it's from."

"If I did, I'm pretty sure I wouldn't be repulsed and scared out of my mind like I am."

"All right, class. I graded the tests from Friday," Mr. Patterson's voice booms over the class as he sets his laptop and bag down on the desk. "For the majority of you, well done. For those who didn't, you better study harder next test. Miss Hayes, please stay after class."

Stay after class? That's never a good sign.

When class does finally end, Mason jumps out of his seat and storms off. It's only then that I realize he never gave me back the offending note. At least he's in my next class, so I can grab it back from him then.

Gathering up my things and putting them back into my bag, I head down to see Mr. Patterson. My nerves are a little uneasy as I make my way up to his desk.

"Mr. Patterson, you wanted to see me?"

"Can you explain to me why you got a zero on your exam?" He throws the printed answers down on the table, and I take a look at them.

"Wait, what?"

"Your answers are answers from last year's test. How did you get last year's test, and did you not think that I would change up the questions and switch them around?" He leans back in his chair, his lips purse and eyes narrow at me.

"Mr. Patterson, I didn't have last year's test. And, yeah, I know my name is on this, but I ... these aren't my answers. I mean the questions are right, but these answers aren't what I wrote."

"Highly unlikely, Miss Hayes."

"I didn't cheat. This isn't my test." I swallow the frustration in my voice down. I'm trying not to lose it with this guy, but he's accusing me of something I didn't do.

"Your test says otherwise." He sighs. "I'm going to have to report this to the headmaster, and like I said, you received a zero for this test. There's also a possibility of an in-school suspension. That'll be up to the headmaster. Future tests, you will have to take under my watch by sitting up here at my desk."

"This is bull—"

He stops me with a finger to my face. "Watch what you say, Miss Hayes. I wouldn't want to have to report to the headmaster about your language as well. You may see yourself out." He dismisses me, and I can't run fast enough out of that classroom.

I realize that by the time I get to my pre-calculus class, I'm late and I have no pass. This day is turning out to be a shit fucking day.

"Miss Hayes, you're late," Mr. Fellows calls out from his desk when I step over the threshold.

"Sorry. Mr. Patterson held me up to talk to me after class," I say as I make my way over to my desk. I notice that Colton and Mason are not in their seats. Great, and now I won't be able to get my creepy note back.

"Did you get a pass?" Mr. Fellows asks.

"Well, since I failed to hand you one, I'm guessing we can draw to the conclusion that I forgot to ask for one. I'm sure you can ask him when you see him in the teacher's lounge. He'll vouch for me."

"Sit down and be quiet."

I plop down in my seat and try to spend the rest of class paying attention. The only problem is that my mind is anywhere but that class. The guys, Chad, the test, the note, just everything is so fucked up.

Rubbing my forehead, I internally groan at everything I have going on and the stress that has got me wound so tight. I have no idea how I'm going to handle that test scandal. I know I didn't cheat. Something else fucking happened there outside of my understanding. Chad is an asshole that needs to stay the fuck away from me. Then the three guys I should be running from, who I can't get out of my mind.

Every touch, kiss, it was so intense. The sensations of having them surrounding me, bringing me pleasure, it was surreal. And that might have been the best orgasm of my entire fucking life. They may have ruined all future orgasms for me.

I clear my throat as quietly as I can and sit straighter in my chair. I need to stop thinking about them. It does nothing but work me up into a hormonal frenzy. My thoughts drift to the note.

How the hell did it get into my bag? It wasn't in there on Friday, and it never left my room. I was home all weekend, and it sure as fuck didn't leave my side when I was around Chad. Who the hell would leave something like that? Is it a sick joke? It has to be.

Class ends, and I stand up to gather my things.

"Miss Hayes," Mr. Fellows calls.

I roll my eyes and walk towards the front. "Yeah?"

He hands me a slip. Detention. Great.

Today is turning out to be a horrible, terrible, and very fucking bad day.

I. Fucking. Hate. Mondays.

## twenty
DAXON

"YOU SAID she found this note where?" I turn to Mason, who left his history class and ran to find me.

He looks between me and Colt. "It was in her bag."

"How do you know she isn't fucking with us?" Colt asks, pulling the note from my hands.

Mase shakes his head and looks around before answering, "You didn't see the look on her face. We've been trying to push her and scare her, but this,"—he points to the note—"made her look sick. This scared her."

"Okay, so then who would do this? Because it wasn't us. Bianca?" I start walking back to the dorms, and the guys follow.

Mason chuckles. "Bianca couldn't find her way out of a paper bag, let alone origami."

"Someone said she slapped Oliver in the dining hall today," Colt adds with a smile.

"She's a lot tougher than we give her credit for. Our normal tactics aren't working. But this? This freaked her the fuck out." Mason runs a hand through his hair.

"No, she plows through everything we put in her way.

Maybe it was your dad? I just don't understand why your dad is so hell bent on getting her out of here. Shit, let the girl go and live her life." Colt shrugs.

"Her dad killed my mother, Colt." I shake my head. "How do I even just ignore that? I'm already confused enough as it is around her. One minute I want to tear her to shreds, the next I want to fuck her into next week. My dick is thoroughly confused."

"That make's two of us. Well, three if I include my dick. Wait, no, four if we include your dick. Colt, you want in on this?" Mason laughs.

Colt rolls his eyes. "But hasn't she lost enough? I mean yeah, her dad fucked up, but then her mom offed herself too. I think she's had enough suffering and that maybe your dad and us need to back off." Colt sticks his hands in his pockets as he looks out at the campus. "Just let her be."

"Don't you think it's a little weird that she's here, at this campus? Where Daxon is? Why is she here? I mean her dad, her uncle, all ties to Dax. Your dad may have good reason to want her gone. What if she knows something? What if she's a threat to all of our families? Part of some big takedown?" Mason runs his hand along the back of his neck and sighs.

"That girl part of a big takedown? She's not that good of a liar. She wears her emotions on her sleeve. She doesn't hide how she's feeling. Get real, Mase. She's a victim in all of this. I'm telling you we should just leave her alone. Tell your dad, Dax, that she's got nothing. Because I don't think she does." Colton turns to me. He may be right, but I still feel like I'm missing something important here.

"My dad still isn't telling me something. There is a bigger reason he's after her. Maybe it has to do with my mom. I don't know. I really need to talk to him. Maybe I'll go make a visit if he's in town." I pick up my phone and text my dad.

**Me: Hey, are you at the office today?**

**Father Dearest: Yes, I am. Come by after your classes.**

Placing my phone back in my pocket, I look up at the guys. "I'm gonna go see him later. I'll see what I can get from him." We head into our dorm and toss our bags onto the dining table and then head into Colt's room.

I throw myself down on his bed and sit back along the headboard. I mull over the death of my mother and the death of Phoenix's family. She's had to deal with a lot of it. Her aunt's all that's left in her life. Mom and dad both gone. I just don't understand the link. What is missing? How does this tie to my family?

"How did her uncle, Ronald Trivits, die again?" I ask Colt.

"Just said natural causes. Autopsy didn't find anything, or they were paid not to find anything." He looks at me out of the corner of his eye. He's always suspicious, which is good. He questions everything.

"Who was the first to pass on in her family? I know her uncle is only by marriage, but who first?"

"Her uncle passed first, then her dad, then mom." Colt swirls around in his chair as he regurgitates the information he has probably gone over a hundred times.

"Do we have any of the recordings from her sessions with the therapist?"

"We do." He turns and types something in and with a few clicks, starts playback. "This is from last week."

*"Phoenix. Please, come in and sit."*

The man, we found out, is Dr. Justin Parker. Graduated, has his degrees, blah blah blah. He's a boring individual who apparently thinks of Phoenix as a mental case if he agreed to continue treating here while she's here.

There's nothing but silence, and I look up at Colt confused. He holds up his hand and just nods.

*"How are your studies going?" She just lets out a small chuckle. "How are things with your roommate?" Still nothing.*

All three of us sit there quietly waiting for whatever comes next.

*"You have to give me something, Phoenix. Tell me how your week has been going."*

*"Fucking hell," she says angrily. The therapist doesn't say anything and just lets it sit for a moment. "Those three, they make my life hell."*

*"Those three?"*

*"The kings. The precious royalty of Dark-fucking-wood. You would think I killed their goldfish or something. They have had me in their fucking crosshairs since I walked on this godforsaken campus. They set the entire school against me. I can't go anywhere without being called names, food dumped on me, trash at my door. Oh, I get drugged at a fucking party, and somehow it becomes my fault. Itching powder shows up in my clothes and suddenly I have an STD. Pushed and made fun of. Everyday I'm on fucking eggshells waiting for the next attack. Just nothing but bullied. Fucking bullshit."*

*"Wait, Phoenix, you were drugged?"*

*"That's what you home in on? I've been bullied relentlessly for weeks, and you're worried about the one time I was drugged?" she bites back.*

*"That's pretty serious. Nothing to ignore. Did something happen to you?"*

*"Yeah, the fucking kings apparently carried me out of the party and took care of me in their castle in the sky."*

*"Did they hurt you?" His voice gets low.*

*Phoenix sighs. "No."*

*"Then why are you crying?" His voice is laced with concern.*

*"Because." She sniffs and lets out a little laugh. "If I tell you, you'll think less of me. Like I'm some horned up eighteen-year-old. In fact, it's probably enough to have me committed. I mean, I might enjoy the vacation. Padded room and all. Hey Doc, do those rooms have a view?"*

*"Well, you're eighteen, but I'm not here to judge," he says softly, as if he's trying to coax it out of her. He completely ignores her smartass remarks.*

*"I don't hate them. Not even a little. When I'm around them ..." She trails off for a moment. "I feel weird around them. This is weird to talk about." She huffs out a laugh.*

*"You know you are free to talk about what you want. It never leaves this room."*

All three of us look at each other and smile, because it's definitely left the room.

*"There's a weird attraction to them. I hate them, but I don't. I want to beat the living shit out of them, but I want to be touched by them. I want to gouge their eyes out, yet I want to kiss them."*

*"Them? As in all of them?" he asks.*

*"Yeah," Phoenix whispers. "How fucked up is that?"*

Colt cuts the audio, turning to us with his arms folded across his chest. Mason sits on the edge of the bed, and I stare back and forth between the two of them. He turns back to the letter that our little Spitfire got this morning.

"Well, that was an interesting turn of events. I mean, I know we had an effect on her, but I guess hearing it ..." Mason stands up and scrubs his face with his hands. "So, what do we do?"

"It's obvious we use that to our advantage," Colt says.

"Well, first, I'll go see my father. See what I can gather

from that. Second, we need to start figuring out who that letter may have come from. Then we keep her close." I run my thumb along my bottom lip, losing myself in thought. The way her skin felt against me. Her moans, her eyes fluttering, fuck.

Colt pipes in, "Keep your friends close—"

"And your enemies closer," I finish.

\* \* \*

I stroll into the lobby area of my dad's office in Downtown. Downtown separates the poor side of town to the, well, rich side. Downtown Black Forest is no Chicago or New York, but it does tout some nice skyscrapers that look out towards the ocean. Go an hour south of Downtown, and you arrive at Baybridge. A drug-infested rat hole.

Politicians have for years tried to clean up Baybridge, but violence, drugs, and sex just don't ever want to leave that town. They have tried bulldozing buildings, cleaning up parks, programs to help the youth, but still, people choose to live in the tattered state that they have always lived in.

Striding towards my father's assistant, Pamela Harley, I give her a wave and crack her a smile. She's been part of this company since before I was born. She was the assistant to my grandfather before my dad took over and is probably close to her seventies by now. I've asked her why she doesn't just retire, since she's worked here long enough and I'm sure they would give her a good retirement. The old bag usually tells me that it's because she doesn't want to rot away on the couch watching soap operas.

"Good afternoon, Daxon. Your father is waiting for

you," she says sweetly as she leans on her desk and rests her chin in her hands.

"Thank you, Ms. Harley," I reply.

"Daxon, sweetie, you know it's Pam."

I smile at her and nod. "I know, ma'am."

"Good lord, there you go making me feel old with that 'ma'am' talk." She shakes her head as I stroll towards the door of my dad's office.

Placing my hand on the doorknob, I take a deep breath and push the door open.

"There's my boy." My father stands and comes around from his desk. You'd never know he's a father by the way he keeps his office picture-free of any family.

"Father." I nod to him, and he points to his couch for me to sit with him. His office is covered in expensive paintings, and his shelves are filled with pretentious awards that were won with just his last name being what it is.

I sit on the stiff black leather couch, and he sits on the other side. A silence stretches between us for a few minutes before my dad breaks it.

"How are your classes?" he asks as he crosses his leg over his knee.

"You know how they are, just fine. I need to ask you something." I pull my eyebrows together.

"Please, go on." He waves his hand at me. He's always so cold, never warm. Never caring.

"What happened to my mother?"

His face is a blank mask. "She disappeared. She took—"

"No! What really happened? Don't lie to me. I know she didn't just leave. That's a bunch of horseshit. I deserve to know what actually happened," I interrupt him.

My dad lets out a long breath. "You already know, or you wouldn't have come here." I give him a curt nod and let him continue. "Your mother, God I loved her, she fell out of love with me. Or she got bored. I … I don't know. But we were not enough." There's a strain in his voice, but I can't tell if it's real or a front he's putting on.

"That's the thing, Dad. Why? I just don't understand how she could leave us, leave me. That doesn't seem like something she would do." I shake my head at the thought.

"Well, she did. She was seeing someone. You know the daughter of the man she was cheating with." He frowns as he fiddles with the buttons on his shirt.

"Phoenix."

He nods. "Yes, but it doesn't end there. It wasn't just the infidelity. They were conspiring to take down Emerson Industries. And this was going on longer than I realized. Right under my nose." My father gets up and walks over to his bar in the corner of the room and pours some amber liquid in a glass for himself. He takes a small sip and then walks back over to me.

"I don't understand." I lean forward with my hands resting on my knees. "Why?"

"Trivits. You know the name, correct?"

I nod. "Yeah. The software guy."

"Well, he was hired by your mother when she thought our accounting process could use an update. I trusted her, since that was her side of things here, handling the accounting department. So, I gave her full reign to do as she wanted. I mean, your mother was good at her job. We had a lot of government contacts come in, and we really did need a better way of keeping track of the financials." He pauses for a moment. "Trevor Hayes worked for us as an accountant. He lived in the town west of here, Fulton."

He lets out a long sigh.

"He was a good employee, well, until he wasn't." He

stands and walks towards the windows that look out towards the ocean. "Your mother and him, they hit it off or something. That software was used to help steal funds from the company. Minuscule amounts at a time, but enough to hurt us. They took the money and had it stored somewhere. I have no idea where. I'm sure some offshore account. I've been trying to have my investigators find where that money is, but they hid it well."

"But why? Why would she do that?" I run my hands through my hair. Nothing makes sense. Why would my mom cheat on my dad and try to take the company money? She had access to all the money she could ever need.

"I don't know. The plan, from what I gathered, was to make it look like I was stealing money from my own company. We would lose our contracts, the defense contracts. Use it to sink us somehow. Wrap the whole town in their mess. They were going to take off, start a life, and avoid the chaos they created."

"But they didn't make it."

"I think your mom got cold feet. Came to her senses and wanted to back out. But when Trevor found out she didn't want to go through with it ..." My dad pauses and looks up at the ceiling. "He was afraid what would have happened had they been caught, so he killed them both."

My heart is racing, my muscles are tight, and I'm ready to punch things. He took my mother from me in a pure act of selfishness.

As I try to make sense of what my father is telling me, I still feel like it's not the full truth. Something isn't sitting right.

"I don't want that girl getting any help in life. Her family has destroyed ours. She deserves the slums. I'm furious the board even let her in on the sole reason because of who she's related by marriage too." He lets out a frustrated growl. "I'm sorry I kept this from you. I just didn't want you to think any less of your mom."

I nod, but I can't find the words to speak. My mind, my heart, everything is being pulled in so many directions I don't know which way is up or down. There's a part of me that wants to ruin her, rip her to shreds for what her father has done. But the other part of me what's to protect her, knowing none of this was her doing. She's an innocent. Her dad and her mom set this in motion. She's probably clueless to it all.

I rub my palms into my eyes. I can feel a headache starting to form. I need to get out of here and try to make some of this, any of this, make just little sense. She isn't after us, she wants nothing to do with us. What the hell is my father afraid of? Her?

I leave my dad's office and head back to campus. The entire drive, the conversation replays in my head. Her family has destroyed mine. My mother may have tried to save us by not going through with it, but that just got her killed. But why did her mom kill herself? What tipped her over that she felt she couldn't move on in life?

And she left her daughter to fend for herself.

Gripping the wheel tightly, I let out a howling scream. For my mom, for Phoenix. There are so many lies, so much betrayal. I'm supposed to get rid of her, but she may hold the key to figuring out why this all happened. She could hold the answers I need to why my mom chose Trevor over me. Getting rid of her like what my father wants will never get me answers.

There's a line drawn in the sand, and I have no idea what side I'm on anymore.

## twenty-one

PHOENIX

"HEY, PHOENIX! GOT YOU A BACON CHEESEBURGER," Liz says as she strolls in with a paper bag in her hand. I could smell the bacon and fries the moment she opened the door. The door slams shut behind her as she brings me over the white paper bag already covered in grease. "Just so you know, I think I gained like five pounds just ordering that."

"Shut up." I laugh as I reach into the bag and pull out a couple of the fresh French fries, shoving them into my mouth.

"How do you eat like that and still fit into your uniform?" She looks at me with feigned disgust. "It's not fair."

I pat my belly. "Good metabolism."

Liz sighs. "You make me sick, woman." She chuckles as she plops down on the couch and eats her salad with minimal salad dressing. No, seriously, it's like a drip of dressing and that's it. "Look, I'm sorry about being pissed off that you left the party. I know you didn't really want to go there, and I made you. I shouldn't have gotten mad. So can you forgive me?"

I unfold the wrapper around my burger and turn to her. "It's okay. I should've said something."

As usual, I'm not one to make conversation, so we sit there in silence until she breaks it. "Any big projects coming up?"

"A couple papers. Oh, and I have to do some performance by the end of the semester for my music class, but that's about it." I take a giant bite out of my burger, moaning as the juices drip down my chin. I focus back on my reading for my history class as I wipe my mouth with my hand.

"It's like I'm watching a porn between you and that burger." She scrunches her face while I chew.

I swallow down the last bite and smile. "You know it turns you on." I run my tongue along my lips and moan more.

"Gross." She throws a wadded-up napkin at me.

"Hey, this weekend, I was going to go into town and get a pedi. You want to join me?" She flips her hair back.

I cock my head to the side. "Um, do I look like a person that usually pampers themselves?"

"That's why you should go. You don't know the heaven you are missing. The warm water, the hot towels, the massages! It's heaven!" She leans back on the couch and closes her eyes like she's having an out-of-body experience.

"Do you want a moment alone?" I chuckle.

She opens her eyes and lunges across the couch to shove my shoulder.

"Okay, I'll go," I say hesitantly, but I give her a smile. My mom had always talked about her and I having a girls' day where we went for pedicures and manicures. Spending the day shopping, eating like pigs, and then coming home to binge out on candy and watching movies. We never got that chance.

"Yay! This will be so much fun! I can't wait!" Liz grabs her bag, takes out her iPad, and excitedly types away on it. "Okay, Saturday at two!"

We sit there for a little longer and study while finishing off our dinner. When it gets a little late, I head to my room to do some writing in my journal. I've been particularly on edge since yesterday when the phoenix-shaped note appeared in my bag. I didn't even go to classes today; I just wanted to separate from the world.

Many of my thoughts have had me wondering if I should just pull out of school and try to enroll myself in my old high school. The problem is where would I live? I don't want to impose on my old friends. They did me a favor when my mom died, and I couldn't do that to them again. Plus, I have no money. Well, minus the money my aunt gave to me, which I refuse to touch. I just can't ask them to do that for me.

No, I need to stay here. Find some scholarships to the local college and just grow my way to adulthood, alone. All the fuck alone. Though, Liz has been a pretty good friend to me since I got here. Strange as it has been. I know she was thrown in here with me having to be her roomie and all, but no one else has really taken the time to get to know me. No one really wants to get to know me. They would rather call me names and try to make my life hell.

They don't realize I'm already living in hell.

I lay my head back with my headphones on, closing my eyes to try and remember the family I used to have. My thoughts drift back to the first time I was about to get on stage for a talent show, the fear that seeped into me. I was twelve, and the uncertainty getting up on that stage and singing for the first time in front of people other than my parents made me terrified.

*"I can't do this, Mom. What if I mess up? What if I don't actually sound good?" I shake my head and try to fight back the tears that I know will ruin my makeup. My mom spent time making me look nice for tonight's talent show. I don't want to ruin it with crying. But that ball of emotion is stuck in my throat, threatening its way out.*

*"Sweetie, look at me." Her hand comes up to my chin, turning my head towards hers. "Get up there and be your best you. It doesn't matter if you mess up or they don't like you. You are not up there for anyone but you. Now, on that note, you have the most beautiful voice, little birdie. Do you know what my favorite part of my day is?"*

*I shake my head. "No, what?"*

*"When I wake up and hear you singing as you get ready for school or whatever you are doing that day. I love hearing your sweet, beautiful voice. Don't worry about what others think. There will always be people who will try to tear you down, or make you feel like less of a person. Remember to stay strong and be true to you." She leans down and kisses my forehead. "Now get out there and sing your heart out, little birdie."*

There is a sudden dip in my bed, and my eyes fly open as my heart leaps from my chest.

"What the fuck?" I yell. Immediately, a hand comes over my mouth as I try to scramble to roll to the other side. But I'm pulled down from my sitting position, pinned down by the weight above me. My arms start to flail as I try to push the mass off me. My eyes start to focus on who's sitting above me, and I start to scream under his hand.

"Shhh, Spitfire. It's just me," Daxon whispers. "Let's not

cause a scene and scare your roomie. I don't want her coming in here trying to save the day and all." He smirks.

My hands wrap around his wrist as I try to pry his hand off my mouth. All the while, cursing him as I try to ask him why he's in here, but my words come out all muffled. Because, of course, there's a fucking hand over my mouth.

"What? What's that? I can't understand you. I'm gonna need you to speak a little clearer." He tilts his head and shakes it. I try to buck against him to push him off me, but he just laughs and doesn't even move an inch.

I narrow my eyes at him and bring my hands up and flip him off.

"God, I love your fight. You gonna be a good girl and be quiet?" he asks, and I nod. "Are you sure?" Dax narrows his eyes. I glare at him as he bites his lip, trying to hold back his smile. Slowly, he peels his hand away from my mouth.

Taking a deep breath, I try to calm my wildly beating heart. I'm failing miserably at it. "What are you doing here, Daxon? How did you get into my room?" My breathing picks up from the heat of his body over my own. His eyes bore into mine as he has me trapped under him. Honestly, not a position I mind being in. I'm just very confused with all of this. However, my body not so much. No, she knows exactly what she wants, hence the hardened nipples and the fact that I'm fucking soaking wet.

Why does this asshole do this to me? Why do all of them do this to me? Fucking dick voodoo.

"Through the door." He deadpans.

"Yeah, but who let you in? It's after ten, and I'm sure my roommate is sleeping," I growl.

Daxon shrugs. "I can't give away my secrets, sweetheart. Besides, I wanted to talk to you."

My face scrunches in confusion. "So, you break into my

room? At this hour? Isn't there a school law about boys in the girls' dorms?"

"I'm a king, baby. Laws don't apply to us." He places a hand on his chest and smiles down at me.

"Oh, that's right, fucking royalty. Well, what do I owe this pleasure, Your Highness?" I fake gag.

He doesn't say anything for a moment but then cocks his head. "I'm trying to understand you," he says softly.

"What's there to understand? Why?"

He asks, "Why are you here?"

"Because this is where I was sent to come to school, Daxon. Why can you not understand that?"

"No one has ever been let in here outside of being a freshman. What makes you so special?" He leans down, and his arms come down next to my head. I can smell the mint from his breath, his face so close to mine. There's a battle brewing inside of me, one I'm sure I want to lose.

My eyes lock with his. "I'm not special. If I had a choice, this would be the last place I'd actually be," I whisper.

"I don't know, Phoenix. I kinda like having you here." His nose nuzzles against my cheek. "Just like this." His touch sends my skin ablaze. My hands grab onto his t-shirt, and I'm unsure if I'm trying to keep him there or push him away.

"You three don't act like you enjoy me even breathing the same air." My voice is hoarse.

"Hmm. I'm enjoying breathing the same air right now."

"Why do you hate me?" My voice comes out soft, my hands clinging to him. And I hate it. I hate how weak he makes me feel right now. I hate that he's here in my room. I hate that he is talking to me. I hate that I'm pulling him closer. I hate that I enjoy him touching me. I hate that my body is betraying me in every way.

Daxon says nothing. He merely stares at me, his eyes studying every inch of my face. Without saying a word, he starts peppering my jawline with soft kisses. His legs shift slightly, and I feel him rubbing against me. I bite the inside of my cheek as I push my hips up slightly against him. Every inch of me is on fire from his touch. And holy shit, he's so hard right now.

Daxon moves from my jawline to nibbling on my ear, eliciting a moan from me as I clench my legs together. He's turning me into a puddle of my own arousal.

"Mmm. You taste so good. Fuck, you shouldn't taste this good." He licks up my neck and hums. My hands find their way to his hair. I grab hold of his black strands, trying to draw him closer as he kisses and softly bites on every inch of my neck. He pulls back slightly and says, "Look at me."

My eyes fling open, and I turn my head. Our eyes meet, and I can see his beautiful green eyes dilating. There's an inferno burning in them. A desire, a need. Our breathing picks up, both of us panting. Suddenly, his lips crash down on mine, swallowing every moan I give him.

This shouldn't be happening. I shouldn't want this. There is nothing about this that I should enjoy. I shouldn't be kissing Daxon. And yet I am. I'm so completely turned on that my body feels like it'll combust at any moment.

Our tongues and lips clash against each other, our hands explore our bodies, and Dax grinds his hardness into me, causing more moans to escape that he swallows up with his mouth.

Shifting my hands between us, I reach down to his jeans and work as fast as I can with my fingers to get them unbuttoned. Once I get them pushed down far enough, I shove my hand down his boxers and grab his very hard and very large cock.

*Holy fuck.*

He hisses the moment my skin touches his. I slowly start pumping my fist along his velvety skin. I can feel him shaking against me, his hips moving in time with my hand.

"Sweetheart," he groans against my lips, "if you don't stop that, I will make a fool of myself in about three seconds."

Before I can test that theory, he pulls away. He removes his pants and boxers, shedding them somewhere next to the bed. He climbs back up and sits, and his hands slowly caressing my hips. His fingers trace the waistband of my leggings, just slightly dipping his finger below it.

His emerald eyes look up at me in question. "If you want me to stop, tell me now." His voice is low and husky.

I shake my head. "Don't stop."

Daxon lets out a growl as his hands grab on to the side of my pants. He slowly peels them down my legs, throwing them to the floor. He yanks my legs apart and settles himself in between my legs, with just my thong separating him from my very wet center.

My entire body is shivering, and I'm not cold. His touch burns me, excites me. I'm looking down at Daxon, seeing only his eyes staring back at me. My heart is racing, and my breathing is erratic. My mind doesn't know whether to tell me to sit back and enjoy the show or fucking take off running.

*I should make him leave.* But I can't. In some sick and twisted way, I don't want him to go.

His arms hook under my legs, and his thumb brushes along the material over my clit. My hips jump at the sensation, and my breathing picks up. Oh my God, he has magic fingers.

He kisses the inside of my thighs as he continues to rub my clit through the thong. My head tosses from side to side as I feel the pressure start to build. The release is so close. I can feel my body start to quiver, start to fall over that wall of ecstasy.

Without warning, he pulls away, and I'm left teetering complete bliss.

"W-Wait—" I stammer as I try to catch my breath.

"Don't worry, I'll get you there. Except, when you come, I just want it to be all over my face." My mouth drops open as he tears my thong down my leg. Moving quickly, he settles right back where he was and before I have a moment to process everything, I feel his tongue travel up my slit and swirl around my clit.

"Holy fuck! Oh my God, Dax," I breathe out. My entire mind misfires. I can't utter a single word beyond that.

"Mm, that's it, sweetheart. I like hearing my name come from that pretty little mouth of yours." He pushes a finger inside of me, causing me to groan from the welcomed intrusion. "I'm going to like that mouth even more when it's wrapped around my cock."

His teeth softly bite my clit, sending shockwaves through my body. His tongue flattens against it, and he inserts another finger inside of me. He curls them inside of me, slowly moving them. The combination of his fingers inside pushing my button and his tongue sucking my clit has me headed towards the fucking light. There's so much sensation, so much of everything, my body tenses as I start to feel a building towards my release, yet again.

"That's right, baby. Come all over my hand and face. Let

me drink you up." He wraps his mouth around my clit, and my vision blacks out.

My mouth opens up, but no sound comes out as I reach complete ecstasy, my orgasm so powerful that my body shakes through it. My head feels light and my body heavy as I come down from the absolute best high I have ever experienced.

My hand hovers over my heart as I try to calm my breathing. I try to ground myself back into this realm. Looking down at Daxon between my legs, I see him lick his lips and then suck on his fingers. I shiver as I watch him enjoy the taste of me.

"Mm. So sweet," he says as he crawls back up my body, kissing me and letting me taste myself on him. He groans as I let his tongue sweep against mine. He is still rock hard, I'm sure ready to explode the moment I touch him.

Reaching down, I run my hand along the length of him as he hisses from my touch. His chest starts to move up and down rapidly, until he is panting above me. His eyes are closed, and I have no doubt he is trying to control himself.

I need to taste him.

"Do you want my lips wrapped around you, Dax?" My voice is throaty and soft.

He nods. "Yes, fuck yes," he moans as he rolls over to his back, pulling me on top of him. I shift myself down between his legs. His eyes are closed, his hands just lightly touching my head as if to guide me to where he needs me.

Wrapping my hand around his cock, I slowly stroke it, causing his hips to buck up. I bring the head to my mouth and kiss it. His breathing picks up, and his hands start to tighten in my hair. I drop my head down and lick up along the backside.

"Oh, fuck, sweetheart." His voice is rough, straining to keep control.

My hand continues to pump him as I wrap my lips around the head of his cock, slowly working him into my mouth. His hands roughly pull at my hair, tugging enough to control my movement but not enough to hurt.

There's a salty taste on my tongue from him. I swirl my tongue around the head, trying to get more from him. Slowly, I work my lips up and down on him. I start to take more of him inside my mouth. When he hits the back of my throat, I gag around his cock and start to pull back. Dax holds me there, not letting me pull back.

"Flatten and stick out your tongue. There you go. Now, breathe out through your mouth." I do as I'm told, and he starts to take control of the movement. His hips buck under me, as his fingers that are weaved in my hair guide my mouth over his hardness. "That's it. Oh, fuck your mouth's so fucking perfect. Suck this cock, sweetheart. Fuck."

As he pushes in and out of my mouth, I use my tongue to push against the shaft and swirl it around. I grab the base of his cock and wrap my hand around the rest of him that I can't get into my mouth, allowing his movement to stroke himself in my hand.

I moan as his speed picks up and his breathing becomes ragged. "Fuck, you have no idea how good this feels. I'm gonna come down that throat of yours, sweetheart. Look up at me. I want your eyes on me as I come in that sweet, warm mouth of yours."

My eyes flit up towards him, and he holds me still while he thrusts into my mouth. My eyes start to water as I try to keep from gagging, his cock hitting deeper inside my mouth. He stops with a silent roar as a warmness fills my mouth. He watches as he continues to pulse inside me, eventually stilling, his head falling back on my bed.

I swallow and wipe my mouth on the back of my hand. Before I can shift off the bed, he drags me up next to him on the bed, pulling me to lay my head on his chest. The moment's way more intimate than I'm comfortable with, but it still feels strangely good. Still, I'm confused as to why any of this just happened. Why am I laying on Dax's chest after I just blew him? Why was he between my legs making me see stars?

"Why are you here, Dax?" I whisper.

For a moment, he doesn't say anything. He just runs his fingers through my hair. Again, the act is completely way more intimate than I would expect from him. He tenses a bit but then relaxes.

"I don't know. I was going to head to my dorm, but then I thought of that letter that Mason said you got and something in me wanted to check on you."

"Why?"

I feel his shoulders shrug. "I don't know." He lets out a deep breath.

"Well, I'm sure the letter is just a cruel prank. This school is definitely not short of assholes, so anyone could just be trying to get a rise out of me."

"Just get some sleep. It's late," he says softly.

I close my eyes and curl closer to Daxon, though I'm not sure why. He has pretty much tormented me since coming to Darkwood. He has been constantly questioning why I'm here. As if I'm here for a nefarious reason.

The three of them have been circling me since I stepped on campus, but no matter how much I try to pull away, we always seem to find a way to be drawn to each other. Right now? Here at this very moment? This is downright scary.

How I feel lying next to him, how comfortable I feel, how not alone I feel, that should raise flags. But it doesn't.

Instead, it makes me relaxed. His presence is relaxing me.

I curl into him deeper and hear him sigh. My eyes start to get heavy when I hear him say, "I'm sorry."

Before I can ask what he means, sleep wins me over.

## twenty-two
PHOENIX

WHEN I AWOKE THIS MORNING, Daxon wasn't there. If it wasn't for the fact that there was a Daxon smell to my sheets and that I was naked from the waist down, I seriously would think that it had all been a dream. Of course, being naked from the waist down could've meant I stripped myself in my dream, but I know it was real. That fucking orgasm was real. The taste of him in my mouth was real. None of that was a dream.

But there is a part of me that is completely confused by the events. Let's just start with how he got into my dorm room, let alone my bedroom. Then I can't even begin to process how I felt with him over me, the weight of his body on top of mine. The heat radiating off him, his soft lips and sharp bites on my skin. Let's not focus on his words, or his confusing actions of pulling me into him after we were done messing around. All of that has left me in utter confusion.

And when I woke up, he was gone. I actually experienced sadness from having that asshole leave me. I mean, he's tormented me and had his goons mess with me, but him leaving my room after what happened last night actually affected me in a way I didn't expect it to.

Oh, and I slept soundly for the first time in a long time. No dreams of my mother in a tub, seeing my father go over a cliff. No dreams of people coming after me and tormenting me. No, I slept peacefully, in his arms after one of the best orgasms of my life.

Bastard.

I slowly slide into my desk in history class, trying to draw little attention to myself, still on edge from the constant tormenting. Mason, already at his desk, turns to me with a huge smile on his face and wiggling his eyebrows. Shit.

"Hey, Red. So, how did you sleep last night?" Mason leans over, his body incredibly close to mine. Heat rolls off from him as he drapes his arm around the back of my chair.

"How I slept is none of your business." I push his arm off my chair and the minute my skin touches his, my breath catches. A weird sensation travels through me. I drop my hand and face the front, trying to regain my composure.

Wow, I'm a horny bitch.

Reaching into my bag, I pull out my book and notebook and do everything I can to focus on anything but the solid slab of hotness next to me. The chair next to me scrapes against the floor, and warm fingers come up to the side of my face and tuck my hair behind my ear.

I feel a heated breath next to my ear. "I bet you looked so beautiful when you came. So sexy as you exploded in pure ecstasy. I'm so fucking jealous he got to see that. To taste you." I shiver from his whispered words. "God, to hear you scream my name as you grind your pussy on my face. Fuck." I bite the inside of my cheek to hold back a whimper.

Closing my eyes, I try to steady my breathing. I use

everything I have to control my heartbeat, because Mason is eliciting a reaction in me that is doing things to my nether regions. Slowly I turn to my right, opening my eyes, and his beautiful blue eyes are locked in on mine.

His hand comes up to caress my cheek, and instinctively, my head leans into his hand before I realize what I'm doing. I gasp at the realization of what I just did. Turning away from him, I push his hand off of me and turn again to face the front.

*Note to self: Bring additional underwear as back up for when I flood mine from just a single touch by of one of these three.*

My mouth dries up, and my heart races as Mason stays within inches of my face. As the teacher walks into the classroom, I feel him pull away from me.

"I can't wait, Red," is all he says before the teacher starts their lecture.

The rest of the class passes in a blur until I head off to pre-calc. I bolted out of U.S. Government, trying to leave Mason way far behind. Of course, I failed. Before I could even get ten feet from the door, his arm came around me, pulling me against his very hard, very muscular body. I look up and see his ocean blue eyes staring down at me with a grin a mile long on his face.

I swear, I'm going to flood the school at this rate.

We get to our pre-calc class, and I pull away from him to run to my seat and throw myself into my desk. He saunters down the aisle, looking at me with narrowed eyes and his lips slightly turned up, like I'm his prey. He slides in next to me, leaning towards me and invading any personal space I assumed I had.

My head jolts towards the front from a scoff and whine that grab my attention. Bitch Barbie number one sways her fake ass into the class and throws me a look. So, I of course flip her off.

"Do you even know who you are messing with? I will destroy you, cunt." She barrels towards me. Before she can even get to me, Mason jumps over his desk and steps in between us.

"Bianca, go sit," he says firmly.

"Don't tell me what to do, Mason. This whore is dying to get her ass handed to her."

"She just sat down, Bianca. You came in here and threw her a look and started shit. What did you expect her to do?"

Bianca's eyes go wide. Her mouth drops open, and she takes a step back.

"Are you defending her, Mason? What the actual fuck?" Bianca's shrill voice feels like it's ripping at my ear drums. Goddamn, she can hit some opera level pitches.

"All right class. Let's take a seat, please." Mr. Fellows eyes our corner. Bianca takes her seat with a huff and starts immediately texting. I'm sure she's letting Skipper and her friend know what just went down.

Colt walks in the room and the air shifts again as his eyes meet mine. He runs over to the desk in front of me and plops down. Then he turns his head and gives me a sly smile. Did Daxon blab to everyone about what happened last night? I turn to see Mason leaning back in his chair, and he gives me a wink. The asshole winks at me.

What the fuck is going on?

The rest of pre-calc is normal, and by normal, I mean Bianca is throwing daggers at me with her eyes and basically plotting my death in her tiny, itty-bitty Barbie brain. I see her continuing to text throughout most of class. No doubt filling in the other brainless idiots of how Mason and Colton are looking at me or some other bullshit.

By the time math ends, I'm hauling my ass out of my seat and flying past the kings and their stalker queen. I need space. I need away from the drama they carry with them wherever they go, with Bianca being a major factor in the drama department. But she's so wrapped up in her text message that she doesn't even see me take off. Thank fuck.

As I walk towards Forthright, it comes to me what class I have next. English. With fucking Dax and one of the bitches, Tiffany. Fuck my life. I stop off at my locker and pick up some of the books I had taken from the library. I need to bring them back when we head in there for class today.

Apparently, in the world of Google and search engines, we still need to learn how to check out books and research. Well, maybe the rich kids do for when they get into Yale and Harvard, but I'm pretty sure I can get by with the internet at a state college.

But whatever.

The moment I step over the threshold of the library, the hair on the back of my neck stands up. Instantly, I know Daxon has eyes on me. I drop my books off in the return slot of the desk. As I turn towards the desks on the first floor, I see him sitting at the table I was assigned. I don't need any more shit today. I groan and make my way over there.

I walk up and throw my bag on the table. "Go away, Dax."

"Is that really all you have to say to me? No 'thank you for the orgasm, Dax? Please give me more, Dax? Let me come on your face again, Dax.'" He tilts his head to the side.

I sneer at him in disgust while my mind replays the events of last night, heating my body up. "If you have to beg me to thank you, then you know you weren't that good. I'm not feeding your already self-inflated ego."

He laughs, and his hand wraps around my wrist as he yanks me down onto his lap. His arm wraps around me, locking me against him. "Sweetheart, you and I both know I had you coming so hard, you passed the fuck out after. Don't play it off like I didn't."

His voice vibrates against my skin. My traitorous body is already responding to his touch, now completely turned on by his words, his voice. His lips brush against my cheek, leaving in its wake a fire burning on my skin.

"Why are you at this table, Dax?" I ask softly, my eyes closed so I can at least control one of my senses.

His lips kiss along my neck and shoulder. "Because I sit here now." I manage to wiggle out of his hold and round the table to the other side. I sit where he can't pull me back into his grasp.

The teacher announces, "Okay, class. Please take a seat. Today, we are going to talk about what to do after you have selected a topic and what steps you use next to research your topic. Now remember, you will actually be selecting a topic and writing a paper on this for the end of the semester, so make sure that you pay attention over the next couple weeks."

Mrs. Gaede points to a white board at the front of where we are all at.

"Once you pick a topic, you first want to get in some background reading. This will help you get an overview of the topic." As she goes on, I stare at the board, but my mind is torn between melting with thoughts of last night and trying to hold myself together being in the vicinity of Dax.

Daxon seems to be the common denominator in all this. I need to get away from him. When Mrs. Gaede finishes her lecture, she sends us on our own to do our research.

Disappearing into the stacks of books on the second

floor, I make my way over to a section that contains books on mental health and depression. A part of me wants to find out if that was what plagued my mom, what caused her to end her life. Why she felt that was the only way out. Even with them both gone, all the shit I have put up with since coming here, nothing could make me want to end it all. I don't understand the psyche or mental state that she seemed to be in. Why leaving me alone without her wasn't more important.

With my head in a book I found, I round the corner and head into a section that continues my search. The air gets thicker, and the hair on the back of my neck stands on end. He's here.

"Spitfire." His voice is low, and I feel him up against my back before I have time to turn around.

"Daxon," I whisper.

He brushes my hair away from my neck, and then his hands travel down to my waist. He hugs me from behind, and I feel his lips along my neck and shoulder, setting my skin ablaze. His hardness presses against my ass, and he lets a groan slip from his throat.

"Is that your cellphone in your pocket, or are you just happy to see me?" I quip.

"Well, my cellphone *is* in my back pocket." He spins me around and shoves me back against the shelves. "Fuck." His lips crash down on mine, and the book I had in my hand falls to the floor. My lips dance against his, our tongues clash, our moans being swallowed up.

There's a sudden realization of where we are. My mind wakes up from the make-out coma to jolt me back to reality. Pulling back, I try to distance our lips from each other.

"Stop, Dax. Not here." My hands push against his chest, but my efforts are completely futile.

"No one will see us, and if you keep quiet, no one will hear us." His hand moves down to my thigh, slowly traveling up under the skirt. Every part of me vibrates with need and want just from his touch. I'm whimpering the closer he gets to my core.

His lips descend on mine again, and slowly he kisses me, taking his time with me. His lips are soft, a strong contrast to every other part of him. He's hard, he's muscular, but his lips are warm and silky. His kisses make me weak, my knees wanting to give out to the ground below me. He is the only thing keeping me from crashing down. He pulls back, and our eyes lock on each other.

"Please, not here." My voice is soft and quiet.

He stares at me, unsure whether he wants to listen to me. But after a moment, he finally speaks, "Okay. Fine. Not here. But on one condition." Dax's lips curl up.

I chuckle and shake my head. "Coming from you, I shouldn't even ask what that condition is. I should turn and run."

He laughs, and his hand comes up and tucks my hair behind my ear. He leans down to kiss my cheek. "Come to the game Friday."

"Wait, what?" My face scrunches in confusion.

"Come to my game. Cheer me on. Cheer Mase on."

"See now, I think you have me confused with those cheerleading bimbos that shake their ass and tits around for all to see. I don't do football games, Dax." I shake my head.

"Please? And then afterwards, there will be a party at my house." He pouts. And damnit if that pout isn't sexy as fuck on him too. What the hell is going on? I feel like I have whiplash with them.

"How about I think about it?" I purse my lips. What is

going on in my brain? Am I really even considering thinking about going to a football game? These three are causing a serious mixup in my head. It's like they use their superpowers of dick sorcery to break down my walls.

"See you there, Spitfire." He smiles as he pushes off me and saunters away.

I roll my eyes. There's no way I'm being caught dead at a football game. No fucking way. Sitting with people I can't stand being around, watching guys tackle each other in tight pants that make their asses looks delicious. The sweat and grunts.

Shit. Okay. Maybe I can get Liz to go with me.

Dick fucking sorcery.

## twenty-three
### PHOENIX

**WHEN CLASS FINALLY LETS OUT,** I silently celebrate because that means it's time for food. And my stomach's fully on the 'needing food because it's starting to eat itself' train. Plus, I think it's a good day for some pizza. I mean most of the chicks here are on some sort of new fad diet, which means more for me.

And honestly, I don't know why they waste so much money on food, half the population here won't even eat. Like I seriously hope they donate the leftovers. I've never seen more people lined up at the salad bars in my life.

I drop my books and stuff off at my locker and head to the bathroom quickly before I walk over to the dining hall. I slip into the closest bathroom nearest to the lockers, finding it's empty and quiet. Locking myself into a stall, I do my business and pull out my phone. I scroll through my messages, though I don't know why I bother. No one ever calls or texts me. No one bothers to ask me how my day was. So, it shouldn't surprise me that my aunt is still MIA.

As I finish, the sounds of the most annoying voices known to man come squawking though the bathroom door.

I freeze, not sure if I should make myself known or stay quiet until they leave.

"Did you see Mason today? He's so yum," Tiffany says.

"Have you noticed Dax hanging around that whore a little more than he should, lately?" Jacklyn asks.

"Yeah, I wouldn't worry. She'll be yesterday's news by tomorrow. He always comes running back to me," Bianca says in the most vile and repulsive voice. God, it's like nails on a fucking chalkboard. Fuck it. If they are going to talk about me, they may as well do it to my face. Because they are all talk.

I slam open the stall door, and it hits the wall next to it. My eyes settle on them huddled in front of the mirror, plastering more makeup on. I wonder how many layers I can peel back until I actually get to their skin. They turn around to see the commotion, and Bianca's eyes narrow at me.

"Who let the town whore in here?" Bianca hisses.

"Well, I think your friends probably held the door open for you, so ..." I trail off and smile at her.

"Oh, you fucking bitch!" Bianca throws her makeup bag down on the counter and a tube of lipstick rolls out and onto the floor. "I'm so tired of seeing your disgusting face here at my school."

"Hm, the feeling is mutual." I turn to wash my hands in the sink.

"You don't get it, do you? No one actually wants you here. You're some charity case they are using to make themselves all feel better. All you do is trash up this school. Hell, you fucked all three kings, you're that easy!" she screams in my ear next to me as I dry my hands.

Turning to her, I smirk. "Are you jealous that all three wanted me, and not a single one wanted you?"

I'm not prepared for it, only because I didn't think she

had it in her. Her hand comes up and grabs my hair, slamming my head against the counter. For a moment I'm disoriented by the blow and the surprise attack.

I'm shoved backwards until I hit a wall that I slid down. My head is throbbing. "What the fuck, bitch?" Before I can say more, Jacklyn kicks me in my stomach, causing me to curl over on the floor. I pull myself into a ball, the pain tearing through me.

"Leave this school, slut. Take your trash and get the fuck out! The guys used you, and that's all you will ever be to them. A used-up whore. Someone they can talk about for years to come on how they got in her pants by just being a little nice to her." She spits in my face. The other girls continue to kick me and step on me. One of them kicks my head and adds more pain to my already throbbing skull.

I lay there on the ground, ready for another attack. I cover my face and curl into myself. But it never comes.

Bianca and her trolls turn and walk out the door, leaving me there, beaten and bruised. I groan in pain as I try to move, but my body is just not ready to move yet. I can still feel the kicks, and my head's throbbing from hitting the counter and wall, while every muscle in my body is tense from being on the defensive. My breathing picks up, and there's a knot forming in my throat. My mind can't think straight with the pain coursing through it.

And then the tears come.

I cry because I'm alone. I cry because I miss my mom. I cry because I miss the family I had. I cry because I lost and miss my father. I cry because I'm in some strange universe left to fend for myself. I cry because my heart hurts. I cry because I'm not wanted anywhere or by anyone.

Tears pour down my face and onto the tile floor. I have no idea if someone will find me in here or whether I'll eventually be able to move. I'm so lost in my self-pity and pain that I don't hear someone enter the bathroom.

"Shit, Red." Mason drops down beside me, and I flinch. "Hey, Phoenix, hey. You're going to be okay." His hand wipes the tears from my face. He studies me, concern etched across his face.

He pulls out his phone from his back pocket and clicks on it.

"Hey. It's me. Found her. It's not good. Bianca did a number on her. Meet me in her dorm." He ends the call and throws the phone back into his back pocket.

His hands come up and sweep the hair out of my face.

"Red, hey. Sweetheart, I'm going to get you back to your room. Okay?" Mason wraps an arm under my shoulders and my knees. I keep my head tucked into him, not wanting to see anyone watching me be carried yet again by a king.

"Everything hurts," I cry into his chest.

"Shh. I know. We got you." I feel him place a small kiss at the top of my head.

Cradling me against his chest, he effortlessly carries me out of Forthright and across the campus to my dorm. When we get to the door of my dorm, I hear the other guys.

"Bianca, that fucking bitch. She's done." Daxon's voice is low. I'm sure that response was from the way I look in Mason's arms.

"Fuck," Colton grumbles.

"Red, baby. I need your code to get into the room. Do you want to punch it in? Or give it to me? Or let Daxon do it?" Mason says with a bit of a chuckle as he lays his head on me as I curl tighter into his grasp.

"Zero, seven, two, nine," I whisper to him, knowing I would have to change it yet again. Shifting me, he punches in the code, and the guys walk in. Daxon immediately heads towards my room, the others following.

Mason lays me on my bed and gets in beside me. His warmth surrounds me, his hand running along my cheek. The tenderness, the softness, cracks whatever resolve I was holding onto once I left that bathroom. A wrenching sob breaks through. Tears cascade down my cheeks, and my vision is completely blurred. Mason pulls me into him, and I wince in pain.

"Shit. What the fuck did that bitch do to you?" Mason lays me on my back. The other two come around the bed on the opposite side of Mason. "Can I lift up your shirt, Red?"

I nod, giving him permission. Mason slowly just lifts my shirt enough that I'm still decent. Colt walks away, his face red and his fists curled at his side, while Daxon and Mason take a look at the damage.

Their hands softly glide over my skin, just taking in the bruises already forming. Colt comes back over to my face with a warm washcloth, wiping the tears from my face.

"You got some blood. I'm just gonna clean it up for you, okay?" Colton stares at me with an intensity in his eyes. Like he's not sure if he wants to go rip Bianca a new one or jump into bed and pull me into him.

I nod, giving him permission to wipe it clean. My mind is overwhelmed with having all three of them in the same room. My body is on the verge of meltdown having all three of them touching me. Caring for me.

This is weird. What earth am I on? What dream world am I in? I'm lost in my emotions and confusion when Dax breaks me of it.

"Fucking unbelievable." Dax furrows his brows as he stares down at my stomach.

"How did you know where I was?" I wince as I turn to Mason.

"Bianca and her minions came into the dining hall beaming." He sighs. "I just had a feeling they were up to something, especially after Bianca was pissed off from class earlier, so when they sat down, we asked them what they were so happy about."

Dax locks eyes with me. "Bianca spilled the beans that they ran into you in the bathroom and that you may actually leave now. When I asked her what that meant, she said that her job was done and she had taken out the trash." He shakes his head. "Without them seeing, I texted Mason to go look for you, and he made up some story about forgetting a meeting with the coach and left the dining hall."

"So, while Mason went back to Forthright in search of you, Dax and I got them to tell us what they did." Colt's face is like stone. "The minute they told us that they ganged up on you ..." he trails off.

"We need to put Bianca in her place," Dax growls from beside me. "Three against one? Having her tramps do the dirty work for her? Fuck!" he roars. "I'm going to go knock her down a peg or two."

"No!" My eyes widen in fear. "Please, no. No more. I just want to survive enough to leave this place. Don't make it worse." My voice is weak, and I've honestly lost all fight in me.

"She hurt you, Phoenix. I need her to pay," Dax says through gritted teeth. I don't understand the reaction he's having. Why does he even care? Why do any of them care? I want to ask them that, but I hold back.

"No." I shake my head.

I see his jaw tense, and he lets out a heated breath.

"What the fuck ever." Dax storms out of my room, pissed I won't let him retaliate on my behalf.

"I'll go keep an eye on him." Colt leans down and kisses my forehead in a weird show of intimacy that stuns me. Mason nods and pulls me into him. He's giving me a weird sense of safety. One of the guys who has been making my life hell, protecting me. And I truly need it.

"How did you find me?"

Mason lets out a sigh. "I ... um ... fuck. I heard you crying, Red. And that's not a sound I enjoyed hearing."

I burrow deeper into him. The heat on my cheeks growing. I don't like feeling needy, or like I need a savior. Yet that's exactly what I need right now. And my weakness led Mason to me.

"I'm sorry you had to come running after me. I don't mean to be a bother."

He pulls back a bit to look at me. "Don't you dare apologize. What they did was fucked up. Don't apologize for them. That wasn't right, and I know we take some of the blame for that. All of it, really."

"Why are you being so nice to me?" My voice shakes.

Mason doesn't say anything for a few minutes. "I don't know," he finally responds. "You're not what we expected, Phoenix. You're an anomaly."

We lay there silently, not speaking. Whatever words need to be spoken can wait until we both have clearer heads. Right now, the pain shooting through me is too much, and I honestly can't think beyond it.

My thoughts immediately drift to my mom. The thoughts that I wouldn't be here in this pain if it wasn't for her. Her actions set off a chain of events that have put me here.

When I was laying on the floor of the bathroom, I

thought I knew what being alone was. But hearing myself cry, feeling the physical pain of that emptiness, it wrecked me. There was no one to fight for me, no one to protect me. Even the guys didn't find me until after. Having no one to love me, to care for me. Being alone is suffocating.

"Please don't leave me. I'm so tired of being alone. Please don't leave me," I sob into his chest. My body shakes with emotion. All the pain, all the hurt and loneliness, is just seeping out and grabbing the closest thing to hold on to. That just happens to be Mason.

"Shh, Red. I'm not going anywhere. You're not alone. I'm right here," he says as he rubs circles on my back. "Close your eyes. Rest."

"Promise you won't leave?" I sounds needy and I hate it. But it's all I know at this moment.

"I promise. I'm not going anywhere. Just sleep." He leans in and lightly kisses my lips. His strong arms wrap around me cautiously tighter.

Nodding, I slowly let out a long exhale and dig further into him. I let his presence and comfort slowly relax me, slowly pulling me to a state of calm.

I listen to the steady rhythm of his heartbeat, his soft breathing, and feel the repeating patterns on my back. I let go and finally let myself cave.

I give in to the darkness.

## twenty-four
### MASON

THE STEADY SOUNDS of her breathing let me know that she finally fell asleep. I pull back slightly and marvel in her beauty. Her skin is so soft, so pale. There are tiny little freckles that pepper her skin. Her lips part slightly, and she lets out a soft moan. That sound instantly goes straight to my dick.

*Now's not the time, fella.*

But my dick doesn't care. There's an extremely sexy woman in my arms, a beautiful set of tits pressed up against me, and it just heard a moan. My dick's reporting for duty.

And that mouth. I'm not gonna lie. I'm incredibly jealous that Dax got to feel those lips wrapped around his dick. I bet she looked incredible looking up at him. Fuck. This is not helping my boner.

I can't help it, though. Phoenix is one of the sexiest women I have ever met. Her fuck you attitude, the way she carries herself, her beauty. I'm in a constant state of hardness when I'm around her. The small little tastes I've had, they just aren't enough. I want all of her.

And that's what has thrown a wrench in every single one of our plans. Her. This woman's a force all on her own. She's like the human form of the Greek Goddess Bia. She's a personification of raw energy, anger and force. Everything we have thrown at her, she fights back with so much power. She never bows to us, never bends.

Yet today, she cracked. Today, she fell apart and completely broke down, and I wasn't there to catch her. Which is a weird thought in itself, that I want to catch her. Don't I want to see her in pieces? Isn't that what we've wanted from the start?

The three of us have been working to tear her to the point of her breaking. To getting her out of here. Bianca and the twits did what we couldn't do. But here I am, with her in my arms, and I'm angry that they hurt her. I'm ready to rage on them for touching her. Rip them to shreds for putting a hand on her. Fuck. This is all fucked.

My phone goes off, and I take it out of my pocket. It's a text in the group chat with me and the guys.

**Dax: Bianca and the canker sores claim little bird started it.**

**Me: That's obviously a lie.**

**Dax: Yeah, I know. Problem is, they already went to the headmaster.**

**Colt: Shit.**

**Dax: Yeah. I'm trying to do damage control, but unless we want to get my dad involved, we won't be able to help her. And I really don't want to get him involved just yet. We don't know the full story. He would absolutely take this as an opportunity to get her out.**

**Me: She could get expelled for this.**

**Dax: I'm trying to talk him into detention. See what favors I can call in.**

**Colt: Do we need to dig up dirt?**

**Dax: No, let's not yet. I have a feeling we'll need it later on with the way these cunts keep acting. How's Spitfire?**

**Me: Sleeping and making these little moaning sounds. It's waking my dick up.**

**Dax: Let her sleep, Mase.**

**Me: I'm not an asshole.**

**Me: Okay, I am, but I know when not to be.**

**Dax: Practice in an hour.**

I close out my messages and turn back towards the sleeping beauty in my arms. Maybe we should let her get expelled. It would get her out of here and off Daddy Asshole Emerson's radar. But then where would she go?

She has no family. Well, she has her aunt. But not that her aunt cares about her. From what I have gathered, her aunt is not interested in being a parental figure. This school's all she has right now. And now that she's eighteen, her aunt would probably throw her out onto the street.

My gut churns at the thought. This is both the best and worst place for her to be. And we really haven't made it that much better for her. We added to the problem.

And that makes me feel like shit. We did this all wrong. We assumed things about her. Honestly, we were wrong.

Fuck we need to figure out what Emerson Sr. wants with her. Fast. Because if he or our fathers find out we fought to keep her here, we'll all be royally fucked.

I roll away, carefully sliding my arm out from under her head. She rolls over onto her other size, her beautiful round ass now facing me, and I internally groan. I want to bite into that ass of hers. Leave my mark. Fuck, she is killing me.

Saint Mason. I deserve sainthood. Fucking goddamn Saint Mason.

She's lying on her blanket, so I head into her closet to see if she has another one to cover her up with. My eyes widen as I take in her closet. It's pretty empty. She has an enormous walk-in closet, and what she owns takes up a small section of a corner.

Her aunt didn't send her with any clothes? Is this all she had from when she moved here? I sort of feel bad for her. She really is out of place here. I bet you if I go into her roomie's closet, it's packed to the brim with clothes and shoes.

And her clothes aren't the top designer brands like most girls here. They are typical find-them-in-your-hometown-mall-inside-of-Hot-Topic clothes. They are perfectly Phoenix.

Like a creep, I lean in and smell them. I can smell the lavender. The sweet smell of her. I adjust myself yet again. Fuck. I'm going to have to jack off in the shower before practice.

There's blanket folded neatly in the corner of the closet, and I scoop it up. My finger hits something hard, and I lift up the blanket to see what I just jammed my finger into. There's a loose board on her floor, not fully put back into place. I crouch down and lift the board up. Inside there's a shoebox with skull and crossbones drawn on the outside. Yeah, this is definitely Red's.

I lean back to quickly make sure that she is still asleep and go back to the box. My heart is beating a million miles a minute. What is she hiding in this? This has to be important for her to hide this in a hole in the back of her closet.

Maybe there are sex toys in here. Oh, please let me find a vibrator.

Removing it from the hiding spot, I open it and see that it's stuffed with letters and trinkets. I frown. No toys. I unfold the first letter and read it.

*My dearest little bird,*

*If you have this box, it means I had to move on from this life. And I'm so sorry. I didn't have a choice. I tried to fight it. I tried to come up with anything other than what I found. But I failed.*

*Especially if you are in fact reading this.*

*Please know I will miss you, and your father, and I love you. I hope you didn't see me at my weakest, and I hope you have grown strong since I've been gone.*

*Your aunt isn't the greatest person, but she will make sure you are in a good school so that you can thrive once you graduate. I don't want you suffering the same fate as me.*

*Protect what's in here. You and I both had our doubts about your father. Pieces are missing, things don't make sense, the story has holes. You can't trust those you should be able to trust.*

*I love you, my little bird.*
*Fly.*

*Love always,*
*Mom*

Shit.

I sift through the box a bit and pull out a jump drive attached to a keychain that says "pictures". I place it back in the box and find newspaper clippings of her dad's accident. They are just the general news of the accident. Nothing like what Colt found. Things were definitely covered up, and it seems like Phoenix's mom knew that they were keeping things from her.

I sift through a folder called "emails" and see they are printed emails from an account that looks like it was Trevor Hayes's email. They are emails to a BTrighton.

My mouth drops open. Fuck.

Trighton.

Beverly Emerson's maiden name was Trighton.

What the fuck is going on here? Why does Phoenix have these? What was her mom doing with these? This has to be some of the reason Emerson wants her gone. Her family is tied to Daxon's somehow.

I find a picture inside the box and pull it out. Turning it over, I see it labeled "Phoenix, age 12." Flipping it back, I study it. It's of her and who I can definitely tell is her mom. They share the same vibrant red hair. The same facial features. And smiling next to them has to be her dad. They are all smiling. Happy. Unaware of the tragedy that was waiting for them in the future.

Fuck, I need to get to practice.

I quickly pack everything back up and place it back in the hole. The guys will need to know what I found. Somehow, we need to dig through what she has hiding in here. I'm not sure when that will happen, but it needs to be on our to-do list.

Grabbing the blanket I originally came in here for, I leave her closet and throw it on top of her, tucking her in. Looking over at her desk, I spot a pad of paper and some pens.

I had promised her I would be here when she wakes up, but I didn't expect her to be out this long, and I have to get to practice or the coach will have my ass.

Picking up the paper and marker, I leave her a little note.

*Red,*

*Sorry. I know I told you I would stay, but I have practice. The guys and I will stop by after with dinner. Get some rest.*

*-Mason.*

I take the note and leave it on her pillow for her to find when she wakes up. Standing over her, I take her in one last time before I leave.

She's fucking perfection. And from here, she looks like she's at peace. Not constantly fighting to just exist. She's beautiful.

I lean in and kiss her forehead before I leave her room and head out of her dorm. Her roommate will probably be back soon, so she won't be alone for long.

Though, I honestly didn't want to leave her. I'd rather still be curled up next to her. Listening to her moan and her little snores.

Fuck.

\* \* \*

"Hey." Dax strolls up to me as I throw my practice uniform on. "You okay? How's Phoenix?"

I shake my head. "I don't even know where to start with how I'm doing. But she was passed out when I left her." I run my hands through my hair.

"Talk to me. What's wrong? Something happen?" he asks as he adjusts his pads.

"Man, I found some shit. And I don't even know how to explain it." I let out a frustrated groan.

"What did you find?"

"I went to go find another blanket for her, in her closet.

I stumbled upon a shoe box she has hidden in a floorboard of the closet."

Dax crosses his arms over his chest. "All right, so what was in the shoe box?"

"Letters from her mom, pictures, a jump drive of pictures, and ... emails."

"Emails?"

"Yeah. Looks like from her dad to your mom." I see the look of uncertainty in Dax's face. He lips turn down, and he shifts his focus to the floor.

I don't think he has had time to deal with the fact that his mother is gone for good. She died in that accident or suicide, whatever you want to call it. He has been hell bent on making Red pay for her death, only to truly figure out she might not even know what has been going on.

And let's face it, she lost a parent that day too.

"What did the emails say?" Dax asks.

"Talked about a meet up. There were more, but I just didn't get a chance to go through them." I let out a breath. "I think this is over our heads, man. There's something bigger at play."

"I mean, if my father's involved, who knows what's actually going on?"

"My father called me yesterday, asked me how the project was coming along. I had no clue what he was talking about, until he clarified that he meant if we were successful at removing Phoenix from the school."

"So, your dad's involved too. Fuck." Dax rub the back of his neck and starts pacing. "This isn't good."

"No, it's not. She may be in more trouble than we thought. Let's not forget the note she got. Though, I wouldn't put it past our fathers to try to scare her out."

"But why do they want her out? Why not just come after her here? What happens if she leaves?"

I shrug. "That's the million-dollar question now, isn't it?"

Maybe her aunt knew what she was doing by putting her here. This was her way of keeping her safe. Because it seems Emerson can't get to her until she leaves this school.

And that changes things drastically. We definitely have been going about this all wrong.

I look at Daxon, and I can see he is putting the pieces together too.

We need to protect her.

## twenty-five
PHOENIX

WEDNESDAY NIGHT I woke to a note on my bed from Mason, but the man was nowhere to be found. My roommate woke me up when she got home because she saw my door open and me lying in bed. Liz said when she saw the bruises and dried blood, that was missed by Colt, she got scared. That's when she woke me.

So, I explained to her what happened and how the guys ended up bringing me back to the room. She of course was shocked to find out that my tormentors were the ones to care for me after Bianca and her minions beat the shit out of me in the bathroom.

Honestly, it was an unfair advantage to begin with, but I hadn't expected it. If I had, maybe I would've been able to defend myself just a little bit. I probably still would've had the shit kicked out of me even if I had defended myself, but maybe less of a head injury. That's okay, though, they will get what's coming to them.

Mason had texted me that night to tell me that they had some things to take care of but to make sure that my roommate went and grabbed me dinner.

In a weird turn of events, I was a little sad to find him gone when Liz woke me up. And I had hoped that they would have come back, but it was probably better that they didn't. I needed to regain my confidence, my strength. Being around those three seem to weaken me every time.

I mean, I cried in front of them. All of them. They saw tears. I save those for my couch sessions with the head doctor or in the middle of the night when I tend to have my anxiety attacks.

But no. They saw me at a low point. Completely beaten mentally and physically. Drained of any fight left in myself, completely in shock. And they cared for me. Mason laid with me, Colt wiped blood from my face, and Daxon was ready to get vengeance on my behalf.

I felt like I had entered an alternate reality.

And all night, they had checked in on me. I had no clue where they were, but they made sure to ask how I was. They even put me in a group chat with them.

It has all been very, very strange.

But then Thursday happened. And the entire dynamic of everything around me shifted. Changed. Nothing was the same.

From the moment I walked into study hall in the library, the three of them walked over to me and flanked my sides. It was like having personal bodyguards. Hot as fuck personal bodyguards who wouldn't leave my side.

And everyone took notice. There were whispers and stares. Having the guys suddenly do a one eighty with me left everyone in complete confusion. Though I'm sure the way I looked also didn't help things.

And it didn't stop when I just walked in.

If I got up to go look at books, one of them was always

with me. Then let's talk about the fact that they're already in all of my classes. I have one of them near me all the time.

They walked everywhere with me, ate lunch with me, even made sure I was fine for bathroom breaks.

At one point, I made sure to mention that I wasn't made of glass. I wouldn't break. But they ignored that fact and continued to act like protective cavemen.

They also went with me and waited while I to talked to the headmaster about the bathroom incident. Apparently, the Queens of Cuntsville went to the headmaster and told him that I jumped them. When I showed up all bruised up and beaten, I quickly put that lie to rest.

It was very obvious I didn't start anything. But also, the headmaster didn't do shit to them for lying and starting the fight. But whatever. At least I didn't have detention, and that was all I really cared about.

Thursday was truly a blur. Besides having three guys up my ass all day long, everything went about like it was a normal day. No one bothered me, no one cared about me, it was nice. I'll take the win.

"You're coming to the game, Spitfire," Dax says as he rolls up next to me, waving to Mason, who's off to his next class. I grab my books I need for English class out of my locker and slam it shut. I turn and stare into those very sexy green eyes. My hands itch to run my fingers through his hair. I clear my throat and remember he just commanded something from me.

"Um, no."

He glowers at me. "Don't fight this, you're coming. I want you there, watching me and Mase destroying the Bucs." Dax runs a finger down the side of my face, and my body instantly goes into puddle mode.

"Dax, I hate football. Besides, it's with people. People I really don't want to be around. I don't want to be there alone." I close my eyes as he tucks a piece of hair behind my ears. The act is soft, comforting.

"You won't be. Colton will be with you, and you can bring your roomie. Then after, we will go to my house and celebrate the win." He winks at me.

"Wow. Got a lot of confidence there, Mr. Quarterback. How do you know you'll pull off that win?"

Suddenly, I'm spun with my back hitting against the locker. Dax's arms box in my head. His lips are almost touching mine. "Because I always win. I always get what I want."

My nipples harden under his stare, the intensity of his presence. If he were to reach up under my skirt, he would find a flood underneath. My breathing quickens. "W-What is it that you want?"

"Right now?" His eyes meet mine for a millisecond before his lips swallow mine. His tongue dominates against my tongue, his body pushing into me. He groans as he pulls on my lip with his teeth. "Fuck, I've been dying to do that."

My breathing's erratic, and I'm trying to come to terms with the fact that he just made out with me in the middle of the hallway around the students who are now standing there in complete shock. Yeah, peeps, join the fucking club.

His thumb brushes against my bottom lip, and the look in his eyes tell me he wants to do way more than what we just did. My lady parts would tell you the same. Holy hell.

"Let's go, Spitfire. Before I take you up against the lockers." He grabs my hand and pulls me out of my trance. We walk, hand in fucking hand, all the way to the library.

I swear to fuck, I'm in a different goddamn reality.

As we stroll into the library, all eyes immediately take in the connection that Dax has on me. And of course, Tiffany is shocked to the point that her mouth drops open and her eyes widen to saucers. She even turns fiery red, and I almost outwardly laugh at the sight. She looks like she's going to blow a gasket.

We spend the class researching our papers, but not without Dax whispering things he would rather be doing than this. All of it includes me, naked.

By the time lunch rolls around, I'm famished. When we get to the dining hall, I split from Dax and go and grab some chicken fingers and fries. I can feel all three of them watching me. Waiting for God knows what but watching every move I make.

I start to head to the table I normally sit at with Liz, who is sitting there waiting for me.

"Hey, where are you going, Red?" Mason comes up alongside me.

I deadpan. "To sit and eat."

"The table's over there." He points to the table that the kings and queens sit at.

"Oh, hell no. Sorry. Not sitting there. You all can do your weird staring thing from there, but I'm going to sit with my roommate."

Mason's lips form a thin line, and he cocks his head to the side. "Hm. Okay." He lets me go and turns back towards the table.

I roll my eyes and head over to the table with Liz. "Hey, sorry. Protective assholes."

"Well, don't worry. You're here now. So, heard a little rumor." She smiles at me. "Someone was making out with someone in the hallway."

My hand flies to my cheek. "No way! Who?" I say sarcastically.

"Oh, come on! Give me deets. What happ—" Liz stops mid-sentence and looks up behind me.

I turn to see my three bodyguards with their lunch in hand. "What are you guys doing?"

"Joining you for lunch. What does it look like?" Dax smiles as he pulls out a chair next to me and sits. Mason grabs one next to Liz, and Colton grabs the last chair next to Mason.

"What the hell?" My brows pull together, and I clench my fists. "You have your own table." I turn and look to see that the Barbie Squad are now shooting me daggers. As well as the rest of the dining hall are staring in complete confusion as their kings are sitting with a commoner.

Awesomesauce.

Mason shrugs. "Yeah, but you didn't want to sit with us."

"Is this fifth grade? Did I circle no? Are you gonna pull my hair and tell me you hate me?"

"Oh, I'm definitely going to be pulling your hair," Dax says in a throaty low voice.

"Oh my God." Liz is flushing pink, and I'm not sure she's all that comfortable.

"Sorry, Liz." I turn to face her, my eyes meeting with Mason's. He's biting his lip and trying to keep from laughing. I can feel the heat rise up in my neck.

"Um, don't worry. It's nice to have company, I guess." She eyes the guys who are now digging into their food.

"So, you going to the game?" Mason turns to Liz.

"Yeah, I was." She smiles at him.

"Good. So is Phoenix, so you guys can go with Colton," Mason says through a mouthful of his cheeseburger.

"O-Oh, yeah, sure. Okay." Liz gives a tight smile. She looks at me, her eyebrows shooting straight up. I try to convey to her my apologies and that we will talk later.

An arm comes around me, pulling me and my chair closer. I feel Dax's lips near my ear. "Is it bad that I want to take you back to my room and make you scream my name until you can't think straight anymore? That I want to kiss and lick every inch of your body? That I want to slide into you, feel your warm, tight pussy wrapped around my cock?" he whispers.

My mouth drops open, and I let out a gasp. Colton chuckles like he knows what Daxon just said to me. He probably does. Mason just continues to eat with a grin on his face.

I'm in so much trouble with the kings.

\* \* \*

Sitting on the bleachers with Colton on one side of me and Liz on the other, I'm honestly freezing my ass off. I still can't believe that they convinced me to go to this game.

"Okay, so what, the game lasts like a half an hour?" I turn to Colton.

He laughs and places an arm around my shoulder. "Nope. Couple hours."

My mouth drops open. "Seriously? You all sit on these metal fucking things in the cold for that long? I'm going to freeze to death. Why? Why would anyone sit here this long and watch this shit?"

"When you see them come out in their uniforms, you'll understand." Liz smiles.

It's at that moment, the announcer calls on us to

welcome the Darkwood Ravens, and everyone in the stands goes wild. This is gonna be a long fucking night.

The team runs out onto the field. Helmets in their hands, uniforms on, ready to go. And now I see why. Fuck, those uniforms do make their asses look spectacular.

"Okay so who's who?" I ask Colt.

"Daxon is number one, and Mason number twenty-five." He points out into the field.

Nodding, I start to look around the field and around me. This is insane. In all my years in high school, I never once have ever been to a football game. And all this is weird.

There's commotion everywhere. People clapping and cheering, food being passed around and shared. The queens are even doing a good job getting the crowd going with their jumping and yelling.

"You all right?" Colton says to me, breaking me out of my thoughts.

"Um, yeah. I think." I really want to tell him that I'm leaving. This isn't my scene. These aren't the people I want to be around. But I don't. "You know, I think I want one of those pretzels. I'm gonna go get one."

"No, stay here. I'll go grab you one." Colton gets up and heads down the bleachers.

"Must be nice having three guys ready to do anything for you," Liz remarks over the noise of the crowd.

I grimace. "It's not. It's annoying as fuck. I needed to pee, too. Fuck. I'll be right back. I'm gonna go head over to the restrooms."

"You are going to have to go to the fitness center. They keep those open during games." Liz points.

"Okay, I'll be back." I get up to run down the bleacher stairs and start the trek across to the fitness center. I turn around and see the boys warming up and getting ready to take the field. As long as I see something, I'm sure the two of them will be happy, so I just need to hurry back.

When I get into the fitness center, I head towards the front restrooms by the gym. Oddly enough, they are locked. I walk down the hall towards the locker rooms and yank the door open. I head over to a stall and handle my business. As I am buttoning up my jeans, I hear the door open and shut to the locker room.

As soon as I reach for the door to the stall, the lights turn off.

"Are you fucking kidding me? Did the rich people not pay their power bill?" I hold up my phone to use as a flashlight, except my phone is such a piece of shit that I can only use the screen.

I open the door slowly and step out into the blackness, my phone only dimly lighting up the ground in front of me.

"This is absolutely ridiculous," I mutter as I hold out my hand and try to reach out to anything in front of me so I can try to get out of here.

As I slowly and cautiously step along, I try to get my eyes to adjust to the dark. I reach out and find a wall, breathing a sigh of relief. Pressing my palm against the wall, I start to follow it around. You would think this place would have emergency flood lights or something. I make it out of the restroom section of the locker room and head down the hallway towards the door. At least I think I am. I can't see shit.

Suddenly, I hit a mass in front of me, and I gasp as my phone drops to the floor. I reach up and touch what I just ran into. It's not a wall. It's person. Before I can utter a single word, a hand is wrapped around my throat, and I get shoved back into the wall.

I try to claw and kick at whoever has a hold of me, but

they're too strong. My head starts to get light as I struggle to take a breath of air. The hand squeezes tighter, and the fight I have left in me becomes me just trying to breathe. I stop struggling against my attacker as I feel myself start to slip under.

"Beautiful," is all I hear before everything goes dark.

## twenty-six
PHOENIX

"PHOENIX! Phoenix! Breathe for me, baby. Wake up."

"We need to call for help!"

"Phoenix, open your eyes for me. Come on, CT. I need you to wake up for me."

I suddenly realize I can breathe and take a huge breath. My eyes fly open, and I see Colton and Liz crouched beside me. My panic flairs as the memory of what happened floods back into my mind.

"No!" I scream as I push back away from Colton. My voice sounds hoarse. My head swivels as I look for the person I ran into in the dark. "Where did he go?"

"Where did who go?" Colton tries to come closer, but I hold out a hand and slide back away from him.

"The guy ... he was here ... it was dark ..." My hand flies to my throat. The pain from just trying to swallow is too much. I can feel the tears start to fall down my cheeks as I try to understand what the hell is going on. My mind is working overtime just trying to make sense of everything.

"What guy, Phoenix?" Colton holds up his hand and

doesn't try to move in on me. "What guy are you talking about?"

I shake my head. My breaths are still coming in hard and fast. I can feel my chest tighten, and the floor seems to shift under me. Did I dream this? Where did he go? I felt him.

He was here. I can still feel his hands on my neck. His hot breath against my cheek. His voice like nails on a chalkboard when he said, "Beautiful." It feels like my lungs can't get enough air in, and I start gasping, trying to suck in as much as I can.

"You need to calm down, I need you to calm down. You are having a panic attack. Look at me, Phoenix." His eyes meet mine as he holds out his hand to me.

"H-He's not h-here." I close my eyes.

"No. It's just you and me. Liz went outside to get some help," he murmurs. "Come here, baby."

I take his hand, and he pulls me up into him. I wrap my arms around him, holding him tightly against me, trying to mold myself into him as I cry into his shoulder.

"Shh. It's okay. It will be okay."

Except it won't be. I don't know who the fuck that was. I don't know who the hell almost choked the life out of me.

Nothing is okay in the slightest.

\* \* \*

Colton brought me back to their dorm, and the guys came straight here after the game. Apparently, the party is still happening, just without their kings.

The cops came after Liz called them. They interviewed me, asking me what I was doing in the locker room. I had to explain that I needed to use the bathroom, that the bathrooms out front were locked so I came into the locker room, and that after I finished the lights went out.

The police proceeded to tell me that the bathrooms at the front of the facility were not locked. That these locker rooms should have been. They also called into question my story about the lights being out, said that the emergency lights would have kicked on. The only thing they couldn't account for was the red handprints around my throat.

After a barrage of questioning that made me feel like I was the suspect and not the victim, Colton brought me back here to Dax's room, where we laid down and waited for the guys.

When they arrived, they immediately wanted to know what happened. Colton recounted the story to them; I couldn't go through it anymore. My mind already wouldn't shut off.

I went into detail about what I could remember. Which wasn't much.

"And you have no idea who this person was?" Daxon paces around the room, his hands pulling at the ends of his black thick hair. He looks like he's about to jump out of his skin.

I shake my head. "No. No idea. I know it was a he, though. But he was strong. He whispered so I couldn't tell who it was. When I slammed into him, I was taken by surprise."

"Fuck! Could it have been Chad?" Daxon continues to pace around the room. "No, there's no way it could have been him; he was there on the sidelines. Though, that doesn't mean he didn't set it up."

Daxon is out of his mind. He's mumbling to himself, trying to piece together what happened to me. But he only knows as much as I do, and that's not much to go on.

"I-I don't know." I wipe the tears from my eyes. We sit there in silence until Colton gives me news that is the last thing I want to hear.

"Your phone is toast, baby." Colton holds up the pieces that remain of my phone. Tears start to pool in my eyes again.

"No, please no," I whisper.

"Hey, Red, we can get you a new phone. Don't worry. We'll get you a new one." Mason comes over and sits next to me, drying the tears off my cheeks that escaped my eyes.

I shake my head. "It's not the phone. It's what was on that phone."

Mason places both hands on the sides of my face. "What was on that phone?"

"My mom," I squeak out before I start to cry again.

"Hey, don't cry, CT. I'll see what I can do to try and get what I can off this. I swear." He places a hand on my leg and squeezes.

I shake my head. "You don't get it. That's the last thing I have of her. I lost my locket, and all I had was the phone with the pictures of us. My mom's gone. She's really gone." Mason's eyes flash with a sadness, his mouth turns down and he breaks eye contact with me. My hands come up to my face, and I lose myself in the grief. Tears stream out of my eyes, puddling in my hands. "It's all gone."

Colt gestures to the phone. "Phoenix, I'll do everything I can to get these out of here for you. I promise."

"Yeah, if there is anyone that can, Colt's the guy to do it." Dax comes and sits in front of me on his bed. He wraps my legs around him and pulls me into him. My body shakes as I let go of everything I've held in.

So much pain. So much sadness. And now I'm sitting here in their presence letting out everything.

Dax orders, "Look at me, Spitfire." I obey, my eyes drowning in his. "We will make sure nothing like this happens again. I swear to you."

"Why do you care? Why do any of you care? You're all supposed to hate me. You should be happy someone's tormenting me. Isn't that what you all were doing? Tormenting me? Trying to get me to break down? Well, here I am. Broken." My voice is still hoarse, my throat still raw. I refused any medical attention because I didn't want to deal with them calling my aunt. "You all have been assholes to me since the day I stepped foot on this campus."

"We deserve that. And yeah, we were trying to. But not now. Not anymore," Dax whispers.

"What's changed?"

"Us," Dax says before his lips brush against mine. I let out a shaky breath.

"Why?" My eyes flutter closed. I feel Mason on my right side, his lips softly grazing my neck.

Mason says against my skin, "We don't want to hurt you anymore."

"You don't?" I whisper as my head tilts back and I feel Dax's lips on my jawline.

"No, baby. We don't." Colton shifts closer to me on my left side. I feel his hand slip into my hair and grab a soft hold. His teeth graze my earlobe, and I moan in response.

"Tell us to stop, and we will." Dax's fingers find my hard nipples through my shirt and gently squeeze them. "Tell us, sweetheart."

My mind has completely left the building. My body has taken over, and it is thoroughly enjoying these three touching and kissing me all over. Everything that has happened up to this point is in the past. My right now is here.

"Please," is all I can muster out.

"Tell us, Red. Please, what?" Mason says as he turns my head towards him, his lips softly brushing against mine.

"Don't stop." I can feel Dax's hardness as my body starts to grind against him. A groan comes from Dax, and he shifts his hands under the hem of my shirt. Slowly, he peels it up and over me, throwing it off somewhere in the room. Fingers of one of them work the back of my bra, which Dax takes off and throws back as well.

Mason crashes his mouth into mine, dominating my tongue with his. My body burns with nothing but desire with each touch, kiss, and moan. When he pulls away, his lip curls up, and I can feel my face flush.

"Have you ever been with more than one guy at a time, Red?" Mason's voice is low and sultry. His pupils are dilated.

"No," I whisper. I can feel the heat in my face. The embarrassment of what he is asking.

"Let us take care of you, sweetheart." Dax lays me down on his bed, and Mason and Colton start to remove their clothes. My head turns back and forth between them, trying to soak in every single inch of their well-defined bodies.

Dax straddles my legs as he bends down and takes turns sucking on each nipple, hardening them into stiff peaks. My back arches off the bed as I feel his teeth scrape against me, pulling slightly on the nipple.

I let out a throaty moan as my head tips back. His lips start to kiss their way down my stomach to the top of my jeans. Colton crawls up next to me, and his lips meet mine. His teeth gently pull on my bottom lip.

Dax's fingers start to work on getting my jeans unbuttoned as I feel Mason's lips on my shoulder, making their way to my breasts.

A low growl comes from Dax as he pulls off my thong and jeans in one shot. "Fucking beautiful, sweetheart." Dax spreads my legs and lays down in between them. "Your pussy's soaking wet. It's so fucking beautiful." His tongue drags up my pussy and twirls around my clit.

"Oh, fuck, Dax." I pull away from Colt's mouth as my hips jump off the bed. My hands find his head as I tangle my fingers in his hair.

"You have no idea how beautiful you look, Red. Fuck." I turn and see Mason now laying back against the headboard stroking his cock. He's watching Dax in between my legs as he slides his hand up his shaft, give the head a slight squeeze, causing him to moan.

My eyes find Colton, who is now kneeling next to me, running his hand over his hardness. His other hand comes up, and his thumb runs along my bottom lip, pulling it down. He sticks it in my mouth, I can taste the saltiness of his skin.

"Suck, baby," he commands as I moan around his thumb. I begin to suck, and Colt tips his head back, his eyes closed, his breathing coming fast. "You wanna do that to my cock? You wanna put your beautiful lips around my cock, baby?"

Suddenly, I feel a soft bite on my clit. My breaths pick up as I start to feel the pressure build. This is all so much. My entire body is ready to release, but Dax is keeping me on edge. I need to taste them, feel them. I release a hand from Dax's hair and wrap it around Colt's cock.

Colt lets out a shuddering breath. His head tips back, and his eyes close in bliss as my hand strokes him.

"Look at Mason, Phoenix. Look at how turned on he is

watching you with us." Dax slides two fingers inside me, and I try to keep from shooting off the bed. "Turn, watch him as I make you come. Don't take your eyes off him. Keep stroking Colt. I want you to come on my face, sweetheart." Dax pumps his fingers in and out of me, and his tongue swirls around my clit, sucking on it. I feel the pressure build again, the tingling in my stomach as I draw near my orgasm.

"Don't stop please." My eyes are on Mason, but I'm begging Dax to keep going. Mason's eyes are hooded as he watches me build to my release.

"Come for us, Red. Come all over Dax's face."

"Fuck!" My entire body tightens. I release my hand from Colt and grab hold of Dax's head. My body shakes as I crash over the wall, riding out the pure ecstasy of my orgasm. My eyes never leaving Mason's.

As I start to come down, I hear a foil rip and I turn to Dax sheathing himself. "Tell me if you want this. Tell me to stop."

"Don't stop. Please. Fuck me, Dax." My voice is throaty.

Dax spreads my legs farther apart and watches himself slide his cock into me, meeting little resistance through my wetness. I feel myself stretch to take every inch of him. I turn my head towards Colt and open my mouth, begging him to fuck it.

As Colt scoots closer, he slides his cock in between my lips. Dax starts to thrust in and out of me, causing me to moan around Colt's cock. I look up to see Colt tip his head back as his hand finds my head and his fingers get tangled in my hair.

"Oh, fuck your mouth is fucking heaven, baby," Colt says as he loses himself to pure fucking pleasure.

"You are so tight, Spitfire. Fuck, your pussy is a fucking

vice around my cock," Dax says as he slams into me. His cock feels like I'm being split in two. It's curved just enough that it hits my spot inside me, bringing me to the edge again.

Dax purrs, "You gonna come, sweetheart? I can feel you tightening around me. You wanna come?"

I muffle out a yes as his fingers start to work my clit.

And it doesn't take long. Between Daxon doing magical things between my legs with his cock and Colton using my mouth to find his release, I'm a live wire waiting to burst.

"Shit, baby, I'm gonna come down that throat of yours. I want you to swallow it all. Every drop as I come. Can you do that for me?" Colt says as he grabs my head and moves me up and down his shaft.

I can't even respond. My entire body is burning with needing a release.

"Oh, she's coming," Dax groans. I start to see stars in my vision as my release careens through me. I scream though it with Colt's cock in my mouth as he finds his release, filling my mouth with it.

"Let me see." Colt holds my mouth open, peering in. "Fucking beautiful. Swallow." I do just that as I feel Dax tighten above me.

"Fuck, fuck, fuck! Phoenix!" he growls through his release. "Holy shit." His entire body is still shaking, his skin glistening with sweat. Dax steadies himself as he tries to come down from his own orgasm.

"Put her ass in the air," I hear Mason order from beside me. Suddenly, I'm flipped on my hands and knees. Colt and Dax both work to catch their breath and come to their senses. Then I hear a foil rip and feel hands on my ass.

"This ass is gorgeous." I feel a soft slap on it. The other two move against the headboard, watching Mason and me.

"Can you take more, Red? Can you take my cock in this greedy little pussy of yours?"

I moan, "Yes, please. Fuck me, Mason."

I hear a throaty groan behind me as he lines up his cock to my entrance. Slowly he pushes his cock in, and I drop my head and cry out into the mattress.

"Look at us, Spitfire. I want to see your face as Mase fucks you." Dax leans over and places his fingers under my chin to lift my head up. "Perfect."

My mind is gone. As in pure fucking mush. I see Dax and Colt, but I have no idea about anything going on except Mason behind me, fucking me like a mad man.

He thrusts hard, long strokes into my pussy, and I can hear the slap of our skin with each one. I let out a moan as I feel his fingers digging into my ass cheeks.

"Goddamn, Red. Your pussy is squeezing me so tight, it keeps sucking me back in. You're perfect. Fuck, your pussy is so goddamn perfect," he grunts as he slaps my ass.

"You look beautiful right now, getting railed by him, Phoenix." I feel Dax's thumb push into my mouth. "Suck."

Closing around his thumb, his eyes become hooded, and his mouth drops open. I see him start to stroke his cock, and my body is burning up.

Mason pulls me up so that my back is against his chest and Dax comes up to my front, sandwiching me in between them. He begins kissing me as he strokes himself.

Dax's other hand reaches down to find my clit and begins to rub it. I moan into his mouth as he tries to coax another orgasm from me.

Pulling back, he locks eyes with me. "Come. Now."

My body detonates. My vision goes white, and I let out a scream as I come all over Mason's cock. I feel him roar as he finds his release through mine. Dax grunts as he comes all over my stomach.

My body gives out, and Mason slowly pulls from my pussy. Dax catches me and pulls me down onto the bed, while Colt stands up and disappears. Mason rids himself of the condom and sits on the other side of me.

I can't speak. My eyes are heavy, my body completely worn out. Closing my eyes, I let out a long breath. A hand caresses my cheek.

"You were beautiful, Phoenix. Just beautiful," Dax whispers in my ear. He continues whispering things in my ear as I feel a warm cloth on my stomach.

"Relax. I'm just cleaning you up, baby." Colt softly runs the washcloth along my skin, cleaning up anything left behind.

Lips graze my shoulder, and I turn to see Mason's blue eyes gazing up at me. "You were incredible, Red. You looked like an angel coming all over my dick. Fucking perfect."

"Get some sleep, baby," Colt says as he lays next to Dax.

Dax turns and pulls my back against his chest. Mason turns to face me, kissing my lips softly.

I can't speak, I can't think. I just exist.

And that's what I do until my eyes can no longer stay open, and I fall asleep in the arms of the men who have me more confused than ever.

## twenty-seven

PHOENIX

THERE'S a warmth on my face, heating it, waking me from me sleep. Ugh, why is it this bright? Though I may have been woken by the furnace along my back. A hot hard body presses against me, and an arm pulls me tighter as someone peppers my skin with kisses.

"Good morning, baby doll," Colt grumbles into my neck.

"Um, morning." A wave of confusion comes over me. The assault, the aftermath, the guys and then the things we did together. And now, I'm being cuddled by Colton. What the fuck?

"You went stiff. What's wrong?" he says as he nuzzles the back of my neck.

"I ... well ... I don't know. You're next to me. In Daxon's bed." I take a deep breath, my eyes still trying to take in my surroundings. I definitely don't think this is a dream. Last night I know wasn't, so this is reality. A very confusing reality.

His arm pulls me tighter as I feel his breath against my

ear. "Are you ashamed of last night? Because you shouldn't be. You were absolutely beautiful." His hand starts to trail lower, and it's that moment I realize we are both completely naked. Memories and the feeling of them against me last night come flooding back. The orgasms, the sex, oh my fucking God.

*Holy shit, I'm still naked.*

His cock is as hard as rock against my back. I don't know if I'm heating up from embarrassment or from being so turned on right now. Of course, my pussy's a needy bitch and didn't get enough last night because I push my ass into him, eliciting a groan.

"Do you want this cock, baby girl?" Colt's words vibrate against my ear, sending a thrill down my spine. I nod and eagerly push against him again. "I need to hear you say it."

"Yes, please Colt." My voice barely above a whisper, my body on edge.

"Are you on birth control?"

"Yes. And clean," I rasp.

"Me too," he says as he nudges his cock against my entrance, and he slowly slides into me. His arms wrap around me and pull me tighter against his body. As he thrusts into me, he moves my hair away from the back of my neck and proceeds to lick and kiss my skin.

"You feel so good, baby. So fucking warm and tight." His words make my core flutter, and I hear him moan in response. "Oh, that's it, squeeze my cock. Goddamn."

He pounds into me, pushing his cock deep inside me. Hitting me in all the right places. Being wrapped up in him, having him lazily fuck me, taking care of a craving and need, it's so much more than I expected. It's overwhelming.

"Colt," I rasp out. My body has completely given into

his touch, his thrusts. My breathing comes quicker as I get closer to release.

"You gonna come all over my cock, baby girl?" he grunts into my ear.

"Yes. Please, yes."

He starts to pick up his pace, thrusting harder into me. His fingers travel lower, finding my clit, as he starts to rub it to bring me to the edge.

The sound of our skin coming together, the heat on my back from him, the pressure on my clit, and the fierceness he is plunging into me with is bringing me to the precipice. My breathing becomes ragged, and I let out a moan as I start to feel the buildup of my impending orgasm.

"Fuck, Colt. I'm gonna come. Please don't stop," I beg.

"Come, Phoenix. Come for me." His voice is hoarse, his breaths quick.

I let out a scream as I explode in complete ecstasy around him. My body shakes, and my vision blurs through my orgasm. Every nerve ending in my body is feeling like a fire has been started inside me.

I'm brought out of my haze by a roar as Colton releases inside my pussy. I feel his forehead on my back and then lips start to kiss my neck and shoulder.

"That was fucking ... fuck. I think you fucked the words right out of me, baby." Colt laughs. "Stay right here." He slowly pulls out of me and gets out of bed. My back feels cold from the loss of his body on mine. I start to shiver a bit until I feel a hand turning me on my back.

"Here, spread your legs and let me clean you up." Colt's holding a wet washcloth, and he drags it softly across my folds, my skin. He is so tender when he takes care of me. He did the same thing after last night and when I was jumped.

"Where are the other two?" I ask as he finishes and then pulls me up to stand next to him.

"They got up early to go work out. They're probably back by now or will be soon. Why don't you go in there, take a shower, and I'll start some breakfast for you?" He smiles at me and plants a kiss on my forehead.

I head towards the bathroom and stop in my tracks at the sight before me. I didn't get to appreciate it the last time I was in here, being sick and all. But now ... wow. This entire bathroom is pure luxury. Granite countertops, high-end fixtures, and there are three shower heads in the fucking shower. Oh, and did I mention that the shower could hold a baseball team in there? The thing is huge. Seriously, you could fit nine people in this thing.

Fucking rich people and their showers.

There's a computer on the wall, which I'm guessing works the shower, so I start pushing the screen and get the water set to a good temperature. And in case anyone is wondering, it's hot. I like my showers scalding hot. If my skin isn't melting off, it's not hot enough.

Just saying.

After washing off, I head back out to the bedroom and find a pair of grey sweatpants and a black t-shirt. Shit, I have no underwear. Well, I guess I'm going without. I pull the pants up and tighten the strings to help keep them up. Combing my fingers through my hair, I try to break up any knots. Grabbing my phone, I pad out of the room, my bare feet loud against wood floors. I hear voices to the right down the hall.

Three heads turn towards me as I approach them. I can feel the heat in my cheeks as I approach.

"Hey there, Spitfire. How are you feeling this morning?" Daxon's lips turn up as his eyes roam over me.

"Yeah, I heard you had a very exciting morning. How was your morning wakeup call?" Mason wiggles his eyebrows, grinning.

Now I really feel my cheeks burning. My head swings to Colton, who stares at me. My eyes are wide, and my mouth drops open.

"Well, I didn't tell them anything, but you just did." He chuckles.

I bring my hands up to my head and groan.

"Aw, come on, Red. There's nothing to be embarrassed about." Mason comes over and kisses my forehead. "Sit. We made you some breakfast. Orange juice?"

"Um, yeah. Please." I take a look around the island and see a gourmet kitchen in front of me. High-end stainless-steel appliances, huge kitchen sink, what the hell? "Can I ask a question?"

"Sure," Daxon says as he leans forward on the island countertop.

"Why the hell do you all eat in the dining hall when you have this kitchen?"

The guys bust out laughing, and Daxon walks over to me, putting his arm around me and pulling me close. "Because we can." He kisses the top of my head.

"Plus, then we would have to do shopping, cook, clean. Yuck." Mason makes a gagging sound.

"Oh, you poor rich boys. Wouldn't want you to have to visit a grocery store." I place my hand over my heart and fake my sincerity.

"I'll have you know that this is the first time we have ever cooked in here," Colton retorts.

My eyes nearly pop out my head. "What?"

"We even went to the grocery store for you, Spitfire," Daxon says into my ear.

"Y-You did?" I stutter.

Colton winks at me. "Well, how else were we gonna cook you breakfast, CT?"

"Okay, I need to ask. CT?" I ask Colton as I lift my eyebrows.

He lets out a low chuckle. "Carrot top."

"Seriously?" I feign being insulted but turn my lips up and smile at him. It's cute. All three have their own little nicknames for me, and I honestly don't hate it.

I look between the three guys, completely stunned. Mason slides over my orange juice. "Scrams and bacon?"

"Scrams?" I say, shaking my head, still not sure of what earth I woke up on.

"Scrambled eggs. Scrams. How do you take your eggs?" Mason smiles that blinding smile at me.

"Scrambled is fine." I nod.

Mason starts to move around the kitchen, and I can feel my heart start to hurt. My mother loved making breakfast for me. Loved to cook me something in the morning before I went to school.

"What's wrong?" Daxon lifts my chin with his finger. He pulls his brows together as he tries to search my face for answers.

"Nothing." I shake my head and try to hold back the tears.

"Tell me. What's going on in that head of yours?" He taps my forehead.

I take a moment and try to compose myself. Everything is so out of sorts. Me, here, with them. About to say what I'm about to say. Everything we did together. My mind is completely wracked with confusion and lust, hurt, and anger.

"I was thinking about my mom." There's a lump in my throat and water gathers in my eyes.

"Your mom?" Daxon whispers.

I nod. "Yeah. She, uh, used to love making me breakfast. We'd sit around the kitchen island like this and laugh and talk. My dad would join us. He'd always have his head in the newspaper, but I'd hear him laughing next to me, at us." I feel a fresh tear roll down my cheeks. "I miss her."

They should know. They need to know.

My lips tremble as I utter the words, "She killed herself. Earlier this year. My dad died too. But in a freak accident. They're, um, both dead." The kitchen becomes silent as the guys stare at me. Tears cascade down my face, and Daxon wraps me up in his arms.

"I'm sorry. We didn't mean to upset you." His hands rub along my back as I sob into him.

After a few minutes, I uncurl from him and spin to rest my arms on the counter of the island. "You didn't upset me. It's just complicated. Both of my parents are dead. And that's all I'm going to say on it. I really don't want to talk about them, if that's alright?"

"Sure, Red. Here, drink this." Mason hands me a cold glass of water, and I slowly sip it. He runs a hand through his blond hair and goes back to cracking eggs. The sound of the bacon sizzling and the smell makes my stomach growl.

Colton winks at me. "Sounds like someone could use some food."

"Well, you did work her up an appetite." Daxon grins. He leans in and kisses my forehead.

I sit there on the stool and stare at the three of them moving around the kitchen. Laughing, joking around, and preparing a feast.

This is all too good to be true. Don't get me wrong, I

want this. I want normalcy, or if you call what we did last night normal. But nothing in my life ever stays. Nothing good will ever happen in my life. I guess I just have to enjoy it while I can. Because I know the truth.

Eventually, I lose everyone.

I will always be alone.

## twenty-eight
PHOENIX

THE GUYS eventually walked me back to my dorm after breakfast. I probably ate as much as they did. I was stuffed to the brim with all the food they cooked.

They were reluctant to have me leave them, and I get it. But I didn't give them a choice. Of course, when they finally relented to letting me go home, then they wanted one of them to stay with me, like a goddamn bodyguard.

Not going to happen.

I needed my space, time to think and process everything. We went from hating each other to fucking each other in under sixty seconds. We needed a cooling off period, a chance for us all to breathe. Everything happened so damn fast.

I also needed to get some fucking laundry done. And there was no way I was having them around while I was doing that. I can see Mason now, playing with my underwear, asking me to model in them for him. Daxon growling and wanting to rip them off. Colton would probably stare at them and hope they combust into flames so I had nothing to ever wear under my skirt ever again.

So, they left me to let me do what I needed to. Plus, Liz was there. We both decided getting a pedicure was probably not the best thing to do in light of what happened last night. Not that I was thrilled about getting one, but I was semi excited to do something normal for once. Still, a new normal doesn't seem to be in the works for me. So, our day became us ordering in and being domesticated and shit.

"Hey, washer is free," Liz calls out as she comes back in.

I grab my basket and run out the door down the hall to the laundry facilities on the floor. I throw a huge load in, not caring what I mix with what. I don't own anything pink, and I don't wash anything in hot water, so one-stop-shop in this washer.

After dousing my clothes in soap, I put my card in, and it starts up the washer. I place my basket on top of it and head back to my dorm.

"So, the kings," Liz throws at me the minute I walk back in the door.

"How long have you been waiting to say that?" I smirk.

"Oh my god, since you walked through the door! But I wanted to give you time to see if you would tell me. You didn't. I can't take it anymore! Spill!" She grips the chair in front of her.

"Um, there's nothing to spill." I shake my head and saunter towards my room.

"Oh, whatever! Those three have been assholes non-stop to you and now are suddenly your knights in shining armor? Nope, not buying it. What's going on?" She crosses her arms as she stands in my doorway.

I slowly sit on my bed as I bite my lip. Rubbing my face, I let out a strangled sound. "I don't know. Okay? I'm just as confused as you are. I want to hate them with every bone in my body, but I can't. They have, oddly enough, been there for me. For some reason that I have yet to uncover. And as strange as it is, for now, I'll soak up whatever they're giving me."

"So, who did you have sex with? Was it Daxon? Oh, it was Mason! Colton's the quiet one, so I doubt it was him." She taps her chin as her mind works out which one I seemed to have slept with.

"Mind your business. I have enough going on in my life, and I don't need any more drama." I roll my eyes. "And this school sure is fucking filled with it."

"That's what I'm worried about." She pauses and takes a deep breath. "You haven't had it easy since you stepped foot on this campus."

"I know," I say as I run my fingers through my hair.

"Phoenix, they set the school on you." Her voice deepens with concern, and she frowns at me.

"Yeah, I know, Liz. Everything is just a mess. It's all so confusing how all this has just played out. I don't understand any of this." I rub the back of my neck.

"What if this is part of their game?"

My eyes shoot to hers. "What?"

"What if this is just another way for them to mess with you? Like, get you to like them? I mean, I don't know, Phoenix." She bites her lip.

Could it be? Could this be just a cruel joke? Another way for them to mess with me? I mean, it's entirely possible and not completely out of the question. I put my walls up with all the shit they threw at me, and then they did a one eighty and I dropped my walls in an instant. The kings went from hating me to fucking me.

And I let them.

I let them all have their way with me. My eyes widen as

I try to process everything. I can feel my throat drying, and I feel like there's a weight on my chest.

"Hey, Phoenix? What's wrong? You look like you're starting to panic." Liz starts to reach out, but I jump up and move away from her.

"I-I just need some fresh air." I start out of my room, with her close on my tail.

"Maybe it's not that good of an idea. You know with—"

"I'll be fine. I don't need a mother. I had one, remember?" I bite back.

Liz stands there, still as can be, and I see the hurt in her eyes. I hate myself for it, but I'll apologize when I've had a chance to get myself together.

I walk to the laundry room and throw my clothes in the dryer. My hands are shaking as I move the clothes over. Everything in my head's moving a million miles a minute. I can feel a headache growing as I rub my temples. I start the dryer and stick my basket on top of it.

Flying out of the laundry room, I head over to the fire exit and push open the door leading to the stairs. I head down the stairs and out the building, walking around to the side and falling down against the wall.

I can feel my anxiety start to grip me again. Fuck. I run my hands through my hair and pull on the ends. I let out an exasperated breath and tip my head back against the stone of the building.

The wind whips through my hair as I stare up into the sky. I shiver, realizing I didn't leave with a jacket. Running my hands along my arms, I take a deep breath. I need to calm myself. I don't know if they're messing with me. But I know I can't let my walls down again. Maybe they truly have had a change of heart. I rub my face and let out a groan.

Whatever. I need to keep pushing forward.

Fuck. A couple months into this school year, and I feel like the end is never going to come. I've been through so much, so much confusion, so much hurt and pain, so much sadness. Then the kings come along and make everything ten times more complicated.

But also ten times better.

I lay my head in my hands and I scrub my face. Whatever this is, I don't even think I can deal with it. Maybe they don't hate me, maybe they do. I came here to get the fuck out of here.

Well, actually, I didn't have a choice. People made selfish decisions that brought me to this point. People's actions have put me in a shitty situation. Since being here, I've been tormented and bullied. I've been called names, had things thrown at me. They tried to drown me and scare me into leaving.

All for reasons I'll never understand.

Pushing up off the wall, I steady myself and take another deep breath. I center myself and find my strength to keep pushing.

I so hope the kings are not playing some sort of sick and twisted game. After being with them, I don't think my heart can take the break. Well, what's left of it.

I have no idea how long I've been sitting out here. But I'm feeling a little stronger than I was, so I run up the stairs to my floor and I head over to the laundry room to get my clothes.

As I approach the laundry room, a foul smell is wafting down the hall. My face wrinkles as I try not to breathe in through my nose. What the hell is that coming from?

The closer I get to the laundry room, the greater the smell. It hits me that the smell is coming from inside there.

I shake my head, and my panic starts to creep up again.

I cover my mouth and nose with my hand and try to keep from gagging. Tears have sprouted at the corners of my eyes.

There's a note taped to the dryer, and I shake my head, knowing that smell is coming from my dryer. It's putrid, rancid, and I haven't even opened up the door yet. I pick up the note and read it.

*Now your clothes smell like the dirty whore you are.*

"No. No, no, no, no!" I open the door to the dryer and immediately I am greeted with a smell so foul I turn to the garbage bin behind me and instantly throw up.

When I stop dry heaving, I run out of the room and down the hall to my dorm room. I burst through the door and run into the bathroom and douse my face with hot water. I take deep breaths and grip the sides of the counter.

"Hey, do you smell that?" Liz says as she enters the room.

The thought of what I saw sends me into a spiral again. I start to heave again and throw myself down against the toilet. Gripping the sides, I gag into the toilet.

"Oh my God! Are you okay?" Liz runs over to me. "Is it the smell?" She grabs a washcloth and wets it in the sink. Handing it to me, she rubs my back. "Just breathe."

"That's the last thing I want to do. Everything is ruined. Trashed," I say through breaths.

She shakes her head. "What do you mean?"

Holding the washcloth on my lip, I close my eyes and try to shake the image from my mind. "That smell. It's from the laundry room."

"What? Did something crawl into the vent and die?" She looks back at the door and back at me. "Wait ..."

I shake my head. "Something did die. In the dyer. With

my clothes. It also managed to gut itself, leaving its insides everywhere. Also, that something's a dead fucking fish." My stomach rolls at the thought. "Everything is ruined. All my uniforms were in there."

"Fuck." Liz's eyes are wide with worry. She bites her lip and stands up. "Who the fuck would have done that?"

"Who do you think?" I stand slowly, trying to make sure I don't need to retch again. "Anyone and everyone at this school!"

"Okay, well, let me call maintenance and get the floor RA on it. Just go relax. I have plenty of uniforms you can probably fit into." She pushes me towards my door.

Entering my room, I suddenly feel like something is off. Something isn't right. I look around my room and see a box sitting on my bed. The air around me goes cold, and my heartrate picks up.

I take careful steps towards the box, my eyes never wavering from it. It's a black box with a white bow on top. My hands shake as I slowly lift the top off. On top of some black tissue paper sits a red origami phoenix, like the one in my bag.

The tears start to pour out of my eyes as I remove the bird. Grabbing the edges of the paper, I carefully peel it back, only to find pictures and a note.

One by one, I grab the pictures, and my stomach turns. The first couple are of me, lying on the floor in the locker room, a hand caressing my cheek as they took it. The last two are of the guys walking me back to my dorm just this morning. I let out a sob as I pick up the note.

*Your boyfriends won't keep you safe forever, Little Birdie.*

I back away from the box and curl myself into the corner of my room. My entire body is shaking, and tears spilling down.

Why? What sick, twisted game is someone playing? What do they want?

Maybe I should have taken Daxon up on that offer to leave this place. Because being here hasn't kept me safe.

I feel like I'm falling apart at the seams. I let out a scream and curl into myself.

I don't know how much longer I can fight to survive.

I'm fighting a losing battle.

## twenty-nine
MASON

WE GOT a call from Phoenix's roommate, Liz, Saturday. Phoenix went into some sort of shock and wasn't responding to her. She was just curled up in the corner of her room shaking. The three of us ran over there, but first noticing the horrid smell that was coming from the laundry room. Apparently, someone decided to throw dead fish into the dryer with all of her clothes.

They are all completely ruined. The entire dryer had to be pulled and removed from the building. She went and saw the headmaster early this morning, and he of course gave her a detention for the "stunt". Red hasn't told us what happened or what he said, but we found out through the grapevine and Ms. Hodgens, the secretary, that was what happened.

She has a new uniform, but I'm guessing it's her roommate's, because it's tighter than hers and her tits look like they are about to burst through it. And while my dick and I are not complaining about that, it's just all sorts of wrong.

I'm staring at a shell of her. And I know it wasn't the dryer stunt that did it. When we ran into her room, we saw the box on her bed with the pictures and the bird that was the same as the one that she found in her bag. She was holding a note that once we got out of her grasp, worried the fuck out of all of us.

I can see why she went into shock.

What's worse, we have no idea who's doing this. This wasn't one of the things we set into motion. This is definitely someone on the outside or someone that went rogue.

As I sit next to her in history, my stomach twists while I watch her just stare out towards the front. I know she's not listening to a word the teacher's saying. She's lost somewhere in her own head.

It's a stark difference from the spunky redhead that was sitting next to me on the first day of class.

"Hey, Red. You okay?" I rub her back, and she turns her head to me. That's when I see it.

The emptiness in her eyes.

They stare at me, but they are not processing anything. She's gone from her own self. She turns back to the front and goes back into her own head. I pick up my phone and shoot off a quick text to the guys.

**Me: She's not doing well.**

**Colton: What's going on?**

**Me: She's staring into space. There's nothing there. Lights on but no one's home.**

**Daxon: Shit. After English, let's take her back and see if we can get her to come around.**

**Me: Yup. Colt, did you get those pictures off her phone?**

**Colt: Yeah, I did. Think that will work?**

**Me: No fucking clue. Worth a shot. Something has to shake her. She's been like this since Saturday.**

Putting my phone back in my pocket, I turn back to her.

I rub my chest, trying to do anything to get rid of the pain I feel in it. The hurt and feeling of worthlessness right now. I just want to make this all better.

Nothing we did would have done this to her. We just wanted her gone. Whoever is leaving these for her, stalking her, has turned her into a shell of herself.

Class ends and she just sits there. I gather up my things and walk over to the other side of her, picking up her backpack, which she never took a thing out of it, and throwing it over my shoulder. She looks up at me blankly and then gets out of her seat, heading out of class.

She walks on autopilot to our next class, pre-calc. I stay behind her, just watching her navigate through the crowds. People are staring at her, noticing that she's not herself. I can hear them whispering, but I can't make out what they're saying.

She passes through the door of the room and heads to her desk. Phoenix slides in the chair and stares down at her hands. Fuck, I can't take this. Watching her like this.

"Phoenix. Hey, sweetheart." I scoot my desk closer to her and reach out to touch her, but she flinches. "Hey, it's me. It's alright. Just me." She looks up and nods. "Hey, I need you to snap out of it. You have us worried."

She doesn't say a thing.

Bianca struts into class with a knowing grin on her face. She immediately homes in on Phoenix.

"Does it smell like trash in here?" she says loudly. Students in the class laugh, and a couple yell out that it does.

"Sit the fuck down and shut the fuck up." Colton come up from behind Bianca and immediately, the room falls silent. "No one will mess with Phoenix. No one with fuck with her. She's ours. Fuck with her, you fuck with us. I suggest not putting a target on your back."

"What the fuck, Colt? She's with you? What bullshit is that? She's trash! How is she with you?" Bianca screeches.

"With *us*," I correct. "As in she is *ours*. Plural."

"What?" I swear her voice just broke the sound barrier. "Does Daxy know this?"

"First off, it's Daxon. He really does hate when you fucking call him that ridiculous name. Second, he was the one who initiated it." Colton cocks his head to the side as he stares Bianca down.

She sneers, "Chad was right. You guys are losing it. Falling for trash pussy."

"Chad said that? That's rich from a guy who has to drug women in order to get laid." I chuckle.

"Well, the only one I know that he drugged was her, and he didn't get to fuck her. So, your accusations are unfounded." She shrugs.

I look up at Colt and see nothing but red. We knew he did that to her. "Oh see, now you are going to explain that. How did he do it?"

"I'm not saying a wor—"

Colt yanks her up out of her seat and drags her out of the room. She's trying to pull away from him, but he's too strong.

The teacher comes in, obviously ignoring the commotion that is going on outside the classroom with Colt and Bianca. He goes into the lesson for today, and I look over at Phoenix. She has her arms crossed on her desk, and her head is laying on them. Her eyes are staring at me, but again, they are empty.

My phone goes off in my pocket, and I take it out.

**Colt: He had Bianca slip it in her drink when she**

**wasn't looking. When she was on the deck that night. That's why she was there. Phoenix caught her but had no clue she drugged her.**

**Me: I'm gonna kill him.**

**Colt: You and me both.**

After class, I do the same as I did in English. I grab both our things and lead her out. This time, Dax meets us in the hall. He wraps his arm around her, but she finches again. Looking up at him, her eyes are wide with fear.

"Hey, hey. Just let me hold you, okay?" Dax says softly to her.

She falls back into her own head, and Dax wraps his arm back around her. This time, she lets him.

I nod to Dax and Colt as they take off to their class. I should be in art, but I need to go find someone and pay them a visit. I head over to the fitness center, knowing where my target is at.

When I stroll up into the weight room, I find him on the bench press. I walk around to the footplate out of his sight and pull the pins out of the bar rests, they fall down along the uprights. That's when he notices me.

"Hey! What the fuck?" Chad looks up and realize he has nowhere to rack the bar. "Fuck, Turner. Put that shit back! This is getting heavy."

"Yeah, that sucks. Listen,"—I lean on the upright—"a little cunt of a birdie told me you had her drug Phoenix at the party, the night of your party where we took her out of your bathroom completely passed out."

Chad starts to struggle to keep the three hundred pounds from falling on his chest. He starts to try to sit up, and I shove his sweaty head back down. I wipe my hand off and grimace.

The bar lands on his chest, and he groans. "Come on, this fucking hurts."

"Hm. That's weird. I still don't hear an acknowledgment to what you did." I lean forward, gripping the bar and putting my weight on it. Crushing it into him.

"Fine," he wheezes out. He grunts and tries to push back up, but he's too weak. "Yeah, I did."

I help flip the bar off him and onto the floor. He struggles to sit up but finally does. I walk around and stand in front of him.

"Are you still fucking with her? Sending her things?"

He pulls his brows together and looks at me for a moment in confusion. "What? No." He rubs his chest where the bar pressed against.

"Better not be. If I see you look at her, talk to her, touch her, even fucking say her fucking name, I will end you."

"Really? That's rich coming from you. All three of you, actually. You don't own her. You can't tell me—" My fist connects with his jaw. His eyes roll back, and he falls back on the bench.

Lights out, mother fucker.

* * *

I skipped class and headed back to our dorm room, and now I'm just waiting on them to get here. It's normally our lunch period, but we all decided we needed to do something to shock her out of this.

And I had an idea. Rare, I know, but I'm good for one or two a year.

I run my hand through my hair and let out a sigh. I'm hoping this works. Otherwise, I'm not sure what we should do. Maybe call that doctor of hers, but that would raise suspicions since she hasn't shared that with us yet.

I hear the door open, and Dax walks in carrying Phoenix. She's clinging on to him, like he's going to let go. Her head rests on his shoulder, her eyes still painfully blank. Colton brings up the rear, shutting the door behind him.

"How's our girl?" I ask.

"Still in her head." Dax runs his hand along her back as he brings her over to the couch and sits down with her in his lap.

"Colt, you got those pictures?" I turn towards him.

He nods. "Yeah, on my laptop."

"Good, bring them out," I order. He takes off to his room and comes back quickly. "Lay her on her side, facing the coffee table. Colt, pull up the pictures and run them on some kind of slideshow."

"Think this will work?" Dax looks at me.

"No idea, but she's emotionless. I'm hoping we can get her to feel something, maybe snapping her out of this state." I shrug.

Dax lays her down on her side, still continuing to rub her back to keep contact with her. Colton turns on his laptop and sets up a slideshow of her pictures. He places it in front of her on the table and hits play.

The computer flashes through pictures of her and her mom, some with both her parents, some with friends. But the ones with her mom are when we start to notice a reaction.

Tears start to form in the corner of her eyes.

"Mom," she whispers. The tears start to fall more, and then she lets out a painful sob. "No! Mom! Why?"

I rush over to her and drop down in front of her. For the

first time in days, she's not staring off into space.

"Hey, baby. Hey, shh. Just let it out. Let it all out. We are right here for you." I wipe some of the tears out of her eyes.

"She's gone. He's gone. I'm alone," she says through her tears. "Why did they do this to me?"

I lean in and kiss her forehead. "You're not alone. You have us."

"This isn't real. What's even real anymore?" She's starting to lose it again. She's so confused, so lost.

"We are real." I lean in and kiss her lips. "You feel that?" She nods. "That's real. This is real."

"But you wanted me gone. How do I know you aren't sending me the messages?" Her mind starts to become clearer with each sentence. The tears are starting to dry up, and her voice has a little more fight in her. "How do I know this isn't another trick? To get me to leave?"

I shake my head. "It's not us. I swear, Red, it's not us. We don't know who's doing that. We have some ideas, but it's not us."

"Why did you want me gone?" She sits up slowly, wiping traces of her sadness way.

My eyes flick towards Daxon, and I'm not sure how we approach this.

"You were an outsider." Daxon looks between Colt and me. "And you were accepted on odd circumstances. We weren't sure what to make of you."

"I don't know what to think of anything anymore," she whispers.

I shift to sit down next to her, and I wrap my arm around her shoulder. She stiffens at first but then relaxes into me. "How about you go lay down? I think you need to sleep some of this off."

She nods, and we both stand. I bend down, tucking my

arm under her knees and lifting her up. Cradling her against my chest. I bring her into Daxon's room, since it's the most familiar. Colton pulls back the covers as Daxon adjusts the pillows for her. I lay her gently in the bed and start to cover her.

She turns to me. "Please stay."

I look up at the other two, and they nod. They walk over to Phoenix and kiss her forehead. I slide in next to her, and she turns to face me, curling into my chest.

"Why did you ask me to stay?" I rest my cheek on the top of her head.

Her eyes flutter closed. "You promised I'd never be alone."

"Yeah, I did." I pull her in tighter and listen to her breathing slow. After a few minutes, she's sound asleep. I look down at her, finding her face is finally relaxed. She doesn't look like she's hurting or in pain anymore. She looks peaceful.

"I'm so sorry," I whisper.

And I am. For the things I've done in the past, and for the things I'll probably do in the future.

## thirty
### PHOENIX

I DECIDED NOT to go to classes today, but I didn't want to miss my therapy appointment. I'm still not feeling like myself, and I'm hoping that Dr. Parker can maybe help get me back to feeling better than I have been. Daxon has skipped our study hall and is waiting outside the office we're in. I finally brought up the reason why I'm not in study hall most of the time. They understood and told me that it was actually a good thing that I was talking to someone.

The three of them have decided that until we figure out who is behind these notes, it's best one of them is with me at all times.

Especially given the last one and its implied message.

"How have you been, Phoenix?" Dr. Parker sits with his leg crossed over his knee.

A laugh leaves me as I try to think of where I can even start on all this. "Not good, Doc. Not good." I cross my arms over my chest as I lean back on the couch.

His brows furrow. "What happened?"

"Well, let's see. I was attacked by someone on Friday.

Knocked the fuck out. No one believes me. But somehow, there are bruises around my neck. No one can explain them, but whatever. Then, every single uniform I owned was destroyed in someone's shitty prank. And by destroyed, I mean there was a dead gutted fish that somehow ended up in the dryer with my clothes, so you can imagine the smell. Oh, and I got detention for it. So, that's cool. And while all that went on and I was puking my guts out, a stalker left a black box on my bed with pictures and a note. Also, the three kings have now somehow gone from my tormentors to my knights in shining armor. That about sums it up. Got any questions?" I smile, seeing his shocked and pale face.

"Actually, I have a lot. First, your safety is paramount. If you have someone attacking you and a stalker, we need to inform your aunt. Not to mention the authorities." Dr. Parker clicks his pen and fiddles with it.

I shrug. "Well, we went to the authorities about the attack. They did jack shit about it. Is there a report? Yes. But they couldn't find video evidence, and they think I'm crazy. So, they can go kick rocks. As far as the stalker, it honestly could be one of the students messing with me. Hell, could be the kings," I say as I run my hand through my hair.

He cocks his head to the side. "I thought you just said they were your knights now?"

"Well, can't really judge a book by its cover, now can you? I may have fucked all three of them, but they could be fucking with me."

An audible gulp comes from Dr. Parker. "I-I'm sorry. What?"

"Wow, did I just make you uncomfortable? When was the last time you got laid, Doc? I mean, I know you just graduated from high school, but it's probably time you lose that V-card." He shakes himself out of his stupor and clears his throat. I ask, "Anyways, what's next on your list on me to tackle for today?"

"Um, let's revisit the kings later, all right?" he offers, his cheeks still flushed.

"Sure, Doc. Whatever you want."

"Now, you said you got in trouble for the fish and your uniforms?"

"Yep. I was told that I did it for attention and that I should have been standing by the washer and dryer while my stuff was in it. Apparently, they are sending my aunt the bill. She'll be happy to see that, I'm sure."

"You haven't told your aunt?"

"I haven't talked to the old bag since she shipped me here. I need new uniforms, and I know that if I pick up this phone and try to call her, she won't answer. She's pulled a disappearing act on me."

My doctor hesitates. "Well, maybe I can call her for—"

"Don't," I interrupt. "I don't want a damn thing from her."

"But you need new uniforms, Phoenix. Those aren't cheap."

"I'll figure something out, Doc. I always do."

He sighs. "Fine. Can I ask you a question?"

"Sure."

"Can you tell me what happened when you got attacked? Go through whatever events you want, whatever you're comfortable with."

I nod as I feel my heart beating harder in my chest. I let out a long breath and then begin. "Daxon talked me into going to the football game, so I went. Colton went with me, to keep me safe or some bullshit. Which was because the students have been bullying me, of course because they told them to.

"Which as I say all this, I realize how idiotic I sound. But I digress. Colton was there to make sure nothing went wrong. Obviously, that didn't happen, but I don't blame him. He went to go get me some food or something and then I had to pee. My roommate told me we had to head over to the fitness center to use the ones there, so I went in, but the ones that should've been open weren't. So, I headed to the other restrooms that I knew of and hoped it would be open, the locker rooms."

I stop for a moment, and my hands start to tremble.

"I finished doing my business, and then the lights when out. I remember taking out my phone and trying to root around for a way out in the dark." I pause and take a deep breath. "I ran into what I first thought was a wall, but then I realized was a person. They grabbed me and started c-choking me."

Tears begin to stream down my face, my breathing coming out in short, panicked gasps.

My mind replays that night, the fear, the pain. Everything. I thought I was going to die, alone. "I-I passed out. I remember him saying something to me. 'Beautiful.' But that was right before I passed out. Honestly, I think the attacker is the stalker."

"Why do you think that?"

"Because the box that was left on my bed had pictures of me passed out in the locker room. So, unless someone found me before Colton did and took the opportunity to snap some pics for Instagram, I'm putting my money on them being one and the same."

Dr. Parker rubs his head. "What was in the box, Phoenix?"

"Pictures of me on the floor of the locker room, and pictures of me walking with the kings. Oh, and a note."

He leans forward. "What did the note say?"

"Um, '*Your boyfriends won't keep you safe forever, Little Birdie.*'" I take a deep breath. "That may have affected me just a little."

His brows crease with worry. "Explain."

I shrug, sighing. "I don't know. I was like locked in my head. Floating. I was there but I wasn't. I don't know, it was like a weird panic attack."

"It sounds more like it was shock. Phoenix, I really think we need to inform authorities. It's my duty and job to make sure you are okay. And you were attacked. I don't doubt you for a minute."

"No. It stays in this room, Doc. I do not want you doing anything. I don't want to piss whoever this is off even more. I will figure it out."

Dr. Parker gets up and grabs a card off his desk. "Look, give this to your … whatever they are, and if that happens again, call me. The attack, the panic, whatever. This is my personal number. Doesn't go to my office, goes right to me."

I stare at him, taking the card when he hands it to me. "I don't think this is necessary, Doc. It's a one and done."

"Well, just to be safe. I don't want anything to happen to you, Phoenix," he says softly.

I narrow my eyes. "Why do you care?"

"I just do."

\* \* \*

Later that evening, the guys and I are inside their dorm room, which is honestly like more of a suite. Well, maybe like a penthouse. It's really fucking huge.

They have decided that they want me to stay a few days with them until they can figure out who is sending me the notes. Daxon hired a PI to help sort it all out. I'm honestly not holding my breath.

Mason walked in the door with new uniforms for me. And I told him no, that I would just find some used ones or something from the office. Or however I got the ones I had. He just laughed and threw them at me. He did mentioned that he was doing the girls' a favor, and then looked down at my tits.

And sure as shit, he did. Just like with Liz's uniforms, my tits are squeezed in and the buttons are barely holding it together.

After hanging everything up in Daxon's closet, I head over to the kitchen island where the guys are putting in an order for some pizzas. Mason, of course, wants to get me the meat lover's pizza. I immediately roll my eyes and try my hardest not to react to his joke.

"How you feeling, sweetheart?" Daxon comes up and runs a hand along my cheek. He leans in and softly kisses my lips.

"Um, I'm a little drained. But therapy tends to do that to me." I jump up on to the stool as Daxon comes over and wraps his arms around me.

Mason runs a hand through his still wet hair from his shower after practice, and Colt is typing away on his laptop.

"So, we have something we want to ask you. And I have something I need to tell you." Mason looks at me, his lips in a thin line.

I look between them. "We? As in a community question? And also, you're scaring me. What is it?"

"Do you promise not to be mad?" Mason pleads.

"No. And I hope that wasn't the question because I can guarantee that if you do something to piss me off, I'll always get mad." I watch him look at the other guys and then reach into his pocket.

Out comes my locket.

My locket. My mother's locket.

My eyes widen as he slides it across the counter towards me. "Mason, why do you have my locket?" I quickly snatch it up and grip it in my hand.

"See, this is kinda the part where I don't want you to be mad at me," he says as he pinches the bridge of his nose.

"No dice. You have my mother's locket. The locket that was fucking stolen from me. The locket I thought I lost forever!" My voice raises an octave with each word. "Why the fuck do you have this, Mason?"

"We took it to mess with you. I was going to give it back sooner, but I just felt worse, and the longer I had it, the worse I felt. It was like a never-ending circle of shit-fucked feelings. I was always going to give it back, I just never thought we would be here."

"Here where? Here as in you just giving this to me now? Here as in I thought I would never see this again?" I sputter angrily. "Do you have any idea how broken I was over this? You stole this to hurt me, and that's exactly what happened. And now knowing you've had it this whole time is a whole level of hurt I don't think you can even understand, Mason."

Gripping the locket, I close my eyes, trying to picture my mom's face. Picture her wearing this. They have no idea how much this necklace means to me, and they treated it as just a way to cause me pain.

I open my eyes and see them staring at me. Mason pleads, "I'm sorry, Red. I really am. I promise I'll show you, make it up to you, somehow. But I never thought we would be here, asking you something incredibly important."

"What is this oh-so-important question you need to ask? Especially now that you finally gave me back my locket that you stole from me?" I narrow my eyes at the guys.

Daxon's lips trail along my ear, sending pleasant shudders down my spine. He takes the locket out of my hands and places it around my neck. Goosebumps form along my skin with every brush of his hand. "We were wondering if you would go to homecoming with us?"

My eyes widen in shock. That's way off from this locket incident. "Whoa. Whoa. Us?" I pull back.

"Yeah. Me, Mase, and Colt." Daxon moves back to me and kisses my neck. I shiver from his touch.

"First, we need to have a conversation about 'us'. Second, you took something of mine to hurt me and think asking me to a dance is going to make it okay? And third, I can think of three fucking Barbie bitches who will be extremely pissed at this. I've already had a hard enough time with them." I scowl.

"What's there to talk about the four of us?" Colton looks up from his laptop. "You're ours, we're yours." He shrugs.

"I second that." Mason chuckles.

"Oh, well, since the almighty has spoken, I guess it shall be," I scoff. "You know this is completely insane, not to mention unconventional. And do I not get a say?"

"Well, we're kinda asking you now, Spitfire," Daxon says into my ear.

I push off the counter and jump off the seat. "This is asking? You stick your dicks into me and I'm yours? That's some caveman bullshit. You can't just shove a dick in me and claim me."

"Well, technically it was three ..."

Colt slaps his arm. "Not helping, Mase."

"Do you have any idea how hard everything is for me already? Then I go and get tied up with the Kings of Darkwood? I'll have every girl on this fucking campus after me. Do you know the looks I already get since you all started just being nice to me? Since you kissed me in the hall?" I turn to Daxon, starting to feel the pressure in my chest tighten. My breaths start to become short. My hand flies to my chest as I try to steady my heartbeat. This is worse than the fucking locket. This will make my days left in this place, however many I have, pure hell.

"Red, calm down. You're sending yourself into a panic attack." Mason runs over to me. "Look at me."

My eyes find his blue ones. I shake my head, and my vision blurs with unshed tears.

"Phoenix, breathe." Mason runs a hand down my cheek, and my mind starts to spiral.

"I can't. You can't. We ... everything will end. No one stays," I spit out. I close my eyes and drop to the floor.

"What's going on with her?" I hear Daxon say from somewhere.

"She's having a panic attack. Just give her space. Let me help her through it," Mason tells him.

They don't get it. If I give myself a chance with them, I will get hurt. I'll end up alone. Everyone ends up leaving me.

"Red, breathe in slowly through your nose and exhale slowly through your mouth. I want you to count on each breath in and each breath out." Mason stares at me.

Slowly, I do as he says as I stare into Mason's eyes. Ever so slowly, I start to feel myself coming down from the attack.

"There you go." Mason tucks a strand of hair behind my

ear. "Red, sweetheart, remember what I told you? I won't leave you. We won't leave you."

Sobbing, I fall into his arms. "But I'm cursed."

Daxon comes up behind me and rubs my back. "How are you cursed?"

"I'm meant to be alone in this world. If I become happy, or feel like something is going to be okay, something bad will absolutely happen."

"I don't think that's true, sweetheart. We won't let anything bad happen to you. Look at me." I turn to face Daxon. "I know things have been shitty since you got here, but let us make that up to you. Phoenix, you have had me all kinds of fucked up since you strolled into here. Let us treat you the way we should have treated you from day one." He wipes the tears from my eyes. "Look, you don't have to walk in there with us, if that'll make it better. But we would love for you to be our date to the dance."

"Yeah, baby. Just show up with your roommate. But save all of your dances for us." Colton stands next to Mason.

"And if I get shit from the Malibu Bitches?"

"We'll handle them," Daxon says firmly.

Looking between all of them, I manage to whisper, "Okay."

Daxon grins from ear to ear, then leans forward and kisses me. "I promise I'm not going anywhere. *We're* not going anywhere."

Famous last words, Daxon. Famous last words.

## thirty-one

DAXON

WE EVENTUALLY GOT Phoenix to relax and calm down. Then we enjoyed some pizza and watched a movie. She fell asleep during the movie, so Mason took her up to my room, where him and I are now lying next to her.

Colt had some stuff to do for his dad, so he took off not too long ago and will probably be gone all night. He was not happy in the slightest that he had to go. But as usual, when our dads call, we go.

Phoenix is facing Mase, laying on his chest with her legs wrapped around him. I have my arm wrapped around her waist, her ass rubbing against my already painfully hard dick.

I get why she freaked out earlier. She's afraid to let anyone get close to her. She doesn't want to have to deal with the fallout of losing someone else. I understand why she has her walls up.

I also want to kill Mason for holding on to that fucking locket for as long as he did. That almost ruined everything. He would have fucked this up, royally.

We can't let anything go off plan.

And fuck. She's right about Bianca and the others. They'll flip their shit when we don't ask them to homecoming. It probably is best that she doesn't show up with us. We can go in solo and just take our turns dancing with her. It will still draw attention, but it'll be much less than our previous plan.

Still keep everything on track.

Phoenix shifts her ass, and I do all I can to contain my groan. My cock's screaming at me right now to just spread her legs and sink into her wet and tight pussy.

I nuzzle her neck and softly leave kisses along the way across her skin. She smells like honey and lilacs. Her skin is so soft, and she has these adorable little freckles everywhere on her body that I want to memorize. Kiss them. Sink my teeth into her skin and leave my mark on her.

She lets out a little whimper and stirs. Her hand grips mine. I continue kissing her exposed skin as her hand guides mine down the soft skin of her stomach and under her shorts, where I find she's not wearing any underwear.

Internally, I groan while my fingers immediately find her warm wet slit. And holy fuck, she's drenched. As I twirl my fingers around her clit, she lets out a raspy moan. She shifts and rolls on her back, her hooded eyes staring up at me. I lean down and capture her lips with mine, swallowing her moans as my fingers work her toward the edge of her release.

"So wet, sweetheart. What were you dreaming about? Huh? Were you thinking about my cock inside of you? Inside your tight pussy?" I insert two fingers inside her, and she is sopping fucking wet. "Oh, you were, weren't you? You were dreaming about me fucking you."

"Yes. Oh fuck, Dax." I love hearing my name come from that sweet little mouth of hers.

"Say my name again. Ask me to make you come."

"Dax, please. Make me come," she begs, her eyes staring into mine. Her hands are wrapped in my hair, pulling me closer.

As I move my fingers inside her, I use the heel of my palm to rub against her clit, and her hips immediately lift off the bed. Out of the corner of my eye, I see Mason shift, his fingers finding her very hard nipples under her shirt before he starts to suck on them.

Her mouth drops open, and I watch as her entire body vibrates from her release. Her cheeks flush, and she bucks against my hand.

"Fucking beautiful." I pull my fingers out and stick them in my mouth, savoring her sweetness. I lean down and kiss her, letting her taste herself along my tongue.

She rolls to her side and runs her hand along the front of my shorts. My head tips back the moment her hand makes contact. Mason starts to help her out of her clothes and then removes his as I try not to cum in my shorts.

"Take off my shorts," I order her, trying to keep my breathing under control.

I shift to my back as she wraps her fingers around the waistband and pulls them down. She takes my boxers with the shorts, throwing them onto the floor. I caress her cheeks and run a thumb along her lower lip.

"Now, wrap those pretty little lips around my cock."

She slowly lowers her mouth and runs her tongue up from the bottom of my shaft and then slowly slides me into her mouth over the head. I wrap my hands around her hair, pulling it back so that I can watch my dick disappear between them. Her mouth feels like heaven around me. I groan as I try to keep my hips from bucking up into her mouth.

"How's that cock taste?" Mason asks her. She hums around me, and I let out a groan from the vibrations. "You want that cock to fuck you?"

She moans, tears starting to form in her eyes as she tries to take me deeper into the back of her throat.

"Why don't you sit on his dick? Be a good girl and climb up there and slide down on him. Let your pussy wrap around his cock." Mason slaps her ass.

She removes her mouth from me with a pop and then slowly crawls up to me. When her face is near mine, I grab her up and crash my lips into hers. Pulling back, I murmur, "You want me to fuck you, sweetheart?"

"Yes, please, Dax. I need to feel you." Her voice is hoarse, and her pupils are dilated.

I grab my dick and line it up with her entrance. She slowly slides down it, letting out a beautiful gasp as she becomes fully seated on me. She starts to work herself back and forth on my cock. I look back and see Mason stroking himself, watching her ride me.

My hands grip her beautiful, silky ass. As I spread her cheeks apart, my finger finds her tight hole. "You ever been fucked here?" I ask as she loses herself on me. Her breathing is coming fast as she shakes her head no.

"You want to fuck Mason too? Have him fuck this beautiful ass of yours? Want to feel us both inside you at the same time?" I press my lips to hers, and she lets out a small whimper. "Tell me what you want, Phoenix."

"I ... yes ... both." Her eyes are closed, and her cheeks are flushed. She's a little embarrassed that she wants both of us. It's fucking sexy as hell.

Mason steps over to my end table and grabs the lube. My hands shift to her hips, and I hold on to her as she grinds on my cock. My head tips back, and I let out a groan.

Fuck, she feels so tight, so wet, and I know that she is going to feel even tighter once Mason slips inside her.

She gasps when he pours some lube on her. "Now I'm going to start with my fingers, okay? Tell me if it's too much, but I need you to relax."

She nods and breathes out, "Okay."

I can tell the minute he has his fingers inside of her. Her pussy tightens, and she stops moving above me. Her eyes fly open, and I look back at Mason, who is smiling like the cat that got the canary.

"Relax for him, sweetheart. Look at me." Her eyes meet mine. "Breathe, and just relax."

"Oh God, Mason!" she gasps. "It kinda hurts."

"Relax. It won't hurt as much if you relax for him." I caress her face. She starts to relax after a couple minutes. Her moans get louder as she grinds harder into me.

"You're so tight, Red. Fuck. I'm going to slip another finger in. Just keep working his cock."

Her mouth drops open, and I know Mason's got a second finger in her. "How's that feel, sweetheart?"

"So very good. Oh god, so fucking good." She rocks against the both of us.

"You ready for him?" I lean forward and capture her nipple, scraping my teeth over it. She fucking tastes so good. Every inch of her skin is sweet, so addicting.

She leans forward slightly, trying to present her ass to Mason. "Please. Please, Mason."

Mason rubs more lube over his cock and then wipes his hands on his discarded shirt. He rubs her back as he straddles behind her.

"Just relax for me. This will hurt a little, but I promise I'll make it feel good for you." She's still on me as she waits for him to push into her tight hole.

Her mouth drops, and she lets out a groan. "Ow, fuck that hurts."

"I know, just relax. You're doing good, baby, so fucking good. Oh God, you're so tight." Mason rocks back and forth a little, trying to slowly work himself all the way in. I start to feel him brush against my cock, the thin wall just separating us. I'm harder than I have ever been, and I'm doing everything I can to keep from orgasming.

"Look at me, Phoenix. Keep your eyes open and on me," I command her. Her eyes lock on mine, and I can see the mix of pain and fire in them. I grab both her tits and softly twist the nipples, just enough to elicit a little pain to distract her.

Suddenly, she starts to rock back a bit, trying to take more of him in. "That's it, work my cock into your tight little asshole. Fuck." Mason tips his head back as she finally gets him fully sheathed inside of her. They both let out groans and I follow, sputtering curse words.

Mason and I start finding a rhythm as we work ourselves in and out of her.

"Such a good girl, Phoenix. You're such a good girl taking both our cocks. Fuck," Mason mutters as he thrusts into her.

"How do you feel, sweetheart?" I say as I pound into her pussy.

"Full. So full," she moans.

I start to feel her flutter around me, and I know she is reaching her release. Her mouth drops open, and her breathing quickens.

"You gonna come for us? Come for us, Phoenix. Fucking come all over this cock," I say through gritted teeth as I try to hold off my release.

"Holy fuck …" She starts to shake, and her pussy grips

my dick so tight that I can't help but follow her into ecstasy. That tingling travels right down my spine, my balls draw up, and then I'm coming inside of her.

"Oh shit, I'm coming." I tip my head back as I pulsate inside of her.

"Fuck, I'm …" Mason leans forward as he groans through his release. I can feel him pulsating inside of her, and I groan as mine feels like it's never ending.

She collapses on top of me as Mason slowly pulls out of her, disappearing to get some things to clean us up with. I smooth down her hair and see that her eyes are closed.

"I think this is the quietest you have ever been," I joke.

"I'm dickmatized." She laughs. "I think I'm worn the fuck out, so I suggest in the future, if you want me to shut up, this … this is the way to do it." She looks up at me and smiles. I can't help but capture her lips in a kiss.

Mason returns, and we both take our time with her to make sure she's good. She gets back in the middle of the bed and immediately passes out. Mason gets in next to her, and she curls right into him.

I rub my hand over my chest and try to dull the ache that seems to be forming.

Is that what it is? An ache? A need? A want?

I have no clue what it is, but it has something to do with her.

I just hope we don't fuck this up.

\* \* \*

You ever wake up in the morning and feel like something is going to go wrong today? Yeah, that was me today. The air felt weird; there was a thickness to it. It made it hard to breathe. Everything just felt off.

Then my suspicions were confirmed when I got a text from my dad.

**Daddy Dearest: You and the boys need to come home for dinner tonight. Dress in your Sunday Best.**

I stare at the text with a nervousness swirling around in me. What the fuck is the old man up to? When I showed Colt and Mase the text, they both gave me a look of unease. They know if we're all wanted at home, it's not good. That means all of our fathers are involved.

And what I should have realized is how quiet my dad has been lately. No text, no phone calls. Eerily quiet. Until just now.

"Did your ... dad say anything last night?" I turn to Colt as we walk across campus to head to the fitness center to work off some stress.

He shakes his head. "No. He had me down at the docks upgrading some of the software for the security systems. They had some extra people there, but I think that was just because I was bringing everything down and they had to do it all manually."

"They brought shipment in and did it all manually?" I cock my head and wonder why.

That's a lot of work to inventory manually, get people in and out of the docks area manually. It's a bitch to get it all entered back in the system. Why not just hold off unloading till the system was back up?

"That late at night?" Mase questions.

"I don't know. I had to take the whole system down to do the updates. There were more than enough people there to unload, but I don't get it. Something seemed off, but I wasn't about to question it. It was your dad's orders that the system needed the upgrade." He turns to me.

I run a hand through my hair. "Fuck. I don't like this. He's up to something."

"You think it has to do with Phoenix?" Mase gives me a worried look.

"No. She has nothing to do with the docks. At least, I don't think she does," I sigh. "I don't have a good feeling about tonight."

"Well. I guess we will find out when we get there." Mason shrugs. "You think she's okay?"

"Who?" Colton asks as he looks down at his phone.

"Red. Like, she was really freaked out last night. I mean, I hate to say it, but we did a number on her. And it's still going on."

"Why the fuck did you take that fucking locket? Better yet, why didn't you just leave it in her room?" I smack his chest.

He frowns. "Like I said last night. It was a vicious circle. I wanted to give it back, but the longer I had it, the worse I felt about having it. Guilty conscience, asshat."

We head into the fitness center, and I find a set of open treadmills for us to warm up with. We get ourselves up to a nice jogging pace when Colt grabs my attention.

"What are we gonna do about Bianca and the other two? We told her we would handle it. If they get wind that she is going there to meet us, all hell will break loose. More so than it already has."

I have no idea. The last thing we need are the queens fucking this up. If they find out, they will torture the shit out of her. Worse than they already have. I can't let them find out about all of this.

I shake my head. "I don't know. We just have to keep with the story that we are going stag. Might piss them off, but then they won't know anything is up."

"I don't like any of this. Something is going to go wrong," Mason says as he pounds away on the treadmill, talking through quickening breaths. "I really think this is all a bad idea. We should just not go."

"The kings not showing up to homecoming? Not a good way to go out, boys," I scoff. My neck is tight from the stress.

"You missed a fun night last night, Colt." Mason waggles his eyebrows.

"Yeah, I figured when I walked into Dax's room to find you three butt ass naked."

We are silent for a moment, and then Mason stops his treadmill and turns to me.

"You think she will ever forgive us?"

I shut my machine down and lean against it for a moment, staring off in front of me. Turning to Mason, I shake my head and shrug. "I don't know."

I jump off the machine and head to the weights. I need to do something to take some of the stress and tension out of me. We failed to do what we were told to do. Get Phoenix to leave school. With the three of us being summoned, it won't be a fun night. We won't hear the end of it.

I can only prepare for whatever fallout awaits.

## thirty-two
PHOENIX

"THIS IS TOO MUCH. Like way too much." I turn to Liz, who is staring at me with her jaw hitting the floor.

"Girl. Holy cow!"

I narrow my eyes at her and point. "Did you just call me a cow?" I crack a smile and turn back to the mirror.

She lightly slaps my shoulder as she turns me back towards her to take me all in. "I knew this would be a perfect dress for you."

"Yeah, and I'll find a way to pay you back. But thank you." I feel my cheeks heat.

"Never. It's my gift. And you can't refuse a gift."

"Says who? There are always gift receipts and a thing called re-gifting. I'm pretty sure I could refuse to take it, too."

"No. Look, you have been through some stuff here. And had to deal with things that I don't even know how it didn't break you. You deserve this. You deserve a chance at being happy for a day or so."

"Just for a day, huh?"

"Well, baby steps." She throws her head back and laughs.

Liz found out that the guys wanted to take me to homecoming. Okay, so not so much found out but rather, I told her and swore her to secrecy. She then insisted that there was no way I was wearing one of my cutup dresses to the dance. That I needed a dress fit for a queen.

I, of course, laughed in her face. I'm far from a queen.

And in true Liz excitement, she went out and got me one. And I'm not going to lie, it's beautiful. This is a classy dress and one I probably would've picked out myself. It's not my usual style, but it's a dance.

The dress is a long ballroom cut with black satin and a mix of lace appliqués and beadwork patches. Most of the lace and beadwork is up top as it fades down the rest of the dress, showcasing the satin. The neckline is a scoop with thin beaded straps, and the back is semi open. Oh, and there's pockets.

I smile. "Well, it's beautiful. And you did pick my favorite color."

"I did want to go for the green, but I figured if there was any chance to actually get you in it, I would have to opt for black." She winks at me, then turns to head back into the bathroom to finish with her hair so that we can make our way over to the hotel for our dance.

It's been a weird week that I'm not even sure how to deal with. First, Dr. Parker didn't show for my session this week. I never got a call or a message that he needed to cancel. I sent him an email to make sure we were still on for next week, but I haven't heard back.

I tried calling my aunt to see if she could get a hold of him. Or if he called her to tell her he wasn't doing a session this week, but she never picked up.

The bitch can go rot in hell.

How do you ignore your niece, who has lost both her parents? Treat her like she's less of a person? She shipped me off to this place and washed her hands of me. Thank God she doesn't have her own crotch goblins. I would actually feel bad for them.

But whatever.

Then there's the guys. And that's been a whole other strange world I stepped into this past week.

They've been distant. A couple times they missed classes, but when they were there, they just weren't. They would look at me, smile, and maybe even say a few things. But that was it. I felt like there were walls being erected between us. And I had no idea why.

I tried texting them on the group chat, but the answers I got were vague and short. And since I don't want to be "that girl", I just let it go.

Even the bullying around school has died down. This week has actually been a nice week. I felt like a normal student at a normal school but still in ugly ass uniforms.

Still, something in me has me worried. There's something I can't put my finger on. Something is very off.

I grab hold of my locket and close my eyes. Their touch, the way they felt inside of me, I know whatever it is, it'll be all right. The way they held me, kissed me, it felt real. That they wanted me. Whatever is going on, they will get through it and then everything will be fine.

With everything that's happened this week, there's a small part of me that's ashamed that I did what I did with them. It's unconventional. Three? Three of them? And the lack of communication has not helped those feelings. Doubt creeps in my mind, embarrassment. I now regret not having them pick me up for the dance.

Closing my eyes, I push those thoughts to the back of mind.

I curl my hair behind my ears and put on a pair of earrings that Liz let me borrow. They are beautiful floating diamond stud earrings. I refused them at first, and then I asked how much I would need to give her if I lost one. She brushed me off and pushed them in my hand.

There's no way these things are cubic zirconias. These are definitely diamonds. I'm wearing fucking diamonds on my ears. I know I'll be nervous the entire night and constantly checking to make sure I don't lose one. Or both. Shit. I probably have thousands of dollars in my ears right now.

"Stop thinking about it. You're wearing the earrings!" Liz calls from the bathroom.

My eyes widen in surprise, and my head turns towards her direction. "How—"

"I can hear your breathing pick up. If you lose it, it's not a big deal. I have like thirty pairs of diamond studs, and I couldn't tell you where I got half of them." She laughs and sighs.

I stand there with my mouth wide open. Fucking rich people. They literally have diamonds coming out their asses.

Such a problem to have.

I didn't do anything special with my hair. Dressing up was enough of me going outside my comfort zone. I let my long red hair fall around me. Liz did straighten it for me, helping to control the fly aways or something as she put it.

Walking over to my bed, I sit down slowly and reach for my shoes. I may be in a dress, but that doesn't mean I can't wear my Docs. I smile knowing that while every other girl in there will be in pain fifteen minutes in with their stilettos, I'll be nice and comfy.

I wiggle my toes in my Docs and jump up to grab my phone and purse. I check it for any messages, but I have none. Nothing from them. No 'see you there' or 'can't wait to see what you look like in that dress', nothing.

I close my eyes and try to push back the feeling of unease. Placing a hand on my stomach, I take a deep breath and try to calm my nerves.

That's all they are. Nerves.

"Ready? The limo's here," she calls from the other room.

*What?* Did I hear her right?

I cautiously ask, "Limo?"

"Yeah! We are showing up in a limo. What, did you want to take a taxi? No. Limo. Besides, my daddy paid for it. So, money well spent." Her lips turn up.

"Kind of extreme, don't you think? This isn't prom." I shake my head as I head into the living area.

She bites her lip and thinks for a moment. "No, you're right. For prom last year we showed up in giant Hummer super-stretch limos and party busses."

Oh. Yeah. Makes total sense. A regular limo is so not prom worthy.

"Why not just get flown in on a helicopter?"

"Oh, that happens too," she informs me.

What the fucking fuck? If I ever have that much money, which I won't, I'm donating it. There is no way I'll ever live like these people. There is such a thing as too much, and when you're taking a helicopter into prom, that's when it hits the too much mark.

Helicopters to a fucking prom. Fuck that.

Before we leave, I reach into the fridge and grab the three boutonnieres that I got the guys. I was so torn on getting them each one, but Liz convinced me that I should. That they probably each got me one. I got them each a black rose. A symbol of rebirth and new beginnings. Which I thought fit well with everything that has been going on between us. Also, it's black, and I do love the color black.

Liz is bouncing at the door waiting on me. She's too excited about all this.

We make our way out to the front of the dorms, and there are other students dressed up taking pictures with each other before making their way to the hotel.

As we walk towards the parking lot, a voice calls out my name, and it sends chills down my spine. I don't turn right away, but I close my eyes and steady my breath. Finally, I turn and see one of the last people I wanted to see tonight.

"Phoenix! Wait up!" I turn to see Chad dressed in a black tux running down the stone path towards me. You know for an asshole, he really is good looking. Especially in a tux, but he's still an asshole. And that ruins the whole thing.

"What do you want Chad?" I roll my eyes. I feel Liz tense up next to me, but she stays silent.

"I just wanted to tell you how beautiful you look." He smiles down at me, and my stomach turns.

"Great. Thanks." I start to turn, but his hand shoots out and grabs my shoulder. "Get your fucking hands off me, Chad."

"Hey, hey, hey!" He holds his hands up in the air. "I just wanted to have a little chit chat is all." His voice is higher than normal.

"I don't want to talk to you. I'd prefer it if you disappeared and went back to whatever it is you do to convince other women to sleep with you." I flick my wrist to shoo him away, but it just makes him angry.

"What, because the kings gave you five minutes of their dicks, you think you're on our level? You're not. You're trash and will always be a whore who will spread her legs just to try and get ahead in life. I mean, that's why you took all three of them at once right? Three times the chance at a happy ever after in riches?"

I gasp, and he laughs at my reaction.

"You don't think we talk about it in the locker room? How they easily convinced you to get fucked in every hole? Just eager to get spit roasted, weren't you?"

I feel my cheeks flush. "Get fucked, Chad." I say through gritted teeth.

"No, no. I believe that was what they were doing to you." He shakes his head. "Oh, Phoenix, Little bird. How naive you are to think they gave two shits about you."

My body instantly freezes at his words. *Little bird*. No. There's no way he could have been sending me that stuff.

"It's you," I whisper.

"Me? What's me?" He tilts his head in confusion.

"You sent the notes. Why? Why are you doing this?" I yell at him, my fists clenched at my sides.

"I have no idea what you are talking about. What notes?"

"The phoenix, the box ..."

He shakes his head. "Wasn't me." His lips tilt up.

"What's that?" He points to the three black roses I hold in the clear plastic container. He pulls me from my mind, distracting me from wondering if he's lying about the notes. He cackles with laughter when he realizes what they are. "Are you serious? Did you really get them flowers? Black roses?" He curls over in a fit of laughter as I feel the heat creep up from my neck.

I suddenly take a look around and see that we have

drawn a crowd of people around us. People are staring and pointing. Some have their cameras out, no doubt getting ready to throw this on social media.

Chad continues to laugh. "You got them death? A rose that means death? Wow, you're all sorts of fucked up."

"It also means new beginnings, fucker." I narrow my eyes at him and do everything I can to keep from smashing the container with roses in my hand. I have no idea why I'm trying to explain myself to him.

"New beginnings? Aw, how sweet. Except, there's no beginning with them, Phoenix. They dipped their dicks in your trash pussy and they have had their fill. I mean, how come they didn't pick you up? Or walk into the dance with you? If they weren't embarrassed by you, they would want to be seen with you." His voice gets low so that only I can hear. "You were just a pawn in their game. Congratulations, Phoenix. You fell for it. Hook, line, and sinker."

Without another word he strolls towards the limo waiting for him with his other friends.

But they asked me. They wanted me. I was the one who said it was a bad idea. Maybe that's what they wanted? That it was my idea that I show up alone? Was this all a fucking mind game?

I feel a hand wrapped around my wrist, and I turn to see Liz mouthing something. Except, I can't hear a thing but the blood rushing in my ears.

My stomach drops, and I try to keep down the bile that's rising. My heart twists, and I feel on the verge of tears. They have been pretty much ignoring me all week.

Did I fall for their game? Was this all a joke?

Fuck.

\* \* \*

The entire ride to the hotel, my mind is lost as I replay every action that I had with the kings. I try to search for clues that would make anything Chad said true. And I have to take what he says with a grain of salt, but still. He knew I slept with them all, and that bothers me more than anything.

They talked about it with the guys in the locker room. Daxon and Mason shared something intimate between us with their football team. The same people who bully me, who push me around and make my life miserable.

I feel so nauseous.

If Chad knows, they all know.

And then he called me "Little bird." I shiver at the thought that he's the one sending me those notes. I mean, they didn't show up until after his party. But how did he get into my room? Even the thought that he has been in my room make me want to vomit. He says he didn't do it, but he knows too much, and he would do something like this. It has to be him. Fuck, I need to let the guys know.

"Hey, are you okay? You look extremely pale." Liz scoots closer to me.

I nod slowly. "Yeah. I just don't know what to believe anymore."

"Look, if they didn't want you, they wouldn't have had you meet them here. And you said it was because *you* were worried about what would happen with the queens. It wasn't their idea." She rubs my back. "They protected you, they took care of you when you were hurt. You don't fake that."

"But it could still be all a game." I bite my lip. I haven't really talked to them all week. I haven't seen them either. That alone worries me.

"If you saw what I saw, you would know that they genuinely care for you. I'm telling you, Phoenix, Chad's lying." Her phone pings, and she picks up it up. She snaps a few pictures of herself and sends it to whoever is on the other end.

I stare down at the three black roses. Then I close my eyes and silently hope that Chad was just trying to get a rise out of me.

As we pull up to the hotel, I can sense the lights and flashes going off from people around us taking pictures. But my mind's too preoccupied to notice much else. Liz grabs my hand, and we walk through the lobby and into the ballroom.

When we get in, my eyes finally make out my surroundings, and I come out of my haze.

It's beautiful. Large crystal chandeliers hang from the ceiling. Beautiful, dark wooden exposed beams run along the ceiling. Tables are scattered throughout with expensive rose centerpieces at each table. Engraved in the silver vase is our school crest. Off to the right there's an archway and a backdrop for us to take pictures at. And a giant wooden floor in the center of the room for us to dance on.

"Wow. This is amazing," I say in awe.

"What? You never went to a dance before?"

I shake my head. "No, but they held them in our gymnasium. And I saw that every day. It was nothing special. They taped a couple balloons to the bleachers and a spinning light by the DJ. This ... this is beautiful."

She tugs on my arm. "Come on. Let's go find your men. We can settle this crazy once and for all so you can enjoy it."

We start to walk around the ballroom in search of the kings. You would think that people would be buzzing about them coming solo to a dance, but no one has even mentioned them since I walked in. As we walk past the dance floor, the whispers start.

*"Oh my god, look at them."*
*"Fuck they are so hot."*
*"I'd give anything to hang off of the Kings' arms."*
*"The queens are so lucky."*

Wait, what?

I turn in the direction from where we came, and my entire world at that moment stops spinning. The wind's knocked out of me, and I'm pretty sure I let out a loud gasp as a result.

I can't believe my eyes.

Daxon, Mason, and Colton come sauntering into the ballroom, each with a *queen* at their side. Bianca is hanging off of Daxon's arm smiling up at him. Mason's arm is wrapped around Tiffany's waist, and Colton has his arm around Jacklyn's shoulder.

*No!*

I look at Liz, and she looks at me; her face has gone pale. She shakes her head at me and then turns back towards the Royal Court entering the dance.

No, no, no. This can't be real. They asked me. They were supposed to go with me. I close my eyes and open them again, hoping that what I saw was a dream.

But it's real.

As if they can sense me, all three kings' eyes find me. They start to make their way over to me, and I'm too frozen in place to make a run for it. Their gazes lock in on me, and I can't read a single one of them.

"Aw, sweetie." Bianca's voice is like a knife to my ear drum. "Did you actually think that they would go with you? How cute." She smiles at me, on the verge of laughing. The three kings stand there, stoically, not saying a word but staring at me with not a single emotion in their eyes.

"What? What's going on? Daxon, please talk to me. This

is a joke, right? Mason, please." I look at Mason and then Daxon, but they say nothing.

"Oh, it absolutely is the best fucking joke ever. You really thought that if you spread your legs for them, they would all fall in love with you?" She cackles loudly. "Best part is you had no problem spreading it for all three at once."

"Let's go, Phoenix." Liz pulls on me from my left, but I'm frozen in place.

"It's cute that you think you had a chance." She places her left hand on his chest, and that's when I see it.

A giant diamond ring on her finger. My mouth drops open and the tears fill my eyes. And then I see all three of the queens have diamonds on their hands. I shake my head. No, this isn't real.

"They have always been ours. Our families have had this lined up since we were kids. Now, we aren't that cruel. We let our fiancés have a little fun, but I think it's time they stop playing with the trash of Darkwood. Don't you think, ladies?" The other two nod in agreement.

"Daxon, please tell me this isn't true," I beg. I look at him and he shrugs.

"Sorry, Spitfire. We got tired. You were too easy. We bet at least November before you put out for all three of us. Didn't we, Mason?"

Mason nods. "Way too easy." Colton stands there with his lips pursed tight.

It's that exact moment that my heart, the pieces that were slowly being put back together by all of them, went up in flames.

I back up slowly, hoping and waiting for them to tell me this was a joke. But they don't break. They just stare at me, waiting to see what I do. So, I do what anyone would. I run.

I run out of the room and to the nearest bathroom. Where I let every single tear fall from my eyes. Every ounce of pain. Every bone in me is enraged. I punch the wall next to me and scream. Pain from the hit surges through me.

It's not a dream. I felt that.

How could this happen? How did I let this happen?

Engaged?

How? When?

My stomach rolls, and I feel like I'm about to throw up. I fell for it. They made a fool of me. I trusted them and all along it was nothing but a game to them.

I was nothing to them.

I'm an idiot for falling for it. And I did. Fast. I let them into my life without second guessing their motives more carefully. I let my walls down. They worked their charm on me, and I bought into it. They had a bet. They bet on me. And it turns out I'm more of a whore than I thought.

I stare at myself in the mirror. My makeup is mostly intact because Liz used waterproof eye makeup. I grab a paper towel and dab under my eyes, trying not to smear or ruin the rest. My lips tremble as I try to hold back more tears.

Steadying my breath, I grip the counters and try to talk myself into a state of calmness. The door opens, and I turn to see Liz slowly walking towards me.

"Hey, how are you doing?" she says carefully.

I shake my head. "I'm fine. Or at least that's what I'm going to tell myself."

"I'm so sorry, Phoenix. I ... I can't believe what just happened! If you want to go, we can go." She places a hand on my shoulder. "You know what, we should go. Let's just go home and eat ice cream in our dresses."

"No," I say firmly. I turn and look at her. "They will not

get rid of me that easy. They can make fun of me, they can pretend to like me and then hate me. But they will not win. I won't let them win. They have taken enough from me. So, let's go back, we'll dance and have fun. Fuck the kings."

A small cautious smile appears on her face. "Okay. Let's go out there and show them we don't care."

Arm and arm we head out of the bathroom and into the ballroom. We start to make our way over to the table when the lights go out.

"Ah, there she is. Ladies and gentleman, the woman of the hour, Miss Phoenix Hayes." Bianca's now standing on the stage in front of the dance floor with her two dogs in tow.

A spotlight shines on me, and I stand there frozen yet again, unsure of what I just walked into. I turn to see all eyes on me. There are whispers, but I can't make out what they are saying. I swallow the lump in my throat.

I should've never come back.

## thirty-three
PHOENIX

"WOW, I'm surprised you came back. Well, a little. You seem to not want to give up. You're an annoying little gnat that just won't go away." Bianca smiles, a wicked curl to her lips.

A voice in the back of my head tells me to run. But I'm frozen solid where I stand, as if the beam of light has locked me in place. I look around at the faces that go from her to me. I notice the chaperones have all huddled against the wall with their back turned to us.

"The kings played their silly little games on you. And I have to say, I did enjoy playing. Watching you as you had to clean out your locker, the dryer incident. I mean, I really pulled out some great ones. Hell, pushing you into the pool didn't even get you to leave. And you almost drowned!" She slaps her leg and laughs. "You play a good game. But I think that's about to come to an end for you. I mean here you are, pining for the kings when all along they were going to be married to us." She flashes her hand again.

The crowd starts to murmur, and some whistle and cheer for that revelation. A revelation that makes me sick to my stomach. Spinning my head, I see people pointing and laughing at me. I bite the inside of my cheek to try to keep myself grounded. Looking around, I don't even see the kings.

She reaches out towards Tiffany, who hands her something. She turns back to me with a wicked gleam in her eye. "You know, you trust too easily. People will betray you for a king and queen in a heartbeat. I mean shit, you trusted the devils themselves. And thanks to them, I think I finally have something that will make you turn and never come back."

Thanks to them? The kings? *No.*

Something clicks and a wall gets illuminated by a white square. Everyone turns to stare at what's displayed on it. A picture of my family is there. My heart clenches and my stomach drops. My mom, my dad, and me. All happy, smiling for the camera.

I'm in a room full of people, but seeing them on that way before me, knowing they're gone ... I'm no one. My chest tightens, and I push the lump in my throat down.

"What are you doing? Where did you get this?" I yell. Why are the chaperones not stopping this? They are standing there, watching this happen. No one is putting a stop to this.

She clears her throat, and her eyes narrow. Her lips curl up. "For those of you who didn't know, Phoenix's dad killed himself. Drove right off the cliff. Bam! Right into the water. Couldn't stand to be around the lie of a daughter anymore and his whore of a wife." I growl and my fists tighten. "But that's not all. Do you know he wasn't alone that night?"

My breathing stops. *What?*

No, my dad was alone. He was coming home from work. It was an accident. I know he would never leave us. He wouldn't kill himself. It was an accident. And I know he was by himself. They said he was the only person in the car …

"Beverly Emerson was a passenger in his car that night. She was also killed when Phoenix's dad drove over the cliff. How selfish is it to take not only your life, but the life of someone else's," she tsks.

My mind starts to turn. Emerson. Beverly Emerson. Oh my God. Daxon Emerson. *No, no, no, no*.

"Oh, look at those wheels turning. That's right, Phoenix. Your dad killed Daxon's mom." She laughs like a hyena. "You should see the look on your face. You had no idea, did you? Aw. Just so innocent. And yet your dad isn't. Well, neither is your whore of a mother."

My arms wrap around my stomach, and I lean against the table nearest to me. I try to take deep breaths, but I feel like my lungs aren't working. I can't breathe. I squeeze my eyes shut and then open them.

I look up at Liz, who has now stepped away from me, staring at me with wide eyes. No, don't. Please. I shake my head and try to speak, but my mouth has gone dry, and I can't find the words. How is any of this happening?

My dad killed Daxon's mom. His mother. There's an ache inside of me.

"You know, I wish it stopped there." Bianca points back to the wall, where a picture of my mother's scene is displayed for everyone to see. And I suddenly feel like I'm stepping into that bathroom all over again. How did she get this photo?

Her body lifeless. Her blue lips. The water stained red. Her wet, matted hair. Those haunted eyes, the fear and acceptance in those eyes for what she did. I can smell the death as I sit here. She's gone.

"No!" I cry out. Tears cascade from my eyes. "Stop it!

Please!" My voice trails off as I plead for her to put an end to this. I'll go. I'll leave.

You won.

"Your mother was so distraught that she killed herself too! You weren't even good enough for her to stick around for. Your dad, your mom, no one wanted you. From what I hear, neither does your aunt. Isn't that why she shipped you here? Because she wants nothing to do with you? That's why it's cute that you think you had our men. But they want nothing to do with you either." She giggles. "But that's not even the best part."

I can't even see anymore. My vision is blurred with my tears. I'm choking back the vomit I can taste in my mouth as I clutch my stomach.

"Do you know why your mother killed herself? Do you know why your dad cheated on your mother? Oh, yeah, Daxon's mom and your dad, they were having an affair. Here's the kicker, and folks, you'll definitely want to get this on camera."

Please make this stop. Please. Why is no one stopping this? *I'll go. Please stop*, I silently beg to those around me who are now just watching me and waiting for whatever shoe to drop.

"Your mother killed herself not because the affair your dad was having, but because he found out you were not his daughter."

Everything stops. The world, time, my breathing. My legs buckle under me and my knees hit the ground. Someone help me.

"Someone, please stop this!" I croak out. But no one does.

I turn to her and clench my fists. "You're lying. You're a fucking liar!" I scream.

"Oh, I wish I was. But your daddy isn't your daddy. Your mother was a whore just like you! Like mother, like daughter! I wonder how many dicks she took at once?"

People around me start to laugh and chatter.

"No! None of that is true!" I snarl back, my fists curling at my sides.

She points to the wall, and I see a birth certificate on it. Where did she get this? My breath catches ... My box. My head spins to her, and she nods. How did she get a copy?

"Yeah, I found your secret hide away. Well, actually, Mason found it. He told Daxon, who told some friend, yada, yada. You get the idea." She winks at me and then points at the wall.

I turn and look at the birth certificate.

"Oh, and look at here, no father listed on the birth certificate. Now, that's weird. If he was your father, why wasn't he listed? Well, see a couple years later, it looks like they started adoption paperwork for Mr. Trevor Hayes to legally adopt you. But then they never finished it. See? He didn't even want you then."

My dad isn't my dad. He was going to adopt me? Why didn't she tell me? My life's been a lie. My entire fucking existence is a lie.

I push up from the floor. I'm trying to process everything. How can they be this cruel?

"Why are you doing this?" I sob. "Why?"

"We have been telling you since day one, we don't want you here. Your family destroyed another. My fiancé's family is broken because your dad couldn't keep it in his pants. Which turns out it's because your mother was spreading her legs around town. You are slut trash just like your mother," Bianca spits.

My hand flies to my chest, and I look around. No one is

stopping this, no one is coming to my defense. Not even the kings. But I still don't see them.

*Where are the kings?*

Fuck them. No, fuck me. This is why they hate me. My family broke his. My family single handedly destroyed his. My dad took his and her life.

Was this why my aunt wanted me here? Does she know this? Is this why she hates me? She's just as bad as these people around me. She threw me right into the lions' den.

She threw me into hell.

I stand, my feet and legs barely keeping me upright. I start to walk backwards and when I finally find my balance, I turn, bursting through the ballroom doors and out of that hell. No one comes after me, no one stops me. I run through the lobby and out to the front. Stopping only when I get to the taxi waiting area.

"Ma'am are you okay?" A gentleman asks me.

I shake my head, "I need to go home. Now. Please. I need a cab or something. Fast," I say through gulps of breaths.

I hear him call over a cab, and I hop in without even thanking the person.

"Darkwood Academy, please," I say to the driver.

As he takes off, I don't turn to look at the hotel. I don't want to see that place. I don't want to see anyone that may have followed me out to continue the laughs.

I close my eyes and try to take a steady my breathing. Tears continue to stream down my face. Then I realize that at some point, I lost the roses, and that's probably for the best.

"Miss, are you all right?" The driver looks at me through his rearview mirror.

"I will be," I assure him, my voice wavering. My mind is reeling from everything.

My mother's gone, the man I grew up loving as my father, gone. And now I find out there is someone out there who is my father, and he has no idea I even exist.

The lies. The fucking lies. What did I do to deserve all this? Why lie to me? Look what the lies led to. It led me to heartache. More fucking heartache. And another reminder that everyone I know doesn't want me.

I'm alone.

There is nothing left for me. They win. I'm leaving. They finally get what they want. Me. Gone.

By the time we make it back to Darkwood, I'm in a state of just existing. I pay the driver and get out, looking up towards the sky. The wind blows my hair in my face, the coolness drying my tears.

"This is the mess you both left me. This is the life you chose for me. Because of your ways, your actions, now I'm suffering. I will always suffer. Your mistakes have defined me."

I head towards my dorm, the campus quiet and eerie. But most everyone is at homecoming. Dancing away, taking photos, making memories. And I know that my downfall will be memorable for them.

No one stopped it. No one came to my rescue. "Adults" sat there and ignored the onslaught on me. My roommate even backed away, not wanting to associate herself with me.

I guess I don't blame her.

My body moves on its own, slowly making its way to the elevators and up to my floor. Walking down the hall, I run my fingers along the smooth wall. The coolness on my skin sends goosebumps along my arm. Each step is a step closer to leaving.

Reaching my door, I mindlessly punch my code in and head straight to my room. I switch on the light of my closet and pull up the board where my box is. It's not there. They did get it. They found it and got their hands on it.

They wanted me gone. They found everything they needed to in order to get me out of here.

I walk over to my desk, my breathing coming fast and heavy. My heart is racing as I pick up a pen on my desk and rip out a piece of paper from my journal that's lying next to it. I scribble out "you win" on the paper and lay it on top of the journal. I slowly step away from the desk and look around my room.

My body becomes numb. If I had only opened that box sooner, read through it sooner. That had to be in the box. The answers were in the box. I reach up, wrapping my hand around my locket, and I let out a blood curdling scream.

I run into my closet and start throwing things around, tearing clothes off the hangers and throwing it on the floor. I run to my desk and pick up my laptop, sending it flying across the room into the wall. I kick the full-length mirror, letting the shards fall to the floor.

My hands run across my dresser, knocking the few items off. A bottle of perfume of my mom's falls to the floor and shatters. The scent surrounds me, and I let out another scream. I grab a shard of the mirror glass and go to my bed.

I slept with them here. I let them hold me when I needed to be held. It was a lie. They weren't my heroes, they weren't my saviors. They were my tormentors, my bullies.

I growl as I plunge the glass shard through the bed, tearing through the blanket and the sheet, down to the mattress. Tears pour into the gaping holes on my bed, soaking into it. I grab the pillow and rip it to shreds with the shard. My breathing is heavy, my chest moving up and down, heaving.

I look down at my dress covered in mattress and pillow remnants. I'm tired. I'm done.

She lied. They lied. My parents lied.

Everything I knew, lies.

Our happy family, lies.

My father, lies.

My mother's love, lies.

My life, lies.

My chest heaves as I try to take deep breaths. I close my eyes and tip my head back. I'm exhausted. So over everything.

I look down at my hands. They are covered in blood from the glass I'm still holding.

A laugh bubbles up through the tears, and I look around the room. It's destroyed.

Just like my life.

Weightlessly, I wander into the bathroom and start the shower. I hum *Ashes of Eden* by Breaking Benjamin. I run my cut hands under the water, washing the blood from the sliver of glass I'm still holding. The sting from the water should hurt, should have me pulling them back. But I'm welcoming it. Let it hurt. I watch the blood mix with the water as it falls to the shower floor and down the drain.

I step in under the warm water, in my dress, and let it soak me. Let it wash the shame away, the fear away. Let it take my loneliness away.

"Just take me all away from this please," I say through my tears.

They burned my heart until it was nothing but ash.

Their touch, their kisses, the whispered words, they

were all lies. The kings let me think that they cared. That it was real.

Lies.

It's over. They win.

They had me so convinced I was fine. That for once I had people that wanted me. I can't do this anymore. I can't fight to live when there is nothing to live for.

Not anymore.

I opened up to them. I let them in. And I fell for their sick and twisted game.

My head tipped back, water pouring over my face, mixing with the tears. I don't want to feel anymore. I don't want to feel this pain.

But I do feel the release on the first cut.

I let out a breath. I welcome that pain. It's a pain to the end. It was deep. I turn to the other wrist and let out a scream as I do, slowly sliding down the wall. My arms fall to my side.

The water washes away the blood as it comes out of me. My dress is plastered to my body.

"I'm sorry, Mom. I'm sorry you felt you couldn't tell me," I say through the tears. "But now I see why you did what you did. You were backed into a corner. Lost, alone. Felt like you caused it all. You caused someone pain. And that hurts to know that.

"But what I think hurts most is knowing that no matter where I go in life, your actions, your mistakes will haunt me. And I can't live like that. I can't live knowing you and dad destroyed someone else's family.

"And I can't live knowing that they took my heart and crushed it to dust. I feel like I'm being burned alive from the inside. And my heart can't take it anymore. I can't live knowing that none of it was real. I thought they cared. It wasn't real.

"Neither was my life. The people I thought were my parents, were you both really? Dad apparently wasn't, and you chose death over me. So where does that leave me? What choices do I have?

"None. It leaves me with nothing, Mom. And I don't want this life you gave me anymore. I'm too tired. I don't want to wake up. Because then I'll be right back in this nightmare you left for me.

"I can't fight anymore. They win."

My head starts to feel light, and I find myself staring at the shower door. I watch the drops travel down the glass. I look down at my wrists, but I can't feel the pain anymore. My body sags, and I welcome the feeling of letting go.

My eyes become heavy as my body starts to feel sluggish. I find myself slowly sliding down until I'm lying on the floor of the shower.

I close my eyes and welcome the darkness.

Where there's darkness, there's no pain.

So let the blackness slip over me and pull me under.

Goodbye to anyone that may have cared.

*from the darkness*

To whoever cares,

It hurts. The pain is blinding. And I'm not talking about the scars on my wrist. It's the wounds bleeding from my heart.

The pain, lies, and heartache.

It's all just too much.

I'm more alone than ever. My past has been exposed for the entire school to see, and the friend I thought I had abandoned me when I needed her most, along with the three guys I opened my heart to. And the moment I did, I was done for.

Daxon, Mason, and Colt brought on this darkness.

Their betrayal and their lies led me to the end.

And that's what I wanted. I wanted it to be over.

I wanted the pain gone, I wanted the tears to dry up, and I wanted the world to go black.

Except, I don't get an end.

My stalker is still out there. I'm still bullied by everyone around me. The only family member alive, ignores me and pretends I don't exist. My life is slowly crumbling around me.

My sanity is holding on by a thread.

My existence can't get any darker can it?

Love,

Phoenix

Preorder From the Darkness

# acknowledgments

To all of my ARC Readers: Thank you. The overwhelming response I received to those who wanted to read From the Ashes was beyond my wildest expectations. Thank you all for taking time to read the first in this series. Your feedback is invaluable and I look forward to our journey through the rest of the Darkwood Academy Series.

Monique Edenwood: Mon, I absolutely love you. Your support and feedback was paramount in helping me finish the first book in this series. I am beyond lucky to have found an amazing friend like you that I know that I can come to when I need feedback. (Or random spicy pictures of guys that should not be opened in public.) I am honored that you chose my book to be your first reverse harem read. DMC forever!

Amara Rae: Let me just say this: is it November yet? Thank you for the continued support through this journey. I can't thank you enough for all that you have done. I remember when I told you about this book series when you came to Vegas. I think your exact words were: "Oh my God, yes! Write this series!" I don't think I would have written this book had it not been for that single moment. So thank you, Amara. I love you.

My family and friends: Thank you for continuing to support my dream. It means the world to me. I love you all.

My readers: Simply put, thank you. Your continued

support and love for my books drives me to keep bringing you these worlds to get lost in. Love you all.

Chanel Johnson: I know we met towards the end of this book being completed, but in that short time you have been such a huge support system for me. Thank you for everything you have done for me.

My editor, Ashley Olivier: Not going to lie, I am always on pins and needles waiting to hear what you thought of my book. Every. Single. Time. Your support, feedback, and friendship is something I value more than I can ever explain. You get my writing, you get my characters, and you understand me. Thank you so much for all the hard work you do on my books. I couldn't have asked for a better partner to help me bring to life my stories.

*also by lynn rhys*

**Scars on My Heart**

For my entire life, my weight and looks have been a hot topic of conversation with my family. I've never felt perfect, never felt like I was enough or even worthy of love. That all changed when I met my husband, Scott. I finally had someone that saw me for who I was, not a number on a scale.

Or so I thought. But then my husband left me for someone more beautiful, someone skinnier. It broke me.

Newly divorced and ready to find myself, I venture out into my single life.

And everything was fine. Until, I met Dr. Nathaniel Bennett . *Of course* I was attracted to him, but he would never see anything in me. I was the big girl. I had flaws. Nothing could ever happen between us.

Oh, and he's also my boss.

**Trigger warning: This book contains strong subject matter that may not be suitable for all readers. This book contains scenes that may depict, mention, or discuss bullying, cheating, childbirth, divorce, emotional abuse, infertility, pregnancy, and suicide. There is profanity and sexual situations. Reader discretion is advised.**

**Safe With Me**

I ran from a monster. A monster I thought was gentle and kind. A monster I thought loved me. I was wrong. So very wrong.

I took a bus out west and landed in a small town in Wyoming.

Ryker, the town's sheriff, has been helping me to settle in. But I can't get that comfortable, even if things seem quiet around here.

I'll keep looking over my shoulder, no matter how safe Ryker thinks he can keep me. I know the monster is waiting in the shadows.

**Trigger warning: This book contains strong subject matter that may not be suitable for all readers. The topics in this book involve domestic violence, abuse, sexual abuse, profanity and sexual situations. Reader discretion is advised.**

### Neighbors

Long ago I learned not to trust people. They are cruel and thrive off hurting others. I was one of those other people. Always the outsider, always the loner. So, I've just learned to keep it that way. I became a recluse, an introvert. If I'm alone, I don't have to worry about getting hurt again.

But then Bryce, who turns out to be my neighbor, came into my life. He flipped my entire world upside down. Every part of me is screaming to turn tail and run. Find a corner to hide in because people can't be trusted.

So why am I not? What is it that draws me to him? What makes him different?

After all the pain and torment I've been through in my life, I'm risking everything I have left in my soul by letting him in. As I bring down my walls, I pray I'll be able to survive the inevitable fallout.

**Trigger warning: May contain triggering content for some readers. Neighbors is a friends to lovers romance book. 80,000+ words. This is a standalone novel with a HEA.**

### What Led Me to You

After graduation, I thought I would have the life I had always dreamed of. But like everything else, it was taken away from me. The people I trusted the most, betrayed me. So, I took the pieces of my broken heart and left Las Vegas. New state, new surroundings, new beginnings.

I was always told, when one door closes, another one opens. Taking the job as a nanny for Alex and his daughter was my new beginning. A fresh start and the closure I desperately needed. Except, just when I think I can move on and enjoy life, my past comes knocking. It's ready to take everything away from me, again.

I thought I was safe and I thought I could start my life over.

I was wrong.

**The Christmas Bet**

*Allison*

This is my favorite time of year. The holiday season is upon us, and I can't wait to celebrate it. After a recent breakup with yet another guy that I just couldn't see my forever with, I plan on just focusing on getting though the holiday with those around me.

Well that was the plan, until a cocky yet very handsome man came into the picture.

Conner is arrogant and pushy. He cornered me into a date with him, even convincing my best friend, Lacy, that it was a good idea.

But behind his very egotistical attitude, is actually a very sweet guy. There's something different about him. Something I didn't see in the other men I dated, a future.

Could Conner be my forever? Is he 'the one'?

*Conner*

Some call me a bachelor, and some call me a playboy, but really, my life is just too complicated to be tied down. Then I walked into the bar and saw her sitting there. The beautiful blonde captivated me. But I don't do relationships and I don't fall in love. I'd never be able to give her the attention she'd deserve. I'm not the settling down type.

Well, until my friends bet me that I couldn't get a woman to fall in love with me before Christmas. Of course, I had to prove them wrong.

So now I have to get her to fall in love with me—and never find out about the bet.

**The Christmas Bet is a holiday romance novella with some adult situations. Reader discretion is advised.**

## about the author

Lynn Rhys is an emerging author in the romance genre. You can find all her books on Amazon.

Lynn Rhys lived in Illinois for most of her life until she moved to Las Vegas, Nevada in 2004. Lynn finished her Masters Degree and decided that she wanted to try for a new adventure, so she decided to take a stab at writing books.

When Lynn isn't writing, you can find her spending quality time with the family. When she has the kids occupied, she loves to read a good book and get lost in it. She also enjoys the daily struggle of trying to get her kids to try to eat different foods other than chicken nuggets and peanut butter and jelly sandwiches.

To keep up with Lynn Rhys, like and follow her on social media. You can also visit her website below.

Visit her at: https://lynnrhysbooks.wixsite.com/lynnrhys